THE KINGS OF W

disobedient
Pawn

BROOKLYN CROSS

disobedient pawn

BROOKLYN CROSS

𝔚𝔄ℜ𝔑𝔦𝔑𝔊

This book is a Fiction Academy Romance story and is intended for mature audiences only, as defined by the country's laws in which you made your purchase. This book may contain vulgar language, dark humor, alcohol and tobacco use, violence, Canadian slang and PTSD.

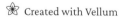

Also by: BROOKLYN CROSS

The Kings of Wayward Academy

(Academy/Slow Burn/Slow Build/Why Choose/Mafia - Dark 1-3 Spice 1-4
the dark and spice will progress more as the series continues)

Disobedient Pawn

Defiant Knight (Coming Soon - Pre Order Now)

Lost Souls MC

(Motorcycle Club - Dark 3.5-4.5 Spice 3.5-4.5)

Malice

Surrender

Showbiz (Coming 2024)

Fealty (Coming 2024)

Handcuffed

Other Books in the Lost Souls World by T.L. Hodel

Adversaries

Frenemies

Warfare (Coming 2023)

The Righteous Series

(Vigilante/Ex Military Romance - Dark 3-4 Spice 3-4)

Dark Side of the Cloth

Ravaged by the Dark

Sleeping with the Dark

Hiding in the Dark

Redemption in the Dark

Crucified by the Dark

Dark Reunion (Coming 2024)

The Consumed Trilogy

(Suspense/Thriller/Anti-Hero Romance - Dark 4-5 Spice 3-4)

Burn for Me

Burn with Me

Burn me Down (Coming 2023)

The Buchanan Brother's Duet & Next Generation

(Serial Killer/Captive Horror Romance - Dark 4-5 Spice 3-5)

Unhinged Cain by Brooklyn Cross

Twisted Abel by T.L Hodel

Unhinged Kallie by Brooklyn Cross (Sept 2023)

Twisted Talon by: T.L. Hodel (Sept 2023)

The Battered Souls World

(Standalone Books Shared World Romance/Dramatic/Women's Fiction/All The Feels- Dark 2-3 Spice 2-3)

The Girl That Would Be Lost

The Boy That Learned To Swim (Coming Soon)

The Girl That Would Not Break (Coming Soon)

The Brothers of Shadow and Death Series

(Dystopian/Cult/Occult/Poly MMF Romance - Dark 3-4 Spice 3-4)

Anywhere Book 1 of 3

Anyplace Book 2 of 3 (Coming 2023)

Backfire Book 1 of 3 by T.L. Hodel

Seven Sin Series

(Multi Author/PNR/Angel and Demons/Redemption - Dark 2-5 Spice 3-5)

Greed by Brooklyn Cross

Lust by Drethi Anis

Envy by Dylan Page

Gluttony by Marissa Honeycutt

Wrath by Billie Blue

Sloth by Talli Wyndham

Pride by T.L. Hodel

To those that believed in me when I didn't believe in myself.

THE KINGS

The Kings
The Order of Kings (Ord na Rithe)

Kings of the Kings
Last Rank Order (LRO) (Ordú Ranga Deiridh)

For the Deserted, For the Power, For the Blood of the Fallen

disobedient pawn

LONELY LONELY - FEIST
RADIOACTIVE - IMAGINE DRAGONS
I THINK I LIKE WHEN IT RAINS - WILLIS
STOLEN DANCE - MILKY CHANCE
MY BODY - YOUNG THE GIANT
FLOWERS - MILEY CYRUS
STRESSED OUT - TWENTY ONE PIOLTS
RENEGADES - X AMBASSADORS
BAD INFLUENCE - PINK
ATTENTION - CHARLIE PUTH
CONFETTI - CHARLOTTE CARDIN
RUN - MATT NATHANSON
DON'T START NOW - DUA LIPA
LAST RESORT - PAPA ROACH
SHE KEEPS ME UP - NICKELBACK
STRONGER - KANYE WEST
DANCE MONKEY - TONES AND I
BEAUTIFUL MISTAKES - MAROON 5
THE GREY - BAD OMENS

No Two
Snowflakes
Are The Same

Chapter 1

R**en**

My headphones were firmly in place as I stared at the priest's mouth. I couldn't hear a word he said. My father was pissed that I was wearing them, but I didn't care. The last thread of my caring snapped the moment he said we were moving. My mum's body wasn't even in the ground, and we were leaving as if she had never mattered. Like the last seventeen years were being wiped away along with her illness and everything else that had happened. I still couldn't think about that night without shaking.

How was I going to visit her from another country? Why did we have to leave our home where all my memories were, good and bad? I was leaving behind everything and everyone I knew.

Father hadn't been around much after he took the new job five years ago, but once mum got sick, he disappeared like a fucking ghost. Maybe if he'd been home rather than pretending we no longer existed, then....

I blamed him for so much, and Mum's death was at the top of the list. He wasn't there that night, and I would never forgive him for that.

I closed my eyes, and a tear trickled down my cheek. I refused to cry like the blubbering vultures standing around Mum's casket. Where were these people when she needed a friend? My mum gave her life to making others smile, but the moment she needed someone, it was too much effort. People were all the same. Selfish pricks and I hated every single one of them. If I never had to deal with another person in my life, I would be happy. Well, except for my best friend, Lizzy.

A strand of my white hair blew across my face. I tucked it behind my ear and snuggled into my dress coat, pulling the collar up to protect my neck from the sharp November wind. I didn't mind winter like most of the other kids I knew. I could ski and skate, and the cold weather was refreshing. Mind you, February in Canada was terrible. If there were one month I could cut out of the calendar altogether, February would be it. I glanced around at the skiff of snow already making its mark and announcing that winter would be here soon.

My eyes lifted to where my father stood beside me, and I couldn't bring myself to care that he had tears in his eyes. He was no better than the rest. I turned back to the priest and tapped my toe to the beat of his mouth moving. This entire day was a joke. My mum was spiritual, but she wasn't Catholic. My father insisted, saying that it would be improper not to have a service.

He made a noise like he was breaking down as the priest finally stopped talking. I glanced at him and wanted to punch him in the face, but that wouldn't do me any good.

He could cry all he wanted. He abandoned us when Mum needed him most. Sure, he had nurses living with us, and doctors paid weekly visits, but that didn't stop the shadows in my mum's eyes whenever she asked where my father was, and I'd have to tell her I didn't know. I had a pretty good idea—none of it was good—but I would smile and say he was working. He never sat by her bedside as she slowly got sicker and sicker until she could hardly lift her head anymore. No, he left that to his daughter. I was twelve when she got sick and took over learning everything she did for the house and then looking after her medical care. I was seventeen now, and I felt like I'd aged fifty years overnight, even had the white hair to prove it.

The priest made the sign of the cross, and one by one, people stepped forward, laying a flower on my mum's casket. I didn't recognize half of their faces. Who were they? Did they even really know my mum, or were they just here for the food?

I spied a man making his way through the crowd as they slowly wandered back to the lineup of cars. I'd never seen him before, but he had a commanding and unnerving presence. He was tall and striking for someone my father's age, what everyone called a silver fox. He reminded me of someone from a mafia movie with his black suit and intense stare. As his dark grey eyes met mine, I shivered, and my insides flipped, but not in a good way. My instincts told me I needed to say away from this man. He was dangerous.

I clicked off my music but left my earphones in so they wouldn't know I was listening to their conversation as he stepped up beside my father. I returned my gaze to my mother's coffin, but my ears were trained on the two men beside me.

They were talking with hushed voices, but I could still make out what they were saying.

"Are you and your daughter packed?"

My father nodded, and I could only assume this was someone from his work. "I wish we had a few more days. This is going to be a hard adjustment for my daughter," my father said and glanced down at me, but I focused on the assortment of flowers that made the black coffin look almost beautiful.

My mum would've loved all the pretty colors but would've hated the fuss. She didn't like it when Father took the fancy new position that came with the massive pay raise. We didn't need the money. My mum had long ago made millions with her sculptures, but she preferred to donate most of it and said that we didn't need for things. They didn't bring real happiness.

Father had wanted to move us from the beautiful yet simple four-bedroom home we lived in, but Mum wouldn't do it. She said all of her memories were here, and all the renovations were just the way she wanted. I could hear them arguing at night about appearances.

I agreed with Mum, fuck appearances. If someone judged me because of the house I lived in and my clothes, they weren't people I wanted to spend time with. They didn't deserve my friendship.

"The movers will be at your home to pack all the items you marked to come. I'm not rescheduling, especially when the jet is here and ready to go," the man I didn't know said, and my heart rate tripled. This had to be my father's boss. Even though his voice was soft, there was a threatening undertone, and I instantly didn't like him.

I'd never flown before, let alone on a private jet. On the surface, it seemed exciting, but the reason for leaving wasn't.

"I understand. We will head home, grab our luggage and meet you at the airfield."

I crossed my arms over the black coat I was wearing, my hand gripping the flower I was holding. I sucked in a sharp breath as one of the rose's thorns stuck into my finger.

"Ouch," I grumbled and shook my hand before putting my finger into my mouth.

"That looks like a nasty cut," the man talking to my father said and stepped around him to stare down at me. "You really should be more careful. You don't want that to scar." He held out his hand, and I stared at it, confused as to what he wanted me to do. It was just a poke from a rose thorn, really not a big deal. When he continued to stare at me, I put my hand into his and immediately wanted to jerk it away, but he closed his hand around my wrist, trapping me in place.

I hated being short. At five foot even, I was considered just under average, but my world was filled with tall people. I felt like a freaking Smurf among giants. Even my mum had been tall and graceful, but I'd been cursed. I felt tinier as he lifted my hand and inspected my finger. For a moment, I thought he might try to kiss it and 'make it better' as he focused on the small droplet of blood that had formed.

"You a vampire or something," I asked, and my father's face paled so much I thought he would faint. That was it. I was going to think of him as Count Dick from now on.

Count Dick smirked. "Some have called me that, but not because I sucked their blood, just their life savings and souls along with it." He smiled, and I tried to jerk my hand away, but he held on until I finally looked to my father for help. This man was creeping me out.

"My name is Lawrence Collier. It's good to finally meet you, Ren," he said. All he needed to do was hiss at the end to complete the whole Satan vibe.

"I wish I could say the same," I said.

"Kayleigh," my father growled.

I tugged on my arm, and this time, Lawrence let go of my wrist. I glared at the two men.

"Don't call me that," I said before stomping to my mum's coffin and laying my hand on the lid. My Mum always called me Ren. It was my middle name and from the time I was little she told me it meant lotus flower and that I was just as exquisite. She always made me feel special and loved.

Leaning over, I kissed the glossy black top and silently made a promise. I would do what she made me swear to her before she died, and that was to live my life the way I wanted.

Her hand was so frail as it gripped mine. Her soft blue eyes filled with agony as her voice strained.

"Never let anyone hold you back, my beautiful Ren. You're as unique and exquisite as the flower you're named for. Let your spirit soar and leave this place. It will only darken your soul."

"I promise, Mum," I said and leaned over her body to hug her, but it felt like I was hugging a skeleton. Her body was cool to the touch, and I was terrified to hurt her. "I love you, Mum. I love you so much."

I tried not to cry in front of her. I never wanted her to feel bad that seeing her sick was ripping my heart out, but I knew she only had a few months left, and each day she slipped away a little more. She hugged me tight, and it was the strongest I'd felt her in so long. My heart lurched in my chest with hope as she held me tight.

Using my bloody finger, I drew a small heart on the coffin. "I'll think of you every day," I whispered.

Casting a glare at my father and Mr. Collier, I turned and marched to the awaiting limo. I had no interest in standing there a minute longer with them. I was actively marking the days on a calendar until I could leave my Father behind for good and never look back. I would uphold the promise to my mum if it was the last thing I did.

Chapter 2

Ren

R "I can't believe you said that to Mr. Collier," my father complained for the thousandth time as we neared the private airport. And just like all the other times, I ignored him and refused to engage in an argument. I knew that was what he wanted. That was the only way my father and I communicated anymore. I took a new approach, the 'Don't say shit approach,'—highly coveted the world over.

We pulled through the gates and drove behind a building toward a black plane. It had a silver emblem on the tail, Mr. Collier's company logo. It was the same stupid logo I'd seen on the folders my father brought home from the office.

Two limos drove past us in the opposite direction, and I cringed with the thought of spending time on this plane with anyone, let alone Mr. Collier. I didn't even get a chance to change at the house. My father acted like we were in some race, ordering me to grab my luggage and ushering me back outside. I had to argue just to pee.

The limo came to a stop, and I jumped out before the driver could get the door open. I hated everyone waiting on me. Of course, my father didn't seem to mind, and I wasn't surprised seeing him order people around. I grabbed my backpack and followed my father up the stairs to the door of the idling plane. Too bad we weren't slower. The plane might've left us behind instead of taking us to freaking Portland.

What the hell was even in Portland? I knew nothing of the place and couldn't muster the energy or interest to look it up. I could hear talking before we entered the plane and internally groaned as I spotted a half dozen people. All of them had been at my mum's service. Great, more of my father's work friends. Could I just jump out the open plane door now and be left behind? Maybe I would get lucky and break my leg. Then I would need to go to the hospital for a while.

Then again, with my luck, my father would tell the doctor to just patch me up and toss me on the plane the same day. He was borderline obsessive with the move and his devotion to Mr. Collier.

Everyone turned and looked in our direction. Their earlier smiles and laughter were replaced with little frowns and fake hugs of remorse for my father. I walked to the back of the plane, where no one was sitting, and tossed my backpack onto the seat, flopping down to stare out the window.

This was it. I was leaving Alberta for good, or at least until I graduated school, then I didn't know. Pulling out my cell phone, I brought up my last text from Lizzy.

R: Soooo, I'm on the plane, filled with a bunch of my father's work friends.

The group laughed, and I could see them opening wine like today was a celebration. It was no celebration, my mum died, and they had no consideration or respect. They were proving my theory that all people sucked.

L: I hate this. I don't know why your dad couldn't just leave you here. My mum said she was happy to have you live with us.

R: I don't know. He's being a pill and so sus about shit. He never tells me anything about his work, and if I push, he orders me to leave the room. I'm not a little kid. It makes me wonder what he's doing that's so terrible.

L: I hate to ask this...but do you think he has a girlfriend or something?

I wrinkled my nose up and glared at my phone. I had my suspicions but no proof, at least not yet. I'd been too nervous to look into it when Mum was alive. I would've felt like I had to tell her. Was that really what someone wanted to find out when they were dying? I didn't think so. Besides, I had too much on the go and couldn't deal with that on top of everything else.

R: Maybe. I don't know. I'm not sure I want to know. We argue all the time now. Could you imagine? I'm sure you'd need to bail me out of jail if I found that out.

L: No doubt. Rylan asked about you at school today. He was acting all retriever-like. LOL!

> R: Sure, now he asks about me when I'm leaving. That figures. Why are guys so dumb?

I had my eye on Rylan for like a whole year, and he never noticed me once. I would pass him in the hallway, and he never looked my way. I tried to sit near him in class, and when the teacher said to pick our groups, he would never include me. He was too busy dating all the puck bunnies that followed the hockey team around.

Whatever. I didn't need or want him. I didn't need anyone.

> L: Yeah, fucked up timing for sure. Do you know where your new house or school is yet?"

> R: Nope, not a clue. I tried looking up Wayward Academy, and nothing came up. It's like the school doesn't exist, which is also sus. How can a private school not come up on a map or an internet search?

> L: Well, it is a PRIVATE school. LMFAO

I smirked at the joke.

> R: Very funny.

> L: Hey girl, I'm sorry I wasn't there for you today. My mum couldn't get the time off work, and...shit, I loved your mum. I'm so sorry.

> R: You need to stop saying that. You've apologized for two whole days about not being able to come.

L: I know, but you're my best friend, and I couldn't be there when you needed me the most.

R: You've been there for me when I needed you. Today was hard, but I knew I was going to be whisked away, and we wouldn't have had any time to talk. Besides, the service was very long. You would've H.A.T.E.D it.

L: You know me so well. LOL! #truth

The tall, pretty stewardess coming along and offering drinks smiled as she reached my seat. She held out a tray that had an assortment of snacks.

"I'm good, thanks," I said.

"Would you like a beverage? I'm sure Mr. Collier would be fine if you wanted a glass of wine."

My eyes flicked to where my father sat, sipping his drink and laughing about whatever. Sighing, I shook my head. I didn't expect him to be sitting on the plane bawling his eyes out, but sipping wine and laughing seemed like he was spitting on my mum's memory.

"Just a bottle of water if you have one."

"Certainly, I'll be right back." If I didn't know any better, I'd say she had walked right out of the movie Stepford Wives. It was next-level creepy how she smiled perfectly and walked away. She returned a minute later with my bottle of water and announced that the plane would be leaving shortly and for everyone to put their seatbelts on. Even though I knew this moment was coming, my stomach flipped and twisted into a knot.

Laying my head against the window, I watched as the plane slowly taxied out to the runway and didn't notice as Mr. Collier stepped up beside my seat. I jerked as my eyes found his in the small window.

"What do you think you're doing," I asked as he picked up my backpack. Turning my head to glare at him, I reached for the bag and expected him to try and pull it away from my grip, but he let go, and I hugged it to my chest.

He lifted an eyebrow at me, his stern jaw set in a hard line as his lips pressed together. "I don't like disrespectful people, but I will let you get away with it because you just buried your mother."

I wanted to say, *aw gee, thanks* but held my tongue. The little time I'd spent around this man was already far too much. So, of course, he sat down and put on his seatbelt. At least the seats were big, unlike the ones Lizzy complained about when she went to Mexico for vacation. I slid as close to the wall as I could and looked out the window. Of all the seats on the plane, why did this man have to sit beside me? I was pretty sure owning it gave you privileges like choosing where you sat.

"Have you flown before," Lawrence asked as the jet made the final turn to the runway.

"Yup," I said, not bothering to look at him. I hadn't, but it didn't matter. I wasn't telling Count Dick anything. I didn't want him to have something else to talk to me about.

The engines got really loud and reminded me of a car getting ready to drag race off the line. They revved, and you could feel the power as the walls vibrated slightly.

"Does flying bother you?"

Why was he still talking? "No, should it?"

"You're going to want to tone down the attitude where you're going," Count Dick said. I looked over my shoulder as the plane raced down the runway, and I was pushed back into the seat from the force. "Wayward Academy doesn't like insubordination." I lifted my brow at him. What the hell did he know of my new school? I couldn't find anything. How did he? "My son attends the school," Lawrence said as if answering the question in my head.

"I'm not worried."

"Is that so, and why is that?"

"I don't get into trouble and have top grades," I said.

"I find that hard to believe with how flippant you've been with me." His dark grey eyes reminded me of a snowstorm. Staring into them left me feeling like I was standing in the middle of a blizzard.

"I didn't realize it was mandatory to give someone I don't know respect. Especially when they practically tore my family apart with how much they made my father work while my mother was ill. Thanks, but I'll reserve my respect for those in my life who deserve it. I don't hand it out for free." I couldn't believe I had just said that, but I wasn't looking away or backing down now. My father worked for him, but I didn't, and I was only on this plane because I was being forced.

Surprisingly, he smiled. "You will do nicely," he said. Mr. Collier undid his seatbelt and stood up as we reached cruising altitude. "It was nice chatting with you, Ms. Davies."

I watched him walk down the aisle and rejoin the group. There was nothing nice about our chat. What the hell did he mean, 'I'd do nicely?' Nicely for what? I caught my father's stare, and it was unreadable. I was alone. Aunt Nadia and Lizzy would be a country away, and Mum was truly gone, never coming back.

I covered my mouth to stop myself from breaking down into hysterical sobs. I was alone with snakes that I didn't trust.

NOVEMBER 3 - WEDNESDAY 4:45 PM (PDT)

Ren

I must have nodded off and jerked awake as the plane's wheels touched down with a bounce. I glanced out the window at the sun in practically the same position as when we left Alberta and remembered that Portland was an hour behind what I was used to.

Yawning, I shuffled to the front of the plane and waited along with everyone else to get off the flying tin can. As I walked down the stairs, there was once more a line of black limos waiting for us. What the hell was it with black limos? Had they run out of any other styled vehicle or even a different color for variety?

I breathed a sigh of relief when Mr. Collier got into his own limo, and we ended up in another. As the cars left the airport, we resembled a funeral procession all over again.

"How far away is the house?" I stared across the seat to my father, who, unsurprisingly, had his nose buried in his phone.

"From here, about twenty minutes, but you're not staying at the house," he said casually like he hadn't just dropped a bomb on my head.

"What do you mean I'm not staying at the house?"

My dad looked up and stared at me. "I swear I told you."

"Told me what?"

"Wayward is a boarding school. You'll be living on campus."

My mouth fell open. "You brought me here away from my friends and Aunt Nadia all so you could dump me off at a boarding school? Mum just died, or did you forget that already?"

The earlier anger I'd managed to tame was back as it burned in my gut so hot that I thought it would burn right through my skin. I gripped my backpack, fists clenching tight.

"Don't be like that," my father said. "Of course, I remember, but this is for the best."

"Don't be like what?" My voice rose along with the quickly building rage.

"Mr. Collier assures me this is a top school, and you'll excel there. You found your old school too easy."

"Oh, Mr. Collier said, so it must be true." I flopped back into my seat and stared out at the world passing by.

"Ren, this is for the best."

"Yeah, for you. As always," I spat out and glared at my father. "You know what, I'm happy to be dropped off. Do me a favor and don't bother to visit," I snapped and then pulled my earphones into place as my father started in on a rant.

I didn't care if I ever heard his voice again.

An hour later, we pulled into the school's long driveway. I could've sworn we stepped back in time as I stared at the architecture. The campus looked like something from an old movie, horrific and haunted, with gargoyles lining the top of the main building.

Jumping out of the car the moment it stopped, I looked up and already hated it. My father got out, still talking to me, but I didn't even glance his way. Slinging my backpack over my shoulder and taking my large suitcase from the driver, I made my way up the ramp to the front door.

"Ren!" My father yelled as he reached the door first and stood in my way.

Grudgingly, I pulled the earphones off and hooked them around my neck. "What do you want?"

"To tell you I love you, and I need to get you signed in."

"You don't love me. If you did, you wouldn't have left me to look after Mum all alone, and you definitely wouldn't have forced me to come to this place to be left like last week's old garbage. Go ahead and sign me in, but I meant what I said. I don't ever want to see you again."

Fuck my father, fuck Mr. Collier, and fuck Wayward Academy.

Chapter 3

Ren

Sitting outside the office, I heard my father and the dean laughing. I smacked my knee and pretended to laugh along with them as I mocked my father's petulant voice. When had I turned into such a bitter person? Was it year one of my mum's illness, was it year three, or was it after she died? I didn't know anymore, and it really didn't matter. The heaviness had settled in my heart and was a part of me. I couldn't stand looking at my father. I didn't want to come to this school and I wasn't going to pretend otherwise.

Fuck, sometimes I wondered if it would've been better if it was me that had died and not my mum.

I felt the sting of tears and quickly blinked them away as the sound of girls laughing reached my ears. A few students walked by the office in casual clothes with classes long done for the day and briefly glanced in at me. I already hated this place. It had a stuffy, disgustingly rich arrogance that wafted off everything like the walls had taken on the personality of those that attended. The place reeked of money which made me more curious as to why I couldn't find them on any search. How did a huge place like this stay off the grid? Who was I kidding? Money bought anything. The more interesting question was why they wanted it to.

The office had perfectly crisp, white walls with wide trim and ornate crown moulding all around the room. The desks were made of the same dark wood as everything else, but there was three windows that looked outside and I could imagine during the day how light would stream through them and lighten all the dark and heavy feeling.

The office was empty, but there were six desks for those here during the day answering phones and doing whatever else secretaries at a school did. I wandered over to the large, framed, greyscale photo on the wall of the grand opening of the school. The small plate proclaimed that it was over a hundred years old. The metal letters over the front archway proudly glittered, announcing Wayward Academy. That was the other thing. Why call a place Wayward? I mean, wasn't that a bad thing? I kept thinking less than two years, and I'd be free.

"Oh hey, you must be Kayleigh. Kayleigh Ren Davies?"

I turned at the sound of the girl's voice. "I go by Ren," I said.

"Well, it's nice to meet you, Ren. I'm Ivy-Rose, but you can call me Ivy or Rose or Ivy-Rose....I prefer Ivy though." She tapped at her chin. "I don't know why my parents couldn't just pick one plant and be done with it. Anyway, I answer to whatever." She smiled, and a little bit of the tension I'd been carrying around since I found out this was where I was heading eased. Ivy had big green eyes and looked adorable with her long dark hair and blunt-cut bangs. A round face with high cheekbones added to her overall cuteness.

"Here, I'll give you this." Ivy held out a thick folder and a book resembling a dictionary. "This is everything you'll need to get settled in, learn the ropes, the rules, and the surrounding area. I added a few of my favorite spots on the property to chill, who the cool teachers are, and who the assholes are. I'm sure you'll figure it out, but this gives you a head start and...." She held up her finger. "I also gave you tips on how to suck up. We can use all the help we can get in this place," she said, leaning in and lowering her voice.

"Thanks, that's great," I said, taking the hefty folder and thick book that weighed a ton.

I turned at the sound of my father's voice getting louder. A moment later, the dean's door opened, and my father stepped out. His eyes were bloodshot from the wine on the plane and whatever he had with the dean for the last thirty minutes.

My teeth ground together at the sight of him. Of course, he smiled like this was fucking Disney Land.

"Isn't this place amazing, Ren? You're going to be so much happier here," he said, slurring ever so slightly. Anyone else wouldn't have picked up on the subtle change, but I did.

"Is that so?"

"I think so. Dean Henry here has assured me that the curriculum is very difficult to keep you challenged, and they have an award-winning arts program." Okay, that got my attention, but I didn't want to hear it, not from him. "I know how much you love your art."

"No, Mum loved her art, and I loved her. Can I go to my room now, or are you planning on hanging out with your new friend for a while longer?"

Ivy's mouth dropped open, but she quickly composed herself. My father's eyes darkened as he turned a violent shade of red. He looked like a volcano ready to erupt, and I was ready for it.

"Ivy, see Ms. Davies to her room and help her settle in. It's going to be a long day tomorrow, and I'm sure you're tired from the trip," Dean Henry said. I hated when people had first names for last names. It was a personal pet peeve, but it always felt like I was being rude without meaning to. Is your name Paul Henry or Henry Paul? This was even worse since he introduced himself to me as Dean Henry. So he had three first names, even though one was a title.

"Sure, I'd love to," Ivy said, smiling wide. I looked away from my father and walked over to my luggage. Putting the folder and book under one arm, I gripped the handle of the rolling case with my other.

"Maybe I can come see you in a couple of weeks to make sure you've settled in and everything is alright," my father said as I got to the door.

I kept my back to him. "Don't bother. I've been fine the last five years without you. What's two more?"

Ivy waited until we were past the main foyer before she spoke again.

"Damn, you really don't like your dad," she said. "If I talked to mine like that, I'd be picking my teeth off the floor."

I looked at her, not sure if she was serious that her father would punch her or not. "Yeah well, my father knows what an asshole he's been. Instead of apologizing, he continues to try and paint over all the bad stuff with fancy schools, clothes, and fake smiles." I gave Ivy a hard stare. "But, I'll never forgive him now. Not ever. So, he can continue to try and suck up all he wants, but I'm doing my time in this place, and then I'm gone, and I'll never have to see him again."

"I wish I was that brave. My dad scares me too much," Ivy said.

"So your dad actually hits you? Why haven't you called the police," I asked quietly so the few people hanging around in the halls didn't hear me. Ivy laughed like I said the funniest thing in the world. "What's so funny?"

"My dad is the sheriff, and his soul was purchased and paid for a long time ago. Just like all of us here." We stopped at an elevator to take us to the second floor, and I stared at Ivy, trying to understand what she meant. "And if you're smart, you'll stay on the Dean's good side. He has the power to make your life a living hell."

That seemed a bit dramatic, before I could ask anymore, the elevator dinged, and as it opened, a group of guys walked out. One of them bumped into me like we were on a football field, and I stumbled sideways. My suitcase fell to the ground with a bang while the folder and book slipped from my hand. Papers scattered in all directions.

"Hey! Watch where the hell you're going," I said, glaring at the group. The guy that ran into me made a sexual gesture with his tongue as they all laughed and walked away. A decent attitude was one thing money couldn't buy.

"Sorry about that," Ivy said as she knelt and helped me gather up the mess. "That was Axel and his boys. He's the captain of the football team," she said, and I rolled my eyes. Could the cliché of this place get any worse?

"It's fine. I just want to get to my room and put everything away. Tomorrow is a new day." It was what I told myself to try and get through the shit, but so far, tomorrow had never brought anything better. "Do you know if I'm rooming with anyone?"

"Um, yeah," Ivy said, her voice apologetic, and I knew, without her saying another word, that I wasn't going to like whoever it was. Not even a full day, and I already wanted to burn the place to the ground.

The dorms were divided once you got to the second floor. The east wing, or Nu Alpha Phi, was the guy's area, and the west wing, Xi Beta Theta, was for the girls. I stared at the double doors and Greek letters that meant nothing to me. We didn't do this in Canada. I had no idea what it meant, but I saw all the hype in movies and how it was supposed to be like a sisterhood or something. Or maybe that was a sorority. I wasn't really sure. The couple things I was certain of was that I wouldn't be out cheering and yelling and all that. I also doubted that everyone got along and sang kumbaya while holding hands.

"You coming," Ivy asked as she held open the door for me.

"Sorry, just looking around."

"There are cameras everywhere except in the dormitories. Each wing is really too big to be a single sorority and fraternity, with how many students there are. The dean is really strict about tradition, so no one dares to try and change it."

Well, that answered that question.

Some girls dressed to party laughed and jogged along the hallway, never giving Ivy or me a second look.

"This is your room," she pointed to the one with a Barbie pink wreath hanging on the door. "I'll meet you here at seven-thirty tomorrow morning. We have first period together, and you can sit with me for lunch if you want."

"Sure, that sounds good. Where is your room?"

Ivy pointed back the way we'd come. "The first hallway we passed, if you turn there and follow it to the very end, you'll find my room. You can't miss it. My roommate and I have little wooden signs with our names on the door."

I looked at the pink wreath again and knew I'd much rather have the wooden sign. "Do I need a key?"

"Vicky already has it." Ivy got close to my ear and whispered. "Find a way to get on her good side. She runs pretty much everything and everyone in this wing. If she doesn't like you, she'll make your stay hell. She loves it when people compliment her clothes and hair."

"So what you're saying is typical mean bitch?"

"I hope you're not talking about me." I closed my eyes and swore in my head before turning around to face my new roommate. She was everything I wished I was. At least five-ten, with a knockout figure, long black hair, and stunning lashes that accentuated her hazel eyes. She could be a model on the cover of any swimsuit magazine.

"Nope, Ivy was talking about one of the teachers." I looked at Ivy, hoping she'd take the hint. She was so pale it looked like she was about to pass out. "Isn't that right Ivy?" I urged.

"Yes, that's right. Mrs. Grey is terrible. She'll find a reason to yell at you even when there is none. Total bitch."

Vicky lifted an elegant brow, she didn't look convinced, but when we stood quietly and stared at her, she seemed to accept the response. "That's true. Although she loves me." Her eyes flicked up and down, and I could feel her gaze as she analyzed and disapproved of me all in one glance. "I'm going to assume you're my new roommate?"

I badly wanted to say, 'No, I just like wandering strange schools with my suitcase.' But I decided I'd already sidestepped one pile of shit, and there was no need to step in another so soon.

"So it seems," I said.

"Well, don't just stand there. Come on in. You can go, Ivy. You're dismissed." Ivy practically ran down the hallway, the navy and gold kilt fluttering behind her before I could tell Vicky that was a bitch thing to say.

I stepped inside the room, and it felt like I was being caged in with a hungry tiger. Vicky stared at me as if she was looking for an opening to attack. It was unnerving. I didn't really care what she thought of me, but we would be rooming together for far too long to start off hating one another.

"So let's get the rules straight, shall well?" I looked over at Vicky as she sat on the edge of her bed, which had fancy little pillows the same color as the wreath on the door. She stretched out, her yoga outfit showing off her lean figure.

I knew I had a nice figure, but when you were barely five feet tall, everyone seemed like a thin, elegant green bean, and I felt like a short yellow bean. Why I thought about myself as a bean was beyond me.

"What rules?"

Vicky held up her French manicured fingernail. "First, never touch my things. I don't like them moved. Second, don't ever eat fish or seafood in this room, it's disgusting, and I can't stand the smell. Third, I need the private shower from six until seven-thirty, so if you like to shower in the morning, you'll have to use the communal one down the hall." Vicky was still only holding up one finger, and I suddenly had serious doubts she could actually count. "Fourth, outside of this room, don't speak to me. I've worked hard to earn my reputation, and I'll be honest, you don't fit in." That was shocking to hear. Not. "Last, don't fuck with or mess with my boyfriend. If you do, then you'll regret it. If you obey those rules, we will get along fine."

Vicky smiled, then stood and grabbed her phone off the desk. "I'll be getting ready and heading out shortly. If I don't get in until late, don't worry." She opened the door to a closet and walked inside, then poked her head back out. "You're not a narc, are you?"

"About you being out?" She nodded. All I could think was the more time that she was away, the better, but I shook my head instead. "Good."

Pulling my suitcase over to the dresser, I peeled off my coat and laid it down before going to the window and looking outside. The leaves on the trees were a vibrant shade of red and orange with a sprinkling of yellow. I always loved this time of year and decided that the first chance I got, I wanted to paint it. The room looked out to a forest, and with the help of the low setting sun I could just make out a body of water stretched out beyond the other side of the trees. It was stunning.

I didn't want to like anything about this place, but I liked Ivy, and the view was incredible. If the art program was half decent, I could find a reason not to want to poke my eyes out every morning.

Glancing at the darkening sky, I wondered if my mum knew we'd left her behind. Was she angry? Was she hurt that we left so soon? I nibbled on my bottom lip, trying not to think about my mum, sad and alone.

"See ya...um...what is your name?"

Turning around, I couldn't believe Vicky had gone from going to work out to partying on the town in just a few minutes. She was beautiful. There was no other way to describe her.

"My name is Ren."

"Like as in Ren and Stimpy? That's a stupid name. Only an asshole would do that to their kid." My fist clenched. Mum loved the name and made me feel special. It was a happy memory for me, and in a single sentence, this bitch was trying to ruin that. "Whatever, see ya."

Just like that, she was gone as she slipped out the door without waiting for a response. I slumped onto the bed and let out a long breath. The room instantly felt lighter without her in here, and that didn't bode well for the next two years if we were stuck together that long.

I wanted Lizzy. I wanted to go home. But most of all, I wanted to bring my mum back from the dead. I couldn't do any of those things. Everything I wanted was out of reach or impossible, and with no one around to watch, I rolled onto my side and cried.

Chapter 4

Myles

"Oh fuck yes!" Pam wailed, yet I could hardly hear her over the loud music of the party happening downstairs. "Myles, fuck. Don't stop," she said as I continued to fuck her hard enough that the pool table was slowly inching across the game room floor. Da would be proud to know that his table was being used for something.

Balling the school kilt in my fist, I smacked her ass hard and thrust into her harder so she had nowhere to jump.

"Ah, don't hit me," she whined as her nails scraped along the green felt I had her bent over. When Pam glared at me over her shoulder, I smirked and hit her again just because. "Ah! You asshole."

I tilted my head back and chugged the rest of the beer down while keeping pace. That should be the new roadside sobriety test. Some hot cop bent over her car...I would be down for that.

"Oh fuck, Myles, I'm gonna come," Pam cried out.

"Ya better fuckin not." Pulling out of her pussy, she whimpered and wiggled her ass back and forth. "I'm nowhere near done yet."

"I can go twice, please," she begged, biting her lip.

As I slid back into her, the door banged open, and the thumping music blared louder as Nash stood in the doorway with a girl under each arm.

"Hey man," Nash said, the girls squealing and laughing. "I need a place to hide from Theo to fuck these two."

I shrugged and looked around the massive room with multiple couches. "Come on in, but I'd lock the door."

"Myles," Pam whined, glaring at me over her shoulder. "I don't want to have sex in front of them."

"Then don't. Nash has two. I'm sure he'd share." She whipped around so fast it hurt my cock. The crack of her hand was loud as she slapped me across the face. The impact lacked strength, but that wasn't the point. No one but my Ma had ever been allowed to smack my cheek.

"You're a fucking dick. We're done," she said, pulling her skirt down and buttoning her blouse.

"We were never datin' love," I said, gripping her waist to hoist her up onto my shoulder.

"Put me down, you asshole," she yelled as I opened the sliding glass door.

"A good rule ta remba is never piss off a McCoy, especially in his own home."

"What are you doing? No, don't you dare," she shrieked, struggling in my hold.

"Heads up below, we got a live one comin' down," I bellowed.

The couple making out in the pool looked up and laughed as I tossed Pam's screaming ass over the balcony into the water below. Fuck I wished I had that shit on film. The way she reached for the sky like she was going to sprout wings, her skirt lifted over her ass, giving everyone around a show. It was a work of art.

Nash came out of the sliding glass door laughing as hard as I was. "Dude, that was the funniest shit I've ever seen," he said as we leaned over the glass balcony to watch a drowned rat version of Pam pull herself from the pool as everyone outside laughed.

"I hate you." Pam shook her finger at me, her makeup running down her cheeks. "Noooo, my phone," she cried as she pulled it out of her bra and held it up by two fingers. Nash was laughing so hard he had tears running down his cheeks.

He clamped his hand down on my shoulder. "I knew it was a great idea bringing you into the group."

"Aye," I said, my accent thicker with the heavy drinking. "Ya also knew that I was da fastest backstroker ya've ever seen. Smart move puttin me on da team."

"Yes, it was."

With the excitement over, we turned back to the game room that doubled as my Da's office when he was home. The two girls Nash had brought with him were leaning against the open door.

"Do either of ya two ladies mind gettin' fucked in front of da other," I asked, and they shook their heads, a wicked smile spreading across their pretty faces. They giggled as we walked toward them. I grabbed the one closest to me around the waist and carried her to the couch.

"Such a gentleman," she said, making me laugh.

"I can guarantee that has never been said about me." Plunking down on the couch with the girl in my lap. "Yer gonna have ta take dat off." I pointed to the condom still on my cock. She made a face, and I thought she would argue, but instead, she grabbed the edge and peeled it off. "Nash, pass dat trash can by ya."

"Here."

"Tanks." I held it for my nameless girl. She didn't have any problem stroking her prize with the thin rubber out of the way.

"I did tell you Pam would be trouble," Nash said as he sat down beside me. "She's the clingy type. They all are from Sacred Heart Academy. It's like they breed them to seek out men to fuck and marry and then get pregnant."

"Well, I got meself a couple good blowjobs out of da deal first. I call that a win."

The nameless girl crawled onto the floor between my legs, and I groaned as she slipped me into her mouth. I could've asked her name, but what was the point? I had no intention of ever seeing her again. Dating was not allowed according to my Da, not when you're entire future has already been planned out, including who the fuck I was supposed to marry. Who the hell still forced their son into an arranged fucking marriage with some cunt on the other side of the world? The stupid McBride girl would be here sometime next year to finish off senior year with me—a get-to-know-me period or some shit.

I would let her get to know me alright, then send the bitch packing right back to Ireland. I had my own plans, and they didn't include my Da's vision of having grandbabies by the time I was nineteen to carry on his legacy.

"Hey man, I have an errand for you to run tomorrow," Nash said, smacking my chest.

"What's that?" I wrapped my nameless girl's hair around my fist and shoved down hard. I snickered as she smacked at my legs and gagged. Nash laughed, but the girl working his cock over was smart and removed her mouth before he could do the same.

Releasing her hair, she came up for air, spitting mad. "You asshole, I could've choked to death."

"And what a way ta go it would be," I said. "Well, come on, get back ta work. I don't have all night." I actually did have all night, but that was beside the point. "So what is it that you need?" I turned my head away from the girl on the floor, knowing she'd continue. That was the perk of coming from a wealthy home and being one of the Kings of Wayward Academy. You could do almost whatever you wanted as long as you kept your grades up.

"I need to attend a boring board meeting tomorrow after classes, but I have the weekend's shipment of party supplies arriving." Nash smiled.

"No worries, I can take care of it, just like...whatever her name is here is taking care of my cock. With sloppy efficiency." I smiled as the cute brunette made an angry noise with my cock still buried deep in her mouth.

Nash laughed hard. At least someone appreciated my jokes.

Loud banging started on the wooden door. "You fuckers better not be in there having sex! I swear I'll tell Coach."

Despite the loud music, Theo's annoying voice penetrated the room. Both Nash and I groaned, but not for a good reason.

"Man, stop being so fucking extra all the time!" Nash yelled as he forced the girl's head on his cock to move faster.

"Not gonna work, man. The race is over." Slumping, I punched the couch and stood.

"Hey, what about us," the brunette asked.

"What about ya? I didn't see me cum, did ya? I don't get off. Then ya don't get off," I said.

"You fucking assh...." She stopped and slapped a hand over her mouth as my brow arched. Her eyes flicked to the balcony, obviously remembering Pam's swan dive exit.

"Wise choice," I said and marched across the floor. "Both of you get out, now," I ordered as Nash stuffed his cock away.

"I swear that guy just wants me to have blue balls forever," I said, smirking as the girls ran my way. I unlocked the door to let them out and Theo in.

He was casually leaning against the door jamb as the girls slipped by. He was all stone and didn't even glance at them.

"You're an asshole," Nash growled and marched to the beer fridge.

"No alcohol either. It's the last fucking tournament and the way Nash has been riding our assess to win, we are not fucking it up with anything. Got it?" Theo meandered into the room as I slammed the door.

"You act like I'm a hard ass," Nash said. Both Theo and I looked at him and he shrugged. "Fine, I am."

I hadn't known any of them long, but Theo was the one guy on the team I had a hard time warming up to. He was like a block of ice all the time. We got along fine, and I trusted him cause Nash did, and I was best friends with his twin Blake, but he kept himself at arm's length.

He flopped on one of the stools by the pool table.

"I hate you," Nash grumbled. "You know how I get if I don't get any. You sure you want to deny me?"

"Coach says no sex and no alcohol three days out from a tournament. Today is three days out, and we need our captain in peak performance. I already threatened Blake and Liam with bodily harm. Myles is a fish with alcohol, so I'm not too worried about him." Theo yawned like he was bored of the wild party downstairs.

"Here, here," I raised my drink and chugged it down, but I knew it would be my last tonight. Fucking water.

"I have a peak, alright. Coach is old school, and you know it. That shit has been proven not to enhance anything. Besides, I'll probably be so fucking horny by then that it'll slow me down with my cock sticking down in the water like a fucking rutter," Nash said.

Theo rolled his eyes.

"I din't know how ya do it," I chimed in. "You're always so chill."

"Someone needs to be the babysitter, and I guess I get the gig since the rest of you dick nuggets can't keep it in your pants."

"That's only cause we have offers, and you don't." Nash pulled a bottle of water out of the fridge and stared at it like it was a dirty jockstrap.

"I get plenty of offers. I simply make sure my quota is full before three days out. Besides, it makes day four that much sweeter."

Nash and I looked at the guy and then at one another. I hated to admit it, but he kind of had a point.

"Fine, get the rest of the team up here. We might as well go over the relay strategy," Nash said, his voice still angry, but the edge was gone. Nash was scary when he was really angry. I tended to punch first and ask questions later, but Nash was 'Rip your head off and eat your brains for dinner,' kind of scary. There was a reason he was the next King in line to take the throne. Being a Collier came with as many problems as it did perks. His father was the biggest one of them all.

We both had asshole das, but Collier was a special kind of evil. We all knew that Nash got knocked around a lot. He never said a word about it, but no one else would dare leave a bruise on Nash other than his old man.

One day that King would tumble, and I was happy to watch when it happened.

Chapter 5

NOVEMBER 4 - THURSDAY 7:58 AM

Myles

I swear Nash was trying to get me killed. When I agreed to do the pick-up, he neglected to mention it was in motorcycle club territory. They weren't the meanest in the area, but the Dark Angels were wannabe Hell's Angels and caused everyone a lot of trouble. At some point, the other families would stomp them out, but until then, I needed to be careful.

Luckily, I liked to familiarize myself with any new surrounding area and had spent the rest of last night scoping out the safest alleys and back lanes to take tonight.

Maybe it was cause we moved so much, but it had become a habit. As soon as we settled in, I would memorize the area. I could sit and redraw an entire map for a fifty-mile radius. There wasn't a spot I couldn't figure out how to get to. But my first problem of the day was how the fuck to stay awake during class? Where the fuck was it again?

"Hey, Myles."

I looked around to see a redhead I vaguely remembered wiggling her fingers at me. "Hey babe, you're lookin fine. You wanna get together later?"

"No, he does not want to get together." I rolled my eyes at the sound of Theo's voice. He wrapped his arm around my shoulders as he came up behind me. "That is a cue to go away," he said, and her face fell.

"Are you a fucking vampire, man? I swear you're everywhere and have supersonic hearing."

"No, but we do have first period together, and the door is there," he said, his voice dripping with the usual arrogance and sarcasm that wafted off him like too much cologne. Theo held his hand out as he guided me toward the open door that felt like a prison.

I hated calculus, and whoever decided that it should be the first fucking class of the day needed to be tied to a set of train tracks. Walking in, I plopped myself down in the seat beside Theo and laid my head on my arms. He was the only reason I still came to this or any class, really. I hadn't met a worse nag. Not Ma, the teacher, or hell, even Coach compared. Theo was like a fucking stalker. He didn't get annoyed or offended and told on you worse than my little brother Lip would.

The door closed with a bang, and I groaned, pushing myself upright before Mr. Willis could yell at me. It would be fine if he simply sent me to detention where I could fucking sleep, but no, he liked to sit me at the front of the class with him where he had a wide assortment of fucking loud bells and buzzers. He was a torture master.

It only took a few times till I never wanted to do that again. I still saw those equations dancing behind my eyes. Nothing was less sexy than math equations popping in your head when you were jerking off. I thought that man ruined me for life.

"Good Morning, class. Actually, let me revise that. It would be a good morning if more of you were passing," Willis said, glaring around the small classroom. "I have your latest test scores, and to say they are abysmal is putting it mildly." Most of the class groaned. I just crossed my arms. I hadn't bothered to study for the last test. I hadn't studied for any of them and knew mine would be shit. Why groan? It wasn't a fucking surprise.

Mr. Willis walked around the class and handed out the papers. He glared at me as he placed the test and the circled mark of one out of a hundred in front of me.

"Although, we do have some good news. I'd like all of you to welcome our newest student joining us today, and thankfully she has a better average than almost all of you combined."

The only new person I could see looked like she could be our school librarian from the back, with the same white hair done up in a bun on her head. I couldn't see her face from where I was sitting and didn't really care. I was tempted to nod off for a few minutes.

"I've decided to mix things up, and we are starting with a tutoring buddy. I will be giving you all designated seating, and whoever you are paired with will be your tutor to help you get your grades to at least a passing level," Mr. Willis said, and I sat up straighter. He better not put me up at.... "We'll start with our class clown, Mr. McCoy. Please stand. Also, Alisha, Leeanne, Tash, Silvia, Robert, Sam, and Elijah."

"Fuck." I swore under my breath as we all slowly stood.

I saw the new girl's hand rise. Her fingers pointed straight up like the fin of a shark. "Yes, Ms. Davies?"

"My answer is no," she said, and the room went dead silent. Not a paper fluttered or pen tapped on a desk. I craned my neck around those standing to get a better look.

"I'm sorry. Can you repeat that?"

"Oh, are you hard of hearing? My apologies. I said, no, I will not tutor anyone," the girl practically yelled. I snorted and cleared my throat as others weren't quite as successful at holding back their snickers.

"I'm not hard of hearing." Mr. Willis put his hands on his hips. "I am still the teacher in this room, so if I say you will help out your fellow students, then you will."

"No," she said again. My curiosity was piqued. I just had to know who this girl was.

"Man, are you not finding any of this hilarious?" I whispered to Theo, who was busy making notes on the day's lesson even though it hadn't started yet.

"Yes, hilarious," he answered dryly.

"Let me be clear, Ms. Davies. You will do what I ask," he said, and we all turned our heads in unison to see what she would say next.

"I'm not sure how better to say this, Mr. Willis. I not only have no intention of teaching those who would rather sleep through class, but I'm technically a student, and you're the paid professional in the room." My mouth fell open. "If it is anyone's responsibility to teach the students that are not doing well, it is yours. Last I checked, I do not have a professor's salary going into my bank account, and I refuse to allow someone else to bring down my grades because I cannot spend the time needed to keep them in the impeccable shape they're in. Now, by all means, feel free to assign these students to whomever you'd like, just not me."

"I think I'm in love," I said to Theo, who'd actually lifted his head to watch what happened next. It took a lot to get his attention.

"Am I going to have to send you to the Dean's Office on your first day?'

"If you do, I will explain the same thing to him, and I'm sure he will be more than happy to rule with me."

"Is that so?" Mr. Willis nodded and pulled out a thick folder from his bag. It took him a few minutes as he scribbled something across the top of the pages and sat them aside. He could've done that for the next hour, and I would've watched to see what he was planning.

"Since I'm the teacher and I've been given permission to change the curriculum as needed, I've decided to add a new points scale. As of today, twenty-five percent of your passing grade will be based on tutoring. All those who are failing will be the opposite. Twenty-five percent of your passing grade will come from your tutoring sessions and understanding of the material. If either partner does not make their new goal, then you will automatically lose twenty-five percent of your grade." The class collectively groaned.

The girl with the white hair burst from her seat, and as she did, I almost sat down. She was fucking adorable. Beautiful in a naughty but good schoolgirl kind of way with fucking silver eyes.

"This is an outrage. You don't even know if I can teach," she said, her hands balling and going to her hips as she faced off with Mr. Willis.

"I took a look at your transcript before coming into the room, Ms. Davies, and you have not only a hundred percent in every single class, you also have the bonus points."

"Damn, man, someone is beating your scores? I didn't think that was possible," I whispered to Theo, who crossed his arms, his face set in a scowl. Theo was competitive to the core, and if someone were even half a point ahead in a grade or a fingertip faster in the pool, he worked harder and focused more until he could beat them. The only person more decorated when it came to the pool was Nash, but no one had beaten Theo academically.

"Just because I'm smart doesn't mean I can or should teach someone else. You're putting their future in my hands. That is not fair."

Mr. Willis smiled, and you just knew he was going to fuck you over. "Then let's consider this your lesson Ms. Davies. You don't seem to need to study calculus anyway. In fact, I'd wager you already have this semester's work all done." She bit her lip, and I suddenly wanted to bend her over her desk. Forget tutoring me. I would fucking tutor her in the art of my cock.

"That is beside the point," she said, and I snickered as Theo swore under his breath. Even he wasn't that far ahead. Double points. Someone that could annoy Willis and Theo...oh yeah, I was in love with this chick.

"No, I don't think it is. You're here to learn life skills, and you never know when you will need to teach someone else. It may be to instruct them on bandaging in an emergency or helping the new person at your job learn so you can move up into a new role. It is a needed skill, and since you're so reluctant to learn, I'm more sold on it than when I first suggested it."

"Great job, new girl," Warren bitched as he shot to his feet, obviously annoyed with his new role as a tutor. I wanted to hit him and tell him to shut up. "Make all our lives difficult."

"Warren, zip it and sit down before he decides to do something else to ruin our lives. Like this school doesn't already try to suck the life out of us," Kelly sniped and flicked her long brown curls over her shoulder.

The new girl looked around the room, and my pulse jumped as her eyes found mine, even if only for a second. Fuck.

She sat down slowly, crossing her arms and glaring daggers at Mr. Willis. I didn't think this would be their last showdown. "Great, now that is all settled, let's pair you up." He began going through the pairs as I tapped my leg.

"Put me with the new girl, put me with the new girl, put me with the new girl," I chanted under my breath.

Mr. Willis waited until each person moved before continuing. "Lastly, Silvia, you will swap with Mr. McCoy and work with Theo, and Mr. McCoy, you will be paired with Ms. Davies."

"Shit," Theo mumbled.

I smirked as Slivia's face turned bright red, her smile beaming in our direction. She'd been trying to get Theo's attention since the beginning of the school year, but that was like trying to get the attention of a rock.

A showdown with Mr. Willis, Theo annoyed, and I get to sit with the new hottie. This just turned into my mother-fucking day.

Chapter 6

Ren

Ivy gave me a sad look, her lips pulling down as she gathered her things and stood to move across the aisle.

"We have lunch together. Come find me in the cafeteria," she whispered.

I nodded. What the hell kind of school was this that made the students teach against their will, and then this jerk had the nerve to make it part of my passing grade?

Was he even old enough to teach? He looked like he wasn't much older than we were. If it weren't for the short hairstyle, glasses, crisp

43

button-down shirt, and khaki dress pants with a pull-over burgundy vest, I would've thought he was a senior. He lifted a pile of papers off his desk and walked over while the student I was assigned flopped into the seat beside me.

Mr. Willis smiled, and if he weren't my teacher, I would've said he was sexy in that nerdy kind of way. What was I saying? I was the same kind of nerdy. Mr. Willis dropped the stack of papers onto the desk with a thud. I stared at them and then up into his hazel eyes.

"What is this?"

"These are Mr. Myles McCoy's failed quizzes and tests and all his repeated attempts to pass." My mouth fell open, and my hand went to the stack, thumbing through the two inches of paper. "Your job is to make sure he passes the class and the next quiz. Myles will also need to retake all these failed attempts before the end of the semester. He needs an eighty or higher on every single one to pass."

"This is a joke, right? Tell me you're joking with me," I blurted out, and the corner of Mr. Willis's lip curved up.

"Not even a little. For each division he fails, no pun intended. Five percent will be deducted from your possible twenty-five percent." I glared at the man claiming to be a teacher and then looked at the guy I'd just been assigned. He was smiling like he'd just won the lottery while I felt like I'd been shackled with a miscreant and a total liability to me getting the hell out of this place. My gaze flicked up and down, taking in his athletic body, and I internally groaned. Great, a typical jock. He was probably lucky if he could figure out what one plus one was.

Myles dropped down beside me with the million-dollar smile that I was sure had won him more than one heart. His dark brown hair was messy yet suited him, but it was the amber eyes that slightly intrigued me. They were the most unusual shade I'd ever seen, like chunks of amber. He could be on any sports magazine cover, but tutor him....Oh, heck no.

"Hey, beautiful," Myles said. Reaching out, he ran a loose piece of my hair through his fingers. I slapped his hand away.

"Oh, this is not happening." I grabbed my bag and marched for the door.

"Class is not over, Ms. Davies," Mr. Willis called out.

"It is for me. You can meet me in the office." I slammed the door hard, and the wood rattled as my heart hammered. "No way, this is not happening."

A group walking down the hall was watching me, and I took a deep breath to calm down before turning toward the exit. I was in Wayside Hall, the The Imperial Wing. They thought they were so cute with the names of the wings tied to what subjects they taught. Personally, I thought it was stupid and lazy on their part.

My shoes squeaked on the shiny marble floor. Who used marble for floors in a school anyway? At least they got the color right. It was grey and depressing like the rest of this place. Pushing my way outside, I wrapped my arms around myself and made a note to take a jacket to all other classes that weren't attached to the main building.

Snowflakes slowly drifted to the ground around me. I stopped and held out my hand for just a moment, my lips curving up as I watched them melt in my palm. They reminded me of my mum. She loved winter. She told me her parents liked to stay in warm places, and she had never gotten to experience snow until she met my father and moved to Canada. My grandparents on both sides of my family passed away before I was born. I always felt like I missed out on the experience of having a grandparent tell me stories or spoil me like Lizzy's did.

I lost count of how many times we'd made hot chocolate and got bundled up to sit outside and watch the snow fall on a clear, calm night. I could feel the tear rolling down my face, leaving a cool line as it went.

"Hey, wait up." Glancing over my shoulder, I saw Myles jogging my way. I wiped away the tear and marched on, not giving him a second look. I had no time for jocks that didn't want to learn. I knew my fair share already and had zero interest in getting to know another. "Wow, ya walk faster than ya look like ya could."

He wrapped his arm around my shoulders, and I stopped walking, shoving his arm off as I spun out of his hold. I didn't care how good-looking this guy was, and he was hot. Tall with wide shoulders, dark chocolate hair, and amber eyes, but that was as far as my interests ran.

"First, don't touch me."

"Ya looked cold. Girls normally like it," he said, and my eyebrow rose as he flashed me another award-winning grin. I did like the hint of an accent. I could tell it was Irish, but it was faint.

"Well, I'm not most girls. So don't do it. Second, you can forget about talking me into helping you. I don't help people that don't want to help themselves." The smile faltered. "So, you can turn around and go back to class, and I'll get this sorted with the dean." Spinning around, I stomped onward for the main doors of the school.

"Wait." Myles jogged beside me and matched my pace easily with his long strides. I was tempted to speed up to see if I could lose him, but I had a feeling that wouldn't work.

"What?"

"Where are ya from? Ya have an accent. I'm curious."

"Says the guy with an Irish accent. What does it matter where I'm from?" I cocked my head and stared at his arrogant face.

He shrugged. "Ya have a sharp mouth, or is that tongue?"

"Sharp mouth? It's definitely tongue. Otherwise, I don't know what that means. I'm from Canada." I crossed my arms, making sure not to shiver.

"Well, that explains it. The cold makes ya feisty," he said and laughed.

"Is that supposed to be funny?"

Myles stuffed his hands in his pants, his broad shoulders rounding slightly. "I thought it was."

"That explains a lot," I said and started to turn away again.

"Okay, wait, wait, wait, please?"

The wind picked up and swirled the loose strands of hair around my face. Myles was staring at me but not saying anything. "Are you going to say something? If not, I'm going inside. It's cold out here."

"Here ya can have me sweater," Myles said, grabbing the bottom of his school sweater to take off.

"No thanks. I just want to know what you want." I bounced from foot to foot to keep warm. I should really take him up on the sweater, but I knew what taking an item of clothing meant to a guy. It was like they were protecting you, you were suddenly theirs, and that wasn't happening. I belonged to no one but myself.

"Tutor me, and I promise I will give it me all," he said.

"No way," I said, and his smile fell.

"What? Why?"

"Because I don't believe you. This is what I know in the thirty seconds I've known you. You can't be bothered trying. I have no idea if it's because you actually don't understand the material or you don't want to. But, you certainly haven't bothered to try, or you wouldn't have been smirking and chuckling at the pile Mr. Willis put on the desk. You would've been horrified or maybe even embarrassed, but it seemed more like a badge of honor to you." I held up my finger, my hand shaking, but I refused to give in.

"Second, you're presumptuous. I don't like to be called pet names like beautiful. We don't even know one another, and you're handsy. Wrapping your arm around me like I'm some damsel. That tells me you're used to getting the hot jock treatment from whatever girl you want something from, whether it be school, money, sex, or whatever. You're probably also used to throwing them away just as fast. But guess what? I'm not interested in being anyone's used garbage. Find someone else to help you. I'm not interested."

This time he didn't call me back as I marched for the door and pulled it open. The warm air made me shiver like a wet dog and sigh at the same time. Day one was not off to a great start, and I could only hope that the dean got this mess sorted out.

Myles

"I don't think I've ever seen you look more pathetic and a girl less interested in you," Liam said as he wandered over, cigarette in hand.

"I think I'm in love," I said, smiling wide at my friend.

Liam screwed up his face. "Um...pretty sure she just told you to fuck off without saying fuck off."

"I know. Wasn't it great?" I looked at Liam and then at the smoke he was inhaling. "I thought ya quit. If Coach sees ya, he'll kick ya off the team, and Nash will have your ass and not in the fun way that Theo taps you." I smirked as Liam rolled his eyes.

"Are you going to tell Coach or Nash?"

Liam put it out before pulling a metal cigarette holder from his pocket and tucking the rest of it inside. One of the school guards wandered along the path, looking like an FBI agent with wraparound sunglasses and dressed in all black. I knew they carried two guns on them, and there were over a dozen on the property at a time.

Liam and I nodded at the guy, and he carried on, his head on a swivel as he took in the surrounding forest that led down to the water.

"They still creep me out," I said when the guy was out of earshot.

"He's just a guard," Liam yawned, making me yawn as I remembered I had only gotten a few hours of sleep.

"Don't be fuckin doin' that, man. It's contagious." The main door to the school opened, and Dean Henry waved to get my attention. "Well shit, she actually went to the dean."

"Good luck, man." Liam quickly escaped in the other direction while I felt like I was walking the plank. Dean Henry was the one person, other than my family, that could make my life a living hell. At least when it came to my studies. Unlike my Da, he was always around and watched everything we did. I swear there were cameras where there weren't supposed to be because the man knew everything that went on. Dean Henry had also been given free rein to do whatever he saw fit to keep us in line, and although I'd never heard of him beating a student, there were other things he could and would do.

I didn't think it was fair, but it was what it was. I'd been tempted to take his car for a joyride but Ilanded my ass in prison a few times before coming to the US and my father warned me to be smart and keep myself out of trouble. Since my father would beat my ass into a pulp if I stole the dean's car, I decided not to push that self-destruct button. Almost everyone here had a record. Some because they liked being a dick, but most due to family obligations. The fun of having a crime family as your blood.

There were a couple that didn't have a record, like Ivy. She was too scared of her own shadow to have any fun, but considering her dad was Sheriff Morrison—who was a total fucking asswipe and worked for our parents—it was safer for his kid to be here too. She was a smaller target than the rest of us but could still be used—another pawn in the larger game.

"Dean, how can I help ya," I asked as he held the door open for me to walk inside.

"Follow me," was all he said, his voice as curt and direct as always. My father thought this man had the best sense of humor. I thought it had run away from his uptight arse a long time ago.

I walked behind him like the good little beaten dog I was—technically, what we all were except Nash. He managed to get away with more than anyone else. The new girl, who I was really tempted to call Snowflake, sat in one of the leather chairs facing the dean's desk, her back straight as a board. Fuck I wanted to loosen her up. See what she was like when she let that unique hair down.

I sat down into the chair beside her, and even though she didn't turn her head, her amazing silver eyes flicked my way. They were such a faint color that the light, for just a moment, made them seem hauntingly translucent.

Dean Henry closed the door and walked around his massive desk. I had all sorts of fantasies about that desk, and none included the dean. I mean, I guess he could watch.

"Myles, I understand from Ren that Mr. Willis has introduced peer tutoring into the curriculum of your calculus class and that Ren is to tutor you."

Ren. I ran her name through my head, loving how it sounded, and had the urge to groan it in her ear. "Aye, that's true."

"I also understand that due to the large stack of failed tests, quizzes, and assignments, she has no interest in helping you," he said, and I looked over at Ren, who just stared straight ahead.

"Aye, that is also true."

"Well then. I've made a decision." Ren sat a little straighter, the corner of her mouth curling up as if she'd already won. "I'm not going to interfere in Mr. Willis's decision to use the students to help one another. Maybe this will finally incentivize those of you treating school as a joke to pass your classes." I smiled wide at the sound of Ren sharply inhaling. Glancing her way, she looked like she was gearing up for round two of the classroom blow-up. "But I'm going to make some changes."

"Um...okay, what changes?" I wasn't sure I would like wherever this was going.

"To begin, you must pass the class with at least a seventy-five percent average, or you will no longer be allowed on the swim and lacrosse teams."

"What?" My mouth dropped open—no one screwed with either Coach Stevens or Coach Bates, they were scary when pissed.

"I'm sure you heard me just fine. I will notify your coaches so they are aware that they could be losing you after the Christmas holiday."

Dean Henry folded his hands on the desk, his eyes going back and forth calmly between myself and Ren. Everything sexy about her outburst was now a fucking pain in my ass. It was all fun and games until the dean started fucking with the only things that kept me sane.

"Now, Ren. I understand that this is a huge ask, especially with this particular student," he said, and I felt like waving and yelling, 'Still in the room, asshole.' "So this is what I will offer you as a compromise."

"I'm listening," she said.

"I am still here, ya know," I mumbled, but neither of them looked at me.

"For helping Myles, I'm going to give you this." Dean Henry opened a drawer and pulled a large keyring out that looked like an old school set you'd see in a prison. Pulling off a key, he handed it over to Ren, who stared at it as confused as I was. "That is a key to the art room door. Your father mentioned that you like art. This will allow you to use the room after hours. I'm trusting that you will be respectful with the space." Ren took the key, staring at it in her palm. "The second thing I'm going to do is offer you this. For every five percent higher you manage to help Myles reach, you can choose something extra to add to your college admission package."

"What do you mean?"

"For example, you will want glowing reference letters from all your teachers. I'm also aware that since you're not legacy, some schools wouldn't consider you for a sorority house, but that would change, and you would be given legacy status."

"Ya got to be joking? I get threatened, and she gets all of that? That's not fair," I blurted out, and the dean's hard stare found me, making my mouth slam shut.

"Then I guess you should've taken your classes more seriously. Oh, and Ren, I've decided to implement this new protocol in all the classes you share with Myles until graduation, which means even more opportunities for extra freedom and college bonuses. That should be more than enough incentive for you to want to help Myles pass his classes." The cell phone on his desk rang and vibrated loudly. "Now, if you'll excuse me, I have a call I need to take."

I stood at the same time as Ren and walked out the door, fuming.

"I hope you're happy now," I growled at her as we left the office.

She spun into my path, and I almost slammed into her. The air felt charged around me with her suddenly so close. Fuck, there was just something about her and her fearlessness that was sexy.

She poked me in the chest, and I grabbed her wrist. "I wouldn't touch me unless ya plan to fuck me," I said, and her eyes narrowed into slits. I let go of her wrist. Her soft skin was making it hard to think straight.

"I'm not happy about any of this. I don't want anything to do with you," she said, and I believed her. Why that made her more appealing was baffling. "I don't even want to be in this place, but I didn't get a say in that matter either. I will make sure you pass your classes so you can have a life outside of shoveling shit for a living." Shoveling shit? "But trust me. There is nothing the dean could give me to make me happy to spend more time than necessary with you." She held out her hand. "Phone, now."

No girl had ever ordered me around like this, and I licked my lips, picturing what she'd be like under me. Reaching into my back pocket, I produced my phone and unlocked it before handing it to her.

"There is my number. Send me a text so I can reach you." She marched away before spinning around to face me again. "Oh, and Myles, I'll have a tutoring schedule for you by the end of the day."

I watched her ass wiggle as she stomped away, the kilt showing it off and making me hot all over. Oh, I couldn't wait to tell Blake about this girl.

Chapter 7

Ren

I'd been in classes for a whopping four hours, and I already hated everything. I chose not to return to calculus class. Instead, I found a washroom to rinse my face off and collect myself before my economics class with Mr. Sharp. Thank god I didn't have Myles in that class, but I did have my oh-so-lovely roommate Vicky.

The only spot left in the class was beside a girl named Chantry, who was so painfully shy that it took me all class to get her to say her name louder than a mouse squeak. Meanwhile, Vicky didn't waste any time making it known that I was her annoying new roommate that snored. Vicky and her friend Raquel would take turns making snorting noises all through class.

I don't snore.

Randomly throughout class, when Mr. Sharp—who seemed older than the next coming of Christ—wasn't paying attention, she made snoring noises while everyone laughed. Joy, oh fucking joy.

I didn't care what the hell she did as long as she didn't mess with my grades. I'd dealt with *Witches of Eastwick* before, and they were all the same. They would bully you until you cried and then bully you some more unless you didn't let it bother you or you punched them in the face. I was trying for the first option, so I didn't end up with a suspension in my first week.

Mr. Collier had been right about one thing. The rules here were fierce. I'd gone to a semi-private school back home, but it wasn't very strict. This place felt more like a jail than a school. Once again, I had to remind myself it was short-term for long-term gain. I needed that tattooed on me somewhere.

At least the lunchroom was easy to find. It was also the assembly area, with a stage on one end. Talking and laughter echoed as I walked into the main hallway from outside. That was one thing I didn't understand about this place. All the main halls where the classes were held were in separate buildings like this was a massive university complex. I didn't care that I had to go outside, but it seemed strange.

Walking in, I looked around for Ivy and spotted her sitting with Chantry who I met in economics. The line wasn't long, so I veered toward it first to get something to eat since I only had a bowl of oatmeal and an apple for breakfast. I wasn't the chicken salad type and gave the greens a dirty look before moving to the hot food.

"Hi there. What can I get for you, dear?" The woman working the hot food station smiled. I glanced at her name tag.

"Hi Betty, I'm not familiar with the daily meals. What do you have," I asked, smiling at the woman.

"I thought you looked new. You seem way too sweet for this place." I had to agree with her there. "We have chicken parmesan or shaved beef on a bun with au jus and fries," she said, and my eyes went wide. Those were the fanciest options I'd ever heard for school lunch.

"Um...."

"The beef is really good today."

"Okay, I'll take that, please."

"I know a different meal ya can have if you're wanting real meat." I'd recognize that whispered voice anywhere. I didn't bother to look, knowing it was Myles.

"Sorry, I'm not into cold, limp sausage," I said, stepping forward as the next person moved.

"Ohhhh damn, you're right. She does have attitude." I didn't bother to look at who the newcomer was. I just wanted to get my food, eat, study, and finish setting up my room. Was that really too much to ask?

"Aye, I love it," Myles said, and I wanted to smack myself.

"Of course you would," I mumbled under my breath.

Another hot jock walked around me and blocked my path, moving with me when I went to step around him. I tried a few more times and had to stop as we looked like we were dancing and drawing stares. I crossed my arms over my chest and glared at the guy. He was taller than Myles with broad shoulders, striking bright green eyes, wavy, blond hair that stopped at his jaw, and deeply tanned skin. He looked like he had just stepped off a beach some-where and should be holding a surfboard under his arm.

"Do you mind? I'd like to get my food," I said.

"Nope, I don't mind. My name's Blake O'Brien," he said like that was supposed to mean something to me.

"Congratulations, now can you move?" Myles draped his arm over my shoulders, and I turned my glare on him. "Haven't I already told you not to touch me?"

I tried to move away, but he gripped my shoulder tighter. "Aw, don't be like that, Snowflake. We're just wanting to be friends."

"Snowflake? Like I haven't heard that before." I jerked away from Myles's hold and ducked around Blake before he could block me again. I know Myles didn't know my past, but the nickname poked at me and scratched at a wound that was still raw. The other kids I went to school with weren't the most understanding when my hair turned white and silver like I'd aged overnight. It was apparently called Marie Antoinette Syndrome, and my hair would never be dark again.

"What's the matter? Don't you like us?" Blake said as he stepped up beside me. I suddenly felt penned in with Myles behind me and the food counter on my other side.

The guy standing in front of me looked over his shoulder. For a brief second, I thought he might help as his eyes narrowed and his mouth opened, but as soon as he saw who was bugging me, he snapped his mouth shut and turned around.

Great. These are the assholes of the school.

That told me all I needed to know about who I was dealing with. My eyes flicked up to Betty, who seemed oblivious as she finished getting my plate. Guess I was on my own. Some things never changed.

"I don't know you, and unlike whoever else you're used to dealing with, I don't want to get to know you to find out," I said. Grabbing a tray from the stack, I held it out to Betty as she put the plate of food and the little dipping sauce on my tray for me.

"Drinks, fruit, and desserts are down that way, dear." Betty pointed and then left to help the next person.

"That's not very nice. We're sweet guys," Myles said as he leaned in close enough that I could smell his cologne and feel his body heat pressing into my back. It made me shiver, and the hair stood on the back of my neck. I didn't like having either reaction to him.

I was tempted to whip around and hit him with the tray, but two Dean's Office visits on the first day seemed like a lot, even for me.

I reached the end of the counter where I could get my drink, and the moment my hand left the tray to slide open the fridge door, it was stolen from my hands.

"Hey," I growled, grabbing a bottle of water.

"If ya want yer food, then yer going to need to come sit with us." Myles smiled as Blake picked fries off my plate and stuffed them in his mouth. They walked away toward a group sitting in the furthest corner with three other guys I hadn't met, but one was very obviously Blake's twin. The only differences between them was a shorter hair cut and the cool, serious stare his brother held.

Vicky, Raquel, and two other girls I could only assume were the rest of her mean-girl clique were also sitting at the table. Vicky was on one guy's lap. He was the most intense of them all. His blue eyes midnight black hair, and dark glare made it feel like he was trying to reach in and rip out my soul. The scar that ran along his cheek made him look rugged and sexy, adding to the feeling that he could rip out my heart and eat it for dinner.

They were all staring at me like I was their entertainment and were waiting for me to blow my stack or maybe run out of here crying.

I was pissed but couldn't be bothered making a larger scene. Screw them. I wasn't playing their game. Besides, the guy sitting in the corner made me shiver with his intensity and what could only be described as a murderous glare. His bright, blue eyes tracked me as I moved like we were predator and prey out in the wild and my stomach twisted into a tidy knot.

Sighing, I looked at the line that was now three times the length it had been when I walked in.

"Screw it," I mumbled and opened the fridge again to grab one of the small yogurts, then wandered over to the table with an assortment of fruit. I picked an apple and didn't spare them another look as I walked to Ivy and Chantry's table.

"Hi, Ren," Ivy waved happily, her face beaming as I got close.

"Hey there." I sat. "Hi, Chantry," I said, and a tiny squeak of a hello could be heard.

"Don't mind, Chantry. She always gets nervous around new people. So how are you finding your first day? I mean, aside from Willis's class this morning?"

I lifted a shoulder and let it drop as I opened my yogurt and then groaned, realizing I hadn't picked up a spoon. Damn, Myles and Blake.

"You need a spoon? Here." Ivy held out the one on her tray. "I don't want my pudding right now and was going to save it til later. You can have mine."

"Thanks." I took the offering and a mouthful of the raspberry yogurt before continuing. "It's going fine. From what I can tell from the binder you gave me, I'm ahead in all my classes except Spanish. I've never taken it before, so I need to start from the beginning and try and get myself caught up."

"How have you never taken Spanish," Ivy asked.

I watched Chantry as she nibbled on a bun like a little mouse. It seemed fitting with her personality.

"I'm from Canada. We take French as our second language."

"Really, that's where you're from? That's cool, no pun intended. My Dad's brother and family live in Toronto, and we visit once a year. Last time we stayed longer and drove north and stayed in this stunning home on the water. The place started with an M, but I can't remember the rest of the name."

I ran through the map of Ontario in my mind and the cities and towns I had memorized. It was a strange habit I had, which was partially why I was so annoyed with this school. I couldn't map it in my head. I still didn't know exactly where we were, but I planned on finding out.

"I think you mean Muskoka," I said.

Ivy's eyes lit up. "Yes, that's it. I loved it there." She took a bite of her chocolate cookie as I ate another mouthful of yogurt. I'd be starving by dinner and was dreading another round of 'Steal my food' with Myles and Blake. They definitely seemed like the type that would keep on poking until I had a meltdown everyone could record. I knew the game, even fell for it a time or two. The last time it happened I promised myself that I wouldn't fall for it again.

"So, what can you tell me about everyone?"

I looked around at the clusters of people, trying to gauge the social groups. No matter how hard schools tried, people with similar interests became units separating from everyone else. I wasn't social, but that was only because I studied during lunch and went home right after school to help look after my mum.

"Well, that far table over there," Ivy nodded in the direction of the long table so loud that I heard them before I stepped into the cafeteria.

I nodded.

"That is the football team and the girls beside them...the cheerleaders," Ivy said, her voice dramatic as she flicked her dark hair over her shoulder and rolled her eyes.

I snickered at the act and looked closer at the group. The one that had practically run me over yesterday, Axel was busy sucking face with a pretty blonde.

"Then the table in the middle of the room, that is the music group."

"Like a choir?"

Ivy smiled. "No, like they all play instruments. The music classes here are really good. They managed to steal teachers from the best schools worldwide for the arts programs."

My ears perked up at that. "All the fine arts classes? I like to paint, but my mum was a sculptor," I said, and there it was, the tug in my heart that I'd managed to go a few hours without. The shadow of sadness washed over me, but I finished my yogurt and licked the spoon.

Ivy nodded. "Yup. Lina Frey is amazing. She came here from France, but she's toured the world teaching."

"Wow, that is impressive."

"I like her," Chantry said, her voice hardly audible with all the other noise. Her hair was like a curtain covering the side of her face, but she didn't say anything more.

Ivy nodded to the table not far away and then leaned forward. "Those are the gamers and hackers, be nice to them, or they will mess with all your devices forever. They are super vindictive." Ivy looked at the table she mentioned and then quickly looked away, her face going bright red.

"Which one do you like?" I whispered, and her cheeks flamed even more.

"The guy with the black hair to his shoulders. His name is Michael, but he goes by Zigzag," she said in a dreamy voice. Ivy's face fell as she looked behind me. "Oh no, Myles is coming this way," she whispered.

I felt his presence before he stepped up to the table, blocking out the overhead light. Chantry slid further away, making sure not to get in the line of fire by accident.

I quickly snatched my water and apple, holding them in my lap. Myles chuckled as he leaned over and trapped me with his arms. His hands were on either side of me, so my only escape was to go under the table. Even I had limits unless it was dire.

His cheek was right beside mine, so I had to lean away from him to turn and look at his smiling face.

"Are you unable to take a hint?" I asked.

"Come on, Myles. It's her first day. Can't you and Blake give her a break," Ivy said, her voice pleading, but I knew he would do whatever he wanted. Myles had that air about him.

She didn't seem to be scared of him, but as he gave her his full attention, she squirmed in her seat.

"I don't know if you're in a position to make any demands, Ivy. Your dad already owes us for bailing him out of debt last week. Do you really want him to be indebted to us anymore?"

It wasn't so much what he said but how he said it that made it sound threatening. The smile never left his face, but I watched Ivy's reaction closely, and she looked down at the table and shook her head no.

"What do you want," I asked, drawing his attention from Ivy.

"I have my first lacrosse practice after school. Would you like to come watch?"

"No, I definitely do not."

"Come on, Snowflake, it'll be fun, and if you get cold, I can give you my jacket to wear."

Had he gotten hit over the head? "Myles, what part of I don't want to get to know you did you not understand?"

"Oh, I don't give up that easy," he said and stood. "You'll cave, I'm sure of it." Walking away, I watched him and the group he was with leave while Vicky shot daggers at me.

"It might be best if you just sleep with him. Then he'll leave you alone," Ivy said, and my mouth fell open. "I know it seems wrong, but he will just keep at you. He and Blake both will make your life hell, and you should pray that their interest doesn't spark Nash. If that happens, your life here is over. Those five will do everything together and I do mean everything. They will torture you like a pack of wolves and they've been known to share in the bedroom if you know what I mean."

My eyes went wide. "All five at once?"

"That's what they say," Ivy said.

"So which one is Nash?" I asked, but was pretty sure I already knew.

"The one that's with Vicky. He's the leader of the Kings of Wayward Academy, and if you get on any of their bad sides, then Nash will come for you. He is the one person you don't want to be caught up with. I haven't met a girl he hasn't made cry or a guy that hasn't run scared."

"So Nash, Blake, and Myles, who else?"

"Blake's twin brother Theo and Nash's right hand Liam." Ivy stood from the table. "Trust me, just sleep with Myles, and your life will be better. Sleep with them all, and you might just be the next Queen."

"Is that what you did?" I was horrified that this was her solution.

"No, but they've never been interested in me. The fifteen-minute bell is about to ring. Just think about it," Ivy said and stepped away from the table before stopping to look back. "Were you doing anything after classes?"

"Just organizing, and then I was going to start my Spanish."

"Chantry has a car, and we were going to sneak off the property to get some dinner in the city. Did you want to come?"

"How about next time," I said, and she smiled before heading out. All I wanted was to get organized and go to bed early.

Standing up, I took a bite of my apple and tried to wrap my head around what Ivy had said. I couldn't imagine paying to be left alone with sex. I was a virgin. The last thing I wanted was for my first time to be a toll bill or with five guys. Thanks, but no thanks. Also, what was that comment about Ivy's dad? Was he a gambler, or did he have another equally dangerous habit?

There were way too many questions, but one thing was certain, I could handle the likes of Myles and Blake. I didn't scare that easy.

Chapter 8

Nash

My arms sliced through the water.

The butterfly was my favorite stroke. The power it took, the speed I got, and the coordination calmed the toxic hatred in my mind. Breathe in...breathe out...breathe in. I could vaguely hear Coach yelling and the other guys cheering me on, but it was nothing but background noise to the sweet silence that came with the sound of water rushing past my ears. Even under the cap, the sound was seductive.

Spotting my marker, I counted down until the two hand touch.

As I pushed off the wall, there was a brief moment I didn't want to resurface. I wanted to sit at the bottom of the pool and let everything above the water disappear as the quiet pressed in on me. But I never stayed. Instead, I pushed harder. Three, two, one. My hand slapped against the wall, and I looked up at the clock. Yes, I cheered in my head with my new personal best.

"Excellent work Nash. We still need to work on a few things, but for tomorrow's competition, you're looking the best you ever have. You all have a really good chance to come away with the win." Coach Stevens clapped a hand on my shoulder and walked away.

Practice was done. There was nothing any of us could do now other than go over our race plans and make sure that we were ready for the weekend. Between Friday and Sunday, we would face a dozen other academies, and one of them was fucking Meadow Grove.

I'd been waiting since last year for this competition to finally get my revenge on Austin Rutherford, who'd taken the gold from me by a tenth of a second. I wasn't allowed to be second to anyone. My father had made that very clear when I got home that night. He said he didn't watch my races, that they weren't worth wasting his time one, and yet...he knew exactly what happened.

All the big-name scouts were at that tournament as well as every television station. I watched that comp play everywhere I went for weeks after, and how I missed out by the tip of my finger. Everyone had gushed over Austin, saying he was the next Michael Phelps. It made me mad enough to kill.

With a push, I rose from the water as the rest of the guys walked over with smiles on their faces. "That was fast, man, you do that all weekend, and you're gonna win for sure against all the other schools."

I grabbed the towel that Liam held out and shrugged. "I only care about one school. The rest I could beat without trying."

"True, but your fly is so much faster than last year," Liam said as I pulled the cap off my head.

"The fly isn't the problem. I know my times have been better than what Austin has posted this season, but the individual medley is still an issue. The backstroke is still my slowest split, and if I can just push a little faster, I'll win the four-hundred for sure. I already know we have the relay covered. I'm aiming for all of us to have all gold."

"That's a huge goal, man," Myles said.

"It is. You also better fucking know I want all you assholes to do the same."

I'd always been competitive, but qualifying for the World's and then onward to the Olympics was my dream. My father's dream was for me to take over and run the family corporation. That was code for you need to take over as the King, which was just a fancy title for Mob Boss.

"Nash, we're already way faster than last year," Blake said, and I glared at him.

"If you don't want to improve every time you're out there, then maybe you don't deserve to be on the team," I snarled.

"Easy, Nash. Blake is only trying to help you feel better. No one is saying we don't want to improve," Theo chimed in, always the voice of reason.

I ground my teeth together but let it go. The guys were not who I was pissed with. My father was insisting that I sit in on the monthly board meeting.

I fixed my stare on Myles. "What the hell was up with you almost being late for practice?"

"Lacrosse practice started after school, first night is always the longest. Chill man, I made it and we will crush Meadow Grove."

"I'm going to shower," I said and walked away, knowing the other guys would follow.

"Ya gonna do an ice bath," Myles asked as I flicked on the shower.

"Can't. Stupid meeting remember? You better not forget to do what I need you to," I said, making sure not to announce what exactly that was. You got good at saying shit without saying anything when your father was the head of the Irish Mob. My father had held power for as long as I'd been alive. Seventeen years and counting. Nowhere near as long as James Bulger or as the public knew him, Whitey, but it was still a long time, and my father had no intention of leaving the position anytime soon.

"I already got it covered and the best route to take. Ya don't need to worry," Myles said, stepping under the spray beside me.

"Are you sure about that," I asked, pushing down my swim brief and rinsing some of the chlorine out before hanging it on the small hook.

"What do ya mean," Myles asked. His eyes were closed, his head under the spray, so he didn't see me raise an eyebrow at him.

"I saw you and Blake with that chick earlier. I also know how you tend to get distracted easily."

"Oh, you mean Snowflake, fuck, she's fine. Makes me want to rub one out right now, thinking about her feisty mouth wrapped around my cock. I think she might actually try to bite it off." He shivered like a dog shaking off water. "Damn, that's hot. I need to stop thinking about it, or I'll say fuck Coach and do exactly that."

"You know I don't believe in that stupid rule right? And I'd ride your ass if I thought it would help."

"Aye, I know, but I can't lie to the Coach for shit. I always look like a nutter when he glares at me. It's only one more comp. I can make it three days," Myles said as Blake, Theo, and Liam walked in.

"Take what," Blake asked.

"Not rubbing my cock out before Sunday night," Myles answered. The sound of the spray and the smell of soap was strong as the heat rose and filled the shower area.

"We on this again?" Theo grumbled.

"I was telling him about Snowflake," Myles said. His face was lit up like a fucking Christmas tree. The last thing I needed was one of my guys being distracted by pussy. Fuck it fine, but don't get too attached was the golden rule.

"Oh yeah, she's fine. I'd tag team her with you," Blake offered Myles.

"Shit, stop making me think about fucking her," he groaned and pointed to his cock that was already standing and confirming my fear of distraction.

"I don't care if you all tag team her, but business comes first, and no distractions this weekend," I said, wanting to shoot my father for making me sound like him.

"I'm pretty sure she wants nothing to do with you, Myles," Liam said. "She told you how many times today to fuck off?"

"She hasn't seen me bust out my charm yet. She'll come around." I liked Myles's confidence. That and his ability to take a punch like no one else were his two most redeeming qualities.

"What's that smell," Liam asked, and we all looked at one another, waiting for a stench to hit us. "No, you assholes, I don't mean someone farted. I mean, I smell a bet coming on."

"Man, the last time I took you up on one of your stupid bets, I lost five grand," Blake whined.

"Fine, you set the bet, then you can stop saying I rigged it even though I won fair and square," Liam said.

I let my head fall back under the spray, allowing the water to drown out the guys talking. I didn't care about a stupid bet. They were always coming up with one thing or another. Instead, my mind wandered to the conversation my father and I had before he left for some funeral the other day.

"I told you, Nash, this is non-negotiable," my father said as he sat down behind his desk.

"I'd like to fucking disagree. Why are we still doing this bullshit arranged marriage crap? Have you seen the date on the calendar? I think I can pick a decent chick to marry." My father rolled his eyes up to me and shook his head. "No, I won't do it. I'm not marrying some girl I don't know. For all I know, you could be setting me up with my first cousin to keep it in the family."

"Not a bad idea, but no, who I have in mind is a much better match to expand our business ties." Father signed another document and laid it aside. "Besides, you don't have a choice. You're a Collier and my only son, making you the next king to wear the crown."

I shoved the back of the chair I was gripping, and it slammed into my father's desk. He burst from his seat, his hands turning into fists as his eyes glared at me with the same murderous stare he'd given countless men. Men that lost their lives for less than talking back or refusing to do his bidding. I'd seen his brutality firsthand. I'd felt it and tasted the blood in my mouth.

"I think ya be missin' da message, son. Ya din't be havin' a choice," Father growled, his accent—that you never normally noticed—coming through strong.

My heart raced as I contemplated what would happen if I pushed. Would he kill me? Would he put me out of my misery? I would rule the kingdom, but I wanted to rule it on my terms, not forced into a box of my father's making. I glared back, and his grey eyes looked black with only his desk lamp on. It was fitting that he looked like the Devil. I'd wondered many times if he was.

Instead, he straightened up and smoothed down his dress shirt before grabbing the drink off the desk and polishing it off.

"One day, son, you'll understand what it means to be in charge and what it actually means to sacrifice. That is the nature of life. Stuffing your cock in a woman and getting her pregnant to strengthen our family's reach is not what I would call a sacrifice. I'm pretty sure you fuck everything but the dog anyway." He grabbed his files and put them in his drawer, locking it before dropping the key into his pocket. "Just be wise and don't get any more of them pregnant. Other than who I want you to, of course, or next time I'll make you pull the trigger."

It was like he punched me in the gut before he walked out, and the anger seethed through my veins. I loved Mya, and I fucked up. I told my father about her, I told him how I felt, and then I fucking got her pregnant, *and she paid the ultimate price. I'd stopped being surprised by the shit my father did, but even I didn't think he'd kill his own grandchild.*

Sadness clogged my throat as I pictured her being dragged from her home. Her wide, terrified eyes stared at the vehicle I was in like she could see me. She was screaming my name and begging me to help her. My father sat across from me, staring at me the entire time. It was his test. What would I do? The gun in his lap sat idle, but at that moment, I knew he'd use it on me if he thought he needed to.

Mya's parents were already dead inside. The flashes and bangs could easily be heard from where we sat by the curb. I could only watch as my father's goons did his bidding and tossed her in a black SUV. I hadn't escaped his anger. I spent two days chained up in his torture chamber, where he liked to do all his hands-on lessons and was beaten repeatedly until I passed out. I ran my finger over the scar on the side of my face. It was a constant reminder of what I'd caused to someone I loved. Now I didn't give a shit about anyone. That was the last time screams would haunt my dreams.

"Hey, earth to Nash, are you in?" I shut off the water and looked at the four faces of my teammates and didn't have a clue what the fuck they were talking about. "The bet. Are you in," Liam asked.

I ran my hands through my hair and walked over to the towel rack with the standard white towels so bleached they felt like I was wiping myself down with sandpaper.

"What's the bet?

"Myles and Blake are challenging each other to see who can get her to fuck them by Christmas," Liam said.

"Liam thinks that Blake has a better shot. I'm going to take Myles for the win. Blake doesn't have what it's going to take." Theo smirked at his brother.

"Thanks, asshole. I'm fucking sexier than you could ever get,"

Blake said, running his hands down his abs. "I bet you wouldn't have what it would take either, looking like that."

I arched my eyebrow at that comment. Theo and Blake were identical twins, making it the dumbest comeback I'd ever heard. I don't even think he realized he just insulted himself.

We all stared at him, but he just shrugged. "Why are you staring at me," Blake asked.

I shook my head. "Sure, I'll take...." I smirked. "Myself."

"What? No way, that's not fair," Blake complained. "You're the King of Kings. Of course, she's going to fuck you."

"Do you want a challenge," I asked, tucking the towel into place. "Or do you want Myles?" I smiled as Myles swore a streak that a trucker would find impressive.

"Fine, I'll take the challenge." Blake crossed his arms over his chest.

"Vicky is not going to be very happy." Theo loved stating the obvious.

I lifted my shoulder and let it drop. I didn't care about Vicky. We dated, we fucked, and that was the end of it. "So what? She can either get over it or find someone else. It's not like I don't fuck around on her already. I told her I wanted an open relationship. It's her own fucking fault if she gets jealous at this point."

"That may be true, but usually those girls are not in the Academy and certainly not her roommate," Theo said, and my ears perked up.

"How the hell do you know that," Myles asked, crossing his arms over his chest.

"I make it my business to know everything," Theo gloated, and even though his tone never changed, his eyes were full of mischief.

"Ha! You didn't give a shit about the last twenty new people. It's because she has a higher GPA than you," Myles said, and Theo's face darkened.

"That may or may not have had something to do with it. I didn't believe it, so I had to find out for myself."

"And...," I asked, intrigued that someone could actually beat Theo academically.

I could see him grinding his teeth from where I stood like he was chewing gravel. "It's true, she has a higher average and is further ahead in all but one class, but I'm fixing that."

"You're planning on sabotaging her? That doesn't seem like you," I said.

Theo scoffed at that. "Um...no. I just plan on beating her. Besides, she'll have her hands full with this one." Theo pointed at Myles. "She is being forced to tutor him. That is going to put her behind."

"Bloody hell, and feck off will ya," Myles growled.

"You're getting tutored, and he has access to her room? This is not a fair fight." Blake crossed his arms over his chest.

"Wait, you can't use being with Vicky to get to her," Myles said.

"Why not? I won't abuse it...much." I smiled. "Besides, I'm not dumping Vicky for this. She gives great blowjobs, and she likes anal. It's a double win. Though I might use it to fuck her quietly while Vicky sleeps beside us." I really had no interest in this girl, but I liked a challenge, and the guys were fun to screw with. They blinked at me. "Oh, come on fuckers, don't chicken out now."

"Fine," Myles and Blake said together.

"Alright, then it's set. Are we going to have anyone else bet on this one?" I could already see Liam running the numbers in his head. The guy was crazy smart when it came to numbers and patterns. Exactly who you would take to an underground poker game and fuck everyone over. We may have already done that once or twice and were banned from a few more.

Pulling my clothes out of the locker, I shrugged. "Don't care. Do whatever you want. Bet is the three of us against one another, and the betters have to pick one of us."

"Then I choose you," Theo said.

"Fucker, I'm your brother," Blake whined.

"How could I forget? I only see your face in the mirror every day."

"Whatever, I'll still beat you all. I have charm on my side. I'm the nice one," Blake said.

"Fuck you all. I saw her first, and we already have sparks. She's mine," Myles growled.

Interesting, he almost sounded possessive. This was going to be more fun than I thought.

Chapter 9

Ren

No one in the world could talk about nothing as much as Vicky. She would make a great politician. She'd been on the phone all night. From the moment I got in from dinner, she'd told the same story ten times to ten different people, and each time it changed slightly. She'd gotten word from her cousin that a girl from another Academy was hitting on her boyfriend. So now she was pulling up every social media account on this supposed girl that liked her man and was in the midst of making her life a living hell. If

73

I had to hear, '*I mean, this is all her own fault. How dare she go near my man,*' one more time, I was going to freak out.

"Hang on. I have another call coming in. Oh, it's Nash. I'll talk to you laters, bye bestie bitch," Vicky said, her voice sounding like a squeaky toy.

I rolled my eyes, happy we had a half wall between us so she couldn't see my face. I wouldn't have been able to wipe the 'Are you fucking kidding me look' off my face.

"Hi, Nash," she said, purring into the phone. Dear Lord, if she started having phone sex, I would be out of here. I had my limits. "A surprise? You know I love surprises."

I glanced at my earphones to see if they were charged. I might need two pairs, so this never happened again. The little light was green, so I unplugged them as Vicky jogged for the door. Was there really a reason to jog? Our room was all of twenty strides long.

Finding a song I liked, I put the earphones on as she opened the door. She jumped and screamed like it was a serial killer at the door before leaping on the guy I'd seen her with at lunch. He was holding a rose, and his eyes found mine for a second before Vicky attacked his face.

"For the love...." I finished swearing in my head and turned my eyes back to the pages of notes I'd already made. Spanish was no joke, and just because I was fluent in French didn't mean a thing. Well, that was a lie, I'm sure it helped some, but I'd never felt this far behind in my entire life.

With the music pumping and focusing on the next set of words I needed to memorize, I didn't notice what was happening with Vicky and her boyfriend until a shadow loomed over me. It was like an eclipse in my room as the desk suddenly became dark.

I looked up at the guy leaning on the half wall, staring at me. The light behind him cast half his face in darkness, but his unique and overly intense blue eyes glowed from the shadows like something supernatural. I couldn't stop staring at the scar on his face. I wanted to know what happened. Was he in an accident, did he fall down drunk and do it to himself, was he in a fight with another guy, or was it something more sinister?

I pulled my earphones off and left them around my neck. "Would you like something?"

The corner of his mouth pulled up in an unsettling smirk that made the butterflies in my stomach want to flit around and hide at the same time.

"There are many things that I would like, but at the moment I just wanted to meet Vicky's new roommate," he said, and before I could stop myself, I chuckled.

"I doubt that. Did Myles or Blake send you? I know you're all friends. You can tell them I'm not interested, and they can go jump in the lake."

The smirk turned up into a smile as he pushed away from the half wall and wandered into my space. I didn't like people in my space at the best of times, but this guy was giving off a dangerous vibe. I definitely didn't want him around my stuff.

Spinning in my chair to keep an eye on Mr. Tall and Scary, I watched as he looked at my photographs from back home. There was one of Lizzy and me and a few others of me and my Mum. He flopped himself down on my bed and for a second I thought he was going to lay back and close his eyes. What the fuck was happening right now?

I looked around and didn't see Vicky. "She's in the washroom getting ready." I glanced at the clock. "I don't care that it's after curfew," he said, his eyes following mine. That was highly unnerving. "You don't like me in here, do you?" His voice was like silk but with an edge that was razor sharp. I felt caught between staring at him and his stupid sexy face or saying something dumb, so I opted to say nothing.

He ran his hand over my pillow but kept his eyes on me. "You don't like it when people touch your things."

It took everything in me to remain quiet. He was poking me, trying to get under my skin, but I couldn't figure out why.

"What if I did this?" He proceeded to lay down, stretching out, and my eyes went to his sneakers that barely stayed off the bed. I licked my lips, my body shaking with the urge to kick him off.

"I'll ask you again, what do you want?" I leaned back in my chair and crossed my arms over my chest to keep myself from shivering as he stared at me. Something about him made me want to jump up and order him out of the room, even though he technically hadn't done anything terrible.

Not yet.

"I already told you there are many things I want," he said, his voice low and seductive.

Even though his hand hadn't moved from where it was on his stomach, all I could picture was it slipping inside his jeans. "But for tonight, from you I just want to get to know you better. You are the newcomer. I make it my business to know who is lurking around the halls."

I laughed at the pile of bullshit that tumbled from his mouth. He might have wanted to get to know me, but I would have placed money he didn't make a point of lounging on every new person's bed.

"Well, that was a pile of sparkly shit if I've ever heard it. You don't want to say, then that's fine with me." I grabbed my head-phones to pull them into place and dismiss the annoying guy on my bed, but he sat up and opened my nightstand.

I was out of my seat and grabbing the journal from his hands before he got it fully out of the drawer. The look of shock was brief, but there was a challenge in his eyes.

Gripping the journal to my chest, I growled. "I don't care who you are. Do. Not. Touch. My. Things."

Nash slowly stood, his eyes locked with mine, but I wasn't backing down. I let him have his fun, and now he could fuck off and go the way of the dinosaurs. I always felt short at five feet, but as Nash towered over me, I had to crane my neck to maintain eye contact. He stepped in closer, but I refused to back away. This jerk was not going to scare me.

"What are you going to do to stop me," he asked, his voice so deep and gravelly that the hair stood up on the back of my neck, and goosebumps rose on my arms.

"Okay, Nash, I'm ready," Vicky sang as she came out of the washroom, the scent of her perfume hitting me a moment later. "What's going on here," she asked, but I didn't look at her until Nash broke the staring contest. That felt like a win.

"Just getting to know your new roommate," Nash said, all too casual, like he hadn't just been borderline threatening me.

He walked away, and the sizzling sensation humming through my body eased off, but it didn't make me feel better. I hugged my journal tighter.

"Why would you want to get to know her?" Vicky shot me a dark glare.

Great, just great. We weren't on the best of terms before Nash's little stunt, and I could only imagine what she was thinking. Based on the look, I guessed it was nothing good. I put my journal back into my nightstand but knew I would be moving it.

"Nash was trying to talk me into giving Myles or Blake a chance," I said. "I already told him no, though. Thanks for passing along the message Nash. So good of you to do it in person, but they really could've made the effort themselves."

They both looked at me as if I'd spoken in tongues. Ignoring them, I put my headphones back on and sat down at my desk. I could feel Vicky still staring at me and heard her say over my low music that she didn't blame me. She wouldn't touch Myles with a ten-foot pole.

"I doubt he wants to touch you either," I mumbled under my breath as the door closed behind them.

Why that comment bothered me, I didn't know. The guy was a pain in my ass and I quickly squashed the feeling. Slumping in my chair, I stared at the door and then at my bed, where Nash had been stretched out moments ago.

Standing up, I leaned over and smoothed out the comforter.

Glancing around the room as if someone had magically appeared, I made sure no one was watching before I leaned over and sniffed the pillow that now had a soft cologne scent. Bloody hell, now my bedding smelled like him.

No way in hell was I ever getting involved with someone like Nash. He was a jerk, and I could already tell he was used to getting what he wanted by intimidating people. He and Vicky were a match made in hell, and I didn't want any part of it.

But the swirling butterflies and thumping of my heart told me I was a liar.

November 5 – Friday 3:03 am

Ren

The sound of the door handle rattling startled me awake, and I stayed still, just listening. I didn't sleep well anymore. Not since my mum...not since those men broke into my old house. Now I heard everything. The tiniest scrape would have my eyes snapping open, and the bang of a door made me jump, but the thump of a boot would make me shake. The memory of the officers marching around the house with their black boots and serious faces somehow haunted me just as much as my mother's death.

Then I heard the giggling and slipped deeper under the blankets just before the door opened, and light filtered into the room. I could just make out the edge of the door frame from where my bed was situated as I peeked around the edge of my comforter, but I heard Vicky and Nash clearly.

"I had so much fun tonight. Thanks for taking me. I really think your dad likes me," Vicky said, her voice all sing-song. I nearly retched as I pictured her sucking up to Nash's father like a cat in heat.

"I'm sure he does," Nash said, and even without seeing his face, I knew that was a bald-faced lie. Well, at least his father had some common sense. Something that his son seemed to be lacking.

"Do you want to come in? I can make it worth your while," Vicky whispered.

Really? You really want to come in here while I'm sleeping and fuck your boyfriend? I was so done. I would find a way out of this place as fast as I could, even if that meant I had to emancipate myself from my father.

"You know I can't. Our last competition is tomorrow," Nash said but didn't bother to whisper.

"Aw, come on, you always say that your coach is stupid for believing that crap about not having sex. Besides, I'm horny." I wasn't sure anyone would believe me if I told them this happened.

"Get your hand off me," Nash growled, making me shiver involuntarily. "If you're horny, take care of it yourself."

Please don't. I wanted to jump up and smack him for suggesting such a thing. Then again, I had a feeling he'd bite my hand off.

"Fine, whatever. Did you want to chill in here with me for a bit, at least?"

"What about your roommate?"

Well, at least he realized I was still in the room.

"What about her?" Not that Vicky cared.

"Isn't she going to be pissed off or wake up? I thought you were going to try and get along with your next roommate."

"She's not my type of friend, besides we can use earbuds so we don't bother the little freak."

Freak? Who the hell was she calling a freak? She was the freak with her overly long arms and legs that made her look like a praying mantis.

"Sure, but I can't stay long."

I sighed, the list of swear words on repeat in my head. The door closed, and the room was plunged into darkness once more.

"I'll be right back," Vicky said.

My eyes were closed, but I could hear the washroom door open and close. She was probably still going to try and talk him into staying. All I wanted was some sleep.

The hair on my arms stood as a soft breeze brushed my cheek a moment before his cologne hit me. "I know you're not asleep, Princess," Nash whispered in my ear.

I couldn't stop myself from shrinking away from him. My pillow shifted on either side of my head, and even though I still refused to open my eyes, I knew he was leaning over me.

"What do you want?" I whispered, asking for the third time. Hoping he'd be honest then run along. I opened my eyes and Nash was right in front of my face, his nose so close to mine that if I moved at all, they would've touched. Ivy's words of warning rang loud in my mind.

"I want you to know that I plan on fucking you, Princess, and I promise you'll scream my name, and beg for more."

I tried to swallow the giant-sized lump in my throat as my heart pounded. Nash pushed away from the bed and wandered out into the dark of the room, but I could still see his eyes and feel his presence like a caress.

Vicky came out of the bathroom, and I still fully expected this to turn into a fuckfest, but Nash shocked me again. "Look, I'm tired, I have to go."

"But you said…"

"I know what I said."

"But you're still going to go?"

"It's never enough, is it?" Nash said, his voice laced with irritation.

"What are you talking about?"

"We weren't even supposed to see each other tonight, but I took you out to my dad's dinner, and we hung out with friends, and yet here you are, pushing for more."

"Shhh, keep your voice down" Vicky ordered. "I don't want it to hear us." It? Now I was nothing more than a thing, not even a freak. How quickly I was tumbling down the ladder.

Vicky squealed, and there was a soft thud. "First, I don't give a fuck who hears us. Second, don't ever talk to me like that again."

My eyes were wide open now, and I couldn't stop listening even if I wanted to.

"I'm sorry." Vicky's voice was so soft I barely heard her. "Can I see you tomorrow?"

"No." His tone had me curling up in a ball and wanting to hide under my blankets. Why would someone ever willingly be with this guy?

Nash offered no explanation as to why Vicky couldn't see him. He was cold and calculating, and I'd never met anyone like him. The only person I'd ever met close to this level of intense creepiness was my father's boss, Lawrence Collier.

The door opened and closed a second later, and I sucked in a deep breath. It felt like the air had been sucked out of the room with him in here.

"Jerk," Vicky grumbled, once the door was close.

I knew I needed to stay as far away from Nash as possible. I was never fucking him, so he could forget about adding me to the notches on his belt. The fear was would he take no for an answer, and why did he suddenly have an interest in me?

Chapter 10

Myles

I breathed into my hand. Yup, still minty fresh. Balancing the two coffees in one hand, I stared at the tippy takeout cups from the cafeteria and raised my other to knock. Snowflake picked that moment to open the door and walked right into my fist. My knuckles rapped off her nose hard enough that they cracked.

"Ow, shit." She stumbled backward.

"Fuck, I'm so sorry," I said and grabbed for Ren, not even thinking about the coffee still in my hand. Of course, one of the lids

83

popped off, and the hot liquid splashed all over the front of her uniform.

"Ah, holy hell, that's hot," she yelped and pulled her shirt away from her body.

"Oh fuck, sorry," I said and quickly sat the second coffee down on a small table and grabbed a towel off the back of a chair. I pressed the towel against the liquid and swallowed hard as Ren's angry stare looked down at my hand and towel pressed against her chest.

I whipped my hand away as Ren's eyes tried to meet mine through the tears streaming down her face from the blow to her nose. I wanted to help but was terrified to move as she glared at me and then down at her outfit.

"What the hell, Myles?"

"Keep it down, Freak. I'm trying to sleep," Vicky complained.

"How about I pour hot coffee on you and see how quiet you remain," Ren growled out, and my eyebrow cocked. No one talked to Vicky like that except us Kings. We didn't give a shit who her family was, but no one else dared to mess with her. I was impressed that Ren didn't seem to give a shit.

Vicky sat up, obviously looking to start World War III, but when she saw Ren's stained and dripping clothes, she burst out in hysterical laughter and grabbed her phone.

"Oh, I need to preserve this," Vicky said.

"Leave her alone, Vicky." I did the one thing I could do to help and stepped between Ren and the camera, holding the towel open to make sure Vicky didn't capture this moment. I was all for being an asshole. In fact, I was great at it, but I figured punching Ren in the face and dumping hot coffee on her was more than enough asshole for six in the morning.

"Come on, Myles, get out of my way."

"Not a chance. Ren, are ya alright?" I glanced over my shoulder, but she was gone. "What the fuck?" Spinning in a circle, I checked every corner of the room. It was like a magic trick. There was no way she would still go to class like that, would she? Dropping the towel on the mess, I darted out into the hall and saw the far exit door closing.

Coach Bates would've been impressed with my speed and how quickly I got through the two sets of double doors that led out of the girl's wing. I got my arm in the closing elevator doors just in time, and with a ding, they opened.

Ren held her bag in one hand while the other wiped at the mess I'd made. I wanted to make a mess all over her, but this wasn't what I had in mind.

"Snowflake, truly I'm sorry," I said as the doors closed behind me.

"What were you doing at my door in the first place, Myles?"

"Ya told me to meet ya for tutoring this morning." I pulled out my phone and flicked through the numerous texts from the guys and a couple of girls I planned on meeting up with after the competition.

"I'm pretty sure the text said to meet me in the cafeteria."

"Aye, but I thought I would do something nice and bring ya coffee and walk ya there. We didn't get off on the best foot yesterday, and I was trying to be nice."

Ren sighed and rubbed at the tears still running down her cheeks. Her nose was already red, and she would definitely end up with a partial black eye. There was a strange stirring in my gut. Guilt was a rare ass emotion for me, but I felt it now.

"It was a nice thought, thanks."

"Are ya okay? It didn't burn ya? We can go to the nurse."

"I'm fine. Nothing that a shower and some ice won't fix."

Oh, she had to go and put the idea of her naked and wet in my head.

The elevator dinged, and I stepped back so Ren could walk out first. She looked like a perfect little librarian, with her hair twisted into a messy bun and a pen stuck in it. Even covered in coffee with a swelling eye, she looked delicious. I wasn't sure how I would get through two hours of calculus twice a week, plus tutoring, and not think about laying her on the desk.

Who was I kidding? There was no world where I didn't picture her laying on Mr. Willis's desk as a fuck you to the ass wipe teacher. Her normally neat blouse would be open, showing off her white lacey bra that I could see through her damp shirt. I'd push that short blue kilt up over her hips and—

"Why are you staring at me like that?"

Ren's voice startled me. Shaking my head, I forced myself out of the fantasy that could become a full-fledged reality if she just said yes. Fuck the desk. I'd pull her back into the elevator and press the emergency stop if she wanted.

"Sorry, I spaced out."

"Are you going to do that the entire time I'm tutoring you?"

Smirking, I rubbed the back of my neck. If she only knew that it was her distracting me. "There is a really good possibility."

"Great." She stepped out, and I was quick to match her stride.

"Are you sure you don't want to get changed first?"

Ren shot me a look. "I would if I had another uniform. The school is waiting on a shipment to come in. I guess it's late. I didn't own any white school shirts and didn't buy any before coming here." We walked into the quiet cafeteria. "I would've had to know where I was going for that to happen," she muttered, which piqued my curiosity.

"I could lend ya one of mine," I offered, loving the idea of her in my clothes. It was a hot fucking fantasy, and I just liked the idea for some reason. "Ya just need to come to my room for a minute." She shook her head no. What was it about her stubbornness that was such a fucking turn-on? I wanted to rip the stained shirt off of her so she'd be forced to take mine, but I had a feeling she'd pull on a garbage bag first. If there weren't a half dozen cameras in the cafeteria, I might have been tempted to give it a shot just to test my theory.

Ren took an apple and a muffin from the various baskets before heading to the coffee station. I liked that she didn't look the apples all over and didn't worry about reading the little card stating the calories in the muffin. I smirked as she dumped three sugars and two creams into her coffee and made a note to make it perfect for next time.

"You not getting anything," she asked.

"No, we leave for a meet today, and I have a strict diet leading up to a competition."

"What time is that?"

"Heading out right after school. It goes all weekend, but tonight's first round of preliminary heats start at six."

"Meet. Isn't that swimming? I thought you played lacrosse."

"I do. I'm on the swim and the lacrosse team." Normally, I didn't give a shit what anyone thought about my athleticism, but I was nervous for her reply.

"That's a lot of training, very impressive. Is that why your marks suffer," she asked, her voice even, and yet it felt like a slap. My back straightened, and I rolled out the tension from my shoulders.

"No, they suffer because I don't care." Ren's eyes narrowed into a harsh glare. It was unsettling and turned me on at the same time. "I mean, I didn't care until doing this tutoring with you," I corrected and winked at her.

"Mhmm."

As we sat down, I couldn't remember ever being in here so early. A handful of people were reading and working on laptops, while a few slept with their heads on the table. I yawned, staring at those peacefully sleeping.

"Wake the fuck up! Ya all have detention," I screamed and smiled as everyone, including Ren, jumped.

"Fuck Myles," one of the guys from my lacrosse team grumbled, making me smirk.

"What the hell was that for," Ren asked.

My shoulders lifted lazily. "If I can't be sleeping, then they can't be sleeping."

Ren was gripping her shirt so tight that her knuckles were bright white. I wasn't sure if she realized it as she held on, her breathing much faster than normal.

"Are ya okay?" I pointedly looked to where her hand was.

"Yeah, of course. You just scared me. That seems to be your MO today, and...oh no, did you invite him?" Ren's voice was exasperated as she looked over my shoulder.

"Who?" Shifting around, I spotted Blake smiling as he strutted over to the coffee stand. Of all the guys in this school, Blake had welcomed me first with open arms to the group. But he was a total show-off and walked around like he was a famous rock star or something. The fucker had no reason to be in here other than the bet and to fuck with me. He knew we'd be here. I made the mistake of telling him before the bet was made. Stupid.

He pretended to spot us and wave as I grumbled under my breath. "No, I didn't invite Blake."

"Is he going to be a distraction?"

"Most likely."

Ren's eyes searched my face and then sighed. "Then he can't say," she said just as Blake flopped down beside me.

"Hello, hello, hello," Blake said.

"What the fuck, do you think you're Matthew McConaughey or something?" I growled and glared at my friend, who continued to smile at me.

"Better than. So, what's happening, beautiful people? Don't we all look like little fucking rays of sunshine."

"Nope, not happening. You need to go," Ren said before I could even open my mouth, and it warmed my heart to see the shocked expression on his face.

But then he pulled out his superpower. I didn't know if Blake knew he had the skill and exploited it or if he didn't, but his face turned into the perfect, sad pout. Even I wanted to say aww, at the fake tears that filled his eyes. Fuck me, he was like a sad puppy, and no girl on this planet could resist that face.

"But I just want to have my coffee with you guys. I'll be quiet," Blake offered and sipped his coffee. "Um...you do know you're all wet, right? It looks like someone had a wet shit all over the front of you." Ren glared daggers at Blake, which made me stupidly happy.

I snickered at the comment but sobered as Ren stood. "No, I hadn't noticed the sopping wet shirt and jacket I'm wearing. Thanks so much for pointing it out. I'm not sure how I would've gotten through my day without you pointing it out or that descriptive visual in my head."

"Wow. Chill. I just wanted to know if you knew." Blake lifted his hands like he was warding off an attack.

"Well, now you know the answer." Her eyes reminded me of a cold winter day when they found mine. "Since you have the competition tonight, we'll reschedule for Monday and meet in the library instead. I'll let you know a time."

I grabbed her arm as she reached my side and loved that she shivered from my touch. "But what about right now?"

"I don't need to tutor Blake, and there is something I need to go do. You've lasted this long in the class without being booted out, so I'm sure a few more days won't make a difference." She looked at my hand, and even though I knew it was a mistake, I couldn't stop myself from giving her arm a hard tug. I loved her little scream as she fell toward me.

Between the momentum and my guiding her, she landed perfectly in my lap, making me groan. Her arm went around my neck, and she felt incredible pressed up against me. Damn, she was worth pissing off Coach. If she wanted, I'd take her right here on the table, take the expulsion, and do it again.

Ren's shocked expression shifted smoothly into a smile, her eyes batting at me, and the same strange tug pulled in my gut. I should've known something was coming, but I didn't. I was too caught up in the fact that her lips were inches from mine, and she smelled like the sweet lilies and cherry blossoms in my family's garden back home. Those silver eyes captured me as firm as any fist.

My semi-hard-on from picturing her bent over Willis's desk was now at full attention, but if she noticed, she didn't say.

Instead, she gasped loudly as if shocked. "Myles, for the last time, I don't want to see you suck Blake's cock!" She yelled, and everyone resting sat up like a fucking dinner bell had rung.

I could feel Blake's shocked eyes on my face as I stared wide-eyed at Ren. "What?"

In retrospect, that was the stupidest thing I could've said, but she took me completely by surprise.

"You heard me, Myles. Stop asking if I'll watch and film you guys. I have no interest in being a porno videographer. You boys have fun, though. I'm sure you'll find someone to help you" She smiled wide, pushing herself up from my lap, and marched away.

"What the fuck just happened," Blake asked.

I took in the stares that were still waiting for a response. "Mind your own fucking business," I barked out. Everyone acted like they hadn't heard a thing, the room getting as loud as possible for two dozen people pretending they weren't watching the show.

"She just made asses out of us, is what happened." I shifted in my seat. I could still feel her sitting in my lap, and a stupid smile pulled at the corner of my lips. "Fuck. Dude, I really like her."

Blake rolled his eyes at me before laughing. "You would, but I don't think you have a chance, my friend." Blake looked over his shoulder to the door that Ren had disappeared through. "She's not like the other girls we go after."

"You saying I'm not good enough?"

Blake smiled and reached out to steal the rest of Ren's half-eaten muffin. "I'm saying that there is a good chance none of us are." He shrugged. "I don't think any of us are winning this bet. If I was you, I'd find another one to really like."

"Giving up so easily. Doesn't seem like you, but I'll happily take the win if you're going to bow out of the bet. One less of you assholes to deal with."

"You're a sucker for punishment, my friend," Blake said as we stood. "Cause if we keep at this game, there is a one in three chance that you're going to lose. Are you willing to take those odds? Because

I'm pretty sure that I'll be the one to win." Blake smiled, his eyes smug.

"Over me dead body." I wanted Ren, that was all there was to it, and I was going to find a way to make that happen, one way or another.

Chapter 11

NOVEMBER 5 – FRIDAY 7:45 AM

Ren

There was nothing quite like washing your blouse in the school's bathroom sink while people walked in and out and stared at you. I could almost hear them calling me Freak, even though no one said it out loud. No matter how much I scrubbed, I couldn't get the stain out, but it was better. Luckily, the jacket was such a dark navy blue that the coffee barely showed. It hung on a bathroom stall door to dry while I held the shirt under the dryer.

I heard the door open again but didn't pay attention until Vicky's annoying laugh made me internally groan like she was running her nails down a chalkboard. I didn't bother turning around or acknowledging her as I continued to dry my shirt.

"Don't you just hate poor people," Vicky said, and I rolled my eyes at the wall. I wasn't poor. I might not be a billionaire, but what did it matter anyway? How much money you have shouldn't be a measure of your social standing. A sink turned on, and I bristled at the thought of them throwing water at me.

"Yeah, they're always looking for free handouts and clothing. I mean, get a real job, and you won't have to look so pathetic," a voice I didn't know answered. "Oh, I love this shade," she added, and I could only assume without looking that she was referring to her makeup or hair.

"Exactly, and then to have them blatantly flirt with your boyfriend like they actually had a chance...so pathetic," a third voice said. I was pretty sure that was Raquel. "Yes, I love that color eyeshadow on you. You should try my lilac shadow. It would really make your eyes stand out."

"Yeah, agreed. It's fine, though. I'm going to teach her a lesson she'll never forget. I will make her life such a living hell that she drops out and has to move to another country just to get away from me and the humiliation."

Fuck. Stuffing my arms into the blouse, I turned around as I did up the buttons. "I wasn't hitting on Nash," I said. Like a scene in a horror movie, all three heads that had been leaning over sinks and staring into the mirror turned in my direction.

Vicky blinked and then laughed. "Oh, sweetie, we weren't talking about you." Her eyes traveled up and down my body. The disgust in her eyes was palpable. "You're not important enough to be bothered talking about." She clicked the lid on her lipstick and turned to the two girls that looked like malicious guard dogs. "Come on girls, let's get to class so Ren here can finish getting dressed." She pointed one long elegant finger at me and wiggled it up and down. "You do know that shirt is stained, right?"

Of course, I knew it was stained just as she knew it was stained.

She was in the damn room when it happened. I probably should've cleaned up the spilled coffee, but I had just wanted to get the hell out of there.

I was fuming as she smiled, but it didn't reach her eyes. "See you later, roomie," she said sickeningly sweet. Holding onto the door, she paused and stared at me. "Oh, and by the way, you'll want to find a mop and bucket before the end of classes today to clean up your lover's mess. I don't clean," she said as if reading my mind.

"He's not my lover," I called after her as the door closed and was met with a string of giggles from more than one person.

I damn well knew that little show was for me, and the fact that she said it wasn't somehow pissed me off more. Then I had to go and make it worse. I fell right into her web, and just like the spider she was, she waited for me to get stuck so she could attack.

Fuck I hated this place.

Tucking the ends of my shirt into my kilt, I grabbed the jacket off the door and put it on as I stared in the mirror. You could still see some of the stain, but it was nowhere near as bad. What pissed me off even more was how Myles had pulled me into his lap like I was his property or something. I loathed the fact that it hadn't felt bad either.

He smelled so good, and there was no denying that the flex of his muscles under my hand had been hot as hell. Then there were those eyes that were so different, and...No, I was definitely not going there. The last thing I needed was the distraction of a boyfriend, or whatever it was he thought we would be. If I could stay focused, there was a good chance I could fast-track my studies and get out of here a semester early. That was my new goal.

Picking up my backpack, I marched for the door and ignored all the stares I got as I stepped out into the hall. Let them stare. They meant nothing to me, and their opinions equally so. I watched the numbers count down to room seven and stepped inside. Ivy lifted her hand in the air and pointed beside her. A little bit of the tension that I hadn't noticed forming in my chest eased at the sight of a friendly face and no Myles, Blake, or Nash.

"Hey, how's it going," I asked as I dropped down beside her in the plastic chair. You'd think an expensive academy like this would have something nicer than the standard issue public school seats.

"I'm doing okay..." Her eyes went to the brown spot at the V of my jacket.

"I know, I have a stain. I need more shirts, but the school doesn't have any in my size, and I didn't bring any. I also don't have a car to go shopping anywhere," I said.

"I'll take you." I groaned at the sound of Blake's voice behind me. I knew I'd gotten too lucky. "It'll have to wait until Monday since I'm gone to the tourney all weekend, but we can make it a date. I can show you the area, and I know this amazing ice cream shop where I promise not to throw any on you." Blake walked around to the desk behind me and sat down. "You can come too, Ivy," he said, and her face lit up.

"Really?" Ivy practically yelled with excitement, making me jump. She looked around the room, her cheeks going red as she covered her mouth. "Sorry."

She was so cute, and I laughed at her embarrassment, even though I shouldn't. Turning my attention back to the problem at hand, I looked at Blake and his all-too-happy expression.

"I don't know. I don't even know you," I said to Blake.

"We can ask your daddy if you like," he said, his lip curving up as his eyes challenged me. I wanted to punch him square in the face but took a deep breath and counted to ten instead. "You know, if you still need to ask for permission to leave the property, that is. That's usually a first year issue, but if you do..."

I glared at him and hated that he managed to find a scab to pick at that would bother me. Having to ask my father for anything was a hell no.

"Please, Ren," Ivy begged, her voice soft. "I rarely get to leave the property, my dad is a total hard ass, and I don't have a vehicle.

Chantry sneaks us off now and then, but we usually only do a quick drive-thru and head back."

My bottom lip would end up bleeding before the week was out at the rate I was biting it. I could feel myself caving as I stared into Ivy's hopeful eyes. God dammit.

"Fine, I'll go. Only because you want me to," I said to Ivy, but that didn't stop Blake from smiling like he'd talked me into it.

"Yes," Ivy cheered.

"Great, it's a date," Blake said, smirking.

I shot him a glare. "No, it's most certainly not a date."

"What would you call it?"

"An outing," I said and crossed my arms. "It just happens to be together."

"So an outing together on a specific date. It's a date." The mischievous grin he gave me had me shaking my head. I could see now why he and Myles were friends.

Ignoring the comment, I turned around as the teacher, Mr. Martelli, walked in. I think I was just tricked and was already regretting saying yes.

November 5 – Friday 1:15 pm
Nash
I released Vicky's face from the tonsil fucking I was giving her. She was a decent kisser, a little sloppy, but that wasn't the talent I wanted from her mouth anyway.

"I hate that you're gone all weekend," Vicky said, her bottom lip pushed out in a pout.

"I'm looking forward to this meet and kicking Austin's ass," I said. There was no point in saying shit like I'll miss you too when it would be a lie. I never missed her, and I had a date with a Grove

Academy girl after the meet was over. I'd never said we were exclusive. That was the label Vicky put on us.

"You'd better get going, or we're both going to be late for class." I could see her gearing up to ask, 'Would you mind if I came to watch?' Or offering, 'I could go with you if you want.'

No thanks.

"Okay, well, good luck, baby," she said.

As she walked away, I turned my head to look down the hall and spotted my target coming toward us. The two women glared at one another as they passed. Before I could grab Ren, she darted into the biology classroom with a group of other students. Smart girl.

"Hey man, how's it going," Liam asked, clapping a hand on my shoulder.

"We're about to find out." I leaned against the locker, not worried about being late or whoever sat where I wanted. They'd move. There were a very select few in this school that dared to push me. The rest scattered like insects running from my boot. "We need to have a meeting when we get back from the meet," I whispered.

"You got it. I'll make the arrangements. I have one that would like to be inducted. You want me to bring him along?"

I ran my thumb over my bottom lip. "Sure, I could use a good hazing." The bell rang, and I pushed away from the wall. "See you when class is over."

The moment I stepped into the doorway, I knew where Ren was. Even if the silvery hair didn't give her away, I felt her eyes on me. The moment mine met hers, she casually looked down at the textbook in front of her. I couldn't read the rest of what she mouthed, but the word *fuck*, made me smile.

Walking over to the long desk, I stared down at the girl in my seat. She glanced up, and her eyes went wide as she gathered her things and took off, almost knocking the tall stool over.

Ren glared at me from the corner of her eye as I sat down. Up close, I could see the appeal that Myles saw. She was sexy in this unique way, and I could also understand why Vicky hated her. It was obvious she had something that almost everyone inside these walls lacked, a backbone.

She didn't squirm under my glare. In fact, she didn't acknowledge me at all. I stared at her face wondering who'd given her the black eye. Was that why she and Vicky had glared at one another? I wasn't sure how I felt about the two of them throwing punches. If they added whipcream I'd be down to watch that shit all night long.

She scribbled across the standard issue lined paper rather than typing the notes into her laptop. Ren remained completely focused on her task, and with a quick glance, I could tell she was much further ahead than the lesson we were on. No wonder Theo was pissed at this girl.

"Hey, don't I know you? I know I've seen you around before," Axel said as he turned around and leaned on the desk. Ren didn't bother looking up. There were no flustered comments or batting of her eyes for the captain of the football team.

"You almost ran me over the other day," she said. "All my stuff went flying, and you made a sexual gesture before you walked away."

"Shit, yeah, I remember now. I might have been a little wasted in my defense." He held out his hand, and Ren's pen stopped as she looked up at him. "Name's Axel. I'm the captain of the football team." Axel looked at me, and I instantly knew he knew about the bet. He was working at fucking things up for me. He must have put money on either Myles or Blake.

"I know who you are," Ren drawled, her tone saying volumes about how unimpressed she was with his title. I snorted, unable to keep the laughter in as Axel pulled his unshaken hand away.

"Wow, bitch much," Axel said, his eyes darkening with anger.

"Yup, that's me, la bitch extraordinaire," she said and flicked the page in her textbook. I had to admit she'd piqued my interest ever so slightly. Very few girls—unless they only liked other girls—refused to bow down to the captain of the football team. The only one higher in the school's pecking order was me, and she wasn't falling all over me either.

"Do you like girls," I asked, and the tables around us got quiet.

Ren finally lifted her head, and I liked that her eyes matched her hair. That was pretty fucking cool. I'd never seen anyone with that combination before other than in movies.

"And what would it matter if I did?"

I shrugged. "It wouldn't, but Myles will be sad."

She rolled her eyes and turned back to her textbook, not bothering to answer the question. Reaching out, I smacked my hand down on the paper she was working on and noticed her fist tightening around her pen like she was debating stabbing me with it. This would be harder than I thought, and I loved that. Before today I would've bet I had her in bed with me by the end of next week, if not sooner, but now...I wasn't so sure.

"I asked you a question." Leaning in close to her ear, she shivered ever so slightly. "I won't tolerate being ignored. Bad things happen to people that do."

"You threatening me," she said, her voice just as soft as mine, but the heated look in her eyes was next-level intense. Suddenly I saw fire dancing in their depths and wanted to know if she would fuck the same way.

"I'm just letting you know the rules. I own this place and everyone in it, which means you as well."

She snickered and then sighed as if I was boring her. Ren clicked her pen, and my eyes instinctively went to the sound. "Don't you have a fancy swim meet this weekend?" I raised my brow at her, not sure where she was going with this. "It would be a real shame if something happened to your hand and you couldn't compete."

The pen she held clicked again, and the look in her eye told me all I needed to know. She would fucking stab me and take whatever punishment was coming to her, just to get me out of her face. I was impressed. I didn't impress easily, but she had drawn a line in the proverbial sand. My lips curved up in a smile as the teacher walked in, giving me the perfect excuse to back off without backing down.

"Don't think I won't remember this," I said under my breath.

"I wouldn't dream of it," she sniped back.

"Our next lesson is Mutations, genetic diversity, and natural selection," Mrs. Grey called out as she wrote on the whiteboard. I wasn't sure why she still did this. We all had texts and laptops, but no matter what, she wrote down every lesson, old-school style. "Also, we will be doing pair work, so look at the person beside you. They will be your partner until the end of the semester."

"Fuck me," Ren mumbled and covered her eyes.

"Oh, I plan on it, Princess," I mumbled back.

Chapter 12

NOVEMBER 6 – SATURDAY 9:33 PM

Ren

Sketch pad under my arm and key in my hand, I silently made my way over to Bowfield Hall. Vicky had invited Raquel and the other girl, who I now knew as Jennifer, over to do each other's nails.

I honestly didn't care that they were laughing, talking, and playing music. What I had a problem with were the constant comments obviously directed at me, but as if they weren't. It was mental warfare that I had no extra energy to fight.

Stepping outside, I took a deep breath of the air. It was the kind of cold we said held bite back home. Basically, it was a sharp cold, and there was no moisture in the air. I shivered in the simple cotton pants and sweatshirt I wore.

I liked how everything here was well-lit at night. All the walkways had old-fashioned street lamps. They also lined the driveway and the outer jogging track that circled the property. I'd seen several people using the track as I stepped outside.

Pulling open the door to Bowfield Hall, I paused inside and took a moment to appreciate the utter stillness. The silence didn't unnerve me like it would other people. This was the sort of quiet I enjoyed.

The main hallway was brightly lit and comforting. Room twelve was near the end of the building, and as I wandered along, an uneasy feeling grew in the pit of my stomach. All the doors were locked, and the windows were black. I felt like I was being watched, and a set of eyes were going to appear in one of the small windows, which was insane. Suddenly nothing about this place felt entirely safe. Then again, would any place ever feel safe after what happened? All the things I took for granted like sleeping through the night, not jumping at the sound of a door slamming, or not shivering when a man yelled, bothered me. I tried to hide it, and ignore it as best I could, but the feelings were always right there waiting to pounce from the recesses of my mind.

Reaching my destination, I used the key that Dean Henry had given me and unlocked the door to the art room. There was a distinct hum when I flicked the light switch as all the fluorescent bulbs came on and warmed up. I closed and locked the door behind me and smiled the first real smile in what seemed like a lifetime.

The room was huge, with stairs leading up to a second story. Workstations were set up with easels and various paints, charcoal, and pencils. When I was here for my first class yesterday afternoon, I didn't want to leave and asked Mrs. Frey if I could stay. She said I could stay as long as I liked, and I'd done just that. Even though I knew I should be studying Spanish, I just couldn't tear myself away from the painting I'd started.

Walking over to my easel, I took a moment to appreciate my work. I'd always loved painting and working with clay. The ability to create something beautiful from nothing filled me with purpose. It made me feel like anything was possible. It also allowed my mum and I to stay connected and gave us something to do as her health declined.

Mum would've loved this piece. I could almost hear her saying I made her look like an angel, but that was what she'd always been to me. Now that was how I liked to keep her in my heart. An angel watching over me so I didn't feel so alone.

I remembered all too clearly the first time she collapsed on the floor and how my heart had raced as I called 911 for help. Her hand had felt cool to the touch, and I had refused to leave her side even when they said they didn't have any space in the ambulance.

They had finally conceded and let me sit up front when they realized they would have to knock me out to get me to let go of Mum's hand.

"Would you like to wait for your husband to arrive, Mrs. Davies," the doctor asked my mum.

"No, that's okay. He's caught up at work." The doctor's eyes flicked in my direction, and I knew the news wasn't good. No one gave the 'Are you sure you want her here?' look when it was good news. "You can speak freely in front of my daughter," my mum said, holding my hand.

Was I too young to be in the room at twelve? Possibly. But I wouldn't have left without guards carting me away. Stubbornness had always been my number one trait.

"Very well. We found a brain tumor, but we are unsure if it is cancerous. We won't have that answer until the tumor is out and the pathology report is back. Due to the size and location, we can't wait to perform surgery, and I've scheduled you for the day after tomorrow."

My hand tightened on my mum's, my stomach flipping and making me feel sick as tears pricked the back of my eyes, but I didn't cry or throw up. I needed to be strong for my mum.

"Oh, I see. What happens if it is cancerous?"

"You may need chemo or radiation. We will also be checking to make sure it hasn't metastasized," the doctor said calmly, while I wanted to scream at him and ask him what all that meant. It seemed very serious by the worry on my mum's face. How could he act so calm?

"What am I looking at, time-wise?" My mum asked as she held my hand tighter. I laid my other hand on top of hers.

"It is too early to say. We're not even sure what we are dealing with at this point." He spoke so evenly and stood perfectly still, like a robot. His hands were neatly folded in front of him with a clipboard in his hand.

"Do you know why this has happened?"

"Again, it is far too early to say. It could easily have been there for years or not long. The fact you haven't had any symptoms until your collapse is very optimistic. I don't want to give you false information or hope, so let's wait and see what the tests say."

My mum sighed and looked at me with silver eyes that matched my own. She smiled at me, but I could see the worry all over her beautiful face.

"Okay, whatever you need to do," my mum said, and the doctor stepped forward with papers for her to sign.

I wiped away the tears that were such a common occurrence this last year that most of the time, I didn't notice them trailing down my cheeks. Grabbing the paints from the cupboard, I opened the drawer at my station to pull out my brushes, but they were gone.

Panic instantly squeezed my throat as I stared into the empty space. "Who would take my brushes? Why would someone even want them?"

I dug around in the drawer, hoping they'd somehow jumped out of the tray and landed in the bottom. I knew it was stupid, but it was the only thing I could think of. Vicky and her friends didn't take this class neither did Myles, Blake, or Nash. They were the only ones that I could see doing something like that.

The tears I'd managed to get control of hit again as I gulped in air. As I stumbled backward, my back hit the wall. I slid down and put my head between my knees as the panic and sadness compressed my chest until I couldn't breathe. The world swam, and little dots floated behind my closed eyes.

"What do you mean you couldn't get it all?" *My father yelled at the surgeon. My father had shown up halfway through the surgery and raced around asking questions that I already had the answers to, but he didn't look at me. He didn't even check on me as I sat alone in my mum's room and waited for word that she'd be okay.*

How had I become so invisible to him? What had I done wrong that he never wanted to be around and didn't offer to do any of the things we used to do? Ice cream runs on Sundays had been my favorite. I loved getting a bag of bread from the convenience store and our favorite ice cream before we fed the ducks at one of the parks nearby. They were so cute to watch, catching the bread out of the air like a dog doing a trick.

That all stopped six months ago. At first, I kept asking, hopeful that the new job keeping him so busy would slow down and we could do things as a family again. But the job didn't slow, and my father was home even less, and now...now it was like I didn't exist at all.

"The tumor has wrapped itself around one of the major arteries using it as a blood supply. I have done all I can until the radiation treatment is complete. We will reassess at that time to see if it's possible to go back in and start again," the doctor said.

Keeping my ears trained on the conversation, I stared at my mum's face. She looked like she was sleeping with one of her beloved scarves tied around her head. At least, that was how I chose to see the white bandages hiding the long line of staples holding the skin on her head together.

I wasn't supposed to know that, but there was no way I was sitting in a chair in the waiting room. Besides, I needed to know what my mum required to get better. It was my only goal now. She needed to live so we could try out the new paintbrushes she'd just gotten me for my birthday.

I always hated that my birthday was on Devil's Night, right before Halloween. It felt like I was getting ripped off, choosing between trick-or-treating or having a party. I now realized that was pretty selfish, considering my mum always did whatever she could to make my birthdays exceptional. I linked my fingers with hers. She was cold to the touch still, and I hated that. I grabbed the blanket folded at the end of the bed to lay over her.

"This is unacceptable. I want a second opinion," Father argued and pulled out his cell phone. He left the room with the doctor, and I was left in silence with only the low beep of the monitor to keep me company.

"Hey mum, it's me. That was probably pretty stupid to say." Glancing around the room, I could feel tears wanting to form, but I wouldn't let them fall. I was old enough now to handle this, and my mum needed me. "I'm here, and I'm not going anywhere, not ever. Dad is fighting to make sure you get the best care." I hated that I didn't know what to say. I didn't know how to say what I wanted as my jumbled thoughts bounced around in my brain while the emotions tore at my chest. "I love you."

Maybe I left them by the sink. Using the sleeve of my sweatshirt, I wiped away the tears so I could see and pushed myself to my feet using the wall to balance. I still felt dizzy, but I needed to know. I had to check.

Stumbling away from the wall, I grabbed a desk to rest for a second and let my mind clear before pushing on. Taking a deep breath, I focused on the lineup of sinks and forced myself to put one foot in front of the other. Anyone who saw this would say I was irrational and panicking over nothing. They were just paintbrushes. But they weren't just paintbrushes and meant so much more than that to me. They were the last gift my mum got me before she got sick. They were my only link to happier times when we argued like mother and daughters did and laughed just as hard. When we would string cranberries for the Christmas tree, bake cookies and stay up all night playing board games on holidays.

My mum was my whole world. One day she was fine, then in a blink, she was sick, and then she was gone.

B*ang.*
I jumped up from the large recliner where I'd been sleeping and looked at my mum. She was wide awake and staring at the bedroom door. So that meant the noise wasn't my imagination.

"Turn on the security cameras," Mum wheezed.

With my heart hammering in my chest, I grabbed the remote and hit the buttons for the television that would bring up the security feed inside the house.

"Oh my god, mum. What do they want?" My hand shook as I stared at the three men wearing black masks, going through rooms and trashing everything they touched.

My mum grabbed my arm and looked at me with her stern expression, the one she used when she needed me to pay attention. I hadn't seen her this alert or with so much conviction in the last year.

"Ren, I need you to go into the closet." She took a deep breath, and I could see her struggling, but the new doctor said she was miraculously getting better, so I didn't understand why she seemed worse. "Are you listening to me?"

"Yes," I said and then jumped as something crashed downstairs.

"Go in the closet. On the top shelf at the back is a red box. Bring it to me. I have a gun," she said, squeezing my arm. I didn't know my mum had a gun or knew how to use one. "Go now and hurry."

I ran across the bedroom to the massive walk-in closet and jumped up and down, trying to see the top shelf. "Mum, I don't see it."

"It's there. Keep looking," she said, and I watched as she opened her nightstand. My fingers hit the edge of a box, and I had to jump back as an old shoebox fell toward me. It hit the floor, and the lid popped off. Mum's old sewing needles and scissors tumbled out of the box.

"Shit. I need a stool."

"No, Ren, stay there."

Her voice cracked like she was crying. I let go of the shelf and stared into my mum's eyes. There was something sad and desperate in the look. My pulse raced faster than it had when I saw the robbers. "I love you, baby, and I always will. Remember, never back down. You've always been a queen."

"Mum?" I stepped toward the opening, and a thick steel door I never knew existed, slid across and slammed into place. "Oh my god. Mum!" I screamed and ran at the thick metal, pounding my fists against it, but it didn't budge.

"Think Ren, think. There has to be a control panel," I said out loud. Moving all the clothes out of the way, I found a small door so well hidden I would never have seen it without looking for it. When I pulled it open, there was a keypad and a small screen. I hit the 'On' button and screamed at the top of my lungs, watching helplessly as one of the men grabbed a pillow and held it over my mum's face. Her arms and legs thrashed, but I knew she was no match for three men.

I needed to get out of here. Why would she do this? Screaming hysterically, I ran to the door and threw all my weight against it. Over and over, I slammed my shoulder into the door until I cried out in pain. But I wouldn't give up and clawed at the metal until my fingers bled.

"Leave my mum alone!" I hollered over and over again. My mum was the sweetest person and wouldn't hurt a fly. She was also deathly ill and not a threat. I couldn't understand why they would want to hurt her.

Movement on the screen caught my attention, and I stared in horror as my mum lay still, her arm hanging limply over the side of the bed, the pillow still covering her face. One of the men was close to the door, looking it over like he was trying to figure out how to get in.

"I hate you!" I screamed and kicked at the door. "Do you hear me? I'll *kill you for this!" As the words left my mouth, I knew they were the truth. I would find a way. It was horrible of me as a person. I should want them arrested and thrown in a cell for the rest of their lives, but all I could see was my mum's lifeless body and what they had done.*

"I'll find you!"

My fear had been replaced with a burning rage, and as I stared into his dark brown eyes, I hoped he would find a way to get the door open. My pulse thumped in my ears, tears trickled down my cheeks, and I walked to the back of the closet. The items that had fallen out of the box were still scattered on the floor. I calmly squatted and picked up the scissors.

My eyes locked on the gray metal door as my hand squeezed my weapon, but all I saw was blood...his blood. I wanted him to suffer. He'd just taken the most precious person away from me, and my hands shook with a rage I didn't even know I possessed—a rage that terrified me.

B efore I could reach the sinks, I collapsed to the floor on all fours. It felt like my heart had been torn from my chest, and I was left bleeding. Then the door rattled, and I screamed as images of that night, of my birthday, came back to me.

"Ren," a soft voice said. I heard footsteps coming toward me, and then someone knelt by my side, placing a warm hand on my back. "My dear sweet girl, what's wrong?"

"Mrs. Frey?" I mumbled before the panic attack consumed my mind, and everything went dark.

Chapter 13

Myles

I paced the locker room, my feet slapping against the damp tile floor as Blake told the other guys the story of my screw-up with Ren...again. Three times was pretty excessive, and I was close to punching him right off the bench.

"So get this. Not only did he do all that, but then he pulled this girl into his lap, and she screamed across the cafeteria that she didn't want to watch us sucking each other off."

Blake laughed hysterically, and Liam followed suit. I didn't think the story was as funny the third time around. Blake had taken to making faces and acting out being punched in the face. If he kept it up, I really was going to hit him and give him a reason to cover his nose.

Nash was in the zone in the corner and wasn't paying attention, or at least I didn't think so. It was hard to tell with Nash when he was this focused.

"I haven't told you all the best part yet. Nash, you listening," Blake asked.

"I'm trying really hard not to," he said, his tone sarcastic as he rolled his shoulders.

"Dude, the final race is not for another half-hour. You need to take a breather," Blake said. "You already beat Austin in the individual events, and we're going to fucking kill them in the team medley."

Nash stood and wandered over to where the other guys were sitting. "If you keep distracting me and we don't win, I'm going to blame you, and then I will drown you in the pool."

"I'll be quick. So I had English with her...." Blake paused, and we stared at him, waiting for the rest of the story. This part was new.

"And?" Nash prompted. "You said it would be fast."

"None of you appreciate a good story. I got Ren to agree to go on a date with me Monday," Blake said. My hands balled into fists as jealousy, another emotion I was unaccustomed to, poked its head up from wherever emotions were stored.

"What?" I growled.

"That's right, suckers. I'm taking her shopping for new shirts. So thank you, Myles, for ruining her only blouse. You made my life really fucking easy. I'm thinking of taking her to the little ice cream parlor down near the river. You know that one...." He paused on purpose again, knowing damn well we all knew which one he was talking about. There was a famous make-out location near there. It had a great view of the water and multiple spots that were completely hidden from those driving past.

"Don't ya dare. I swear to god, Blake, if ya screw this up for me," I said and then bit my tongue from saying any more.

I didn't date girls, not really, but Ren made me want to make an exception, and now I had a stupid bet involving my two friends. We had a rule about not going back on a bet, so I was stuck between a rock and complete humiliation for the rest of my life.

"Are you wanting to back out of the bet," Theo asked, his eyebrows mocking me.

"Naw, of course not. I just mean I was going to use what happened to take her shopping, and ya stole it out from under me." I wasn't sure if they believed me, but they let the topic drop.

"You snooze, you lose." Blake smiled wide and showed off his perfectly white teeth that I wanted to knock down his throat.

"So that's it, that's all that happened," Nash asked, and Blake's face fell.

"I'm further along than either of you two assholes, and I don't have access to her room like you or tutoring like him." He crossed his arms over his chest.

I grabbed my bottle of water from the locker and took a sip.

"I told her I was going to fuck her," Nash said, and I spit the water out all over the floor. I glared at Nash as he smirked at me.

"And did she agree," I asked, unable to contain my curiosity. I wasn't sure I wanted to know the answer. This girl was doing weird things to me.

"Not exactly, but she will. It's only a matter of time before she caves. I can see it in her eyes. She wants me."

I snorted. "That's not desire. It's called annoyance. You've just never seen the difference from a girl that's not a soul sucking leech like Vicky."

"Alright, I have a tally going, and as of right now, Myles, you're trailing the other two by at least four points," Liam said as he wrote the numbers in his betting book. "Nash, you have two points, and Blake, I'm saying you're ahead by four. I'll make sure to update the odds for everyone."

"I bet I'll have her in bed before I reach five points. I have the charm, just wait and see. After our date, she'll be all over me and begging for it again."

Before I could come up with a comeback, the speaker crackled and beeped with an announcement.

"Group nine, come to the deck. Group nine to the deck."

All the antics and teasing stopped as we marched for the door. The odd man out of the relay was Liam. I went first with the back-stroke, and Theo went second with the breaststroke. Nash was third with the fly, and Blake was our closer with the freestyle. We'd crushed all the other competition this weekend, but now it was down to Meadow Grove, Hawking Shores, and us for the final event.

We didn't care about Hawking Shores, but Meadow Grove was an athletic academy. Their students were all top athletes, which was why we were so pumped for this competition and to beat them. We only faced them once a year, and this was it. The bragging rights lasted three hundred and sixty-five days and came with perks. We got free coffee and food from the local shops, random gifts, and of course, our pick of the girls.

We sat down on the deck in line, and I checked my cap to make sure it was perfectly in place. My norm was to go over the strokes, and how I could gain an edge on my opponent, but instead, my mind was wandering. All I could picture were Ren's pretty eyes and how her lips had been so close. It had only been a few days, but she took up every moment of my thoughts. I'd never thought about a girl other than was she fuckable.

I glanced along the line and couldn't help wondering what they thought about this arranged marriage bullshit. We never talked about it, but we were all paired up to better our families. We were nothing more than expensive cattle that our mothers had birthed. I dreaded the day. I'd met mine once and she could be the nicest lass in the world, but she wasn't who I chose.

"Hey, wannabes, ready to have your asses kicked?" Austin walked in from the second locker room with his team and sat down beside us as we waited to be called to the blocks.

Nash glared at Austin, surprising me when he kept his mouth shut and looked away. Nash rarely backed down from anything, especially the likes of Austin.

"If by assess kicked you mean mop the fucking floor with ya, then ya," I said. I lowered my voice so only Austin and his teammates could hear.

The swimmers from Hawking Shores had the least points of the three teams. They were the last to enter and sat down beside Meadow Grove. The Captain of Hawking, Sabastian, gave Austin a look, and I didn't like it one bit. I was good at knowing when there was some dirty shit going on.

I leaned toward Austin and whispered, "Don't forget Austin. I know where all of ya live. Ya try anything shady out there, and I can promise ya, you'll never swim again." I smiled as if we were having a friendly conversation, but there was a good chance that I'd break his kneecaps one day soon. That was what I was good at, according to Da. He was good at wearing a suit during the day and murdering people and taking their money by night. I didn't want to be him, I didn't want to become that. We took care of banks which meant money and muscle for those that couldn't pay.

The bank had been in the family four generations and had gone from one to multiple all over the world. He loved to send me out to collect. He could send Devin, my older brother who loved to kill, but no he sent me. I'd decided it was all part of his sick game, but I refused to be his pawn forever.

Now did that mean I wouldn't kill someone for Nash? Fuck I would do it without question, but that was out of respect and friendship, not because he was my boss. Nash never treated me any differently and never asked me to do something that he, himself, wouldn't take the fall for. With that, he'd earned my undying loyalty.

"Are you threatening me, Myles," Austin asked under his breath.

I pointedly looked between him and Sabastian to make myself

clear. "Naw, just reminding you of the order of things. All of your family's wealth is built on the backs of ours, but with that comes certain secrets that I'm sure your families wouldn't want shared. I know you. I know all of you, and I know how to destroy each of you in ways you'd never recover. Don't fuck with us, have a fair swim, and we will get along just fine. If not...well, I'm sure you can piece together the rest even if you do go to Meadow Grove."

The smile slipped off Austin's face, and with a glance, I noted the others wore the same worried expression. They may have suspected what we were capable of, but now they would be terrified of all the secrets they held dear to their heart. They would wonder which ones we knew and how we would attack them. That fear was more sustainable than killing one of them. I reserved that for extreme circumstances only.

Austin leaned over his teammates and said something to Sabastian that I couldn't hear, but as long as it was calling off whatever shit they had planned, I didn't care.

"Teams, to the starting blocks," the announcer said. There was no point announcing schools anymore. There were only three of us left. Twelve swimmers determined the fate of the coming year and their school's reputation.

The crowds were always rowdy for this comp, but tonight even the standing-room-only section was filled and loud. The colors of each school were proudly on display. Yellow for Hawking Shores, green for Meadow Grove, and blue for Wayward Academy. My eyes scanned the crowd, and even though I shouldn't be disappointed, my stomach sank as, once again, my father didn't bother to show up.

I hopped in the water between the other two teams and got into position. Gripping the bar tight, I readied myself, my mind going blank as I waited for the buzzer. I focused on my breathing and visualized the hard arcing push. You needed to be as agile as a jungle cat to get a good lead.

The buzzer was low and always hard to hear, but I was used to blocking out background noise. The water glittered back at me, my muscles twitching with anticipation. When it finally buzzed, I pushed off hard, smoothly gliding under the water before leveling off. As I broke the surface, I kept an eye on the little flags that singled the halfway mark of the pool and counted down until I reached the other end.

With a quick twist and flip, I was off again back the way I'd just come and knew I had a whole arm's length on the guys beside me. I let the sound of the screaming crowd fill me. I pictured what it would be like to have someone I cared about here to support me. I couldn't help wondering if Snowflake would come, and would she sit quietly or scream like the rest. The thought of her screaming her heart out gave me an extra burst of adrenaline. I put all I had into the final few strokes to give Theo the best advantage possible. As soon as my fingertips touched the wall, Theo was off. Nash was stoic as he stepped up on the block. His face looked like he was made of stone while Blake yelled and screamed for his brother.

"Fucking move it!" I screamed at Theo even though I knew he'd never hear me. The excitement was pumping through my body as I pushed myself up and out of the water. Cupping my mouth, I yelled. "Move your ass! They're catching you!" It wasn't true, Theo had pulled a little further ahead, but it was a good incentive if he did hear me.

Nash rolled out his shoulders and got into position. I'd never seen a better jump as he smoothly slipped under the water and rose with a vengeance. I thought I'd seen him at his top speed in the singles, but before he even reached the wall, he'd pulled a full length ahead.

"Shit, he's killing them," I said to Theo as Blake stepped onto the block.

"He looks possessed," Theo said, which was the perfect description.

"Better not fuck Blake," I said and smirked at Blake who glared back.

"You mean like how you did with Ren?" This time he smirked as he adjusted his goggles and then turned his focus on Nash who was only a few strokes away.

If this comp didn't mean so much to Nash, I would've pushed Blake in the water.

When Nash touched the wall, the guys in the other two lanes still had a length and a half to go.

Theo and I leaned down, and each grabbed one of Nash's hands to pull him from the water. Gripping his shoulder, I shook him.

"Fuck man, that was impressive."

"Thanks," Nash said, but his eyes were still filled with a murderous glare as he looked over my shoulder.

"Forget about Austin. You embarrassed him," I said, and the corner of Nash's mouth lifted ever so slightly.

The cheering got unbelievably loud, and we looked up to see that Blake had lost a little ground, but he was still a length ahead and had just reached the final quarter.

"Come on, Blake, let's go!" We all cheered and hollered with excitement. Blake's arms sliced through the water for the final strokes of the freestyle and touched the wall. He looked to either side as the other two competitors touched so close together that they would require a photo finish.

We pulled Blake from the pool as we celebrated. The moment was a rare one for us. To simply be teenagers, and forget who our fathers are. To cheer and act immature and let the moment just breathe all on its own. It meant something for all of us, even if only for a little while.

Coach Stevens pulled each of us into a hug before moving on to shake the other coach's hands.

"Congratulations, I wouldn't get too comfy on that throne. You never know when it will be yanked away," Austin said and held out his hand to shake Nash's. I still didn't like his cocky tone. He had a gleam in his eye like his shit didn't stink.

Nash gripped Austin's hand and smiled for the cameras filming us, but I wanted to kick his ass and hold his head under the water, preferably in a toilet bowl.

"Top three teams, please come to the podium."

We made our way over to the large blocks set up like an Olympic medal ceremony, but I kept my eye on the other two teams the entire time. My senses were tingling, I didn't know why, but I didn't trust them.

Hawking Shores was called up first, and then Meadow Grove. We were the last to take the center spot and waved for the crowd as the officials came over with the medals. We'd no sooner had the medals placed around our necks when someone approached one of the officials and whispered in his ear. As his eyes flicked up to us, I knew this was it. Whatever they'd put into motion hadn't been stopped, and my knuckles cracked as my hand rolled into a fist.

Like a slow-mo horror movie, the official held his hand out for the microphone and asked for quiet.

"It has come to our attention that illegal substances may have been used. Pending further investigation, Wayward will not receive the gold medals this evening. We will require all the medals from today until our investigation is complete."

"What the fuck!" Nash exploded off the block and stomped toward Austin. I jumped in his way and gripped him hard.

"Don't. Not here. There are better ways to deal with them," I whispered.

Nash stopped pushing against me, but he growled under his breath. "This is not over. I worked too hard for this. If you fucked up my chances for the world's qualifier, there will be no place you can hide, that I won't find you Austin. No one humiliates me like this. No one."

Chapter 14

NOVEMBER 7 – SUNDAY 10:00 PM

Nash

Crack.

The punch snapped my head to the side, but I didn't move from the spot.

"No one humiliates this family!" My father bellowed. "Ya, let that sniveling piece of shit humiliate us on national television." I knew the second hit was coming. He always did them in twos or threes.

He hit me again, and once more, I held my ground. My jaw was used to the abuse, and what would've knocked me on my ass a year ago now felt like a tickle against my skin.

"I'll teach him a lesson," I said.

My father's finger, with the wide gold ring of our family crest, was pointed in my face. He'd left an impression of the ring in my skin more than once.

"You'll do more than that." The bookcases rattled like they were terrified of my father's wrath as he stomped across the floor to the small bar in his office. Grabbing one of the decanters, he poured himself a glass and glared at me across the room. "I want you to kill him."

It was sheer will alone that kept the shock off my face. "You want me to kill Austin for making an anonymous call to officials about my team? We don't even know if it was him."

Taking a healthy gulp of the dark liquid, he walked behind his desk and sat down. "Nash, even if it wasn't him we need to remind all those pompous pricks who they are dealing with. What they did was signal to every other influential family that they could walk all over us. He made a fool of you which means he made a fool of me. You should've known they were planning something. So this is your mess to clean up. You will kill him, and it will send a message that we are not to be messed with."

"I know he was is an asshole and did a fucking piece of shit thing, but this is excessive even for us," I argued. "I can break both his legs and teach his family a lesson without killing them."

My father's fist slammed down on the desk, and a little bit of his drink spilled out over the side of the glass.

"You will do as I say, and maybe you'll learn to be prepared for an attack from anywhere. We are the Collier family, and one day you'll sit where I am. You have to be prepared for anything."

"How was I supposed to know what they were going to do?" I held out my arms in disbelief. Did he think I was a fucking mind reader?

"You know, by knowing your opponent." His finger stabbed the top of the desk. "When you sit in this spot, everyone is your enemy. We don't have friends. We barely have family. What we have are alliances and agreements. The girl I plan on marrying you to will strengthen our hold, but that won't happen for a couple more years. In the meantime, you need to be vigilant in how you represent the family."

The white-hot anger that was boiling in my system was getting ready to spill over, and I knew that would only lead to more punches to the face or a trip to the torture room. My father wasn't above torturing his lessons into me. Instead, I marched for the door.

"Where do you think you're going?"

"To follow orders like the good little soldier I am," I said and flung the office door open with a bang. "I won't be back tonight."

Pulling out my phone, I hit Liam's number, and he answered on the first ring. "What's happening?"

"The initiation has been bumped up to tonight. Have everyone meet me at our spot in an hour, no excuses." I hung up the phone, not wanting to hear any possible objections. I stomped down to my room and hit the button for the fake drawer in my dresser to pop out, revealing an array of weapons. Pulling out two nine mils, I loaded the clips and tucked them in the back of my jeans before concealing the drawer once more.

My father said dead, but he didn't say how. He wanted a public display, and I'd give him one.

November 8 – Monday 1:00 am

I was the first to arrive at our cottage. We'd pooled our money together and purchased it. Any one of us could've afforded this spot, but we didn't want our parents to know about it. This was the one place off-limits to chicks or anyone else not being initiated into the group. Our numbers were slowly growing, and soon there would be enough of us to pull back on the strings that bound us. We may only be pawns right now, but we would be The Last Rank.

I shut off the headlights, and the entire area was plunged into darkness. The tall, old trees surrounding the cottage loomed over the place as if purposely blocking out the light. The additions I'd been slowly making would one day make this hideout impenetrable from any attack. My father didn't think I thought ahead or wanted to be prepared. In that, he was very wrong. I was preparing to take over, just not the way he envisioned.

As I got out of my car, the cold night air made it look like I was breathing fire. It was quiet enough that you could almost hear the sound of rushing water. The Columbia River flowed to the north of the property. This spot was perfect for so many reasons. It had come with almost six hundred acres of land. We had no neighbors, and anyone hiking in the national forest would be used to gunshots around here. We had a few canoes in a shed closer to the water if we ever needed to escape. It sounded stupid until you realized that the last hundred acres of this property were on the other side of the Columbia River with an old shed that we'd been fixing up and a pair of trucks ready to go. My father may think I'm stupid, but that would be his downfall.

I stepped up onto the cabin's porch just as multiple headlights flashed, announcing the guys' arrival. Liam pulled up and opened the driver's side door, allowing me to see the boy in the passenger seat with a black hood on his head.

His name was Rory O'Hea, and he'd just arrived with his family from Arizona. His father wanted to kiss my father's ass, a regular occurrence for some families that were not as large or had lost favor at some point. From the little bit I knew from Liam and my father's conversations with other council members, they thought this family was too small and their dry cleaning businesses were a joke. I saw value in every member. No matter how influential, the one thing I needed was loyalty and dedication. Even the hands that others ignored I put to use.

If he made it through tonight, he would become one of my moles. He'd already told Liam that he was great at getting in and out of tricky situations and had a memory like an elephant. I already had three spies constantly collecting and relaying information from the other influential families in the school. It was amusing that they believed they were the only ones with a secret group. The difference between theirs and mine was that I didn't treat it like a fraternity. I treated the Order like my father handled the mob.

"Bring him up," I said, waving Liam forward.

Liam and Theo guided Rory up the steps to the top of the deck and then let him go.

"Hello, Rory," I said, smirking as he took a tiny step back. "I wouldn't go back much further, or you'll end up tumbling off the stairs to your death. If I decide to push you, you'll be equally dead." Rory didn't say anything, which I liked. "So tell me why you want to be part of The Last Rank?"

"It's time for change. The snake's head needs to be removed," he said a little too perfectly like he'd been coached.

"Is that the real reason, Rory? I will shoot you right now and leave you for the animals to eat if you don't tell me the whole truth." I didn't need to see his face to hear him swallow as his body shivered.

The last set of lights pulled into the driveway, and Myles jumped out, giving me a thumbs up before he walked to the trunk of the car.

"So let's have it, Rory, what's the real reason you want to join? After all, I am the King's son."

"Can I speak freely?"

My brow arched. I'd never had anyone ask that before and my interest was piqued. "Yes, say what you want."

Rory stood as still as a statue. His head was bowed like in prayer. I had no idea what was happening and looked to Liam, who shrugged. Only as his head lifted and he began to speak did I realize he was collecting himself and had been crying. The cracked voice and emotion were as physical as the late fall breeze biting into my skin.

"Your father is the reason. He is a plague set upon us and needs to be beheaded." My eyes went wide, and I hated that I felt a tiny bit of conflicted emotion. My father was all that and more, but he was still my father. There was a level of respect and love that just naturally happened with family. If and when the time came, I would be the only one to take his life.

My fist clenched, not because I wanted to hit Rory, but because I wanted to rip out the damaged piece that had marred my heart and kept me tied to the man that had destroyed the good in me.

"My parents didn't have much money when they arrived in this country, but they had a dream for me and my sister and needed to move here. My da knew someone who knew how to reach the King of Kings, and your father made it possible for us to move, but he didn't do it without a price." Rory was shaking, and I could feel the intense rage coming off his body. "My sister was his price. Every time he had business out in our area, he...used her in horrific ways. The last time was so bad that she was hospitalized for over a week, and we didn't know if she would live."

"Then why move closer? Why bring your sister closer to him?" I crossed my arms.

I knew what my father was. I also knew that his desire to punish didn't stop with me or those that wronged him. I'd been forced to watch him do far worse, and the council members had become versions of him. The last meeting I attended had been nothing more than a reason to have an insane sex party. The night had started with twelve girls, but it ended with only five still breathing. As was my father's way, I was the one that needed to remove the dead bodies and dispose of them. I was better at hiding and destroying evidence than baking a cake. That was sad and said a lot about my home.

"My sister took off. She checked out of the hospital and left without a trace other than to leave me a note. My parents don't have anything else to offer so your father demanded we move closer and my father work off his debt in other ways. I don't know what that means, but it can only be something evil." He put his hand in his pocket and produced a square piece of paper that he held out in my general direction. I plucked the square from his fingers and unfolded it like it was a death sentence.

Ro

I can't do it again. I'm sorry. We came to this country for a chance at a better

life, but this is not better. I feel like I've been plucked from the emerald gem that

we called home and dropped into a fiery hell. Ma and Da are in too deep,

but there is still time for you. Don't become a puppet like them. You still have time to

get out. Do it, run, and never stop running from the monsters that seek to turn

you into one of them. You're better than that.

I love you, Ro. I will take you in my heart wherever I go.

Leah

Folding up the letter, I placed it back into Rory's hand. "She was my best friend, and I let that man hurt her in ways that will haunt me forever. So, I started looking for a way to take him out and kick him off the throne by any means necessary." Rory put the letter back in his pocket and stood tall. "If you wish to kill me for speaking the truth, then that is the risk I had to take to do what is right and avenge what he did to my sister. The brightest soul I've ever met became a shadow scared of herself. He broke her."

I believed him. The conviction in his tone told me that he wanted my father off the throne, but more than that, he wanted him dead. Would he keep his emotions in check and do what needed to be done for however long it took to be able to take over properly? That was the question. We called ourselves The Last Rank for a reason.

"And what makes you think I'm different from my old man? You've taken quite the risk coming here, not knowing where you were going or what I'd do to you."

"You're right. I don't. You could be as big of an asshole as your father, but it was a risk I had to take. I'd heard whisperings of a group that was pissing off the Order of Kings. I didn't know it was you when I came here, but I've spent every second trying to find out who you are. You wanted my answer. The short version is revenge."

It was good to know that what we were doing was having the desired effect. The elders were getting annoyed and would start making mistakes. I would be there to pick up all the little pieces.

I stepped in closer to Rory. "You do know that could take time. I can't have you going rogue. If I accept you into the fold, what guarantee do I have that you won't ruin the larger plan?"

Rory shocked me as he lowered himself to the ground like a knight looking to be touched with a sword. "I swear to you on my sister's life that I will do whatever I can to help and won't do anything without your say. I am your pawn. Use me as you need. As long as it's to take down your father, I will do anything you ask."

A glance at Liam told me that he'd already looked into Rory, and as far as he was concerned, he was clean. I turned to look at Theo, who'd sat down on one of the cabin stairs, and he nodded his acceptance.

"Alright. I choose to accept you if you pass the initiation tonight, but from this moment on, you are sworn to secrecy about anything to do with The Last Rank. You don't so much as glance my way if someone brings us up. You will do what I say, when I say it, without question."

"I swear," he said.

"Get him up."

Walking away, I knew that Liam and Theo would bring Rory. Marching down the dimly lit path, I followed it until it opened into a half horseshoe shape. We had a fire pit built in the center with benches and a small stone podium. I wasn't one for sacrifice like The Kings, but there was something to be said for tradition. The fire was low, but the glowing embers and orange flames danced, casting shadows in every direction. I'd spent many nights sitting around this fire with the guys or alone. It was my safe space and the one place my father didn't know how to find me. I always shut off my phone and had removed the tracker in my car ages ago. That argument quickly got volatile when I refused to put it back in.

It wasn't the fire that kept my attention tonight, though. No, it was the man tied to the big Oregon White Oak tree with Myles and Blake guarding him. We stopped in front of my wide-eyed prisoner, who had already pissed himself. The wet spot on his pants and the stench of fear wafting off of him proved how brave he really was.

"Unhood him." I looked over my shoulder and recognized the guy under the black hood. Sandy blonde hair and brown eyes, he was good-looking enough to fit in with any of the popular crowds but didn't stand out so much that people would recognize him at first glance. I watched him closely as his eyes left mine to stare at the man tied to the tree. He'd either make it through tonight or die where he stood.

"Austin thought it would be funny to make a joke of me on national television. He tried to have my medals stripped from me and make me look like a cheater, ruining my chances of making a national team."

I nodded to Myles. He ripped off the tape and pulled the gag out of Austin's mouth.

"It was only supposed to be a joke, I swear."

The corner of my mouth lifted with the ridiculous answer. "No, I'm pretty sure you accomplished exactly what you wanted. You thought there was a good chance one of us would be taking steroids just because those of us at Wayward are known for getting into trouble, and even if we weren't, it would discredit anything we did." I held my arms out. "The damage would already be done, and that would be all people remembered. You win, we lose, no matter what."

"No, man, I promise that's not how it happened. Sabastian and I just thought they'd check your shit, throw you off your game, you know? We wanted to rattle your cage. We both saw the times you've been putting up all season and...shit. I didn't think they'd wait until we were all on the podium." His body shook as I stepped closer to the worm on the end of my hook.

"Do you know who I really am," I asked, my voice no more than a whisper. Austin nodded slowly. "Yet, you chose to set us up anyway." I smiled. "You're either really brave or really fucking stupid. Which is it?"

"Really fucking stupid," he blurted out, and all the guys snorted as they tried to contain their laughter.

"Well, that is one thing we can agree on."

"I promise we'll never cross you again. Whatever you want from my family, it's yours," he rambled. "We have lots of money, stocks, homes. I have a big family. Are you looking to marry someone?"

I shook my head. "You think I need any of that?"

"I...I...I...please, man," Austin begged, and I wondered what his fancy model girlfriend would think if she saw him now.

I slammed my fist beside his head, the bark biting into my hand with a thud that rustled the remaining leaves above. "I'm the fucking heir to the Kings. That means your money is useless to me, your favors and begging mean nothing, and I certainly don't need you whoring your family out for me." I leaned in a little closer. He closed his eyes and turned his head away. "Your family will be better off without you."

Pushing away from the tree, I strolled toward Rory, who seemed a little nervous, but he wasn't running and didn't back away when I stopped in front of him. Reaching behind my back, I pulled one of the guns I'd taken from home. With a touch of dramatic flare, I wiped down the grip and held it out to him by the barrel.

"This man tainted my image earlier tonight. That is something I can't let slide. If being part of The Last Rank is what you really want, you will shoot him right here," I said.

Rory looked at the gun and then at Austin, who was begging louder than I'd ever heard a girl wail through sex. I wasn't sure that was a good thing.

"Do you know how to shoot?"

"I lived in the Arizona desert my whole life. Of course, I know how to shoot." I could tell he was stealing himself for what was to come. His dedication to the Order and his sister's revenge were stronger than his morals, and that was what I needed from my members. There would always be blood on our hands, and the only way to ensure we all survived was to know that someone else had just as much blood dripping from their hands as we did.

Rory took the gun from my hand and stepped around me.

"Oh god no, please, I'm begging you. Anything you want, I promise I'll make it happen. I'll owe you for the rest of my life." Rory raised the gun, and his hand shook. It was a hard thing to take a life but to take the life of someone in a vulnerable state who hadn't done anything to you fucked with your psyche in a totally different way. "Please, man, I don't want to die."

Tears and snot streamed down Austin's face, his chest heaving with each terrified breath. Myles and Blake stepped away from the tree.

"Please, man, Nash, please."

Click

Austin jerked like he'd been shot, and the scent of fresh shit filled the air before he slumped against his bindings and cried.

"It didn't fire." Rory looked at the gun and then at me, confusion written all over his face. Pulling my black gloves from my pocket, I put them on and held out my hand for the gun.

"Did you really think I would make you kill someone for your test?"

"Um...well...yeah," he said.

"I'm a monster, but I'm not a heathen. I did need to see if you would do it, though. If you would go against your instincts and do what needs to be done. Because there will come a time that you set aside your morals for the greater good. Let him go," I called out to Myles and Blake.

"So this was all just to see if I was trustworthy?"

"Yes," I said, pulling the clip from my back pocket. "I didn't need you to step over that line tonight, but the time will come when you will."

"Thank you, thank you, you won't regret letting me go," Austin said, standing still and staring at me.

"What? Do you think you're going back to the city with us? With shit and piss in your pants? No, I don't think so. The trail is that way. Run along." I waved my hand in the general direction of the water.

Austin hesitated for a moment longer than he should, which once more told me his true nature. He was a worm and nothing more. He took off jogging, his legs lifting at an odd angle from the shit I was sure was running down his legs. I checked the chamber of the gun, lifted it, and without even a blink of hesitation, pulled the trigger just like I'd been taught. The bang of the gun was loud in the silence of the night. The echo coming back at us was as haunting as the first night I'd done this.

Austin crumbled to the ground. I walked over to his writhing body as he rolled over, looking at me with his mouth gaping as he tried to get air through the lung that now had a bullet in it.

"The lesson here, Austin, is that you should never fuck with The Last Rank," I said and shot him between the eyes. "You know what to do with his body."

Rory's face was green as I walked over to where he was standing. Liam opened a black lock box, and I laid the gun carefully inside.

Liam locked the lid, and I smiled as Rory stared at the box. He sucked in a gasp, and I knew he was putting all the little pieces together.

"That's right, Rory, it doesn't matter if you didn't kill him, your fingerprints are all over the weapon, and that weapon is now my insurance policy. Understand this. I'm fair, and I'm loyal. But if you give me any reason to mistrust you or if you try to ruin me, then I don't care which way you're facing. I'll kill you and crush what's left of your family." My lips pulled up into a smile as I clapped a hand on his shoulder. "Welcome to, The Last Rank."

Chapter 15

R**en**

Why did I agree to this?

"Oh my god, look at the cute outfit in the window," Ivy squealed from the backseat of Blake's car, reminding me how I got rooked into this mess. "And that store is new and that one."

She sounded like an exuberant child. I was afraid she would jump out of the moving car as Blake parked at the giant mall. I hardly got my seatbelt off before Ivy was out the door and opening mine like an overeager chauffeur or a carjacker as she grabbed my arm and

137

pulled me to hurry up. I just managed to get the door closed on the sleek Maserati.

"It's just a mall girl," I said as I was dragged along.

"No, it's a slice of heaven." My eyebrows shot up as she raised her arms in the air as if she'd been freed from jail. How long had she been trapped on the property? "We are going in every store."

I looked to Blake for help. He'd been oddly quiet, and so far, there had been no teasing comments. He just shrugged.

"Is there any place you want to shop," I asked Blake as Ivy speed-walked away.

"Not really. I order most of my stuff online," he said.

"Okay." We lapsed into silence as we followed Ivy. The first store was huge, with clothes, shoes, and a wide assortment of other items. Ivy had already disappeared among the racks.

"She's that way," Blake said, pointing. I envied all those taller than six feet. It must be nice to reach shit on the top shelf in a kitchen without needing a stool.

I wasn't going to say it to Blake, but I was happy to get off the property, too. It had been less than a week, and my roommate was showing more of her crazy with each passing day. She had zero consideration or empathy for anyone else. After Mrs. Frey found me Saturday night, which wasn't a great moment for me, I was brought to my bedroom, where I stayed under the blankets all day Sunday. Vicky paraded so many people in that I lost count. Each had a rude comment or sarcastic remark about the fact I wasn't up or how my side of the room looked sparse. A few went so far as to sit on the end of my bed, pretending to jump and scream when I asked them to move.

That got Vicky laughing the loudest. I wasn't sure if Vicky was really bad at hiding her true intentions or if pretending to be oblivious while talking about me was part of her bitch act. Honestly, I didn't have it in me to care anymore.

I figured I was entitled to my mini-break. There wasn't time for me to process all that had happened or how quickly the investigation

DISOBEDIENT PAWN

was wrapped up before we buried my mum. The police said that it was a robbery that got out of control, and there had been several in the area. They would let us know if they found who killed my mum, but then they released the body, and before I had time to catch my breath, the funeral was planned, completed, and we were on a plane. Five days had passed from the day my mum was murdered to us leaving everything I knew behind.

As it turned out, Mrs. Frey had taken all the brushes home to give them a thorough cleaning. As soon as she understood why I was in the middle of a breakdown, she pulled the bundle from her bag with an elastic around them. I clutched them to my chest as if they would somehow transform into my mum. Relief washed over me, and the sheer terror that had gripped me faded.

Of course, she wanted to report the incident, but I begged her not to. I'm sure she did anyway, but the fact that they didn't knock on my door and cart me off in a white jacket gave me hope that she'd kept her word.

"Where was Myles this morning," I asked.

"What?" Blake's eyes took a moment to focus like he'd been off on a totally different plane.

"I was asking where Myles was this morning. We had a tutoring session, but he didn't show up and then missed class."

Blake shrugged. "Despite popular opinion, I don't always know what he is up to, but we were out really late after the tourney on Sunday, so he probably slept in." Stopping at a rack, he thumbed through the dresses, and I assumed he was looking for a gift.

"What does she look like? I can help you find something," I offered and went to another rack close by that was a whole boho collection. Why I was offering help, I had no idea. I seemed to have that problem a lot lately.

"About five feet." I nodded. "Really pretty, has a great smile."

"Do you know her size or style?" I asked and pulled out a fun dress. It had an embroidered flower pattern and little tassels that lined the deep V of the neckline. It was the kind of dress you could wear on its own in the summer or put on a pair of tights with boots for the colder days.

"This is stunning." I held it up, and as Blake looked but didn't say anything, it dawned on me that most guys preferred short tops, skintight pants, or skirts that left nothing to the imagination. I put the dress back on the rack. "I'm going to help Ivy and then find some shirts for school."

My stomach knotted as I walked away. The last thing I needed was to give this group of overly popular jocks something else to make fun of me over. I may not care, but why give them ammunition on a silver platter. I was no fool, and he was not my friend.

Ivy had completely disappeared, and even jumping up and down, I couldn't see her dark hair among the rows. Ugh. Marching toward the large hanging sign that said tops, I scanned the racks and the walls for anything that passed for a plain white dress shirt. You'd think something so simple would be easy to find, but I felt like I was playing a game of *Where's Waldo*.

"Isn't this incredible!" Ivy exclaimed behind me. I jumped, clutching my chest. I hated that this was happening to me. I'd never been skittish, but lately, I ducked or jumped at the slightest noise.

Turning around, I smiled as Ivy spun in a skirt and top outfit that was both sexy and adorable, just like she was.

"I love it, Ivy. Are you going to get it?"

Her smile fell. "No, my dad doesn't like me spending money. He gets pretty mad about it."

"I'll get it for you." She shook her head, but I cut her off before she could refuse. "Girl, I would've been lost without you. You made an entire binder to help me fit in, so the least I can do is get you a gift to say thank you. This way, it's something you want."

She smoothed her hands down the material. "I don't have anywhere to wear this. I don't want you to waste your money."

"We will book somewhere to go so you have someplace to wear it. I'm buying it, no arguments." Ivy rushed me and gripped me in a hard hug.

"Thank you!"

Ivy sprinted off for the dressing room, her ponytail bobbing behind her. I'd never seen anyone this excited about shopping before. I couldn't relate unless it was art supplies. Then I was in a little slice of heaven.

I tried not to make it obvious as I glanced around for Blake. "You looking for me?"

"Geez us, Christ," I swore and jumped again. At this rate, I would need medical attention for the fucking heart attack everyone was trying to give me.

I whipped around to face Blake, who was leaning against the wall with a stupid coy look on his face that made me want to smack him. He looked hot standing like that, but I kicked that thought out before it could take root. It didn't matter what he looked like or how sexy his dimples were. He was the enemy.

"No, I was just looking for the white shirts," I said, crossing my arms. "I still haven't found them."

"Uh-huh." Blake pushed away from the wall, and my heart sputtered a little. It was just an aftereffect of two scares so close together.

"What did you get?" I pointed to the store bag.

"Couple shirts. I'm going to take this out to the car, but the dress clothes are down that way," Blake said and nodded at a row I'd yet to go down. I stared at his hand, terrified as it came toward my face.

"What..." I started as he tucked a strand of hair that had fallen in front of my eye behind my ear.

"Don't hide your face," he said, then turned and walked away.

I felt the heat in my cheeks and took a deep breath to try and calm my galloping heart. What the hell was that? Shaking my head, I walked down the row Blake had indicated and, sure enough, found rows of them neatly folded in large stacks. Thumbing through the sizes, I found mine in plain white and pulled out four—no point in coming back to town if I didn't need to.

Ivy and Blake were waiting by the register when I came down the aisle, and even though it shouldn't have shocked me or bothered me, the fact that Blake was leaning over the counter, flirting with the girl working, irked me. That was the only way to describe it. I didn't feel wholly jealous or angry, we weren't a couple, but it did irritate me that he'd been flirty with me and was now giving this girl the same treatment. It merely proved that I was nothing more than a number. Someone for him and Myles to toy with, like a cat playing with a mouse.

Stepping up to the checkout, I laid my shirts down and tried really hard not to feel like a total idiot. But the angry little voice in my head was telling me off. For just a moment, I thought this guy was interested in me. When was I going to learn?

"Ren, is everything okay? You look upset," Ivy said, grabbing my arm. Her brows knit with worry.

"I'm good, just overthinking shopping. I'm not a shopper," I said, which wasn't a lie. At least not entirely.

"Oh. Well, you'll be happy about this. Blake's cousin Lisa was just telling us about a party at her sorority house this weekend and invited us all to go."

The pretty blonde—with the name tag screaming Lisa—smiled at me. So she was his cousin.

She held out her hand. "Nice to meet you, Ren. I love your name. I wish my parents had given me a cool name. Lisa is so common."

She shook my hand enthusiastically. "Nice to meet you too, Lisa."

"So yeah, I never see my cousin enough. You should come and bring whoever you like. The parties are always huge."

I could see Blake smiling at me from the corner of my eye. "What school do you go to?"

"I go to Sacred Heart Academy."

"Yeah, and we just kicked your school's ass at the swim meet over the weekend," Blake gloated.

Lisa rolled her eyes at her cousin, and I liked her a whole lot more. "And I still don't care," Lisa said back. "Ignore him. Swim guys are all the same. I haven't met one yet, that you can trust."

"Hey! I'm trustworthy, don't be telling her that." Blake scowled at his cousin, and I suddenly loved her.

"I mean, you all look hot in your little swim trunk things, but watching you all wet getting in and out of the pool is where my interest ends." Lisa smiled at me and Ivy. "So what do you say? You wanna come? The girls will love you. My house is very chill."

"Um, I don't know. I don't even know how we'd get there."

"Hello, still standing here," Blake said, crossing his arms over his chest like he was sulking.

"I'm not going to assume you'd take us to a party." Truth be told, I'd never been to a party. By the time I was old enough to start going to things like that, I was looking after my mum and never felt comfortable leaving her alone.

"Fine, fair point, but we will have a bus going. It's just a given you'll come," Blake said as Lisa rang up my shirts and the outfit Ivy wanted.

"I'll think about it. Spending any length of time on a bus with you sounds like pure torture," I joked, making Lisa and Ivy laugh.

"Oh, I like her already. Do you two like mani-pedis? We always go and have our nails done before a party. If you arrive early enough, I'll take the two of you." Foolishly, my excitement grew. Deep down, I knew this was a bad idea, but I'd never been able to be a teen and do all the shit other teens do. Going to a party, getting dressed up, and having my nails done sounded like a lot of fun.

"You would like her. Oh, you'll love this. Ren has a higher GPA than Theo," Blake said, and I didn't know why that was so funny, but Lisa burst out laughing until she couldn't breathe.

"Oh, I really like you now." I looked at Ivy for clarification, but she shrugged. Lisa placed all the clothes in a bag and handed it over. "I gave you my employee discount."

"Thanks, that's really nice." I pulled out the shiny platinum card my father had given me. I hadn't used it yet and suddenly wondered what the limit was. Just how much trouble could I get into with it? My lip curled up at the thought of maxing it out.

Blake whistled. "Wow, your father trusts you with platinum? My dad refuses to give us anything more than gold. He's terrified that Theo or I will max it out. No...that's not right. He's only worried about me," Blake said, making me smile.

"My dad won't give me any," Ivy said.

"It's just a card, not magic," I said, brushing it off, but Blake's comment really made me want to call the card company.

My father may have found a way to shove me off and forget about me like he'd forgotten about Mum for the last five years, but I was about to remind him that I existed. What better way than hitting him in the only place that mattered to him? His wallet. Some self-care was needed to cope with my deep-seated trauma.

Spinning the card in my fingers, I stared at it like cowboys would their gun in old western movies. A giddiness bloomed in my chest.

This was a terrible idea, but I knew I would do it.

Chapter 16

NOVEMBER 8 – MONDAY 7:21 PM

Myles

Shifting into fifth, my baby revved and flew around the final curve before the long straightaway to the city. The Ferrari was my pride and joy, and I showed her off whenever I could. Another week and she'd be put away for the winter, so this might be my last chance to take her out.

A miniature lacrosse stick swung from the rearview mirror, reminding me that not only had I missed my lacrosse practice—Coach was going to have my ass—but I'd missed my tutoring session with Ren.

I'd crashed as the sun was coming up and stayed at home rather than going back to school. Austin's remains being found was all over the news, and I smirked thinking about how The Kings would react when they saw their signature on the body. Nash was gonna be in huge shit for it and likely take a beating from his father, but he didn't care. It was what he wanted. Austin needed to be a dual message. So that was what we did. Blake and I turned him into a swinging pinata for the world to see.

It was simultaneously sad and thrilling that we were so good at getting rid of bodies. I was eight when my father first made me watch him kill and dispose of a person. It didn't stop at that. My twelfth birthday gift was my first kill. Nothing says family celebration like shooting someone.

I'd tried to run afterward but failed and had gotten my arm broken for the effort. Calling the police seemed like the smart thing to do, but the cop was on Da's payroll, and I was beaten severely for ever picking up the phone. After that, I was resigned to the fact that this was my life...it was the same for all of us.

So I treated those we killed like props in a movie, easily disposable.

Grabbing my phone out of the cupholder, I stared at the little dot on the screen and knew exactly where Blake had taken Ren. One of these days, he'd remember to shut off the 'Find My Phone' feature, but until then, I would use it to my advantage.

There was no way in hell I was letting him have an entire romantic date night alone. Crashing his date seemed like fair payback. Payback for what? I didn't really know, but it felt like he was kicking me in the face by pursuing Ren. Agreeing to be part of a bet in the first place was my own stupidity. Now to win her over, I was up against Blake and Nash. Blake, I could handle, but Nash...he worried me.

"Fuck I'm such an idiot," I mumbled and turned the radio up, hoping to drown out the voice telling me off in my brain.

It was dusk by the time I crossed into the city limits and veered off the main road to head for the restaurant we all loved. You could get anything you wanted there, and they even had a special section with favorites from back home. Their Steak and Guinness pot pie was to die for.

It would close for the year at the end of this month since most of its revenue came from seasonal traffic. We didn't get as cold as other parts of the country, but we still got a ton of snow, and no one was hanging out on the river or hiking in the winter. My first year here was a huge shock to my system. I was used to rain and damp days, but this was bitter cold, and it felt like I could never get warm.

If it weren't for the guys in the Last Rank, I'd find a way to move back to Ireland as soon as I turned eighteen. For no other reason than to get away from my father...if we hadn't killed him by then.

Hitting my blinker, I pulled into the parking lot and spotted Blake's car right away. I parked beside him, surprised that the lot was almost full. I was getting out of my car when the restaurant door opened, and Blake's voice caught my attention. He was too busy telling his story to notice me, but I noticed him and the two girls with him.

"Son of a bitch," I mumbled under my breath. Either Ren brought Ivy because she didn't want to be alone with Blake, or Ivy was invited the entire time, and Blake made it sound like a fucking date to mess with me. That seemed more likely. I had a hard time picturing the girl that embarrassed us in the cafeteria suddenly agreeing to a date.

Ren was the first to notice me, the smile on her face slipping, but she didn't seem angry, more shocked. Fuck she was pretty. Every time I saw her, she took my breath away a little more. Her hair was hanging loose and blowing in the breeze coming off the river, the long strands whipping out to the side. It reminded me of her personality, beautiful and a little wild.

"Fancy meeting all of ya here," I said. Blake finally looked up and noticed me, his smile turning into an annoyed frown that I'd found him.

"What are you doing here? Have a hot date with that chick from the other night," Blake asked, and I ground my teeth together.

"Nope, just came for some takeout, but since you're here, Ren, would ya mind if I spoke to ya for a moment?"

"We were just heading back to the academy. Can it wait til our next session, or are you planning on skipping that one too?" Her tone was even, yet she still managed to sound sarcastic. Ren crossed her arms. I smirked, wanting nothing more than to kiss that smug attitude right out of her. Fuck she got my blood hot.

"No, it can't wait and...." I drew an X over my heart. "I promise I won't miss another session if we can chat right now." I held up my finger. "If for some reason I have to, I will make sure to let ya know like I should've this morning." I was trying for sweet and sad, but I couldn't tell if it was working from the look on her face. "I can take ya for a ride in my car. This is the last time I can take her out, and I'll have you back long before curfew."

"Hey man, butt out of my date. We were having a good time," Blake bitched, but I ignored him and kept my eyes trained on Ren.

"It's not a date," she corrected and didn't bother to look at Blake. I wanted to smile but kept it off my face. "I can't leave Ivy."

"No, you go ahead. I'm fine with Blake," Ivy said, and I could see Blake getting more pissed by the second, which warmed all the evil little parts of my heart.

"Blake, ya don't mind taking Ivy back to the academy, do ya?" He glared at me. "I mean, you were heading there anyway."

"No, of course not." His voice was tight, but he smiled wide as the girls looked at him. "I need to get to bed early. We were up way too late last night. Did you ever get that girl's number?"

It was official. I was gonna kill Blake. "Ya mean the one to detail my car? Yeah, and her rates are lower than my other guy, so I'm going to give her a chance. I really hate that he scratched my car with all the money I paid." It was the first lie I could think of.

Blake lifted an eyebrow, his lip pulling up, letting me know he was impressed. We hadn't gotten to party at all with the Meadow

Grove fiasco, so there was no random girl last night. It was a good try, and I had to give him credit for pulling out all the stops.

Ren nibbled on her bottom lip, and I couldn't stop staring. I could tell she still wasn't sure, so I threw out my last ditch effort.

"How about this? There is a great coffee shop not far, and we can all go there for a coffee. Then we can talk on the way back to the academy. Ya can keep me company, and we can follow Blake so ya can make sure that he's not driving off into the wilderness with your friend."

"Unbelievable. Always ruining my dates," Blake grumbled.

"Lord tunderin Jesus, it's not a date," Ren said as she glared at Blake.

I burst out laughing. I couldn't hold it in, that was the cutest shit I'd ever heard a girl say in my life, and the confused look on Blake's face made it like sweet icing on the cake. As her glare found me, I tried to suck it in but couldn't and ended up laughing all over again.

"That was amazing." I choked out and realized that at least Ivy had been giggling too.

Ren rolled her eyes at me, but she couldn't hide the hint of a smile that played along her lips. "Fine, let's do the coffee thing. I don't want to ditch my friend completely, and Blake was nice enough to bring me to town."

I so badly wanted to say if you only knew the real reason for his interest, but that would lead to the bet, and she couldn't find out about that. I was already sweating with the possibility. I could hear Blake grumbling as he got in the car. Ivy grabbed Ren's hand and smiled. I assumed that was girl code for 'I'm all good.'

As she walked toward me, my heart pounded a little harder. Giving myself a kick in the arse, I met her around the passenger side of the car and opened the door for her.

"What are you doing," Ren asked.

"What do you mean?"

"You're being all...nice," she finally said.

"I am nice." I had to stop myself from leaning into her as the delicate scent of cherry blossoms hit me. "Just only to select people."

"Ah, and how did I get to be one of the lucky ones?" She crossed her arms over her chest.

"How about ya get in since it is freezing out here, and you can interrogate me all ya want?"

"It's not cold. You don't know cold until you've spent a February in Alberta." Ren stepped in closer to get into the car, and I lost the battle leaning into her like she was calling me.

She immediately leaned back and scowled at me, which was fucking adorable. "I like the smell of your shampoo. It reminds me of home. My home before coming to America."

"Oh. Okay." Her cheeks pinked, and I gripped the door tighter to keep from kissing her. I was pretty sure she would knee me in the balls for it, and yet I was still fucking tempted. It was good that she slipped into the car before I took the chance.

"Fuck," I mumbled, walking around the back of the car. I needed to get control, but she made me so damn hot. Blake glared at me from the driver's seat of his car, but I ignored his irritating ass. He might be my best friend, but there was no way in hell I was going down without a fight. I saw Ren first, and I wanted her before the bet. As far as I was concerned, he could fuck right off.

Getting into my car, I glanced over at Ren. She looked liked like a little snow queen. It was a ridiculous thought, yet she sat so perfectly. Her face was serious and commanding without even trying, with her long silver hair and white coat. Her eyes questioned every little thing as she looked around the car and then at me.

"Are we going to go? You do know you have a strange habit of staring at me, right?" She said, putting on her seat belt.

"Aye, I do." Starting up my pride and joy, I backed out of the spot and pulled in behind Blake, who was already waiting for me.

"So, what did you want to talk to me about," Ren asked and settled back into the seat like she'd been in here a million times.

Was I upset that she wasn't impressed with my car? She wasn't asking to fiddle with the heat or music. Did I like that she was so chill? I wasn't sure of anything, and she had me all over the damn place.

"Um...can we just talk about random stuff first? The coffee shop is just up there," I said as I racked my brain for a legit reason for dragging her away from Ivy and Blake.

"Sure. I hear that the swim meet didn't go so well. Any truth to what people are saying?" She glanced over at me.

"None. We don't do that shit. The other teams were jealous that we were taking all the gold and wanted to tarnish our names. Bunch of fucks," I growled. I wondered what Nash decided to do to Sabastian. He said he would take care of him.

"Did you hear that they found one of the guys dead?" I looked over a Ren, unsure if she somehow knew and was poking at me to see my reaction or if she was genuinely curious. It made me wonder a little more about who her family was. Which family lines did she belong to? Nash would already be digging. It was his thing, looking into every new person that walked through Wayward's doors.

"I did hear that. I'm not going to say that I feel bad, though. That guy made a lot of enemies by being a piece of shit. He was bound to piss off the wrong person."

Ren didn't acknowledge that she agreed or disagreed, and I wiggled in my seat. I normally didn't give a flying fuck if a girl cared about the things I did, but I found myself wondering what she'd think if she knew it was me that had hung Austin by his neck from the bridge. Would she be impressed or maybe scared? Would she run for the hills? Would we have to silence her? That last thought was a gut punch. All the kids at the school were from one crime family or another, but Ren seemed different. I couldn't put my finger on what or why, but there was this innocence to her. She didn't seem marred by the dark crap that the rest of us were.

"Do you like the car?" I finally asked, unable to take the silence anymore.

"You mean, am I impressed by your Ferrari 296GTS convertible with hybrid technology, extreme power, agile handling, magnificent steering, and scintillating speed? You mean the car with a twin-turbocharged 3.0-liter, V-6 engine, and an amazing 819 horsepower, married to a battery-fed drive motor placed between the engine block and an eight-speed dual-clutch automatic transmission. The car that can reach 60 mph in sub-three seconds, has a quarter mile sprint of under ten seconds, and is almost four hundred thousand to purchase. With the customizing specs and paint job you've chosen, it would certainly be at the higher end of the scale." My mouth fell open as I stared at Ren, and she shrugged. "It's alright," she said, the corner of her mouth lifting in an adorable smile.

"Holy fuck, you can talk dirty like that to me anytime." I pretended to shiver, which made Ren laugh. I loved the sound, and she had the best smile. That old saying about lighting up a room applied to her, and now I had a fantasy of her screaming car stats while she rode me. I needed to adjust myself when I got out of the car. Ren was so sexy she was killing me. "I take it you like cars?"

Ren shrugged. "I'm indifferent."

"But you can recite the stats of my car off the top of your head?"

Ren turned in her seat and looked at me. Her eyes were not exactly playful but weren't as guarded as normal. She cocked a brow as she drew her bottom lip into her mouth. "I'm a walking mystery," she said, and my brain screeched to a halt.

"Watch out," Ren squealed and pointed out the windshield.

"Fuck," I growled out as I had to slam on the brakes so I didn't ram into Blake. My heart hammered as the car came a hair's breadth away from colliding with the Maserati. "Damn, that was close." Blake stuck his arm out the driver's side window and gave me the middle finger. "Please, for the love of god, don't make that face at me while I'm driving."

"What face?"

"That sexy as fuck look you've got going on."

"You're crazy," she said, shaking her head like I was ridiculous. Could she really not see how pretty she was? That seemed impossible. She was a knockout. The rumblings among the guys in the school regarding the bet were loud, but the comments about how hot she was, were a close second—just another reason for me to get her locked up before they could get ahold of her. The thought of someone like Axel touching her made me want to cut his dick off.

I followed Blake as he pulled into the coffee shop, the brown and green sign announcing the name. EEFFOC. Ren stared up at the glowing sign as we drove by.

"It spells coffee backward. Everything in this place is amazing. They have coffee puns and jokes written on the tables and framed coffee images on the walls. This place is the best, and when I stay at my house, I make sure to come here before heading back to the academy. Their coffee doesn't compare."

"So you live around here," she asked, and I nodded as I pulled into the empty spot beside Blake. If he didn't love his car so much, I could see him opening his door so I'd hit it.

"Most of the parents do. Where is your family living, or did they stay in Canada?" Ren's facial expression turned as cold as the weather outside.

"I don't know. I didn't see the house before I was dropped off at the academy," she said, getting out of the car before I could question how the hell that happened. Every time I learned something about her, I wanted to know more. Another first for me.

I got out of the car and locked it but couldn't stop staring as Ren and Ivy walked just ahead of Blake and me.

"I'll get it," I said and reached around Ren to grab the door, holding it open for the girls to walk in, but Blake stopped as he reached me.

"Smart ruining my night, but don't worry, I have other ideas to get her alone." My teeth clenched tight as Blake winked and walked into the coffee shop. Before this bet was over, I might actually kill my best friend.

Ren

This place was the coolest coffee shop I'd ever set foot in. The selection of coffees and sweet treats was overwhelming, but I finally settled on a French vanilla latte with a piece of Triple Threat Chocolate cake. Hello sugar high. Now I was sugar high and couldn't stop laughing. As annoying as Myles and Blake could be, they were also extremely funny and had stories that kept Ivy and me in stitches.

"Nope, no arguments. I get the bill," Myles said, slapping his hand down on the table as the waitress came around and dropped it off.

"You won't see me complain," Blake said, leaning back in his chair.

"This is not a date. I'll pay for my own," I said to Myles as I grabbed my purse, but his hand landed on mine, stopping me.

"It's my treat for all of you. I know it's not a date," he said, linking our fingers under the table. His hand felt so incredibly hot, and my traitorous pulse pounded harder as our eyes locked.

I'd never had a guy be this persistent. What was I thinking? I'd never had anyone show this kind of interest. It was confusing. I was momentarily frozen, unsure what to do, but he only squeezed my hand and let go. He got up and went to the front to pay, and I found myself following his movements.

"I'll be right back. I need to use the bathroom before we leave." Ivy scooted away from the table and left Blake and me alone.

"So, did you want to head back to the academy with me or Myles?"

Blake crossed his arms, seeming genuinely annoyed, and I had no idea why. Blake didn't seem like the dating type, and I didn't think I'd be his first choice. If Lisa weren't his cousin, I would've said she was exactly what he liked. Tall with long blonde hair and a glowing pageant smile.

"I promised Myles I'd talk to him on the way back to the academy, so I'll go with him. Unless, of course, there is some reason you don't think I should go with Myles?" My brow lifted slightly as I wondered what Blake was up to with his questioning. We'd discussed this and it was already decided.

"No, it's just that I don't want to see you get hurt." Blake leaned his arms on the table and lowered his voice. "Myles has a reputation with the girls. I just wouldn't want you to fall prey, is all."

I smiled at him. "Well, isn't that sweet of you." My tone dripped with cynicism. "I'll be honest, that comment seems funny coming from you." Blake's friendly, 'I'm only here for you, kid' smile slipped.

"From what I hear, other than your brother Theo, you're all the same. I'm pretty sure I heard you bragging that you slept with five different girls last week. Needed to cram them in before the meet." I made little air quotes with my fingers. "Thanks for the warning, but I learned a long time ago how to take care of myself. I'm certainly not going to...fall prey, as you put it, but I appreciate your concern, even if it is self-serving."

Blake's mouth fell open, while the look in his eyes was caught between baffled and annoyed.

"Is everything okay here," Myles asked as he stepped up to the table. I could feel his gaze flicking from Blake to myself and back again.

"All good," Blake drawled out.

"Yup, I'm good too," I said and stood as Ivy returned.

"Why is it that I'm getting the feeling ya aren't being completely honest with me?" Myles challenged, his eyes going to Blake and narrowing into a glare.

Blake pushed away from the table. "Come on, Ivy. We better get you back before your father knows you escaped."

"Ain't that the truth." She smirked, but it didn't reach her eyes. Standing, I hugged her before we followed Blake outside.

Myles was still staring at me again, but I wasn't going to say any more about my conversation with Blake. There had to be a reason for how Blake and Myles, and even Nash, were acting, but I hadn't figured out what that reason was yet. They all seemed a little too interested, way too quickly and all at once. Was it a challenge of some sort? I didn't get that feeling off Myles as much. I couldn't put my finger on why that was, he just seemed more genuine, but it was hard to tell with the other two. Blake was trying too hard, and Nash was terrifying. It made it very difficult to get an accurate read.

As soon as we got inside the Ferrari, Myles looked at me. "What did Blake say that had ya upset?"

"Nothing, I promise. He was giving me a rundown on who I should avoid in the school. I told him I didn't need that as I planned to stay away from everyone until I graduate and get the hell out of here."

Myles's eyes hardened. "Ya wanna leave?"

"Don't you? I mean, what is tying you here?"

"Nash and the boys and my work," he said.

"I didn't know you had a job. What do you do?" I snapped my seatbelt in place.

Myles rubbed the back of his neck before starting the car and pulling out of the parking spot. "I do deliveries and sometimes guard."

"You're seventeen. How did you get a guard job?"

We pulled out onto the main street and headed toward the academy. My mum used to have me memorize the route we took to get places and then map in my head how I would leave and get myself home. My mum would say that you never knew what could happen, and if I was ever kidnapped, I wanted to remember everything I could. It seemed like a strange exercise and one that was designed to scare me away from talking to strangers, but I did as she asked anyway. Now it was habit.

"It's for my Da and sometimes for Nash's father. It pays well."

I flicked my gaze around the car. "I can see that."

I waited until we were outside the city limits before asking, "So, what did you want to talk to me about?"

Myles drummed his fingers on the top of the steering wheel. "I wanted to apologize for missing our tutoring session and class this morning. I was working late last night after the swim meet and crashed at my Da's place and forgot to set my alarm." He looked over at me, and even in the shadowed car, I could see the hint of gold in his amber eyes. My instincts were telling me he was sincere. It was only one tutoring session, not the end of the world, and it wouldn't kill anyone. But could I trust that? Could I trust him?

"You're forgiven. But Myles, I take my classes seriously. I want to have my pick of any university in the world. So, if you start missing all the time or don't put in any effort...."

"Naw, I swear. I will do better." He cleared his throat and shifted in his seat like he was nervous. "There is something else I want to talk to you about."

"Okay."

"I wanted to ask ya out on a proper date. Not a friend outing, but a real date. I want to get dressed up and take ya someplace nice."

"I don't know, Myles. I'm not looking to date anyone." I crossed my arms and stared out the window, but I could still see his reflection in the glass.

"Okay, let's call it a getting to know ya, and I promise I'll be on my best behavior." He held up his hand like he was swearing on a bible, and I smirked.

I knew what he was like, and what I told Blake was true, but it had been so long since I laughed like I did with Myles. It was difficult to remember smiling over the last five years, let alone laughing and feeling like everything would be okay again somehow. What would be the harm in one outing?

Blake tapped his brakes, the bright glow flashing at us. "What is he doing?"

"Oh, ya think so, do ya?" Myles said. Before I could ask what he meant, he pulled out into the oncoming lane and pulled up beside Blake.

"What...what are you doing?"

Myles looked over, but he wasn't looking at me. He was staring at Blake. I looked out the window as Blake held up three fingers. Fear swept through my body as he folded one down.

"Don't you—"

I didn't get the rest of my sentence out before Myles stomped on the gas. The sports car leaped forward like we'd been shot out of a cannon, and my head slammed back into the headrest.

"Oh my god, oh my god." I kept saying over and over as we flew along the two-lane road. We crested a slight hill, and I screamed, closing my eyes at the sight of the car coming at us. Myles swerved, and my eyes snapped open to see we'd slipped in behind Blake again.

"What the fuck, man! Can't ya see I'm racing here?" Myles yelled at his rearview mirror before pulling back out and whipping up beside Blake once more.

"Myles, can we slow down?" If he heard me, he ignored me as we streaked around a corner at speeds I'd never dreamed of traveling in a car, let alone at night on a winding road. My heart hammered like a scared animal, and my adrenaline spiked.

"Myles, please," I said, pushing my feet into the floor and gasping as a pickup truck pulled out of a driveway. We would've hit it if the person hadn't swerved onto the gravel shoulder.

Suddenly images flooded my mind. I was in a car when it swerved off the road and crashed. I gasped and shook my head with the sudden flash that seemed real and like a dream at the same time. I'd never been in an accident, so it had to be my fear screaming what could happen. My nails dug harder into the leather.

"Woohoo!" Myles yelled as we edged in front of Blake. Glancing out my window, it didn't look like Ivy was having any more fun than I was. Her face was as white as a sheet of paper. "I'm gonna kick your fucking ass," Myles growled.

I sucked in a sharp breath as the car somehow found another gear, and we blew by Blake, cutting him off just as red and blue lights pulled out of a sideroad. The siren was loud as the police car raced after us.

"Ah fuck," Myles groaned and let his foot off the gas. He pulled over at the same time Blake did behind us. I crossed my arms and glared at the side of Myles's head. I'd never been so happy to see a cop pull someone over before, especially when I was in the car.

My shaking hand gripped the front of my puffy jacket as I tried to calm the panic that had me on the verge of passing out. I wasn't the type to faint, but it had happened twice in a couple of days, and I was beginning to worry that something more serious was wrong with me.

"Fuck, well, at least it's Morrison," Myles mumbled as he stared into his side view mirror. I didn't know who Morrison was, but he better not let the guys off. They were racing and driving dangerously.

Myles's window lowered as the officer walked up to the car, and a middle-aged man leaned down and stared in at us.

"Myles McCoy. I should've known you'd be the other idiot," Morrison said.

"Aye, ya know how it goes when ya take a new girl out on a date. Ya gotta show off just a little," Myles said, and my teeth clenched for ten different reasons. At the top of the list was being lumped in with all the other new girls that had gotten into his car. In one sentence, he managed to undo all the work he had put in and crush my spark of hope by making me feel like I meant nothing more than the next notch on his belt. Knowing it and hearing it were two totally different things.

The Sheriff chuckled which further set my teeth on edge. "Yeah I get it but, Myles, no more racing. Just because the car can go that fast doesn't mean it should. Don't you want more dates with other girls?"

Myles laughed and looked at me, but I didn't laugh back. I didn't say anything. Not only was he barely getting a slap on the wrist, but they were joking about all the girls he'd take out in the future. I stared out the front window grinding my teeth, barely containing the hurt and rage inside. All I wanted was to get back to the academy and put space between us.

"I mean it, Myles, no more racing, or I'll impound this thing and make sure the guy treats it like a junker."

Myles sucked in a horrified breath. "Ya wouldn't dare do that to my Black Beauty?"

"If I catch you racing again, I guess you'll find out," Morrison said, walking away. Un-fucking-believable was all that was running through my head.

"Well, looks like we got out of that one easy enough," Myles said, his voice all cheery as he pulled away from the shoulder. "Ren? You okay?"

Now he cared? He didn't care that he almost killed us, didn't care that I was scared or that he'd grouped me in with all the other girls he'd dated, fucked, and tossed aside. But he cared now that I wasn't speaking to him? Well, he was going to get a lot more of that.

"Ren, come on, talk to me."

I tuned him out as he babbled about how he just wanted to show off a little and how sorry he was. I didn't care. When it meant the most, he showed his true colors. He was still begging me to talk to him when we pulled through the gates of the academy property, and my eyes snapped to the men walking around dressed in all black. I stared at them as we drove past, but Myles didn't even acknowledge they existed. I rubbed my eyes and looked in my side view mirror to make sure I wasn't losing it, but they were still there.

I wanted to ask who the hell they were, but that would've required me to speak to Myles, and that wasn't happening.

"I'll pull up front and let you out. Then I'll go park." I nodded. "Ren, please talk to me," Myles begged as he pulled up to the front doors.

I looked at him and hated the stupid sad look on his face, but I wasn't going to be played. He made me want to hit him square in his sexy face. "You wanted an answer about a date or outing? The answer is no."

"Ren."

I opened the door and got out but glared into the car at him. "I'm sure next week there will be yet another new girl you can take out and impress. Maybe one that will actually be impressed with your fancy car, how you almost killed us, and just how much experience you have, but I'm out."

Flicking the door closed, I walked over to Ivy, who'd already gotten out of Blake's car. She looked as terrified as I felt.

"You okay," I asked and spotted the police car pulling up the long drive.

"Oh no," Ivy said, sucking in a shuddering breath as she grabbed my arm in a death grip. "That's my dad." I stared at the driver as the car pulled up, and the man glared at us. I recognized Morrison, and it dawned on me why Myles knew who it was. It wasn't because he had gotten in trouble with the cops before, but because he was Ivy's father. The window on the passenger side of the car slid down, and Ivy's hand shook on my arm.

"Ivy-Rose, get over here right now," his voice boomed and didn't hold any of the light teasing it had with Myles. He seemed like two different people, a total Jekyll and Hyde.

I didn't care who this guy was. He wasn't scaring me, and he wasn't hurting Ivy. I took a step forward, but Ivy stayed rooted to the spot, her eyes as wide as saucers. What the hell had he done to her? Anger burned in my gut, and I glared at Morrison as he hollered for his daughter again.

"Come on. I'm going with you."

"No, you don't want to do that. Stay on his good side. You don't want him to know you exist," Ivy said, but I grabbed her hand as she started away.

"No. I do what I want, and no one intimidates me." She held my hand tighter as we walked to the side of the car.

Morrison flicked his gaze to me as we stopped beside the car door. "Do you mind? I'd like to have a private discussion with my daughter?"

"Actually, I do mind. Anything you have to say to her can be said in front of me, Mr. Morrison, or do you prefer Sheriff Morrison?" I leaned on the edge of the window.

"Depends on the context, I guess. At the moment, it would be Sheriff Morrison, and you're lucky I didn't arrest you."

"Oh really? For what exactly," I asked. He glared, but I couldn't give two shits. "Let's get something straight, Sheriff Morrison. I may only be seventeen, but I know my constitutional rights and am already studying university-level law. If you want to threaten me, then by all means, but I can name at least a half dozen laws you broke by letting Myles and Blake go earlier. I also happened to be filming the race and caught you letting the guys go on my phone, so unless you're the one that would like to be in hot water, then I suggest you say what you want to say to your daughter, with me standing here and then be on your way."

His nostrils flared, and his hands gripped the steering wheel so hard it looked like he would rip it right off. Ivy was clinging to my hand so hard as she trembled that I could feel her nails digging into my skin. That was all the fuel I needed to stare this man—who was obviously a bully—down.

"You really shouldn't make an enemy of me. What is your name?" He made a point of pulling out his notepad and pen like that would somehow intimidate me. Instead, I smiled.

"Kayleigh Ren Davies, would you like me to spell that for you?"

His pen paused. "As in Neal Davies' daughter?"

I had no idea why my father would've had a reason to have dealings with the local Sheriff, but I decided to keep the shock to myself.

"Yes."

He set the notebook aside, his entire personality changing. "Fine, both of you get inside, and I don't want to see you in Blake O'Brien's car again. You know the rules. You stay away from the kings, that's an order." Morrison pointed his finger at Ivy and then hit the button to close the window. I had to jump back or be caught in it. So he knew the guys nickname which I thought was strange. Then again there was a number of things at this place that were strange. We watched the car leave just as Blake and Myles walked up the sidewalk from the student parking around the back.

I had no interest in going round two with Myles over a date. Whipping around, I dragged Ivy with me. I glanced over my shoulder as I opened the front door, but he was looking down. I was a little shocked that he didn't try to chase me down. Maybe he got the message. A wave of disappointment washed through me, and I really hated how I didn't want him yet could still feel disappointed. As soon as we got inside, I pulled Ivy into the girl's bathroom. The automatic lights flicked on as we pushed through the second door.

"What the hell was that?" I whispered. "Why was your dad treating you like that?"

Tears welled up in Ivy's eyes. "Talk to me, Ivy. That wasn't normal. He looked like he was going to drive off with you to knock you around."

I felt bad for pushing her as tears fell like a dam had burst. "I don't want to talk about it," she said as she ran out the door.

I was going to run after her, but I knew when someone had been pushed too far. She needed her space. Glancing up at my reflection in the mirror, I sighed. What had started as a fun evening certainly didn't end that way. I really wasn't looking forward to heading back to my room to deal with my bitchy roommate, but unless the room transfer I put in for happened, I needed to sleep at some point.

Chapter 18

N **ash**

Vicky was all talk. She put on a good show and acted like she would make a great porn star, but when it came to sex, she was as dull as one of my father's three-hour board meetings about the fiscal quarter. At least those had colorful graphs. All I was getting was a limp body that flapped like a dying fish and moaning that was more like a pig's grunt or maybe a goat's—no that had to be a donkey. I couldn't distinguish farm animals well enough to know for sure, but she was definitely of the petting zoo variety. I pet, she brayed. I wanted to stuff a dirty sock in her mouth and if she choked on it, would be a bonus.

It was so much better when I shoved my dick down her throat and shut her up. Nothing made me go soft faster than listening to the squeal and moan that ended with a throaty grunt. Seriously, what the fuck was that?

"Oh yes, Nash, you feel so good," she said, and I rolled my eyes.

"Oh yes, I'm the best," I drawled out.

I knew shit had really taken a turn for the worse when I started imagining what it would be like to fuck strange things. I'd gone through normal items and even tried a couple, but my latest fantasy was a stuffed turkey. That had some serious possibilities with it being warm and gooey. I could rip off a leg like a caveman and eat at the same time. Okay, that was some funny shit, and I had to stop myself from laughing out loud.

I'd avoided having sex with her for the last month, but this was the best way to get under Ren's skin. I had one goal with this maneuver, Ren would forever have me burned into her brain. I didn't do hearts and flowers, and I certainly wasn't going to charm her into bed. But annoy the fuck out of her, make her remember me, have her wonder what it would be like to be the one under me...now those were all things I could do.

Best case scenario, she got jealous, but the end goal was to stick with her. Whenever I walked into a room, she would remember hearing and seeing me. It was a mindfuck that I enjoyed, and this was only act one. The long-game plan was to make sure she looked in every corner to see if I was there, wondering what I'd do next. There was a power that came with being on someone's mind all the time, which I planned on using to my full advantage.

Now the question became could I manage to stay hard until she got back? Fucking Blake and Myles, they better not have won already. I'd never live that shit down.

"Please never stop fucking me," Vicky cooed in her high-pitched voice. She ran her nails across my shoulders, and I leaned into it from side to side, wanting to tell her she missed where I was itchy.

"Oh, I love it when you wiggle back and forth like that."

"Yeah, so do I," I said and moved my shoulder up and down against her nails.

And what the fuck was up with these sheets? They were terrible. I had no idea how she slept on them. My ass felt like I was rubbing up against Velcro while being bitten by fire ants with every thrust. I would've whipped them off my back, but in typical Vicky fashion, she said she got too cold and it would take her longer to come. Fuck I would layer the bed in fifty heated blankets if it made this bitch come faster.

If Ren didn't show up soon, I would have to fake an orgasm. I'd never had to do that before, but I was going to give it the good old college try just to get the hell out of here. My adrenaline spiked as soon as I heard the key card beep in the door. Fucking yes! She was back.

I started thrusting harder until Vicky's head hit the wall. "Ouch, Nash. Not so hard," she complained, but I ignored her. My full attention was on a different girl.

The door opened, and I smirked as I stared at the shadow cast on the floor. "Fuck Vicky, you feel so good," I groaned and then glanced over my shoulder to see the full effect of her shock.

The look on her face was a beautiful thing. Ren's mouth hung open, her eyes wide as she stood frozen mid-stride. Now all she had to do was run off and think about what she saw. Like planting a seed, the thought would grow with a little water and eventually become what I wanted.

What I hadn't expected was the rage that came over her face. It actually turned me on, or did until she opened her mouth.

"Get the hell out of here, Freak. We're in the middle of something," Vicky yelled.

"Oh fuck no, this is not happening," Ren said, her voice a low growl.

My movements slowed as she propped the door open. What the hell was she doing? Ren pulled out her cell phone and held it up. Even from my compromised position, I could tell the recording light was on.

"Hey, everyone! You want to see Nash and Vicky fucking? I'm live-streaming that shit on my channel, *For The Love Of Art*, or come out into the hall and see it for yourself. I mean, it's a pretty weak show, but I'm sure you'll get some worthy blackmail material. I give Vicky a solid two out of ten, Nash maybe a three and a half."

I couldn't believe what she was doing. I'd never seen a girl act like this before and especially around me. I was the next King, people ran scared, bowed at my feet, or wanted to fuck me, but this girl stared at me with pure hatred.

"Freak, what the fuck? Go away!" Vicky screamed in my ear, making me wince.

There was no fucking way she was putting my face on a live-streaming channel. If my father saw that, I'd be beaten for a week. I quickly pulled out of Vicky and grabbed my T-shirt off the floor, holding it up like a shield to cover my face. I snapped the condom off and purposely dropped it into Ren's trash. Thank god that was over, at least.

Grabbing my track pants, I yanked them on and shoved my feet into my sneakers before marching for the door. Keeping my head covered, I leaned down close to her ear. "Turn the camera off," I growled low enough that only Ren could hear.

"It's already off. Like, I actually want your ass on my art channel? I like to inspire people not horrify them. I've seen old men at the park with better asses than yours. If I were going to film anyone, it would be one of the guys from Meadow Grove," she said.

My lip lifted in a snarl. She managed to say the one thing that would really piss me off. I glanced at her phone, and sure enough, it was pointed at the ground. She smiled at me when I grabbed her arm.

"Careful, Nash, you have a bunch of witnesses watching and

filming," Ren whispered, her silvery eyes flashing with the same intensity of hatred I felt in my chest. What did Myles see in this girl?

"You think you're pretty smart, don't you? That you have me all figured out." I let go of her arm but leaned in, bracing my arm against the door to block out the view of the cameras with my back. "You have no idea the kind of monster I can be. Consider yourself on notice."

"I'm trembling in my boots," she snarked and crossed her arms. Her face was a mask of stone, but I could see the slight uncertainty under the layer of anger. I wanted more. Ren didn't have a clue who she was dealing with, but she was about to. I'd make sure of it.

"Watch your back, Princess. I'm coming for you."

Pushing away from the door, I turned to walk away.

"At least you'll be coming for someone!" She growled back.

The hallway ohhhed, and I froze. Looking over my shoulder at her, my jaw cracked as I ground my teeth together. No, this was not the time, but she had it coming.

"What the fuck are you all looking at?" Doors slammed, and people jumped back inside to get out of my way.

This bet may have started as a stupid little game, but now I didn't even care if I won as long as I got to make Ren's life a living hell.

R en
I slammed the door so hard that it shook the walls, and I heard the stupid pink wreath hanging on the outside fall.

"What the hell is your problem?" Vicky yelled as she stomped toward me with a blanket wrapped around her body. Her hair was a mess, and her face was red as she fumed, but I was just as pissed off. All the crap I'd managed to hold back the last few days of living with this woman had erupted to the surface. Between the shit with Myles earlier and now this, I was done.

"Me?" I growled. "We're not even supposed to have a guy in the room, let alone have sex with him, and it's after curfew. You didn't even mark the door. My eyes are permanently scarred," I growled and stood my ground as Vicky got in my face.

"Spare me. That is the closest you'll ever get to action with a real man. No one of Nash's social standing would ever touch the likes of you, Davies. You and your family are nobodies." Vicky said this like it was an insult, but in reality, I couldn't be happier. It just proved that she didn't know or didn't want to see what an asshole her boyfriend really was. The fact that he'd already threatened to fuck me twice screamed it all.

"Oh no," I gasped and clutched at my heart. "I won't have the opportunity to be with a cheating piece of shit that treats everyone like crap? What ever will I do?"

Vicky's eyes narrowed. "Nash is not a cheater."

"If you believe that, you're a bigger idiot than I thought. That guy is so far from faithful that he'd have to look the word up in the dictionary to know what it even means." For just a blink, Vicky looked like I slapped her. She had to know the reality. How could you not? I'd been here less than a week and heard the rumors about the wild parties the guys threw. To know all the shit people said was why I purposely wore my headphones without any music playing when I wasn't in class. It was the perfect way to make everyone think I couldn't hear them.

One of the girls in my art class had been whispering to her friend about how much fun she had a few weekends ago when Nash ate her out while her friend rode him. That was pretty specific to be fake news.

"Just because you want to die dried up and alone doesn't mean that I have to," she said, and even though there was no way for her to know about my mum, the statement hit hard. "I plan on marrying Nash. He is a King."

I screwed up my face. There was nothing kingly about that guy. Asshole thug whose family happened to have money, sure, but a king? No. I hated how everyone walked around calling the assholes in the school kings like they were something special. Lets get real people, were on a swim team, they didn't rule a country.

"Setting your standards low, I see. Good for you, Vicky. Then he can permanently fuck around on you while you stay in your fancy home with your two and a half kids wondering where he is. If you think you're going to change him, you'd better give your head a shake. That guy isn't changing for anyone, no matter how many girls you threaten, rings you put on his finger, or tantrums you throw."

Her face went so red I thought she was going to be the one to erupt. Vicky raised her hand like she was going to poke me.

"Don't touch me, or you'll find out how much of a freak I can be when I shove it up your own ass." I wasn't sure I'd actually do that to her, but the anger and hatred boiling inside me was lethal and scared me.

She dropped her hand but stepped in closer until she stared down at me like Nash had. I didn't know what it was about tall people thinking this was a good intimidation tactic, but it didn't work with Nash, and it wouldn't work with Vicky.

"I'm going to ruin you."

"You already did. I saw you naked, remember? I thought I was going to go blind." She sucked in a deep breath, and I could tell she was getting ready to go full steam into another rant about how pathetic I was. It was the only song she knew how to sing, and it was already getting old. "I don't care if you are fucking Nash, just don't do it in our room. Literally, go anywhere else, and I would cheer you and your stupid ambition of marrying him on."

Vicky snarled like a dog. "I'm going to make your pathetic life hell. You just made an enemy of the wrong person," Vicky said. She marched toward the bathroom but tripped on the sheet, and I once more saw her naked tits as she screamed and let go of the blanket to break her fall with her hands.

"Ow," she whined. I snickered, sauntering over to my side of the room, and pulled out my phone. I didn't turn it on but pretended I did and was taking a bunch of photos.

"Yup, I'm terrified. Great shot of your bouncing tits." I pointed.

"Put the phone away! Or else."

"Or else what? Oh I should post these on the school website."

"Don't you fucking dare." I smiled, as Vicky pushed herself to her feet and gripped the blanket to her chest. An evil smile curled up the corner of her mouth. "You're a nobody, Davies. No one would miss you if something terrible were to happen. No one would care if you lived or died, and no one would bother looking for your body."

Now I wished I had my phone on. That threat would've been nice to have recorded. "I have an idea for you, Vicky, it's novel and will be hard for you to understand, but I think you should give it a try. Fuck off and leave me alone. I don't want anything to do with you, your boyfriend or your life, but if you come at me..." I smiled. "I'll come for you. Don't say I didn't warn you."

"Bitch." The bathroom door closed.

"Try looking in a mirror," I yelled back.

Grabbing the back of my desk chair, I slowly sucked in a breath and fought to beat down the anger. My tongue had always been sharp, but now I wanted to lash out. I'd pictured grabbing the scissors off my desk and stabbing Vicky with them. That wasn't normal. I wasn't normal. Maybe, I never was, but something inside of me was switched off or broken, I could feel it.

It happened to me while I was locked in that panic room, waiting for someone to arrive and let me out. It was like a part of me died, but I wasn't the same when I got out.

Chapter 19

Ren

"Earth to Ren?"

I jerked at the sound of my name. It was as if I went from complete silence to being in the middle of a concert. Okay, it wasn't that bad, but Ivy and Chantry did have the music loud.

"I'm sorry. What did you say?"

Ivy tilted her head and stared at me. "What's going on? You keep spacing out."

"Nothing, I swear, just tired. My roommate is not exactly the respectful type." I smiled, and the girls chuckled. Everyone had

175

already heard about the confrontation with Nash and Vicky last night. The place was practically buzzing with the news. There were even a few memes of Nash stomping down the hall with different captions. I'd inadvertently made him into a meme, even I knew that didn't bode well for me.

Vicky was playing the victim, crying over what I did to her and saying I violated her privacy. But it wasn't Vicky I was worried about. It was Nash. If he'd come at me in biology class with anger and intimidation, I wouldn't have been suspicious, but he'd done the complete opposite. He barely spoke, answered any direct questions with respectful, intelligent answers, and was the perfect lab partner. He even had his half of the in-class project done and handed it to me to hand in before class was over. What the fuck?

There was only one thing that I knew for certain...he was up to something. His asshole attitude was easy to deal with, but this sneaky and quiet Nash scared me. I searched every corner for him when I walked into a room and made sure there were always people around when I went to and from the cafeteria or my locker. I had no idea what he'd do, and that was unnerving. He could be planning anything. I could picture him humiliating me, or stealing all my stuff. Hell I could even imagine him beating the shit out of me in a dark corner. He had a ruthlessness that burned in his eyes and every minute that passed that something didn't happen only made my nervousness worse.

"Are you still thinking about the blow-up yesterday?"

I looked between Ivy and Chantry. "I'm a little worried about what Vicky and Nash will do to retaliate."

Ivy gave me a sad look. "Any luck on the room transfer?"

I shook my head. "No. They said all the other rooms are taken, and no one wants to switch. That's a shock. Not even her so-called best friends want to room with the Queen Bee."

"That's more like Queen Bitch if you ask me," Chantry whispered, shocking me as much as it looked like it did Ivy. We both stared at her with our mouths hanging open. "What?"

I couldn't stop the laugh from tumbling out, and soon we were all in hysterical tears.

"That is very true." I leaned over and looked at the nail polish Chantry had chosen. It was a pretty shade of pink that I never would've expected from her. "I like the polish. It looks so pretty," I said, admiring the little rhinestone that Ivy had put on.

"Thanks." Chantry blushed and looked down so that once more, her black hair covered her face.

"What color do you want," Ivy asked, and I shifted around to face her.

"Hmm, do you have any silver?"

"Have you seen this basket?" Ivy's voice was playful as she held up the large basket full of nail polishes. "Duh, of course, I have silver." Smiling, I held out my hand. I missed doing stuff like this. The last time I had a girls night was months before Mum was killed. My Aunt Nadia, Lizzy, Mum, and I had sat around my mum's bed laughing and talking like everything was normal. We knew it wasn't, but my mum hated when we acted differently around her. I'd done my nails silver then too.

"Could you do one nail black," I asked.

"Yeah, that will look awesome."

I smiled at Ivy, but the joy didn't reach my heart. It was a little symbol of my mum's passing. Before I could stop it, a tear fell from my eye and landed on my sweater. I was hoping that neither of the girls had seen, but they were both staring, and I had to look away from their concerned eyes.

"What's wrong? If this is about Vicky, you can stay in here with us. I basically curl up in a ball anyway. You can share my bed."

I giggled, picturing the look on Myles's face if he heard I was sleeping in the same bed as Ivy. Why it was his stupid face that came to mind, I didn't want to analyze too closely.

Wiping away the tear, I sighed. "No, it has nothing to do with the Nicky ship." The girls smiled.

"Nicky?" Ivy laughed. "I like that. We can use it as a code word for them. Sorry, go ahead. I'll be quiet."

"It's okay. My mum passed away not long before I came here, and it's been really tough. My dad and I don't get along at all, and we haven't for years."

Saying it out loud confirmed the truth of just how alone I really was. My Aunt and best friend were in another country, and I was trapped in this place with a group of people I hardly knew. Most of whom didn't like me or wanted to mess with the new girl.

"Both my parents are alive, but I only see them on holidays," Chantry said. "They drop me off and forget about me only to over-compensate with lavish and unwanted gifts. Then during summer break, they ship me off to visit a family member. The truth is, I was a mistake. They never wanted kids. They never wanted me."

Leaning over, I hugged Chantry, but she just sat there rigid. It was easy to tell she wasn't used to contact with other people. I just held her until she relaxed into the hug. Straightening, I looked at Ivy. She had her head down, playing with imaginary fluff on the blanket we had spread on the floor.

"Ivy, will you tell me why you're so scared of your dad?" I reached out to lay my hand on her knee. The mood of the room had shifted, and I felt terrible for that. It also didn't match the sweet and welcoming atmosphere created with decorative lights, flower arrangements everywhere you looked, and pretty photographs of rainbows and waterfalls on the walls. It was as if the girls had preferred to live in a garden and wanted the room to feel like we were sitting outside.

"He wasn't always an ass. I can remember my dad bouncing me on his knee, reading me stories, or taking me to movies when I was really little. My mom was amazing, or she was until she took off. I was ten when I came home from school and found the house empty, not just of her but of everything. She had it all set that she was leaving and had movers lined up to take the furniture. My dad was served divorce papers at work." Ivy shrugged. "He was hurt and sad at first, but then he got mad and mean. Now he doesn't care who he hurts or if he takes money from bad people. When he gets angry or drinks, he hits me and calls me my mom's name."

This time we both hugged Ivy. "I hate going home. I never want to go home for holidays or for summer. This place is like a prison, but it's still safer than what's waiting for me out there."

"I'm so sorry." Standing up, I wandered over to Ivy's phone and the speakers playing music. I found the song I was looking for and hit play. Cyndi Lauper's, *Girl Just Want To Have Fun* came on, and I cranked the volume. I held my hands out to the girls. Their smiles were slow but eventually spread as they stood up and came to me.

"This song was one of my mum's favorites. We both loved Grey's Anatomy and would dance it out whenever Merideth and Christina would on the show. Then it became our thing. We would always put on music, dance around and sing whenever we felt sad. I don't want to give up the tradition. Would you like to be my new dance partners," I asked, wiggling ridiculously.

"Heck ya!"

The room descended into a dance party of three. We laughed and sang, and when the song ended, we hit play again until we were out of breath. Lowering the volume, we flopped on the floor pillows we'd been sitting on earlier and giggled at the ridiculousness, but it felt good. I hated that little things like this seemed so big and left me with a hint of guilt. In my heart, I knew my mum would want me to live my life, but doing anything fun seemed like I was spitting on her memory.

Completely out of breath, I leaned back on my arms and stared at the ceiling. The simple white had been painted with tiny stars that made up constellations. My fingers instinctively went to the side of my neck, and the eight freckles my mum said looked like the Phoenix constellation. From memory alone, I traced the symbol feeling like I'd been reduced to ash by everything that happened and was still waiting for my rebirth.

"Thank you, I didn't know how much I needed that," I said and smiled at Ivy and Chantry.

"Same." They looked at one another. "Jinx." They said in perfect unison again, which reduced us to a fit of giggles.

"So, are you excited about the party next weekend," Ivy asked as we settled back into her doing my nails. It took me a moment to remember what she was talking about.

"Oh, you mean the one Lisa mentioned?"

"Yeah, it's at Sacred Heart Academy, which is a little over an hour away, but we don't have a curfew on Saturdays," Ivy said, smiling wide.

"I thought your dad wouldn't let you go to things like parties?" Ivy's cheeks flushed.

"He doesn't, but Sacred Heart is outside his patrol area, and I know he's off duty. There shouldn't be any reason for him to see me."

That still sounded risky for her, but it was her decision. I wasn't sure a party was the best spot for me right now, but even Chantry looked excited. I was such a sucker for those hopeful faces. As hard as I tried, I couldn't even remember the last time I was at a party. My mum insisted I have a special night for my sixteenth, but I'm not sure you would consider that a party.

Mum had bought me a pretty dress with blue sequins, and I had my hair and makeup done. A huge limo had taken Lizzy and me to a fancy restaurant and then an all-ages club. We felt like superstars for the night.

It felt like they were holding their breath for my answer. "I'm not sure if you want me at a party, I tend to run my mouth in public, but if you really want me to go, then I'll go."

"Yay!" They cheered, and Ivy almost knocked over the open bottle of nail polish. "I can't wait to figure out what I'm going to wear. I know that Zigzag likes the goth look. Do you think I could pull it off without looking washed out?"

Oh lord, I hadn't even been thinking about something to wear. I should've done more shopping when I was out with Blake. Dammit, I didn't want to call my Father.

"What about you, Ren? What are you going to wear?"

"I'll look when I get back to my room. I don't even remember what I brought with me," I said and smiled. "But, I love the goth idea for you. I can do an excellent smoky eye if you want?" I said, quickly changing the topic.

The last thing I wanted to talk about was my father. We'd just gotten off the sad topics for tonight, and there was no need to rehash. The situation was what it was, and it was obvious that my father didn't care about me. Even though I'd told him I didn't want to see him, my heart held out hope that he would reach out and prove that he wanted to be in my life. Prove that he loved me, but instead, he remained silent. Not a call or text in almost a week.

I wiped away the stray tear that leaked out before the other two girls saw it. There were some things in life you wish you weren't right about, and your father not loving you was on that list.

Chapter 20

Myles

My pen made a little tapping noise as I bounced it off the table, my mind torn between the lesson in front of me and Nash. He had fumed all swim practice. Ren was getting under his skin and not in a good way. I didn't think he'd randomly kill her, that wasn't what we stood for, but there were a whole lot worse things he could do. I was genuinely worried for her, and everything was a mess. I wanted Ren, but this bet had turned everything on its head, and now I wasn't sure what was safer for her.

I was so deep in thought that I didn't hear Ren until she stepped up to the desk. "Wow, you're even early," she said, and I lifted my head to stare at her. Fuck, my reaction was always the same. My heart would leap in my chest, and my stomach would tighten into knots while my pants suddenly became a little more snug. "You're doing it again."

"Doing what again?"

"Staring and not saying anything."

I smirked. "Aye, I guess I am. I got ya a coffee." I pushed the coffee across to her and grabbed the brown bag handing it over with my surprise.

"What's in here? It's not something gross, is it?" She poked at the bag, and I chuckled.

"What are we in elementary school? I wouldn't have done that even then." Leaning back in my chair, I crossed my arms, but Ren arched one of her sexy eyebrows as she did that thing where she silently questioned me. It really did freak me out and held some sort of power over my mouth. "Okay, fine. I would've done it in elementary school, but not now."

She still gave me a look like she wasn't sure if she should believe me, but sat down and unfolded the top of the bag. I watched her face as she looked, and my heart warmed as she smiled wide.

"It's a muffin." Ren reached into the bag and pulled out the mammoth-sized muffin.

"Not just any muffin, that is a raspberry, sour cream muffin from Coralee's Bakery in town. They are always sold out, so you have to get there super early if you hope to get anything. Lucky for me they open at five."

She pulled off the top, and I couldn't look away if I wanted to as she took a sensual bit of the soft muffin. I licked my lips as she did hers, and her little moan had my cock at full mast. Fuck, I'd get her a muffin every day if she moaned like that for me again. I'd get her anything she wanted if she moaned like that in my ear. Every muscle flexed with need as she took another bite and licked her lips.

Watching someone eat a muffin should not be this sexy. Oh my god, what would she do with whipcream?

"Myles, this is amazing," she said, and as stupid as it was, my chest filled with pride. I'd finally done something right. She still had the hint of a bruise from where I'd given her the accidental black eye. On the plus side, you really only could go up from punching her in the face and spilling hot coffee all over her.

"Ya really like it?"

Ren took another bite and moaned again. If she kept that up, I was going to drag her to a storage room or just lay her out on the table.

"Freaking eh!"

I didn't know what that meant, but the dreamy look on her face said it all. "Well, that's good because I actually got ya a couple of different ones to try. I didn't know what ya'd like." I pulled three more bags out of my backpack and handed them over. "There is a fruit delight, triple chocolate threat, and a zucchini muffin which is my personal favorite."

Ren stared at the bags and then up at me. "I know it's over the top, but I genuinely didn't know which one ya'd like best, and I really needed to make up for some shit, like hitting ya in the face and...well, all of it," I rambled and rubbed the back of my neck. Why did she make me so sweaty? I hadn't been this nervous to talk to a girl since losing my virginity, and that was years ago.

Her cheeks pinked, and for just a few seconds, her eyes which were always so guarded, softened. Before my brain had time to register what I was doing and that it was most certainly a horrible idea, I stood and wandered around to her side of the desk and sat down.

"What are you doing," she asked. Her voice was once more as cool as a winter breeze, and I wondered who'd hurt her.

"It's easier to study this way." Pulling my notes and textbook across the table, I turned them for her to look at. She gave me a wary glance, and I wanted to kiss her until the look disappeared.

Being this close was definitely a bad idea. She popped another piece of muffin into her mouth, and I watched her lips move as I wondered what they would feel like. The soft scent of her cherry shampoo had me shifting closer as she concentrated on the books.

"Your notes are great. All your formulas and answers are correct except this one graph." She tapped the page and then pulled a pencil out of her updo and made the correction. I smirked when I noticed she still had another pencil in her hair like a fashion statement, even though I knew it was practical. She didn't wear makeup or try to dress up the uniform with her own flare like other girls.

"You forgot to answer part c. Suppose the curve $y = f(x)$ has tangent line $y = 2x + 3$ at the point x = 2. So true or false, $f(2) = 7$?" I tore my eyes away from staring at her face to focus on what she was talking about.

"The answer is true."

She smiled, and my breath caught in my throat as she looked at me. Our eyes locked from inches away, and all I could hear was my blood pumping through my body as my heart pounded like a drum. It felt like the air was charged between us.

I loved that her eyes were unsure, yet they flicked down to my lips like she was silently asking me to kiss her. At least, that was what I was hoping for. As I leaned in a little closer, she looked away and shivered.

"Myles, what are you doing?" Ren's voice was shaky, but she didn't sprint off or punch me.

"I wanted to get a closer look at this," I whispered, running my thumb down the patch of freckles that looked like a constellation on her neck. "They remind me of something."

"Phoenix," she said, her voice soft and breathy. Goosebumps rose as I continued to caress her skin.

"What's that," I asked, purposely letting my breath fan her neck and loving it when she shivered. I caught sight of her hands clenching into fists on the table like she was trying to fight the reaction, and I smirked. I wanted her as undone as she made me feel.

Nothing stopped the thought of her. Not work, not practice, not hanging with the guys. From the moment she got out of the car the other night, she was all I thought about. When I closed my eyes, I could almost smell the sweet scent of cherry blossoms and feel her soft skin under my fingers.

"The..." Ren paused and cleared her throat, which made me smile. "The freckles...they are the shape of the constellation Phoenix."

She was right. It did look like that. My ma would've loved that. She'd always been into nature and the stars. "I love the stars. When I was ten, my ma got me a fancy telescope for my birthday. My da thought it was a stupid gift for a boy, but I still have it, and it might be nerdy, but I take it out when there are going to be shooting stars."

"I like that," Ren said and turned her head to look at me. She was so close that our lips were almost touching, and I wasn't even sure why, but I wanted her to make the first move. "Can I ask a favor?"

"Anything."

"I need to go shopping tonight for the party on Saturday at Sacred Heart Academy. Would you take me shopping?"

"Ya trust getting into a car with me again?" I smirked and then laughed as she glared.

"No more racing."

"Scouts honor." I held up my fingers.

"I think that's the peace symbol," she said and smiled. It took everything in me not to lean in the last inch and kiss her.

"I'd be happy to take you, but under one condition. No one else comes, and you have dinner with me. Whatever you want, burger and fries or a five-course meal, I'll take you wherever you want to go."

Ren nibbled her bottom lip, a habit I found way too enticing. "Please don't do that, Snowflake. It makes me want to drag ya to a dark room and devour that mouth of yours." Ren's cheeks flamed a bright red, and I loved that I was finally getting a big reaction from her. My heart was going wild.

"Fine, I'll do dinner, but it's not a date. I don't date guys that plan on using me and tossing me aside." All the flirting from her stopped like she'd just slammed a door in my face. She turned away, looking at my calculus that I'd forgotten about.

"Who says I plan on doing any of that?"

She wasn't wrong. I didn't normally date. In fact, I couldn't remember an actual girlfriend of any kind. What was the point when I'd been told from the time I could walk that I'd be forced into an arranged marriage? I at least knew who I was supposed to marry, unlike Nash and Liam. I'd met her before we left Ireland to be closer to the Colliers, and she was a fine enough lass, I suppose, but it was the premise of the thing. I wanted to choose someone I genuinely connected with, someone I couldn't live without, not someone I settled for.

Although Ren was making me want to test the waters, and who knew, maybe my father would love her and cancel the stupid arrangement. One could hope.

Ren didn't bother to look up as she checked off each equation I got right and made little notes beside the ones I didn't.

"Myles, I know who you are and what you are. I know what you all are." I lifted a brow, not exactly sure what she was talking about, and figured it was better to stay quiet. Her hand moved quickly, the pencil she used as accurate and sharp as her mind. "You're all players, and I'm not talking about sports."

She flicked the page and continued. "I have been through too much to let myself fall for that crap. So if you were only taking me tonight because you thought you could check off another box in your little black book...." She looked up at me, and her eyes held so much pain that it was shocking. "Then I will find someone else."

I opened my mouth to ask what had happened to her when I heard the front door, and a moment later, Nash wandered in.

"Well, isn't this cozy?" He walked over and stood behind Ren, looking down at my notes. "That looks fucking boring. Then again,

I'm not surprised. You are mid. I'm not sure what my boy Myles here sees in you."

"Bro, who pissed in your cereal this morning?" I laughed, hoping to diffuse some of the building tension that felt like it could explode at any time. I wasn't sure if his tactic was to try and piss her off to make her want him, but if it was, I didn't think it was going to work.

Ren lifted her eyes from the notebook and stared up at Nash. "Trying to be cool now, I see. That's a switch from jerk mode. Not sure it suits you any better."

"You have quite the mouth on you, Princess. I wonder what it will be like with my cock shoved down your throat."

"I'd bite your shit off," Ren said. "I would then stuff it in a garburator and feed it to the first pigs that can be found. A fitting end to your cock, in the belly of a hog."

I shivered as she said the word cock, and as fucking horrible timing as it was I wanted to ask her to say it again.

"What the fuck is a garburator," Nash asked as he leaned over Ren, grabbing one of the bags I'd given her, and looked inside.

"How do you not know what a garburator is? You put your left-over food in it."

"You mean a garbage disposal."

"No, I mean a garburator. Try looking it up, or is that too difficult for you?" Ren growled, while Nash chuckled. I had to give it to her. She held her own with Nash, and I fucking loved that.

"Whatever, not worth my time. Damn, Myles, you got the good shit. I'm taking this one. You don't mind, do you, Princess?"

"What I mind is you here at all," Ren said, and the intense anger between them rose to another level.

"I see now why your family sent you here. I wouldn't want you around with an attitude like that either." Ren jumped to her feet. Her face contorted in rage as she glared up at Nash. I stood and placed my hand on Ren's shoulder.

"Nash is purposely trying to get under your skin," I said. "He loves to see how much he can push, don't ya, Nash?"

This felt strange. I was caught between standing up for Ren and my best friend, who also happened to be my boss, and the next King of Kings. We could disagree, but anything more, and we were as good as dead. It had never been an issue, and I never thought it would become an issue since all of our ideals had lined up until her. Now I was conflicted, my brain screaming at me from two different directions, and I wasn't sure what to do. They just stared at one another like they were in a contest.

I snatched the bag with the muffin I'd gotten for Ren from his hand. "Come on, man, just chill and get your own damn muffin. Don't be a cheap ass," I teased, once more settling on humor to try and break the building storm of tension that was swirling around them.

Nash glared at me but didn't seem angry, just curious about my reaction. I didn't know what was worse at this point. It was a fifty-fifty split. Either way, he could play with my emotions where Ren was concerned, and I didn't like feeling that exposed.

"Fine. I'll go, for now." Nash leaned past Ren, getting into her personal space as he grabbed the last bit of muffin Ren had been eating and popped it into his mouth. He smiled at Ren as he stood up straight and licked his fingers. "But I always get what I want."

Fuck I hated this bet.

"And that's my cue to go. I can only take so much on my asshole meter," Ren said and turned to stuff everything into her backpack. As soon as she had it zipped, Nash grabbed the bag and then her arm.

"Let go of me," she growled out as he yanked on her arm hard enough that she tripped over the chair she'd been sitting on and would've landed on the ground if Nash hadn't held her so tight.

"What the hell, Nash?" I said, my hands balling into fists. If he wanted me to throw down with him, all he had to do was ask. He didn't have to put Ren between us. It was the look on Nash's face while he stared at Ren that was so confusing. It was like she'd beaten his pet and stolen his car or something equally horrible. He was glaring at her like she needed to be eliminated, and that was what was chilling.

"I told you I'd be coming for you, Princess," Nash said, and my muscles tensed.

Shit.

Could he really be that pissed about the other night? Nash didn't take to being embarrassed well, but this seemed out of character, even for him. Nash stepped back and dragged Ren with him, but that was when her composure slipped, and she pulled back, trying to break Nash's hold.

This was going from tense to volatile in a blink.

Smiling, I walked over to Nash and wrapped my arm around his shoulders. "Nash, man, come on. This seems pretty extreme for an embarrassing stunt, and this is not us. I mean, we're assholes, but not like this."

"Says the guy that threw a girl off a balcony," Nash shot back, and Ren's eyes went wide.

"It sounds worse than it was, I swear. I was only tossing her into a pool," I quickly said and prayed Nash didn't finish the story of why I tossed Pam over the railing. "Point is that was for fun, but ya seem...." I turned my head away from Ren. "Like yer lookin to really hurt her, ya seem like yer dad," I said under my breath so only he could hear.

Nash sucked in a sharp breath, letting Ren go so fast I thought she would fall back over her chair and made to grab for her, but she caught herself with her hand on the table. She quickly righted herself and glared between me and Nash, like I was okay with this. I wasn't. I just didn't know what else to do other than knocking his ass out, and that came with more issues and maybe more problems for Ren. I needed to diffuse without escalating.

"Bag." Ren held out her hand, her eyes glacial as she glared at Nash. It took him so long to hand it over that I thought he was going to hang on to it out of spite. Like it was painful, he stretched out his arm and let go.

Ren stepped away from us but kept her eyes on Nash as if he might still try and attack. "I'll meet you in class," I said.

"We don't have class together today." She flung the bag onto her shoulder, and I mouthed, *I'm sorry.*

She marched away, and I waited until I heard the door to the study hall close before I turned on Nash.

I gave his shoulder a hard shove, forcing him to step back. "What the fuck was that man? Ya looked like ya were gonna kill her."

Nash ran his hand through his hair. "I don't know. She makes me so angry."

"For what? Ya, Snowflake has grit and sandpaper to her, but she didn't start that shit. We were minding our own fucking business." He shrugged and shook his head. "Is the bet getting to ya? We can call it off."

"Fuck no, it's not that. Just stressed, I guess." Nash walked away like nothing happened, but I'd felt the rage rolling off him. He was so not okay.

"We need to talk about this. Yer acting weird, man," I called after him.

"No, we don't. I'm fine."

I'd seen him get assertive and even aggressive, but this felt different. The look in his eyes was the same one he got whenever he had to fuck someone up.

"Tomorrow night, you're going to be busy, so don't make plans," Nash yelled as he opened the door.

"I have lacrosse practice."

"Then show up at our spot when you're done." The door closed with a thud.

"Fuck." Why the hell couldn't I have one moment with Ren that didn't go sideways? Stupid fucking bet.

Chapter 21

Ren

Vicky was at cheerleading practice when I got to my room after study hall, and I was thankful to change in peace. I didn't realize how much I enjoyed having my own quiet space until I was forced to share it with that bitch. Not to mention that every time I opened the door, I held my breath waiting to see if Nash would be there. Would he be camping out in my bed next, just to mess with me? Or maybe behind closed doors, he'd actually knock me around. It sure seemed like he wanted to hit me this morning. I hadn't seen him for the rest of the day, so I hoped he just woke up on the wrong side of the bed.

I pulled out my phone as I rode down the elevator to the main foyer and hit up Lizzy.

R: Hey girl! How's my bestie?

L: Okay, stop that.

I stared at my phone, not sure what I was supposed to stop doing.

R: Okay...?

L: Stop acting like you're completely fine and nothing is bothering you. You always do that when bad shit is happening. And!!! I don't want to hear this crap about how you don't want to burden me or bring me down.

I sighed as the elevator door opened. Lizzy was right. I wasn't fine, but I also couldn't let myself think about it too much. If I started crying, I was afraid I would never stop.

R: I'm not pretending. I'm okay. I won't say I'm great or that I'm loving life or this crazy ass school or that things are suddenly good with my father and me, but I'm okay.

L: Hmm

I smirked.

R: I'm sensing that you don't believe me.

L: It's not that I don't believe you, Boo...I just know you take on way too much and don't let anyone in. I hate that you're so far away. I miss your damn face.

I smiled as I pushed through the door to wait outside for Myles. Lizzy was the only one that could get away with calling me that nick-name. She'd started using it when my hair first went white, and we thought that it would go back to normal. She said that I reminded her of *Casper, The Friendly Ghost.* I had to admit it was cute, and it stuck. Then calling someone your *Boo* became slang, and now it just looked like we were trying to be cool. Trying was the keyword.

> R: I miss your face too. I'm going to try and come home for a visit, but I don't know when yet. I'll keep you posted.

> L: Okay, give me the deets on the hotness, and don't you dare tell me there isn't any because I'll know your ass is lying.

> R: There may be one or two that are…cute.

> L: Cute? Are they fucking puppy dogs?

I laughed and pictured Myles. He could definitely pass for an adorable puppy, just one that tended to piss on the floor. Blake wasn't much better, and I had no clue why I suddenly pictured him licking windows. Nash, on the other hand…there was nothing even remotely cute about him. He was lethal, like a fighting dog beaten into aggression. He had a killer instinct. I couldn't say for certain how I knew that, but maybe it was because the blank dead stare he got matched the look of the guy that had tried to get into the panic room. Even though he wore a black mask, I could see his eyes. I'd never forget that look. It was the same one Nash had given me a few hours ago.

> R: No, they are not dogs. I'll see if I can get a shot of Myles. He's picking me up to take me shopping.

> L: Cute, and he'll go shopping with you? Damn, he's a keeper.

R: Ha! He's also a hardcore player.

L: Girl, all men are hardcore players until the right girl comes along.

R: I'm pretty sure there is a guy somewhere out there insulted by that comment.

L: Oh please, you know it's true.

R: What I know is that I'm not looking to be anyone's girl, and I'm certainly not looking to change a guy.

L: We could go round and round on this one.

R: It's gonna have to wait cause Myles is pulling up.

L: P.I.C.T.U.R.E

R: LOL!

Myles jumped out of the car and ran around to the passenger side to open the door. Bowing low, he held his arm out. "Your chariot awaits."

"You're crazy," I said. Looking around, he was drawing stares from other students that were outside.

"Aye, I am. Who was making ya smile like that a moment ago? Do I need to kill some guy?"

"It was just a friend." I crossed my arms and smirked as he narrowed his eyes.

"That didn't really answer the question. Was it a girl friend or a guy friend," Myles asked as I slipped into the car. He leaned on the roof and looked in at me.

"What would it matter either way?" I snapped the belt into place.

"Well, if it's a guy, I'd have to hunt him down and cut his dick off, but if it's a girl, then maybe she can join us." He laughed as my smile fell. "I'm joking...unless ya're into that, then I'm totally down. Just say the word."

"I'm thinking it would be best for you to stop talking and close the door before I get back out."

"Good call." Yes, he was hot, but he definitely had some cute in him. He had this warmth that I couldn't quite put my finger on, and he oddly made me feel better when he wasn't being an ass.

Myles got in the driver's seat, and I grabbed his arm before he could start the car. "I thought the last time we were out was the last time for the Ferrari before winter?"

"There is still no snow, and I love me, Black Beauty." Myles caressed the dash, his face staring at it like it was his girlfriend.

"You named your car after a children's book about a horse?"

"She was more than just a horse. That's an insult."

I watched him closely to see if he was joking, but Myles seemed serious about his declaration.

I held up my hands in surrender. "Okay then, I stand corrected." Myles smiled. "So I need to ask you another little favor."

"Another one? Better watch out. Soon ya will be owing me a date." He flashed a wide grin that showed off his dimple, warmed my insides, and made my stomach turn to goo.

"You're funny. Look, I was talking to my friend Lizzy from back home and...oh lord. She asked me to get a picture of you."

I didn't think Myles could look any happier, but he pulled it off and ran his hand through his hair. "Oh yeah, ya've been talking about me with your girlfriend. I'm in the good books."

"Who said what I had to say was good?" I gave him my best deadpan look while hysterically laughing inside as his smile fell. "I'm joking. I may have said that you're not too bad when you aren't being an ass."

"It's a start. Gimme your phone."

"Can I trust you?"

He cocked a brow as he held out his hand for my phone. I wasn't sure this was smart but, I unlocked it and gave it to him. He went to the camera, and I thought he would just take a selfie, but he wrapped his arm around my shoulders and pulled the two of us together instead.

"You're going to have to pretend ya like me," he said, and my eyes flicked up to him, unable to stop my mouth from pulling up as he smiled for the camera.

Myles turned his head and looked at me, and the air instantly charged around us. He was giving me that look again, the one that made me feel like he wanted to eat me...or something.

I quickly looked away and smiled at the camera as he snapped a few shots that looked great before he handed the phone back. I looked happy. I hadn't seen myself like that in so long that I forgot what my smile looked like. Myles really was sexy. I didn't dare admit that to him, I could only imagine his reaction.

But, I found myself fantasizing about his unique amber eyes, dark lashes, and equally dark hair. I hated that when I closed my eyes I could still see how he filled out his school uniform and I wanted to see what he looked like under his shirt. But, it was his smile that warmed me from the inside out.

I didn't realize he took so many pictures and paused when I reached the one where we were looking at one another. My pulse spiked with the intensity of the image and the look in his eyes.

"Are they okay?"

"Yeah, they look great. Thanks."

"So where to?" The Ferrari revved, and Myles made a face out his window as Theo and Liam walked along the sidewalk. Liam tapped his wrist, and Myles shook his head. I didn't know what that meant.

"I need an outfit for the party, and I need to go to a large sporting goods store." Myles gave me a quizzical look, his eyebrow lifting.

"Are ya planning on fishing while at the party?" A playful grin danced across his lips. "Cause if ya are, I know a big...."

I held up my hand, laughing. "Okay! Enough of that. No, I'm not fishing, I like to hike, and this area has a ton of trails. I need some new gear, so I figured I might as well make the most of the trip."

"Hmm. I can only think of one place for the outdoor stuff. Liam is big into rock climbing and camping, so I'll take ya to the spot he always goes. I think there is a mall across the road from it, if I'm not mistaken."

"Perfect."

I sent off one of the images of me and Myles to Lizzy and immediately got a gif of Jim Carrey from *The Mask,* where his mouth drops open, and his tongue rolls out. That made me smile.

> L: Holy fuckin eh girl! You said cute. You didn't say drop-dead fucking gorgeous. I think I need to move to Portland.

"What did yer friend think? Do I pass her approval," Myles asked. I glanced over at him and purposely gave him a little shrug and a non-committal noise.

> R: Okay, fine, he might be hot. Happy now?

> L: No! I want allllll the deets, like allllll of them. You two look so fucking cute!!!

"What does that mean," He asked, his eyes wide.

> R: Later, got to go. LUV U

> L: LUV U MORE

"Lizzy says you're cute," I said.

His brows drew together as his lips made a little pout.

"Cute? We need to take more photos. Maybe those got my bad side."

I couldn't hold back the laugh as I put my phone away. "No, we don't need to take more."

"I'll take some later and send them to you."

"No, I swear, you're all good." I pictured getting a million naked flexing shots...on second thought that wasn't a horrible idea.

"Fine...cute. I'm not cute," Myles mumbled as we left the school. I loved the miniature rant, it added to the adorable factor, but I bit my tongue from saying that. "Tell me something about yourself, Snowflake."

"What do you want to know?" I gripped my mini backpack harder, worried about what he might ask.

"How did you end up at Wayward? I mean, no offense, but almost all of us were arrested by age fifteen. We're not exactly a wholesome school if you know what I mean?" I stared at the side of Myles's face in disbelief. Did I get sent to a boot camp? "You just don't strike me as the type to have gotten into trouble with the police before."

"Wait...are you telling me that Wayward is like a boot camp?"

"No, more like a spot for rich and powerful families to put their kids that is safe, especially those that tend to get themselves into trouble." He smiled wide.

"You say that like it's the greatest thing since sliced bread. It really isn't," I said, suddenly wondering what the hell everyone had done. I couldn't picture Ivy or Chantry killing a fly, let alone doing something that warranted reform school. Vicky, on the other hand, I could definitely picture her keying cars she thought were ugly.

"I don't know what that saying means," Myles said.

I crossed my arms, more annoyed than ever with my father. Did he really think that I needed a school for delinquents? I was a top student, and even when Mum was at her sickest, and I wasn't going to class, I always handed my homework and projects in. Just when I thought I couldn't be more fucking livid with the man, he found a way to do something that would make me hate him even more. Was it possible to reach a point of anger where there was no coming back? If so, I thought I was reaching my limit.

"It means you act like this is great, but it's not. What the heck did you do? Am I out with a murderer or a rapist or..."

"Whoa, I'm not a rapist," Myles said, and I noticed he left off the murderer part, which made me inch further away in my seat. "Okay, look. I was arrested for theft before my family left Ireland. Even before I could drive, I liked fancy cars, and I may have pinched one or two to take on joyrides. The owners didn't find it as amusing."

I relaxed in my seat but looked around the inside of the Ferrari. "Naw, I didn't steal the Ferrari. I worked hard to get this car," Myles said.

"I didn't say anything."

"Ya didn't have to. The look on your face said it all." He ran his hand through his hair, and the messy look got messier and somehow looked better. "The world can be a dark place, Snowflake, but it doesn't mean those that do dark things are bad people."

The ride was quiet as I contemplated what Myles said and how I ended up at Wayward. There were so many questions, and I knew there would be no other choice than to break down and call my father. I didn't want to, but this would eat at me until the mystery was solved.

"Do you want to talk about something else," Myles asked, pulling me out of my brooding thoughts.

"Sure, why did I overhear a couple guys talking about you and using the name Echo?"

Myles cringed and rubbed his hand on his jeans. I didn't think I was going to like the answer.

"Well...shit." My brows lifted. "If I tell ya this, promise me yer not going to run away?"

"Now I'm worried." Myles looked over and sighed.

"I guess it's better ya know, now. My family moves a lot of money and holds books for families all over the world, and they may have ties to money that could potentially be from crime and or from gambling," he spewed the run-on sentence out.

My mouth fell open as I stared at his worried expression. "Did you just tell me your family finds ways to wash money and are bookies?"

"It sounds so much worse when ya put it like that."

"And the nickname?"

"I may or may not be the person they sometimes send to collect. The name comes from them screaming so loud." Myles cleared his throat. "Okay, stop looking at me like that."

My brain couldn't even compute what he just said with who I knew him to be or at least thought he was. Myles was goofy and funny and, yes, even sweet, but muscle to collect on debts...no.

"Are you serious?"

He nodded. "Yeah. I mean, it's not what I would've chosen to do with my life, but it's the family business." Myles gave me a hard stare. "Ya really don't have a clue about the school, do ya?"

I didn't say anything as my brain reeled, skidded to a stop, and then started again.

"Snowflake, you only get into Wayward if your family is involved in crime. That means either your Ma or your Da has ties to a connected family. You're not able to step foot on the property otherwise."

It felt like the blood drained from my body. I was suddenly light-headed and shaking.

"No, that...that can't be. My father is a jerk, but a crime family? No way."

Myles shrugged. "I don't know what to tell ya. It's the school's rules, and they are very strict." I covered my mouth as tears sprang to my eyes. Had my father done something to get my mum killed? Was that why they were at the house in the first place? Is that why there was no real investigation? Is that why he whisked me away to this academy and dumped me?

Myles laid his hand on my shoulder. "Are ya okay? Do ya need me to pull over?"

I shook my head, but the tears were falling like rain, and I couldn't speak as the possibility that my father had caused my mum's death raced around in my mind. I was gulping for air as I tried to hold back the pain and stuff it down as I'd done so many times before, but it was getting more difficult.

I didn't notice that Myles stopped the car until he pulled me into a hug. His arms were warm, and even though I knew I shouldn't, I hugged him back.

"I got ya, Snowflake. Whatever it is, I've got ya."

Chapter 22

NOVEMBER 9 – WEDNESDAY 5:23 PM

Ren

I looked down at my hand, still linked with Myles. He refused to let go, and like some sort of trick device, the more I tried to pull away, the tighter he held on. He didn't say anything after my little breakdown, but something had changed. He seemed more serious, and I was pretty sure he thought I'd gone insane and was worried I was planning on jumping out of the moving vehicle.

I finally gave up asking him to let go of my hand, and swallowing my embarrassment, I leaned back and stared out the side window.

209

All I could think about were the hundreds of conversations with my mum over the last five years. If she knew about my father, she never said a word. I didn't understand any of this, and it felt like I'd just stepped into an alternate reality. There were two things I knew for sure. First, if I wanted out from under whatever my father had going on, I needed to be more dedicated than ever to my studies. Second, I needed to re-evaluate everyone I'd come into contact with since arriving at the school.

Fear tickled down my spine as I thought about the look Nash had given me this morning. Had he killed before? I thought he looked lethal, but now I didn't know why he was sent to the school in the first place or what he'd done since. The idea of being surrounded by criminals made me feel like I was floating on an island of my own. Glancing at Myles, I just couldn't see him dragging some guy off into a dark alley to beat the shit out of him.

"You sure you still want to go shopping? If you don't and want to go back to the academy, I'll turn around," Myles said.

"No, I want to do this. I'm not sure I want to go back there at all."

Myles looked at me like I'd hurt him. "We're not all bad people, Ren." I noticed he used my name and not the nickname. I thought it bothered me, but I was disappointed when he didn't use it.

"I know, I'm sorry, that was a jerk thing to say. I just...this is a huge shock for me. I had no idea my father was involved in anything criminal. Now every time I hear a siren, I'm going to wonder if it's coming for me because of something he did."

"Well, I don't know what family you're part of, Davies is not a name I know, but it doesn't matter. I will look out for you, and I know the guys can be asses, but they will too. Okay?"

I chewed on my lip as I stared at the side of his face. What did looking out for me mean? Would he hide evidence? Lie to teachers or police? Sneak me out in a getaway car? Beat the snot out of someone? Did I even want any of that? Did I even want to know?

"Thanks," was all I said. There were too many things to unpack to make a logical decision.

"Well, here we are." Myles pulled into a parking lot of a giant store with a car sized fish on the sign. The parking lot was busy, and we ended up in a far corner taking up two spots so that no one parked too close. Myles squeezed my hand as I reached for the door handle.

"Are we okay?" Myles asked.

"You mean because of what you said you do?"

He nodded, and I stared out the front windshield at the people coming and going from the store. Completely oblivious to the shit I'd just learned. I wished that I could go back and not ask about the nickname. A finger touched my chin, and Myles made me look at him.

"I'd never hurt ya. Please don't think that or worry about it. I'm not some psycho who loves to hurt people, and you're the last person I'd ever hurt."

"Except for punching me in the nose," I teased.

"Well yeah, there was that, but that was an accident." Myles' face flushed red.

"And throwing hot coffee on me."

"I get it, my track record is not very good, but I promise both of those were not on purpose. I just can't seem to do anything right around ya," he said.

There were a million things he could've said to try and win me over, but he struck a chord with that statement. I was the first person to hold my hand in the air and say I understood what it felt like to feel like I was failing no matter what I did. It sometimes seemed that the harder I tried, the more I failed until I was drowning and barely able to hold my head above water.

Myles lifted our joined hands, and the thumping of my heart rose with each inch closer my hand got to his lips. The kiss was so soft that I barely felt it on the back of my knuckles, but a piece chipped off the case my heart was sealed in. I didn't want to like him. I didn't want to like, love, or date anyone. Lizzy was right about that. My default was to hide away from the world and surround myself with books and my art, things that couldn't hurt me.

"I mean it," Myles whispered. Those amazing amber eyes lifted to find mine, and it was all I could do to draw a breath. "We better head in before I lay the seat down and keep you in the car instead." He got out and jogged around the car to open my door. He made me laugh with his constant chivalry. I was suddenly thankful for the colder temperature as I stepped out of the car. It felt like the heat had been cranked on high.

As Myles and I approached the store, a couple walked out the front door. They seemed happy to anyone walking by, but the cool body language and how they stayed far enough apart not to touch said more than screaming would. There were also the dark looks they gave each other.

People-watching was a habit I'd picked up back home. I would sit outside my home and watch the neighbors from a distance. You could always tell which family members were fighting or who was in a dispute with the neighbors. Sometimes it was as easy as watching how they smiled.

"What are you doing," Myles asked, and I whipped my head around to look at him.

"What do you mean?"

"You're analyzing people, but why?"

My feet stopped like they had a mind of their own, and Myles jerked to a stop. "How do you know that?"

"I just do." He shrugged. "I could tell by the way your eyes searched them. Like ya were inspecting a threat."

"I didn't think they were a threat, but I do watch everyone." I stuffed my hands in my pockets and flicked my eyes to the door as it opened again.

Myles smirked at the two guys walking past. "Ya did it again. Ya may not have known what yer family does, but it's in yer blood, trust me."

I wasn't sure that was a statement I was happy about. Did I really want criminal enterprise blood running through my veins and making me see the world differently than everyone else? My body shook as the sudden blast of warm air hit us, and I let the action carry all the questions I had away. This moment shouldn't be filled with so many heavy questions.

Myles already had a buggy, and I giggled as he pushed it along and then stood on the back until it slowed and did it again. "You're a goof," I said.

"I just like to have fun. Come on and try it." He held the handle of the buggy and smiled at me as he waited for me to try.

"I'm not doing that."

"Ya know ya want to."

"You don't take no very well, Myles. Noooo."

"If ya don't, I'm going to sing at the top of my lungs as I follow ya around the store." His smile was wicked as just the corner of his mouth turned up like he was daring me to challenge him.

"You're determined to get arrested again?"

"Pfft...by mall cop? Not a chance. He'd let me go just by slipping him a hundred. They pay them like crap here. Now come on, let's have some fun. Ya, look like ya could use a smile."

"You're crazy. You know that eh?"

Myles gripped my shoulders and laughed. "I love it when ya do that."

"Do what?" I laughed at the exuberant expression that could brighten anyone's day.

"When ya say eh, it's so fucking cute. I just love your accent."

"I like your accent," I said before I could stop myself and immediately felt my whole body getting hot, which meant my face was red.

"Is that so," he said, lowering his voice, and my stomach somersaulted. "Den maybe I should be talkin ta ya like dat all da time. I could even be talkin dirty ta ya. Tell ya all da tings yer makin me wanna do to ta ya."

Okay, that was hot. I stood staring at his smiling face far longer than I should've and finally managed to look away. Clearing my throat, I grabbed the buggy. "Come on. I'll try this."

Stepping up onto the buggy, Myles trapped me with his body as he gripped the bar on either side of my hands. His body was brushing my back, and if I weren't already hot, I would be now.

"Admit it, ya be thinkin' me accent is sexy," he whispered in my ear. My hands tightened on the handle of the buggy. "Say how ya be wantin' me ta talk dirty to ya in class and get ya all hot. How naughty it would be if Mr. Willis heard."

"I'm not saying that, and I definitely don't want Mr. Willis over-hearing," I said, but my shaky voice gave away that he was not far from the mark. I'd never heard anything that made my stomach tumble like he did with a few words.

"Den tell me ya dinnie like it, go ahead and say da words, but I know ya will be lyin'." His breath brushed against my skin, and even after all I'd learned and all the questions I had, nothing could've stopped my body's reaction to him. I'd only ever kissed one boy, and it had been a tween peck on the lips. I wanted to kiss Myles the way I'd dreamed of. But the fear of letting myself fall that far for someone that would undoubtedly hurt me in the end, kept me from turning in his arms and kissing him now.

"Fine. I find it sexy. Can we go now?" I gripped the buggy so hard that my nails were leaving little indents in the palm of my hand.

"I know ya can do better den dat. Ya can keep tryin' to deny it, Snowflake, but we have something between us. I plan on making ya mine." Myles let go of the buggy, and I took a deep breath and tried to settle the wild jitters that had my body trembling. It wasn't fair he made me a stuttering mess while he looked as calm as ever. It was so annoying.

"So what are ya needing," Myles asked as he walked beside me. It hit me that we must look like a couple as an older woman passed by and smiled at us.

"Um...everything."

"Captain, I think we're going to need a bigger buggy," he said, and I couldn't help laughing at him and his *JAWS* impression.

"Okay, maybe not everything. If you want to wander on your own, you can. Don't think you have to stay with me."

"Why would I want to wander on my own when watching ya smile is the highlight of my night?" He smiled wide, and I rolled my eyes.

It was official. If I were made of snow, I would be a puddle on the floor by now as another wave of heat flashed through my body. What did one even say to that statement?

The hardest part was picking a new pair of hiking boots. I couldn't decide if I wanted summer or winter, so I just got both. Myles was as enthusiastic when we were ready to check out as he was when we arrived. The issue came when we went back to the car and realized there was little to no space to put everything.

"Well, shit on a stick, this is going to be an issue," Myles said as he wandered away on his phone. "Give me a second."

I didn't know who he was talking to, but I hoped it wasn't Nash.

"Okay, it's taken care of. My father's driver will be here with the limo in ten minutes. Do you want to sit in the car where it's warmer?"

"No, I'm good. I'm warm from shopping anyway." We chatted a little, but I kept thinking about the lineup of black limos at my mum's funeral. I figured that was normal at the time. It was what you saw in movies, and I'd only been to one other funeral that I was too young to remember. The black limo was easy to spot as it pulled into the parking lot, and Myles waved at the driver.

It was identical to the one that had picked me and my father up from the airport. Was being part of some large crime family what the limo meant, not just that they had money? What else in my life was a lie?

As the car came to a stop, the trunk popped open. Suddenly I couldn't stop myself from wondering how many bodies had been back there. I quickly snuffed out that thought before it could take root.

"Sir, would you like help with the bags," the elderly man asked as he stepped out of the car.

"No, I'm good, Frederick. You stay in the car." He waited until the older man was in the car with the door closed before he whispered. "He's really getting too old for this, but he refuses to retire."

Grabbing a few bags, I went to the back of the limo and helped load the trunk. It would be full by the time we were done.

"You're not planning on getting a bunch more, are you," Myles asked as he closed the trunk. "I'll need my pickup truck if you do."

I shook my head. "No, I just need one outfit."

Myles knocked on the trunk, and the limo drove away. "Frederick will take the bags to my house, and tomorrow I'll swap everything over to my truck and bring it to the academy for you. Or are you planning on hiking away from us tonight?" Myles smirked.

"Not a bad idea, actually, but no, that works fine. Thanks for all the extra hassle. I wasn't even thinking once we started shopping."

Myles waved it off as he opened the Ferrari door to let me inside. "No worries, I'll let you pay me back later." There was nothing wholesome about the look he gave me.

I needed to be stricter with myself if I was going to keep my heart safe from his grasp. I could feel my resolve slipping, and Myles McCoy was dangerous, now in more ways than one.

Chapter 23

Myles

The other guys I hung out with were stupid, that was the only explanation, and I could say that with certainty. None of them liked to go shopping with a girl, but not only was Ren proving to be a lot of fun when she finally let her guard down a little, but she was sexy as hell. I was having way more fun than I should be, grabbing outfits by the handful and handing them into the stall for her to try on.

The other thing I figured out was that the more complicated the outfit, the more she needed my help. I was getting really good at

217

helping with zippers on tops and dresses. I loved watching her shiver as I brushed my fingers along her neck or down her back when I unzipped her. I was so fucking hard after half an hour that I was tempted to drag her into an empty stall. Ripping the mini skirt and low-cut top off her were vivid images in my mind as she did her little turn at the end of the aisle and walked toward me.

She was a fucking wet dream, and there was no doubt I would need a cold shower when we got back to school.

"What do you think," Ren asked. She pulled on the bottom of the skirt, and as she bent over, the low-cut top gave me an unobstructed view of her tits that made my mouth water.

"I think it's too revealing," I said, picturing all the guys at Sacred Heart Academy and what they would try when they saw her in this outfit. I hadn't planned on going to the party, but I sure as fuck was now. I wasn't leaving her alone with that bunch of horny fucks. I'd end up ripping their arms off their bodies.

"You think?" She looked up and sighed.

Unable to stay seated any longer, I stood and stepped into Ren's personal space. Grabbing her hips, I growled low and pulled her into my body. Her eyes widened as she leaned back, staring up at me like she was frozen by shock or fear, maybe both. I liked her off her game. I liked this as much as her sharp wit and sass. Every muscle flexed as I leaned down close to her ear.

"I want ya so bad that all I can think about is ripping this outfit off of ya and fucking ya against the wall. I'm barely able to contain myself, yer so fucking sexy, Snowflake. So whether it's right or not, trust me when I tell ya it's too revealing to be wearing to the party. Unless ya want every guy begging to fuck ya hard all night long," I whispered and then groaned as she shuddered in my hold and swallowed so loud that I could hear it.

"I...I...I ah," Ren mumbled, and I smirked.

"Get the outfit ya had on before this. It's hot, but not so hot that ya will blow the end of everyone's cock off, and ya won't be fiddling with the tight jeans like ya are with the skirt. Ya seemed the most comfortable in it." She nodded but didn't try to speak.

I needed to let her go, but my fingers didn't want to work, and we stood there like two statues, each waiting for the other to make the next move.

"Oh, I love that group. How did you get tickets?" A girl was talking on the phone as she walked into the changing room. Saved by the bell? I wasn't sure. My body was craving a whole lot more, even though I could feel that it would be too much too fast. Ren wasn't acting like someone with a ton of experience, and I finally had her out alone, having a good time. The last thing I needed to do was fuck it up again.

"I know one of the guys that runs the ticket place, and I gave him a little extra payment to be the first to purchase," the voice coming through the girl's phone said.

I stepped away from Ren as the girl passed, telling her friend to be quiet and that she was on speakerphone. Luckily, she went to the far end of the changing room to continue her conversation.

"You gonna get changed," I asked Ren, who still hadn't moved. Her eyes were glued to mine, and even though she wasn't trying, she was testing my resolve. Those silver eyes of hers sparkled under the little spotlights above us. "Go before I do something like kiss ya, 'cause if I start, there is a good chance I'm not gonna stop."

Ren's cheeks flamed a vibrant red before she dashed into the changing room and closed the door with a bang. I smirked as I glanced down to still see her heels on the other side of the door like she was leaning against it. Forcing myself to look away, I leaned down and picked up our jackets before sitting down and laying them on my lap to try and hide what was going on in my jeans.

I needed to think about something else. Anything but the feel of Ren's soft skin and the sweet scent of cherries I smelled every time I leaned in close. Or how I was dying to wrap her long hair around my hand. Closing my eyes, I pinched the bridge of my nose and started running through all the school projects I needed to get done by

Sunday. It took a few minutes, but my body began to cool off, and I could think straight.

Fuck, she just did something to me.

"I'm ready. Are you okay," Ren asked, and I jumped as her hand touched my forehead.

"Yeah, I'm good." She had the outfit for the party draped over her arm. "You're still getting the skirt outfit too?" I lifted my eyebrow in question.

"I might have a place to wear it one day. I like the way it looked." She smiled, and I almost jumped out of the seat to leap on her like a fucking animal. She was making me nuts. "I have an idea. How would you like to help me spend an exorbitant amount of money?"

Pushing myself out of the seat, I followed her. "I'm always up for spending money, but why?"

Ren handed over the clothes to the woman behind the counter. "Let's just say I have a score to settle with my father." She pulled out the fancy credit card with a minimum hundred thousand limit.

"Okay, in what way exactly?"

The girl bagged the clothes and handed over the receipt. When we stepped outside, Ren pointed to the massive chain store with multiple levels of everything. They had clothes, electronics, and even food.

"I'm still not getting it."

"They do delivery, right," she said.

"I think so...I don't really know."

"Let's go ask. If they don't, we'll find someplace that does."

"Snowflake, what are ya up to?"

The smile she gave me was devious as fuck, and just like that, my jeans were snug again. Dammit, this girl could never come to one of my swim meets, or I would have a permeant problem for everyone to see.

"Come on." Ren shockingly grabbed my hand and dragged me along as she walked so fast that we looked like we were racing. Panting, she walked up to the first person she saw wearing a name badge. "Hi, do you offer delivery service for a large quantity of items?"

"Pretty sure we do." The guy pointed to a customer service sign. "They'll know for sure."

"Thanks." We were off again, and I didn't care as long as she kept holding my hand. It was official I was whipped. I hadn't even fucked her yet, and I was panting at her heels. Ren asked the customer service desk, and the next thing I knew, we were being whisked away to a manager's office.

"Have a seat," the manager said. "I understand you'd like to make a substantial purchase and have it delivered. What are we talking about here?"

Ren pulled out the fancy card and handed it over as she unlocked her phone and opened a few apps. "I would like to use two-hundred thousand dollars of the limit on this card." The manager's mouth fell open. "I'm going to divide it into two delivery locations, and we will choose what to send to each location."

"I'm sorry, but I'll need to check with the credit card company before I can authorize anything of that size."

"Go ahead."

The manager picked up the phone, and I turned to Ren. "Okay, fill me in. What are we doing?"

"My father and I are not exactly on speaking terms, even more so after what you told me tonight."

"Okay..."

"There is only one way to get his attention, and that is through his money. I looked online, and there is a large homeless shelter and an abused women's shelter not far from here. I won't spend the money on something he can take back. I'm going to spend the money on whatever seems the most useful and have them delivered as a donation in his name. He's never going to be able to collect it back, and that makes me all warm and fuzzy inside. Besides, these are both good causes that don't get near enough help. So it's a double win."

"You don't care that he'll be fucking pissed?"

"That's what I'm hoping for."

My lips turned up in a grin. "Then ya brought the right man for the job. No one can spend like I can."

We were still laughing by the time we reached the restaurant for dinner. I'd never had so much fun with a girl ever. Maybe I hadn't given others a fair shake, but no one sparked me to want to do anything more than have sex and move on.

We picked out everything from clothes, food, beds, and blankets to shampoo, soap, and anything else Ren could think of. Once the manager had gotten the okay from the credit card company, we ran through the store with two scanners and four helpers a piece. What had become blatantly obvious was that Ren was fearless and had a heart as pure as her snow-white hair. I didn't think she saw it in herself, though.

"I still can't believe we did that. What a rush." I was so tempted to wrap my arm around her shoulders as we walked inside the pub-style restaurant.

"I can't wait until he gets the bill. Too bad it won't be for weeks. The surprise when he turns on this computer to pay off the card...so sweet. Now the question is, do I ignore the ranting phone call?" She tapped her chin, her eyes full of humor.

The hostess gave me a flirty smile as we stepped up to be seated. Usually, I would flirt back, get her number regardless if she was dating anyone, and very possibly hang around to fuck her when she was done with work before never seeing her again. But I wouldn't be doing any of that.

Her name tag said Sheila, but she reminded me more of a Jennifer for some reason. Sheila batted her eyes at me, but I didn't feel the usual need to have sex. She was pretty, I hadn't suddenly gone blind, but there was simply no desire to bend her over a table. But the heated annoyed look in Ren's eyes...that was a whole other story.

An idea was slowly formulating in the recesses of my brain. Leaning against the wooden stand, I smiled back at Sheila but kept an eye on Ren's expression out of my periphery.

"Good evening Sheila. Do ya happen to have a booth left with a window?"

Sheila looked a little flustered as she stared down at the squares with Xs through them and names written in others.

"Um...I don't think so. I'm really sorry about that." Reaching over the stand, I grabbed the seating arrangement of the pub. "Hey, give that back."

"Relax, Sheila, I'm only having a peek. There's nothing wrong with looking, right?" I purposely deepened my voice as I stared at her from under my lashes. Yeah, I knew I was a dick. I also knew the look worked. Well worked on everyone but Snowflake, which was simultaneously aggravating as hell and fucking sexy.

Right on cue, Sheila blushed a deep red and bit her bottom lip as she silently invited me to meet her around back later. I looked away from her hungry stare to the seating plan, but the subtle shift in Ren's energy pressed in on me. She was getting more jealous by the second. Had I finally found her kryptonite?

Using my thumb, I wiped off the word reserved for the corner booth. Grabbing the black marker, I added reserved to a booth a couple down and added my last name to the corner block.

Smiling wide, I handed the seating plan back to Sheila. "There we go, all fixed."

Sheila looked at what I'd done, and I knew she would try and say something stupid like, 'But I'll get in trouble.' "When did you start your shift, Sheila?"

"Oh...um...only like half an hour ago," she stammered as she flicked her eyes between the seating chart, my face, and the furious glare that Ren was now giving her. I was fucking hard as a rock all over again, and it was for the girl that was shooting daggers at Sheila. The 'I'm going to rip your hair out' stare was better than any drug.

"Then, how could ya possibly get into trouble for something that was done before ya arrived? I mean, that's clearly not yer handwriting. Come on, just this once, and I promise to leave ya with a really large tip."

Sheila looked like she might pass out as I licked my bottom lip. Ren, on the other hand, looked like she was going to murder someone. I wanted to sit that furious and sexy as hell ass on my lap and fuck her here in the restaurant so bad that I would've paid any amount of money to have that as an option on the menu.

"Alright, I guess it couldn't hurt just this once. Let me just mark it down." I glanced at Ren as Sheila worked, and although she hadn't said a word, I would've put money down on her to knock Sheila out if they were in the same boxing ring. I wonder if I could get her to mud wrestle or whipped cream wrestle, then I could lick it off her body.

"Right this way." I shook my head to rid it of the way too sexy image of Ren naked and covered in cream, not all of it from a can.

Sheila led the way to the booth I'd confiscated from some other couple. Scooting into the booth, I watched Ren closely as she sat across from me, loving that she continued to glare at Sheila.

"Here you go. Your waitress will be by in a few moments." Sheila gave me one last smile before she left. I pretended I didn't notice Ren giving me the death stare and picked up my menu, only to have a piece of paper fall out from inside with a number on it.

I held it up between my fingers. Ren mumbled something under her breath that definitely had a few choice words as she picked up her menu, and I suddenly couldn't see her face.

Smirking, I slipped out of my side of the booth and slid in beside her. She was fucking adorable as she tried to ignore me. Ren still didn't look at me as I stretched my arm out to rest on the back of the bench behind her or when I leaned in to see her menu. She bristled, and I could see the muscles in her jaw working as she held herself back from giving me a piece of her mind.

"Do you mind? You're crowding my personal space. Why don't you run along and call your new friend? I'm sure she'd love to have you all up in her business." Every word from Ren's mouth was so sharp they were like a bunch of tiny cuts.

Dropping my head to her ear, I whispered, "Are ya jealous, Snowflake?"

"No."

"Are ya sure, cause ya kinda seem like ya are, but I thought ya didn't want to date me?"

"I don't want to date you." She didn't so much as blink in my direction.

"Hmm, I don't believe ya Snowflake," I growled softly and loved that her jaw clenched tight. "Because yer tone tells a different story."

"I think you need to learn to read people better." Ren turned her head, and our eyes instantly locked.

"Do ya want me to call her?" I traced her lush bottom lip with my thumb and savored the softness. I leaned in a little closer. "Cause I don't think ya do." Her glare softened slightly as she looked away only to stare at my lips. "Have I told ya tonight how pretty ya look?" Ren was wearing a shimmery silver top cut just low enough that it kept drawing my eyes down. "I wanna kiss ya, Snowflake." My blood was racing through my veins as I closed the distance. "Tell me ya want me to kiss ya," I growled softly, so close to her lips that I felt the warmth of her skin.

"Well, isn't this adorable." My eyes went wide. This could not be happening.

My body jerked straight at the familiar voice. I turned my head, and sure enough, there she was, my sorta ex wearing a waitress outfit. I didn't know who hated me upstairs, but someone enjoyed fucking with me. That was the only explanation.

"Pam? What are ya doing here?" Stupid question, but I had no idea that she worked at all, let alone in a pub.

"You see, Myles working in a place like this is what one of us lowly, not-rich kids have to do to pay our bills, especially when our boyfriend decides to throw us from two stories up into a pool and ruins our uniform."

Like a fucking laser beam, I could feel Ren's eyes on my face, and I was suddenly being stared at by two women that I was sure wanted me dead.

"Ya were never my girlfriend," I argued.

"Well, what do you call two people that go out on dates and have sex?" She crossed her arms over her chest.

"We were casual, just having fun, or were until ya put a label on us."

She rolled her eyes. "Please spare me. You didn't mind being called my boyfriend as long as I sucked you off and let you fuck me. It wasn't until I said I didn't want you to smack my ass and fuck me in front of people that you decided I was no longer interesting. But I see you already moved on. Not surprised, good for you." Pam's eyes went to Ren. "I feel sorry for you. If you're smart, you'll run for the hills and never look back. Myles McCoy only knows how to do one thing well other than fuck, and that's fuck you over. He will stomp on your heart and leave you crying in a corner."

"Thanks for the warning, but I can make my own decisions, starting with asking for a new waitress since you obviously can't separate your work and personal life. So if you could get your manager, I'd appreciate that," Ren said.

Pam's eyes narrowed at Ren, but she didn't say anything more and stomped off.

"That was really impressive..."

"Don't think you're off the hook. I don't like people who can't keep their shit together and be professional when called for, but she said exactly what all the little flags in my gut have been telling me. You've been playing me. I'm just another notch on your bedpost, and I have no interest in being your next score. Just wait a week. I'm sure there will be another new girl you can get with." She pointed out of the booth. "I want to head back to the academy. I've had my fill for tonight."

My heart raced with panic, my brain stuttering and not coming up with anything good to say. "But we haven't gotten anything to eat," I spit out and internally cringed. "I mean, let me explain over our meal."

"Do you really trust her not to spit in our food or worse? No, I'm leaving even if you're not."

"Ren, at least let me explain my side of events," I said as I scooted out and stood.

"Myles, you only need to answer two questions. The first is, were the two of you involved in a relationship, and second, did you throw her into a pool because she wouldn't have sex with you in front of other people?"

"We were casual, and I'd been drinking. It seemed like fun at the time." My gut twisted with the look Ren gave me. It spoke volumes about what she was thinking.

"I see. Then we don't have any more to talk about. I appreciate all your help tonight, and I genuinely had a great time until this moment. But we come from two very different worlds, and I don't want anything to do with this game you play. Please take me back to the academy."

Ren zipped up her jacket, and that sound held finality. I would be lucky if she ever spoke to me again.

"Please, Snowflake..."

"Don't make things worse, Myles. Maybe one day we can talk about it, but..." She looked away. "I'm not in a good head space for any relationship, and I definitely don't want to try and navigate whatever this is."

Spying Pam across the room, I wanted to do a whole lot more than just throw her in a pool, and all of it was dark.

"Fine. I'll take ya home."

"The academy is not my home. I don't have one of those anymore." With that, Ren marched away.

I couldn't believe that this was happening again. All my good intentions were crushed in a matter of minutes. My head was doing the backstroke in the sea of insanity.

"Aw, such a shame you won't be staying for dinner. I hope I didn't ruin your appetites," Pam sniped as I walked up to where she was standing near the door.

I stared down into her smug face. Smiling, I leaned a little closer, but she knew this smile. It promised pain, and her smile fell. "I shoulda cut out yer tongue before I tossed ya over the railing, and if ya keep it up, I'll do more than that."

"Are you threatening me, Myles?" She crossed her arms.

The darkness in me was seeping out like fucking Pandora's box. I tried very hard to keep it where it belonged, but sometimes the temptation became too much. Blood had coated my face for the first time when I was six, stemming from a lesson that only a father like mine or Nash's could come up with in their sick and twisted brains. That very first lesson was to kill the new kittens that were born in the shed. I cried and cried and took the smacks to the face, but he still snapped their necks in front of me. No matter how hard I'd tried not to let his evil seep in, some had. It slipped through the cracks filling the little gaps in my soul, and then tried to spread.

My lip curled up as I whispered. "If I need to answer that, yer far stupider than I thought. Push me again, Pam, and I'll make sure ya know why people don't mess with those from Wayward." I lowered my voice a little more as her eyes went wide. "There are parts of me that would love to see ya bleed before that little home on Blueberry Lane goes up in flames. I wonder if yer family would make it out in time or if something would happen to them too."

Pam gasped, a hand going to her mouth. "Like I said, keep it up, and the fun-loving guy ya wanted to humiliate will become the monster that hides under your bed and rips the soul from yer body. Is that clear enough for ya?"

She nodded quickly, and I backed away. "Good."

Pushing open the heavy wooden door, I stomped outside only to skid to a stop as Ren yelled at Sheriff Morrison. Could this night get any stranger?

I moved slowly, totally focused on the conversation.

"I don't care what my Father says. I shouldn't have to have a curfew earlier than the other students. So, you can either arrest me or tell him that if he wants to talk to me, he can be man enough to do it to my face," Ren snarled.

She glared up at Morrison. He was a scary man in his own right, but Ren seemed unaffected by him. Pride soared in my chest, but I didn't trust Morrison. There was no way in hell I was leaving him alone with my Snowflake.

"I don't make the rules. I just enforce them," Morrison said.

"Unless you're moonlighting as a pompous ass babysitter, wearing a badge doesn't give you the authority to order me to do anything when I'm not breaking the law. Which I'm not." She pulled out her phone, and the screen lit up. "Curfew is not for another two hours and twenty-three minutes."

"Like I already explained, your father wants you to be inside the academy gates by no later than seven-thirty for your own safety."

I reached them just as Ren stepped up close to Morrison like she was going to take a swing, and I gently laid my hand on her shoulder to keep her from crossing that line. Morrison wouldn't dare put a hand on me, but he had a reputation. I genuinely liked Ren, and no one was ever hurting her, even if she never let me take her out again. That realization was staggering, but more so was the fact that I'd never felt protective over a girl before.

"And like I said, if he wants to tell me that, he can get off his ass and come speak to me himself. Otherwise, you can run along and find someone else to harass."

Morrison's face went bright red.

"Sheriff, we were just heading back to the academy anyway," I said.

Morrison's eyes flicked to mine. "What were you doing with her here in town in the first place, McCoy? The second time in two weeks."

"What business is it...." Ren started, but I squeezed her shoulder, and she took a deep breath as she tried to rein in her anger.

"Shopping. There were some things Ren needed, and I was the one free to bring her. I'll make sure she gets back to Wayward safely."

Morrison looked between my calm face and Ren's furious one before shaking his head. "I don't get paid near enough to put up with shit like this. Fine, get going, but straight back and no speeding."

"Yes Sir." We stood quietly as Morrison stomped off to his police car, got in, and drove away before Ren jerked her shoulder out of my hold.

She turned on me, and I swallowed as my eyes met the steel in her silver depths. "I don't need a hero, and if I did, I wouldn't call you."

The words hit harder than any physical attack. Ren stepped around me and got in the car, the door closing behind her, and my gut churned with a million and one emotions that I couldn't decipher. Sadness and anger at myself were at the top of the list, but so was longing for something different and regret, which I never felt.

Just like the rest of my screwed-up existence, one moment, my life was amazing, and the next, it was shredded right before my eyes.

Chapter 24

NOVEMBER 10 – THURSDAY 7:12 PM

Nash

The twelve of us stood around as my father landed another blow to the ribs of the man hanging from chains. The chains and cuffs my father had installed in the underground meeting room were straight out of something medieval. He had since expanded his toys to include a stone dais that was supposed to be for final executions. Most of the time, he used it to become the center of attention when he was beating and raping some girl.

I hated every fucking second I had to be down here with this

231

group. The others were lucky. They weren't eighteen yet and not allowed. I'd happily be anywhere else, but not showing up would end with me hanging from a wall.

Only one man of the bunch never played any of the Order's sick games. Theo and Blake's father, Ethan O'Brien, was the only one with any morals as far as I was concerned. Of course, my father hated that. He hated that they had the next strongest family holdings and that Ethan and his family were respected. Most of all, he hated that he couldn't force Ethan to participate in the corruption and blatant abuse of power.

I had no problem with killing traitors or those that looked to tarnish our image. This was business. The family I was born into was not like other families. We were groomed from a young age to rule and make hard decisions. There was no call to the police when someone stole money or product. We didn't hire lawyers and sue when another family or organization humiliated us. In our line of work, you learned what you needed to know and killed off threats, no matter the risk.

The man's screams had dulled long ago, but a fresh wave of yelling and begging began as my father pulled out the long nine-tails whip with the barbed wire ends. The sharp metal dug into his skin and tore pieces from his body with every strike. Blood flew in all directions. I dropped my head to look at my feet but still felt drops and things I didn't want to know about hitting the long dark robe.

Sadly, this would continue for days, if not weeks. Father would stop before the man died, have him doctored and healed enough to start all over again. If the traitor were lucky, he'd go home with all his limbs. If my father was in a particularly evil mood, he cut off fingers, toes, maybe a whole hand, or a bullet to the head for stealing.

My father didn't need an excuse to hurt someone, but there was very little he put up with. Stealing was a fuck no. He repeatedly preached how if someone stole from you, they were capable of anything and needed to be taught a memorable lesson or taken out for good. Again, I understood his reasoning, and maybe it made me a fool, but I preferred to look at the entire picture before inflicting punishment.

This man, Geoff Humphries, stole five hundred dollars to pay the remaining amount on his mortgage payment so he didn't lose his home. If he had no place to live, then we would lose him and his small business to launder money through. So wouldn't it be better to slap him on the wrist and tell him that he needs to contact us first next time? That way, we could collect interest instead of blood and flesh. Just one more decision I didn't get a say in until I took over as the next King.

Glancing to my left was Devin McCoy, Myles's older brother. He stood a few feet away, and just beyond Devin was their father, Owen McCoy. Both watched what my father was doing, their faces were passive, but their eyes held excitement. Ethan was to my right, and the look in his eyes was a stark contrast. We shared a look, and even though no words passed between us, we knew that neither of us wanted to be here. He was the only King I was tempted to bring into the Last Rank. But with what we were planning, the answer was always the same. It was too dangerous. As much as I liked him, I didn't know if I could trust him, and if my father found out what I was up to, then my life was over.

That wasn't some teenage drama. It was a fact. My father would never let me live if he knew I planned on removing him and dismantling part of his legacy. He would keep control until he was ready to give it up, and nothing, not even me, would ever stand in his way.

"Have you learned your lesson," my father asked. Geoff was reduced to a sobbing mess and in so much pain that he didn't answer anything more then incoherent blubbering as he hung from the chains.

My father looked at me, and I knew he would ask if I wanted a turn. It was a test. If I said no, I was weak. If I said yes, then I was no better than him and I had to hear their screams when I closed my eyes at night. Sometimes I didn't get the opportunity to say no, but tonight I had an excuse to get the fuck out of here.

"My King," I said, the words more sour than sucking on a lemon. "It is nearing time for my errand this evening. If it pleases you, may I take my leave and be of greater use to the Order?"

We were forced to talk like we lived in a different era, as if we were upholding some ancient laws. Another fucked up rule my father or one of his favorites had decided on. There was an old order, but all those who ruled had died generations before my father was even a sperm shot. The fact that he took ancient books, twisted the rules and doctrine to suit what he wanted and then sugar-coated it with words like righteous was an abomination. You could put a dress on a pile of dog shit, but it was still a pile of shit.

My father's glower told me exactly how he felt about me asking to leave, but I also knew he would let me. He valued money above all, and not meeting with a buyer, especially one who regularly spent large sums, was a huge no.

"You may be excused."

"Thank you, my King." I desperately wanted to spit on the ground but turned and marched for the exit instead.

"Hold on." I froze mid-stride, my hands balling into fists inside the wide arms of the robe. "I want Devin to go with you."

When I turned around, I looked from Devin to my father and then to the man hanging by the chains. Where would I end up if this all failed? Would I be hanging from those chains? Was this another test? My boys were the only ones I ever did errands with and my father knew that. So why did he want Devin to come with me?

"Are you coming, Devin, or do you need a reminder of what a disobeyed order from the King means?"

My father smirked, and I knew that I'd hit the chord he was after. I'd bet the right way and rolled snake eyes for a win.

Devin was three years older, and I recognized the insanity in him. The same insanity that my father had and his father had. It was the same look that said he would do whatever he could to earn my father's ear and force me out, but Devin didn't know who he was dealing with or what I'd do to ensure that didn't happen.

I pulled open the heavy metal door and my father called out, "oh and Nash, try not to embarrass the kings again. The stunt with those from Meadow Grove was quite enough for one month."

I bit my tongue from snapping back and nodded. "Yes, my King."

My father had asked me how the Kings symbol ended up on the chest of Austin. I told him I didn't know, and the last time I saw him he was naked. Which was the truth. There was that moment between us where I wasn't sure he was going to let it go or press, but his phone rang which ended the conversation.

As we left the gathering hall, I stripped off my soiled robe and wanted to tear it in half but instead folded it to fit under my arm. Devin tossed his into the communal laundry hamper. I didn't trust putting my shit in that hamper. I controlled my fate, and leaving behind my DNA was a fuck no.

"Are you not washing yours," Devin asked.

"I like to hand wash mine. My Father always says that you must take pride in your cleanliness. I take that very seriously." Devin ate up my lie and glanced at the hamper, and I knew he was thinking of pulling his back out. "We better get going. These guys get twitchy if I'm late."

"Anyone else coming," Devin asked.

"Liam." I didn't elaborate any more than that. The less I told Devin, the better.

After laying my hand on the palm reader, the lock clicked and released, and the heavy door opened. I let Devin go in front of me.

"I'll be right back," I said, walking away, leaving Devin by the front door to wait.

Once in my room, I stuffed the robe in a bag and hid it behind the trap door I had secretly built myself. I'd deal with it when I got home. Grabbing my gun, I tucked it into the back of my jeans and pulled on my leather jacket to cover it before heading out. I heard Liam's voice as I approached the front door. Devin didn't look too happy to see him, but that wasn't a surprise. He had hated Liam since the family picnic last summer when Liam beat him in the obstacle course. Devin lost every round of running, shooting, and fighting. Such fun times with bloody noses and burgers to wash it down.

"We'll be taking the truck."

I didn't bother to slow down as I whipped open the front door and jogged down to my black truck.

"What the fuck do you think you're doing," Devin growled as Liam grabbed the front passenger side door.

"I'm getting the front seat. What the fuck does it look like I'm doing?" Liam stood toe to toe with Devin. My second in command was quiet and reserved most of the time, but when pushed, Liam was one scary fucker.

"I'm older," Devin argued.

"Coulda fooled me."

"Enough. Liam gets the front since he was already part of this drop," I said, ending the argument.

"Why exactly are you coming anyway," Liam asked as we all got in and our doors closed. "You've never been interested in the grunt work before, so why the sudden change?"

"I do what my King tells me to do, and he wanted me to come with the two of you. Maybe he no longer trusts that you can do the job properly," Devin said.

I glared in the rearview mirror. I didn't know how two brothers could be so different, but Devin was nothing like Myles. Then again, Devin had been sent here to attend school from a young age and was completely cut off from his family, including Myles.

"If my Father lost faith in me, he'd put a bullet between my eyes. Maybe he plans on moving me up the ranks, and you'll get this job," I said, smiling as Devin's smug smirk fell. His brown eyes looked black in the dark as I held his stare.

"I doubt that. I'm too valuable."

"Whatever you say." It was amusing fucking with him. He was an ass-kisser with 'Yes Man' disease, which was why he'd only make it so far before hitting a wall. What Devin neglected to learn about my father was that he was not stupid. Even if he praised Devin and patted him on the head, he knew Devin was just trying to suck his dick. Did I trust either of them to do the right thing? Fuck no.

Construction made it take longer to reach the agreed upon warehouse. Some of the roads were ripped up, and others you couldn't pass at all.

"I've met with this guy a few times. He's fucking twitchy, so no sudden moves, and if he asks who you are, you give a straight-up answer, no smart-ass comments. Understood?"

"No argument from me," Liam said, checking his gun and hiding it under his jacket.

I pointedly looked in the mirror at Devin when he didn't answer. "Yeah, I get it."

"Is that the same attitude you'd give if my father were here?"

"You're not your father."

All the darkness and evil my father instilled in me filled my chest as I smiled at him.

"Not yet. Careful who you make an enemy of Devin. It's unwise to assume you're always on an island and safe from harm."

"Are you threatening me, Nash?"

"I'm reminding you that there is a pecking order, don't forget it, or I'll find a reason to forget about you." I held Devin's stare until he finally looked away.

He was always an ass, but there was something extra tonight that I didn't like. I was tempted to order him to stay in the truck, but he'd run back like a pansy ass to my father and tell him that I'd treated him like a child. It was a coin toss with fifty-fifty odds on how that would end.

Stepping out of the truck, I glanced around. My eyes and ears strained to make out anything unusual past the paved parking lot and the lights that created more shadows than were actually helpful.

Hammer was a member of one of the larger motorcycle clubs in the area. When I asked why he was called Hammer, all I got from him was that there was one in every MC. What the fuck that meant was beyond me. I found out that his real name was Harold Johnston. He was thirty-nine, had a woman he wasn't serious with, and a teenage daughter who didn't speak to him. I also knew what double-wide he lived in and how many times he'd been arrested and let out. I could imagine him squealing on us to save his own skin like he'd done many times before, but my father insisted that we deal with him. So here I was, but that didn't mean my foot wasn't ready to cut off his air supply.

Pressing the button on my keys, the little pad outside the door lit up before I punched in the thirteen-digit code. The pad wouldn't turn on without one of the activator keys. With a click, the door released, and I pulled it open, waiting for all the lights to turn on.

I didn't scare easily, not anymore, but stepping into a black room made the hair on the back of my neck stand up and sent a trickle of fear racing down my spine. Some lessons were harder to forget.

With a loud hum, the rows of lights systematically began to turn on. The massive warehouse was empty except for the four crates waiting for us to make the deal.

"Liam, keep an eye out for Hammer."

Nodding, Liam pulled out his gun and stayed by the door.

"What time is this guy supposed to arrive," Devin asked.

"Why? You have a hot date you need to get to that is more important than what we're doing?" I crossed my arms and leaned against one of the crates. Devin glared, his eyes narrowing as he crossed his arms as well.

"No, just wondering if he's late."

"That's not your concern."

Devin opened his mouth, probably to say something else stupid, but Liam whistled to let me know that Hammer had just arrived.

"Apparently, he's right on time." Smirking at Devin, I hit a different button on the remote that looked like a car starter, and the bay door began its slow ascent.

Pulling my gun from the back of my jeans, I remained relaxed, and the gun pointed down, but you could never be too safe. A short box truck backed in and parked as the bay door rumbled and rattled, lowering back into place. Hammer was in the driver's seat and hopped out while another guy I'd seen once or twice at these meets jumped out of the passenger side.

"This the goods," Hammer asked, not one for pleasantries or small talk.

"Maybe. Where's my money?"

"Already been sent," Hammer said, and I cocked an eyebrow at him.

"Is that so?" I made sure my tone said just how much I didn't believe him.

"You calling me a liar?" He puffed out his chest and put his hands on his hips.

"Hammer, how stupid do you think I am," I asked. "You never send me shit in advance, and..." I pulled out my phone, unlocked it, and held up the glowing screen. "I have no notifications from the bank about a deposit." I tapped the gun off my leg as I watched him closely.

Devin was quiet by my side with his arms crossed and Liam not far off, but even with the extra man, I could feel the tension rising like a hand pressing on my chest.

Hammer finally smiled and then laughed. "You're right. I was just fucking with you."

I didn't smile. "So I'll ask again. Where's my money?"

"It's in the back of the truck. I couldn't do our norm, so I needed to bring cash. Feds sniffing around and shit."

I bristled as little alarm bells began to scream in my head, and red flags were waving in front of my eyes.

"Then you'll have to come back when you're ready to do business properly. This was not what we agreed on, so get back in your truck and get the fuck out of here. The deal is off."

"What the fuck, man? Is my money no good to you," Hammer

asked. His eyes snapped with anger, and the brief moment of calm that had settled was gone.

"Watch your fucking mouth, asshole," Devin yelled, and I couldn't help staring at him. *What in the actual fuck?* "Do you think you can come in here and order us around? Change shit whenever you feel like it?" Devin marched forward and got into Hammer's face.

"Who the hell is this punk," Hammer asked, and I felt like asking the same question.

"Yo, D. Back the fuck off of Hammer." How the hell did I end up defending my lying ass purchaser?

"Why are you letting him walk all over you? I should put a bullet between his eyes right now," Devin said, and all hell broke loose.

Devin reached for his gun while the guy Hammer worked with flicked the latch on the roll-up door on the truck.

The first thing I noticed was boots, and I knew we were fucked. "Look out!"

Just as the gunfire started, I jumped over the crates. We were sitting ducks, and there was nowhere to run or hide. Wood splinters exploded as the crates were hit, little pieces raining down on me. Arm over arm, I crawled to the side of the crate and saw one of the bikers shooting at Liam, who'd managed to get behind one of the large steel support beams. I didn't see Devin anywhere.

Aiming, I pulled the trigger and watched the man collapse to the floor with a bullet in his back. The sound of boots on wood had me rolling over, and I caught a glimpse of another man I didn't recognize. I didn't hesitate and put two in his chest when he raised his gun.

He tumbled off the crates, his body landing on one of my legs. "Fuck!"

"Get the closest crate," Hammer yelled over the loud bangs echoing in the empty warehouse. The sound was so loud that it vibrated back at me and felt like an assault all on its own.

"Oh, no you fucking don't," I growled as the sound of scraping was added to the rest of the noise. Liam was firing at the truck, and there was a yell and a thud just as I got my leg out from under the asshole that fell on me. Popping up, I used the crate for cover and shot the guy closest to me. He dropped his side of the crate and grabbed at his bleeding neck wound.

I dropped behind the crates again just as bullets ripped more of the crappy plywood apart. Shuffling around, I moved as fast as I could to the other side and just caught sight of Hammer shooting Devin in the leg. Then he ran toward the front of the truck, yelling for his guys to leave the crates.

Devin yelled and rolled around on the ground as the truck started. I fired at the tires and saw Liam reloading his gun. Tires squealed as Hammer raced for the closed door, and even though one of the back ones popped, it wasn't enough to stop the truck from crashing into the bay door and ripping it right off the hinges.

Jumping to my feet, I assessed the damage and realized that my heart was slamming against the inside of my ribcage. All the guys lying on the ground were dead—five in total.

"Liam, call the cleanup crew and Sheriff Morrison. Someone had to have heard all that gunfire," I said and jogged over to Devin.

"On it."

"Fuck, that hurts. I knew something was wrong," Devin said, groaning. I was tempted to let Devin bleed out. He was fucking annoying, even with a bullet in his leg. Grabbing my knife, I flicked it open and cut through Devin's jeans. "What the hell are you doing?"

"Do you want to bleed out before we get you to a doctor? If not, then shut the fuck up." Taking the material, I tied it around the wound as tightly as possible, making a tourniquet like I'd been taught. Medical training in an emergency was one of the few classes my father forced on me that I thought was helpful.

"Ah, fuck!"

"There that should hold."

"Five min out," Liam said, walking over.

"This is what happens when you're too weak to rule. You lose control of a—"

Crack. Liam slammed his fist so hard into the side of Devin's jaw that he was out before he fell back onto the ground.

"Fuck he's annoying," Liam said and shook out his hand.

"Yeah, he really is. Thanks for shutting him up."

As I stood, I played back over the entire interaction. Something was off. But what piece was I missing from the puzzle?

Chapter 25

Myles

There wasn't a more boring job than switching the drugs from the latest shipment I picked up to baggies with the Kings' logo. I didn't understand Nash's reasoning at first and questioned why we were wasting our time with something so tedious.

Nash explained it was a form of Lingchi, but I had no idea what the hell that meant. *"It means death by a thousand cuts. It's a Chinese torture technique, and we need to utilize this mentality to take down the giant."*

Now I got it. Sales had slowly started to dip for product sold by the Kings. It was an inferior cut, less of a high, and they charged a lot for it.

We re-packaged the Kings' drugs with The Last Rank symbol and sold them exclusively to a few trusted dealers. They sold for us at a reduced price to those who usually couldn't afford this high-grade party favor. We were raking in the money. The dealers sold out in a matter of days rather than weeks. All the money was put into a shell company's account in the islands, and we only used the funds to advance our cause.

The guns were trickier. We were only involved in the final pick-up of those, and the warehouses where the crates were stored were locked down like Fort Knox.

"For the love of my fucking eardrums, can you stop singing?" Theo grumbled at Blake.

"Why? Mom says I have the voice of an angel."

"Mom is fucking deaf. She doesn't count."

I snickered. Blake glared. "Yer terrible, my friend," I said, and Blake muttered that we had no taste before getting up and leaving the room. "Make me a coffee," I yelled after him.

"No."

Theo and I shared a look and then chuckled. Blake would make me the coffee. He couldn't stay mad long. It was one of his most annoying and best traits as a friend.

"What do you think is taking Nash so long?" Zipping the little baggie, I tossed it into the box and started on another.

"Don't know, could be a million things."

What Theo didn't say—but we were both thinking—was that he'd done something to piss off his father and was now being beaten to within an inch of his life. We'd all offered for Nash to move out and stay with us, but he said it would do no good and only anger Lawrence, further. He couldn't run and he couldn't hide.

Our latest recruit Rory was right when he called Nash's father a vicious piece of shit that needed to be stopped. Lawrence only had one good quality, and that was his business acumen.

"Hey, look who I found," Blake said, walking in with Nash and Liam following. As predicted, he handed me a coffee and even brought bags of potato chips.

"What took you two so long," Theo asked.

Liam flopped down in a chair while Nash paced like we'd locked him in a cell. "Your brother Devin got shot tonight."

"Did he die?"

"Naw, it was a leg shot. He lost blood, but he'll survive."

I looked Nash in the eyes. "Too bad, it was almost my lucky night."

Devin was a prick of the highest order. I could deal with jerkish behavior, but Devin took it to another level. He hated and resented me for having Ma and Da for as long as I did while he was shipped off to school here in America. As far as I was concerned, he could keep Da, the man wasn't much better, but I was happy that Ma wasn't forced to see how Devin turned out.

He was ruthless, conniving as a snake, and would happily skin a cat for fun. He had a strangeness to him that was darker and sicker than anything that Lawrence did or would do, but Devin couldn't control it. He couldn't hold back when needed and wasn't as good with business, building alliances, friendships, or furthering connections. Devin wanted blood, and the more of it, the better. He was a straight-up psycho, and if my father wasn't controlling him, I had no doubt he'd be a serial killer by now.

We'd thrown down a few times since I arrived here, and even though Devin had his own house on the property, I still locked my bedroom door at night with two padlocks and an emergency stopper when I was home. You also learned never to wander around in the dark. Thankfully Lip lived at his academy as well, or I'd be home every night making sure that sick fuck didn't mess with our little brother. I had visions of him pushing Lip or me down the stairs and claiming it was an accident.

"Yeah, I agree." Nash tapped his chin.

"I wish I could've seen what you saw, but I was on the other side of the truck," Liam said, rubbing his eyes. "Is there any more coffee?" Blake nodded, and Liam disappeared.

"So are ya gonna tell us what happened, or are ya planning on keeping us in suspense for the night?"

"I'm just thinking." Nash sat down, but the energy coming off his body was as jittery as when he'd been moving. "I was getting ready to leave the Order meeting when my father told Devin to come with me."

"That's weird. Do you think he suspects anything," Theo asked.

"I don't think so. It felt more like a pissing contest. Devin has been poking at me since I turned 18 and started attending the meetings, questioning my ability to lead or complete jobs. I think my father saw it and wanted to see...something. I'm not sure what. I never know for sure with him ."

"Okay, so then what happened?"

"Hammer showed up like normal but said he had cash and wouldn't do a wire. It was all bullshit, and there was no money. Anyway, Devin got in his face, and they both went for guns. Then the other guy with Hammer opened the back of the truck, and a bunch of guys jumped out."

"Oh shit. How did you guys survive at all," Theo asked.

"You know, that is what I keep going over. Don't get me wrong. Liam is a crack shot, and I'm no slouch, but it was just us and Devin, who disappeared into the walls like a fucking ghost when the shots started. We killed five, and Hammer shot Devin before he ordered his guys to retreat without the crates of guns."

I screwed up my face as I thought. "You said Devin disappeared?"

"Yeah, but that's not the craziest thing. Hammer was six, maybe seven feet away from Devin when he shot him in the leg. Why not just shoot him in the chest and run? Why leave him alive at all?"

"Ya think he has a deal with Hammer," I asked, and Nash looked up at me.

"How would he even know who Hammer is?" Nash held my stare.

"Aye...who the feck knows." I looked around the room at my friends. "Ya fucking better not be thinking I had anything to do with this." My mouth fell open as Nash watched me. He was definitely questioning me but didn't seem angry. Meanwhile, rage burned in my gut as I rose from the table. "Spit it out, what are ya not sayin?"

Liam chose that moment to walk back in and stopped as he spotted the two of us. "It just seems strange that I didn't have any problems until a year ago. We've had one weird thing happen after the other. This is only the latest."

"I see." I peeled off the latex gloves I was using to handle the drugs and tossed them in the trashcan. "And it couldn't have anything to do with the fact that my Da contacted Devin and brought his piece of shite ass into the Order. It couldn't be that our group is growing, and we have more people to watch over and ensure they are keeping their mouths shut. And, of course, it couldn't have anything to do with yer Father testing you or other groups wanting to fuck with yer Father. No, couldn't be any of that, just me?"

"Where are you going," Nash asked as I grabbed my jacket and shrugged it on.

I walked toward Nash as he stood, but if he planned on intimidating me, it wouldn't work. "I have been nothing but loyal to ya. I'd go to my grave holding any secret or deed done by anyone in this room. I have been a fucking great member of this group, and I thought we were a family, building something different from our parents. Something based on more than money, mistrust, and threats, but I guess I was wrong. Yer just as mistrusting as yer father, and after what I saw yesterday morning in the library, I think yer turning into him more every day."

Nash's eyes widened and then narrowed into thin slits as he ground his teeth.

"Ya want to know where I'm going? I'm fucking going home to bed. Ya want to know why? Because ya just fucked up and hurt me." I looked around the room. "I might be the newest member, but I've never disobeyed an order or narced on anything we've done. My belief in what we are doing is strong, and I would die for ya, and yet ya just made me feel like I never belonged."

I marched for the door.

"Myles."

Looking over my shoulder, I locked eyes with Nash as he said, "So you don't want to know what I think happened?"

"Naw, I wouldn't want ya to think that I'd go running to my Da. If ya need me to do a run, ya know where to find me."

"What the fuck, Nash?" I heard Blake yell as I stomped up the stairs to the main floor of the cottage. "Myles, hold up." Blake caught up to me just as I reached the front door. "Man, don't mind Nash. He's just under a lot of stress."

"Ya don't think I am? Look, it doesn't matter. If Nash doesn't trust me, then I can't trust him. It's that simple. Without trust, we have nothing. He needs to apologize for what he just insinuated. I'd never open me mouth, and ya know it."

"Yeah, I know." Blake crossed his arms, but there was no fight in the gesture. "You going to the party Saturday at Sacred Heart?"

I shrugged. After everything that happened with Ren last night, I wasn't sure. She refused to talk to me on the way back to the academy and told me no to a date and goodnight kiss when we arrived. I sent her multiple texts saying sorry, but she left me on read. Even I was starting to think she was done with me for good.

"I hadn't decided yet," I grumbled.

"You not pursuing Ren anymore?"

"She's made it very clear that she doesn't want me to. I'm surprised she hasn't had a restraining order put against me."

Blake laughed. "When has a little opposition with anything, especially a girl, ever stopped you before? I didn't figure you for a quitter."

"Are we still talking about Ren?"

Blake's mouth curved up. "Take it as you will. Night."

As he wandered back downstairs, I thought about what he said, my hand on the cool metal of the door handle. Fuck. He was right. I was no quitter. Spinning around, I marched for the stairs. Nash would apologize, or we'd end up in a huge rumble. Either way, I got something I wanted.

No one disrespected me like that, not even Nash Collier.

Chapter 26

Ren

The moment I stepped into English class, I knew it was going to be a bad day. Blake was sitting in Ivy's spot even though no one else was here. I looked up and down the busy and very noisy hallway, but no one was making a move to walk into class early.

Shit, shit, shit.

"You going to stand in the doorway all class?" Blake called out, his bright green eyes were full of humor. I hated that he was so good-

251

looking. Why did all the annoying guys have to be hot? Was there some rule in the universe that I was unaware of?

"No."

Called out. I marched in and stopped at the desk to stare down at Blake. Of course, he looked as relaxed as a cat in the sun—another annoying trait.

"Why are you sitting in Ivy's spot?" I finally asked when he didn't say anything.

"I asked Ivy to switch spots with me, and she agreed." I crossed my arms. "I didn't threaten her if that's what you think."

"It had crossed my mind."

Blake smirked. "I may have bribed her a little, though."

"Is that so?" I looked over my shoulder as one of the kids I didn't know walked in and took their seat. "What could you offer Ivy to make her want to move seats?"

A wicked grin pulled at the corner of his mouth, and for a moment, I thought he'd offered something sexual. Why that poked at me, I couldn't explain. All these damn emotions were getting to my head. I blamed Myles. He started this crap.

"Ivy and I have a two-hour computer class together, and I sit beside Zigzag. I also happen to know that she is all...." He held his hands to his chin like he was hugging something and sighed as his eyes fluttered at me. I tried not to smile, but the look was ridiculous, and I gave in and giggled. "So I offered to switch her seats in comp class if she swapped me seats in English."

"Devious." I unwrapped the scarf I was wearing and laid it on the desk as I sat down.

"I like to think of it as smart."

"Okay, smart guy, then answer me this. Why would you even want to sit beside me? I hardly know you, and let's be honest, I'm not exactly your type, yet you keep persisting. So...my guess is you want to annoy Myles. The question is, why is annoying Myles so impor-tant to you?" I finished pulling out my text, binder, and laptop before looking at Blake.

"Who says you're not my type?"

"The other day in the cafeteria, was that not a cheerleader that walked over and sat on your lap?"

Blake's cheeks pinked, which of course, only enhanced his tanned skin. "Well, yes, April is a cheerleader."

"And she also seems very close to Vicky, who hates me. Are the two of you together?"

"Not like on a regular basis."

I arched my brow, and he looked away from my eyes and cleared his throat. "Blake, I don't care if you are having sex with the entire cheer squad. What I do wonder about is why you're trying to get up into my business when I'm clearly not who you'd choose to date or whatever it is you do?"

"Um...I like spending time with you. I had a lot of fun until I screwed up and was a dick about Myles." He shrugged, and I wasn't sure how to take what he said. Did he mean he liked hanging with me as if I was one of the guys or something more? See, this was why I didn't date. Everything was always so confusing.

The only guy I'd ever been interested in was Rylan, the Captain of the school hockey team back home, and he acted like I didn't exist. Getting a hello out of him was shocking unless he wanted something. A couple of times, he did have the gall to ask me to help him with an exam. He quickly forgot my name again after.

"Are you going to the party with Myles?"

"No, was I supposed to be?" I watched Blake's expression closely, but he didn't give anything away.

"I was just curious. You two seemed to be getting pretty close."

"Your spies are lying to you," I joked. Blake did have a layer of adorable under the cocky persona.

"I got this for you." Blake reached down beside him and produced a beautifully wrapped box. The paper was blue with tiny little snowflakes all over it. I looked at the box and then up a Blake.

"Um...okay. Why?" At that moment, I realized that I didn't trust anyone, and now I had the added worry about what each of them was capable of. I'd been suspicious of the bag of muffins from Myles, and now I wondered what the hell was going to crawl or slither out of this box.

Blake's brows drew together as he mimicked me and then laughed. "Why are you staring at it like it might be a bomb?"

"I don't trust anyone," I said, and I hated that his eyes lost their humor as they studied my face. "Don't look at me like that."

"Just open it. I swear it's nothing weird, strange, or gross."

Glancing around, a few students had sat down and were talking, but I could tell they were watching to see what would happen next. I wiped my sweaty palms off on my kilt and gently ripped at the tape holding the paper in place. His wrapping job was really nice, which I admit was shocking. He didn't strike me as the perfectly folded corners type when his shirt was always half untucked.

Getting the paper off, I lifted the lid on the box before moving the tissue out of the way. I recognized the pattern on the dress I loved from our day out shopping. As I ran my hand across the soft material, a smile played across my lips. I remembered him holding a bag and how he lied and said it was stuff for him. Or had he gone back? Either way, I wasn't sure what to make of the sweet gift.

"You got this for me?"

Blake leaned closer, and I wiggled in my seat as a mass of fluttering started in my stomach. "I said I liked spending time with you, and I meant it. I thought maybe you'd like to wear it to the party tomorrow." I opened my mouth, and he held up a hand to stop what I was going to say. "First, I'm not taking it back, so don't ask. Second, there is no obligation to me or to wear it to the party. You saw it, and you liked it. I wanted to do something nice for you since you're new, and...you seemed to need a smile. Don't look so shocked, I can be a nice guy, and that is all there is to the gift." He could really pull off the sad puppy look. He was looking at me from under his lashes with a slight pout to his lips. I could only imagine what his and Theo's mother had to endure with the two of them.

Then again, I couldn't picture Theo as the pouting type. He

seemed more like the kid that would use big words you didn't know he knew and give an argument that would make any lawyer proud.

Heat rushed to my face, and my throat constricted as I tried to swallow past the lump that had formed.

"Please put that away, Ms. Davies. Class is about to begin."

I whipped my head around to see the classroom had filled up, and I hadn't noticed Mr. Martelli was standing at the front of the room.

"Yes, of course. I'm so sorry." It was hard to embarrass me, but I felt way out of my element, and as quickly as I could, I put the tissue paper back in the box with the pretty dress and set it on the floor.

Once class was underway, I scribbled on a piece of paper, feeling like I'd stepped back in time to my elementary school days as I held the note out to Blake under the table.

A little electric shock raced up my arm as Blake's fingers brushed against mine. He smiled at me as he gave me a quick look and then quietly unfolded the paper under the desk.

Thank you. I love it.

Was all the note said, but Blake flipped the paper over and began writing back. I shouldn't feel this giddy, but it was hard to contain my smile. The little voice in my mind kept chanting that this was a very bad idea.

Blake handed the note back, and as I gripped it, he wouldn't let go. I glanced over at him as he ran his finger over mine, and my cheeks flamed hot as my pulse jumped. He finally let go, but his cheeky grin made me want a water bottle and a fan.

As stealthily as I could, I unfolded the paper while keeping my eyes on the board where Mr. Martelli was writing our newest assignment. I wasn't paying attention to what he was writing. My mind just wouldn't focus.

I smoothed it out on the desk, then froze as Mr. Martelli turned around. "I want you all to pick one person you admire to do this project. It can be someone living or deceased. They can be famous or a family member, but this is not a free pass assignment. I want to see a real effort to make these projects special. They should genuinely mean something to you."

He turned back around to finish writing his notes, and I looked down at mine.

Will you go to the party with me? Just as friends if that is all you want.

I nibbled on my bottom lip and could feel Blake staring at me as he waited for a response. Twirling my pen nervously, I debated what to do. On the one hand, I'd already promised to go with Ivy and Chantry, and they would still be going. If it was terrible or Blake turned into a raving jerk, I could leave with them. But...I didn't want to date, and he was Myles's best friend. That was a huge downside.

At the thought of Myles, all I could picture was Pam's angry face as she stood by our table. I didn't like how she handled herself, but she was hurt and lashing out, which I did understand. If Myles could hurt Pam and be so callous about it, what would he do to me?

My body jerked as Blake's warm hand wrapped around mine on the desk. I gently tugged my hand out from under his but looked at him and sighed. Saying yes was a horrible idea, but I circled, as friends, and slid the paper back.

Blake smiled wide. My stomach flipped, and I wondered what the hell I was doing.

Chapter 27

NOVEMBER 11 – FRIDAY 4:50 PM

Ren It was official. I was going to kill Vicky before the month was over. I would end up in jail and not be released until I was old and...well, I was already white-haired, so I had one part ready to go.

Fridays seemed to be the night she invited everyone over and got ready to go out or partied in our room all night. Two of the four girls in our room were sitting at my desk. They'd moved all my things out of the way and had their makeup all over it. I looked like a total bitch as I ordered them to sit at the small communal table with two chairs.

Then I had to stick around and make sure they didn't move back while Vicky talked about how great Nash was like a broken record skipping and repeating the same line. I finally put on my headset and ignored them until they left. I'm sure insults were tossed my way. I then got changed and used the washroom...that was when I found all my bottles emptied. My shampoo, conditioner, soap, and perfume were all turned upside down in the sink.

Fucking childish. I glared at her bottles and was tempted to do the same, but I shook my head. She was trying to drag me into a fight, but I wouldn't bite or lower myself to her level. I had small travel-size bottles of everything in my suitcase. I would use those until I could get more.

Instead of creating a huge scene, I decided to go over to the art room. Hopefully, I could get some painting done this time. The last time—due to my panic attack—was a bust. Pushing my way out the dorm doors, I took a deep breath and held it. The feel of fresh air hitting my lungs had a different meaning for me now. It seemed more precious, after my mums murder I savored every second.

Cars were coming and going from campus, and I found myself looking for Myles' Ferrari, then kicked myself for doing it. My phone dinged, and I pulled it out to look at it.

I: Hey girl, what are you up to?

R: Heading to the art studio for a while. What are you up to?"

I: There is a small party happening with some of the girls from the drama club, and ZZ is going to be there 😊

R: Sounds great, but I need a quiet night.

I: You sure?

R: I'm sure, but thank you for the invite. I hope that ZZ takes notice of how awesome you are.

I: I'm really sorry about switching spots in English class.

I shook my head.

R: Stop apologizing. I'm fine with it. You're right behind me.

I: I know. I just feel bad that I totally dumped you to get a spot near ZZ. I'm a terrible friend.

R: I would've done it too.

I: I doubt that. Besides, you don't need to. You have all the guys panting after you.

R: No I don't.

I: Yes you do.

R: ...

I: Why do you think Vicky hates you so much? I mean, other than the obvious. LOL! You're a threat to her. She hasn't had anyone challenge her for queen status ever, and you're doing it without even trying.

R: You're crazy. Go have fun. If you need me, I'll be in the art room having a nice quiet night with me, myself, and my painting. I want all the details later.

I: Hopefully, he'll ask me out. Not that my father would let me go, but that is problem number two. The first one is getting him to acknowledge me. Night girl.

I stuffed my phone in my pocket as I walked into the open art room. The lights were off, and the blinds were drawn, but I liked it like this, so I didn't bother to turn them on. I only got a few feet inside when a hand clamped over my mouth and strong arms pulled me back into a hard body much larger than my own. I tried to scream, but the sound came out muffled. I twisted and fought, but my attacker never gave me an inch.

"Hello, Princess." I shivered as Nash's distinct voice growled next to my ear. "I told you I'd pay you back for embarrassing me." His arms tightened slightly, letting me know just how weak I was next to him. "You're lucky you didn't live-stream anything online about me. This wouldn't have ended as pleasantly for you as it will now." He chuckled. "None of it will be pleasant, but I'll enjoy this more."

Fear lanced my heart. Was he going to rape me? He had promised to fuck me, and it was the only thing I could think of him wanting to do.

I tried to scream again as he picked me up off the ground. The door to the art room slammed closed, and my heart raced in my chest. Panic was steadily rising inside of me as he stomped across the floor to the teacher's leather chair.

Sitting down, he laid me across his lap and removed his hand from my mouth.

"What the fuck, Nash? Let go of me," I said, trying for menacing, but Nash only laughed.

"No, I don't think so. You need to be taught a lesson."

"A lesson? What are we five?" I asked sarcastically.

"Fine you need to learn your place."

"My place? Ow!" A loud crack sounded as his hand connected with my jean-clad ass.

"One."

"Are you fucking spanking me, you ass...Ah!" I screamed as the second blow was harder than the first. A torrent of fury was spinning inside me, and I wiggled and twisted as hard as I could to get out of this ridiculous and humiliating position.

"Two."

"Fuck you!" Smack. I jerked on his lap. I was going to kill him when he let me up.

"Three."

"I swear to god, I'm telling Vicky about this," I said, but Nash kept on laughing.

"Go ahead. I'd love to see her reaction." Smack. Tears sprang to my eyes. The strike so hard that it made me gasp. "Four"

"Oh, God," I cried out and clenched my teeth.

More than the sharp bite of pain from the smack, I hated that I didn't entirely hate this. My stomach clenched tight, and with each hit, I was torn between yelling and moaning. For that, I wanted to kill him. A strange heat was filling my body, and I couldn't decide if I was wiggling to get away or because I wanted more.

How dare Nash do this, touch me like this and make me feel like this. I didn't want to feel anything for anyone, let alone have sexual thoughts about him, while he treated me like a spoiled brat. It was degrading and humiliating.

"Five."

It made me hate him even more.

Nash

Oh fuck, this was a lot hotter than I ever thought it would be. I saw Ren texting on her phone, not paying any attention to who was around her or what potential threats there were. In this case me. I didn't have a solid plan on paying her back yet, but sometimes god just tossed shit in your lap, and you had to take it.

I followed her right into Bowfield Hall and down to room 12 without her ever lifting her head. Who was she texting, and what were they saying to keep her so preoccupied? The anger from the other night and my plan going sideways had continued to simmer in my soul. With each passing day, the urge to get payback had grown until it felt like a living thing in my chest.

Her angry stare and smug grin danced and twirled behind my eyes like a decadent show. So when the opportunity presented itself, I wasn't shying away. What I would do to her...I didn't know until this moment, and fuck was it ever sweet.

"Let go of me," she growled, like a little she-demon, and the sound made my cock twitch.

"Not a fucking chance."

She was wiggling back and forth against my cock, and I had to bite back a groan as it began to harden. I stared down at her firm ass, which tempted me to grab it and get a better feel with each slap. Slipping a finger between her legs was a need that came out of nowhere but made my pulse race.

"Six," I said. Ren jerked hard, and her snowy hair fell around her face. I couldn't see her expression, but the sounds she made were confusing. I couldn't tell if she hated it or was as turned on as I was.

This was not supposed to turn me on, and the anger roared through me. Grinding my teeth together, I slapped her for the seventh time. Ren looked over her shoulder at me, her eyes furious with a hatred I understood. I felt the same level of rage on a daily basis.

"Fuck you, Nash. I hate you!"

"Good, I hate you too." I smacked her again, and this time I had to hold back the moan as she arched and bounced down on my fully hard cock. Finishing this bet and taking her right now was a whole new fantasy coming to life.

Without much thought, I released her body and wrapped her hair around my fist. Ren snarled like an animal when I pulled her back, and she struck out with her fist, which harmlessly bounced off my shoulder. I watched her face as my hand connected with her ass again, and the glare turned to white-hot hatred, but under that was lust. It flashed in her eyes a moment after my hand connected, and all my muscles tightened with the desire to bend her over the teacher's desk and fuck her until she screamed my name.

"You like it don't you?"

"No." She said, clenching her teeth as my hand connected for the tenth time. A tear glistened as it rolled down her cheek, and I licked my lip, wanting to lick it off her face.

"Liar."

"You're sick." Her silver eyes caught the little bit of light shining in around the blinds, making it look like they glittered with fury. That was hot. Way hotter than I ever intended for this moment to become.

"Most definitely." I smacked her again, and this time there was no denying that moan. My whole body flexed as I thought about spreading her wide. She was breathing fast, and I could feel her tits brushing my leg, and I realized my heart was beating like a drum inside my chest.

In theory, she could've rolled off my lap since both my hands were occupied, I had nothing to hold her and keep her from running, yet she didn't move. This was dangerous. It wasn't meant to turn sexual but...fuck me. Now that it had, I couldn't think of anything else.

I smacked her ass again, knowing exactly how she'd react, and anticipated the movement, flexing up into her body to get a better feel.

Fuck I was hard. The servicing I'd given myself this morning in the shower wasn't taking the edge off. I needed to let her go. I had to get her away from me.

"Fuck," Ren said and slumped on my lap. My hand was resting on her ass, and no amount of internal arguing would stop me from squeezing. My breath shuddered as I took a gulp of air and tried to push the thought of her bouncing on my cock out of my mind, but it did no good.

Unraveling my hand from her hair, I forced myself to let go of her ass. I was positive if I got her out of her jeans, she would be wet for me, then I could win this bet and get her out of my mind once and for all. So why wasn't I picking her up and laying her on the desk to do just that? I didn't know. I couldn't figure out what I was feeling.

"Get off of me," I growled. Ren was slow to move, so I gave her a push. "I said get off my lap. Your punishment is done."

Ren stiffly pushed herself up and off my lap, and I'd never been so relieved and disappointed in my life. Those silver eyes locked with mine, and before I knew it, her hand connected with the side of my face. The slap echoed as loud as my father's whip, but the sting was far different.

"Don't ever fucking touch me again," Ren said, her eyes full of venom as she growled the words at me through clenched teeth.

Jumping to my feet, I grabbed her wrist and yanked her body flush against mine. Everything about her body language told me to go fuck myself, right down to the way her mouth was set. Her hair was fanned out on her shoulders like she'd just been fucked hard, and once more, I was toeing a very dangerous line.

"What are you going to do? Spank me again for being a bad girl?" Her words were dipped in sarcasm and then sugar-coated with anger. It made me smile.

"Don't tempt me. I quite enjoyed myself."

"At least one of us did."

"You lie, Princess. I bet if I rip those jeans off you right now, your little panties will be soaking wet for me."

"Not a chance," she said, but she couldn't deny the flash of desire in her eyes.

I should just do it. I could take her right now. It was just sex, no different than the thousand other times, but...I couldn't seem to make myself cross that next line. My feet stayed rooted to the floor as Myles' earlier words rattled around my brain. I was acting like my father.

"I know you want me. I saw it in your eyes. You can't deny that."

Her eyes flicked down, the sass evident in everything she did. She had less fear than most guys I dealt with daily. "I think you have me confused with yourself unless you make it a habit to walk around with a hard-on."

I smirked. So she had felt it. Again she could knee me, hit me, or scream the building down now, but she wasn't doing any of that. She didn't even fight my hold on her arm, and with each passing second, the air felt more charged around us.

I let go of her wrist just as the door opened, and Mrs. Frey walked in. She stopped when she saw the two of us.

"What is going on here?"

"Just a disagreement about technique," I said, and Ren mumbled something under her breath as she took a purposeful step back and crossed her arms over her chest.

"Is that what's happening here, Ren," Mrs. Frey asked as she placed her hands on her hips.

Ren looked at me and then at Mrs. Frey. "Yup, that's all that is happening. You know how passionate I get about my art. Nash made his point, but he was just leaving," she lied, and I smiled, giving it my best innocent look.

"Until the next disagreement, Princess," I whispered.

"There won't be a next time," she smoothly whispered back, and I wished she had just kept her mouth shut cause now I was even more determined to make sure there was.

"We'll see about that." Smiling, I crossed the room and ignored the glare from Mrs. Frey. She could believe whatever she wanted. I already knew Ren wouldn't say a word. What I'd said was true. She did like it, I know she did, and that created confusion for her perfect little morals.

The further I got away from Ren, the more I felt like I'd accomplished nothing other than frustrating myself and gaining a raging hard-on that I now needed to take care of. Of course the one night I could've really used Vicky's mouth, she was off to the movies with her girlfriends. How had this gotten so turned around that I was the one with a fucking hard-on, and she seemed as unfazed as when I started.

I wasn't sure if I liked that or didn't like it.

"Fuck, nothing is going the way I plan lately."

Chapter
28

Nash

The party was loud, but the laughter from Vicky and her friends as they showed off was somehow louder. I avoided parties with her for this reason. Vicky got overly excited, and I kept expecting her to pee on my foot. I wasn't a fan of being touched or draped on, and had my father to thank for that, yet Vicky couldn't go a second without trying to sit in my lap or cling to a body part. I could only take it for so long before needing to get the fuck away from her.

I clenched my hand into a fist, it still fucking tingled like Ren's ass

267

was a ghost limb. Opening my hand I stared at my palm, wondering what her skin looked like afterward. Did her ass tingle like my hand? I wanted to know if she pulled down her underwear and glared at the handprints in the mirror. I bet she did. The scowl on her face was so clear in my mind. She deserved every single one for mouthing off to me, embarrassing me, and making me look like an idiot. Anyone else would have gotten far worse. She got off easy as far as I was concerned.

I untangled myself from the octopus Vicky and pushed myself up off the couch. She grabbed my hand, instantly pissing me off.

"Where are you going?" Vicky's lower lip was pushed out as she tugged on my hand to sit down. It was a good fucking thing she came from such a powerful Italian family or I would've killed her by now.

I could feel her friends' eyes on us. They all annoyed me. Every single one of them had tried to sleep with me, even though I was with Vicky, but they had the nerve to call her their friend. Not that I really gave a fuck—it wasn't like I'd ever told Vicky we were exclusive —and I even took a couple of them up on the offer, but that wasn't the point. I felt like I was in a school of piranhas, the way they hungrily focused on me. I'd never admit this, but it was fucking unnerving.

"Piss, drink, and find my boys, not necessarily in that order," I said, jerking my arm out of her hold.

"Oh, can you get me a new drink when you come back?"

She swung the red plastic cup between her fingers, her pout exaggerated. Vicky was already half in the bag, and it wasn't even nine o'clock. I was suddenly very fucking happy that I hadn't given her a ride.

"I don't know when I'll be back."

Walking away, I went on the hunt for Liam and Theo. I'd seen them come in earlier, so I knew they were here. Poking my head in all the rooms, I ignored the flirty stares and whispers from those that only knew me by reputation. The girls from Sacred Heart Academy seeked me out at other parties, but this was not a place I typically came to, yet... here I was.

Laughter was coming from the basement as I jogged down the stairs. I found a rec room with a bar, pool tables, dartboards, and a small dance floor. Okay, this was fucking cool. We didn't have separate houses back at Wayward, so it was impossible to do something like this. The most we had was a communal sitting area, but we were limited to one television and a couple of tables.

Myles and Theo were playing pool while Liam sat on the couch watching with a cigarette hanging from his lips. His eyes were unfocused as he stared at the hockey game on the television. I stayed on the outer edge of the room so he wouldn't see me coming and stopped beside him. His arm was resting on the couch and I grabbed it as I spoke.

"Didn't quit, I see," I growled.

I'd never seen him jump so high or look as guilty. Chuckling, I let go of his arm.

"Fuck man, don't do that to me." Liam pulled the unlit smoke from his lips and held it up. "It's not lit. I miss the habit and the stress relief. This helps."

I glared at the guy sitting across from us in a leather chair.

"Get out of here." He jumped and took off into the crowd so I could flop down. "You know I only ride your ass 'cause I care." Liam's sarcastic stare made me smirk. "Okay, I care mostly about the swim team, but I still care. I'll even buy you a spinner."

"So generous of you." He smiled.

"Fine, I'll make it two." I smirked.

Liam had been my best friend for as long as I could remember. His family handled imports and exports. They owned multiple airfields, planes, and even a cargo ship. More than once, we'd ordered and snuck something we shouldn't have into the country with Liam's help. Forging documents in his father's name was a valuable skill that we would need in the future.

"You're a fuckin' cheater, man," Myles said and slammed his stick down on the pool table.

"Why do you bother to play him? You know you're going to lose," I said, and Myles glared at me.

"He cheats. I know it. I just need to figure out how."

"I'm not cheating. It's called skill. Now pay up. I won."

Theo held out his hand, and the smug grin tugging at the corner of his mouth was the only indication he was amused. Theo was one of those obnoxiously good at everything types, and we'd all made the mistake of challenging him at some point.

Grumbling, Myles slapped the hundred down on his palm. Theo's green eyes were full of his typical arrogance but mixed with humor that only we would notice. Everyone thought Blake was the bad boy, but the shit Theo came up with was the best, and he was the first to start a bet between us. At least the girls stopped asking out the wrong brother now that Theo had cut his hair short.

"Cheater, I swear I'll figure ya out." Myles pointed at Theo.

Theo enjoyed riling Myles up as much as the rest of us. He was like an enraged hornet when he got going and kept us laughing.

I fucking hated that I had to apologize to Myles the other night after suggesting he leaked info. I'm not even sure why I did it. It wasn't like I thought he would, but I was pissed and Myles was a great target. He always fought back, and I never knew if I would actually win the fight. Myles had a load of skill that we never talked about, but both knew how he'd acquired it. Most would decide that was a good reason to avoid a fight, but I loved the challenge.

Apologizing wasn't something I did. My father had beaten into me that apologizing even when wrong was a sign of weakness. Even though it went against my nature, I apologized and still owed him a beer.

"Where the fuck is Blake," Myles asked as he wandered over and grabbed a handful of chips from the bowl on the table. "I need to make my money back."

"He's coming with Ren," Theo said, and Myles choked on the chips he was swallowing.

"What the fuck?" Myles shook his head. "No, there's no way. I don't believe you."

Theo shrugged. "Believe me or not, he said he'd be late 'cause he was bringing Ren."

"Son of a bitch."

Myles' fists balled, and because I was an asshole in a mood, I decided to add to his misery.

"I'm sure nothing will happen. Unlike me spanking her yesterday. She loved every second of it."

"What?" Myles looked like he was going to have a heart attack as his face flamed red and his eyes bugged out. "There is no fuckin' way she'd let ya willingly spank her."

I shrugged. "Who said anything about willingly? I told her I'd pay her back for what she did." I leaned forward and casually grabbed a handful of chips while Myles looked ready to erupt like a volcano. "I found her after school, and she felt real good under my hand." I held up my palm to show Myles. "It still tingles, and she has the cutest moan. I was tempted to fuck her on the teacher's desk. She might've let me, but Mrs. Frey walked in."

"Yer fuckin' lyin'. There is no way she'd let ya do that."

"She protested, but it's always the ones that argue that want it the most." I popped a couple of chips in my mouth, enjoying way too much how this was irritating Myles. "And I do mean she moaned. She got my cock hard. That tells you all you need to know."

Myles scoffed. "Please, ya git hard over any hole ya think ya might be able to stick yer cock in. Besides, I've seen the way she looks at ya. She wants to rip yer cock off, not kneel in front of it." Myles pointed at me. "That's how I know yer lyin'."

"Am I?" Total exaggeration, but to get that look on Myles' face was worth it every time.

"It looks like you're falling further behind," Liam said, pulling out his little black book. I wondered just how many bets he was managing for the school. There was always something going on. "I'll give you three points for taking her shopping and almost going to dinner, but that did end in an epic fail," Liam drawled as he scribbled.

"Fuck ya. It wasn't a fail. We had a connection."

"Define connection for me," Theo said. Liam smiled while I laughed. There were no four words better, to sum up Theo.

"I mean that we talked and laughed and...shit, we had a thing going until Pam." Myles pinched the bridge of his nose. "It was real. I'm not making it up," he added when none of us said anything.

"Did she say she liked you," Theo asked.

"No."

"Did she say she'd like to go out again?"

"Uh...no."

"Did she give you any indication that you'd be able to get her into bed before Christmas break?"

"Fuck...."

"Well, that answers that. I wouldn't even give him three points. Two is more accurate. His odds are getting longer, but I might put this fancy new hundred down on him as a long shot," Theo said, handing Liam the money he'd just won from Myles.

"Yer all a bunch of fuckin' pricks. I just want ya to know that," Myles said, making us laugh.

"Hey guys, I overheard you have a bet going on. Can I join in?"

I recognized Evan from family parties at Blake and Theo's. He was Lisa's brother and already a senior, but he seemed more of a gamer than a partier.

"Sure, pull up a seat." Liam offered.

As the guys talked, my mind drifted to how I would access my father's office and his drawers. He never left the door unlocked and always locked his desk, even on the rare occurrence he forgot the door. I needed to get into those drawers. We were into much more than local drugs, guns, and washing money. We had an entire network, and from the look of some of the girls my father brought

272

to his 'special ceremonies,' we were trafficking as well. I had to find a way to gain access to all that information and then find ways to stop or disrupt it enough that my father was viewed as incompetent and unfit to lead. My talk with him after everything went down with Hammer had left me with more questions than answers.

"*What the hell happened out there, and how did you let Devin get shot?*"

My father stomped around his desk. It was strange to see him without a suit on and even stranger that he didn't lead the conversation with a punch to the face. Such wonderful family traditions. Not that I wanted him to hit me, but I had failed to complete the deal, and failure was never an option. It didn't matter how I failed or if it was even my fault. None of that matter to my father.

"*I don't know what Hammer was up to. He didn't have any money with him, and the back of the truck was filled with men. I thought Liam and I did a good fucking job chasing them off and keeping our product.*"

"*You mean you, Liam, and Devin.*"

"*No, I mean me and Liam. Devin evaporated into thin air and only reappeared to be shot.*"

"*I doubt that. Devin is a dedicated member of our Order, and you should be happy to have him with you.*"

I screwed up my face. Did he just compliment Devin? I couldn't remember the last time he complimented anyone. He certainly never complimented me.

"*How is Devin doing?*"

"*I don't know. I don't give a fuck about him. I kept him alive until the doc came to get him, and I haven't heard since.*"

"*You should care about him. Devin is a rising asset to the organization and can be utilized,*" *my father said, and I glared. "He makes the perfect weapon.*"

I wanted to yell, "I fucking know that already. You just sent him after me." I wish I had proof, but that would take some work.

"I wouldn't hold out too much hope for that happening. He is volatile, unpredictable and the only position Devin wants is yours. To get that, he has to go through me and I will not let that happen," I growled and clenched my fists. My father's brows rose and I could see the shock in his eyes.

"It's good to finally see you passionate about your legacy."

I wasn't passionate about the order or my legacy, but if that's what he wanted to think, I wasn't going to correct him. .

"I can't prove it, but I think Hammer only shot Devin to make him look like a victim," I said, not acknowledging what he said.

My father snorted. "I find it stranger that neither you nor Liam has a scratch on you, but Devin is in the hospital with a hole in his leg."

My hands balled with the accusation.

"You must be joking?"

"I don't joke when it comes to business."

"And I don't screw up deals. In fact, the only deal that has gone wrong is the one where I was forced to take Devin. That's a mighty big coincidence."

My father smirked and leaned back in his big leather chair as he steepled his fingers. It was an intimidation tactic but had long lost its effect on me.

I took a step toward the desk. He'd laid his keys down, and I wished he'd leave me alone long enough that I could copy a couple. I had all the shit to make duplicates but could never get close enough. He was always watching me.

"Son, you know very well there is a group actively working against us. Your job is to find out who they are and take whatever measures necessary to stop them. So far, you've come up empty-handed. Not only that, but you let them humiliate us by painting our symbol on Austin's body, if what you say is indeed true and you know nothing about it."

"It is true," I lied, and crossed my arms.

It was hard to hand over information about yourself. I would have to give him something soon to lead him down another path.

"The group is well hidden, and I haven't found anyone who knows who they might be affiliated with. My guess is a rival gang in the area that knows our routines, but I can't say for sure. Besides, I've been saddled with other responsibilities, but I will make it my top priority from now on."

"You better, or you just might find Devin is a more permanent fixture around here."

"Are you threatening to make Devin your heir?" I stepped closer to the deck and glared down at my father. "I'll never let that happen. Even if you order it," I growled, and my father smiled.

"I don't know what has gotten into you Son, but it's good to see you have grown some backbone." He reorganized some papers on this desk and then laid a folder on top of them. I narrowed my eyes at the pile, what was he trying to hide? Or was this another mind game? "I have a couple of calls to make. You may leave, but remember what I said, Nash. Find who is messing with us, or else."

"Hey man, this is supposed to be a party. Lighten up," Liam said, holding out a drink. "I promise I didn't spike it."

"Better not. You taking advantage of my ass might make Theo jealous."

"Not if I can join," Theo added, never lifting his head from his phone.

"I'll be back," Myles said and walked away.

"Where do you think you're going?" I yelled after him, but he only shot a middle finger back.

"Probably to embarrass himself or fuck up his chances of winning even more." Liam took a sip of his drink. "But, he does make this far more entertaining."

Myles

Every curse word I could think of came out of my mouth as I stomped up the stairs to the main level of the sorority house. It was too pretty in here for a kegger. Guaranteed the shiny hardwood floors would be sticky by morning, and they'd be lucky if their beds weren't permanently stained with one fluid or another.

I couldn't believe that Snowflake agreed to come here with Blake. Seriously, how did he always manage it? My best friend was pissing me the fuck off. I marched over to the large bar and mixed myself a drink. I'd never acquired a taste for beer and preferred whiskey.

"Hey, how's it going?"

I looked over to see Lisa leaning against the bar. Blake's cousin was fun to hang out with, and we'd done so a fair bit when I first arrived the summer before grade ten. Shockingly, we'd never fucked. Our relationship was completely chill.

"Fine."

"Doesn't sound like you're fine."

Someone threw a football, and a moment later, three guys sailed through the air as they tried to get to it first. Cheering erupted as one of the guys I didn't know stood with it in his hand as he howled like a wolf.

"Hey! No one breaks anything, body part or otherwise," Lisa yelled, scolding the guys.

But they weren't paying attention or didn't care. I'd been that guy more than once, but Nash and his strict rules to remain on the swim team had curbed most of those tendencies. Most people would've walked, but I loved being on the team more than I cared how sloshed I got.

"Sorry about that. Apparently, inviting rival football teams was not such a good idea. Those idiots have been at it since they arrived." Lisa shook her head, her blond hair waving as she did, but all I saw was my Snowflake's hair blowing in the wind. I shook my head to get rid of the image. "So you going to spill the tea?"

"Nothing to tell," I said, as the front door opened, and my heart stopped in my chest.

Ren looked fucking gorgeous, and suddenly I couldn't draw a breath. She'd left her hair down, and it glittered under the flashing lights. She was wearing a pretty dress, but nothing about it should've set my blood on fire, yet I couldn't look away. The short combat boots Ren wore with it made me smirk. It was so like her, the perfect combination of sweet and badass.

"Oh, now I know what's biting your ass," Lisa said.

As I glanced at her, I realized I was holding my cup to my lips, smiling like an idiot. Clearing my throat, I turned around and sat the stupid cup down. I wanted to punch Blake.

"Yer wrong," I said.

"No, I'm not, and they're coming this way."

"I need to make her jealous," I whispered.

"What? Myles, that's a stupid plan. Jealousy is crazy, unpredictable, and it will backfire on you."

"Ya don't understand. The only time I get any real emotion out of Ren is when I make her jealous. Please help me," I begged Lisa.

"Oh, heck no. I'm not getting in the middle of whatever shit you and my cousin have going on with her. I've seen your games, and I don't approve."

"It's no game. Lisa, please, I'll owe ya a favor, and ya know Blake would never extend the same gratitude."

"I'll think about it," she said, her voice low and barely able to be heard with the loud music.

I knew Ren was close as the air around me electrified.

"Hi there, cuz. Good to see you again."

Lisa pushed away from the bar, and my entire body shook with the energy coursing through my veins. I could feel her behind me, and I wanted Ren to reach out and touch me so badly that I would've paid any amount to make it happen. I didn't do love or anything mushy because it all seemed like false advertising. But there was something about Ren that drove me insane.

"Do you mind passing me the ginger ale," Ren asked from right beside me.

She was so close I could feel the warmth of her body caressing mine, or maybe I was having a hot flash. Either way, I needed to get control of myself before I pushed her up against the wall. Wondering how she'd taste and the feel of her body under my hands was a continuous loop in my brain. Grabbing the large bottle, I dared to look at her. I figured she'd take it, make her drink, and walk away. Instead, we stood with our fingers touching, holding onto the green plastic, Ren didn't pull, and I didn't let go as we stared into each other's eyes. I wanted to stand like that forever. Fuck, I was turning into a hopeless romantic.

"I'm sorry," I managed to blurt out finally. "For the way the other night went. I swear I'm not playing ya, Snowflake."

I was tempted to tell her about the bet and lay all my cards on the table, but if I did that, it could lead to a shitload of other issues. I'd never been so intimidated by someone's eyes searching mine, but to have her take a moment and listen was worth a thousand interrogations.

"I'm tellin' the truth, I...I do have a rep, but..."

Blake chose that moment to wrap his arm around my shoulders, and just like that, the moment between us burst.

"Hey bud, where are the rest of the guys?"

A thousand bullets could cut him down where he stood, and I would still spit on his body for how furious I was. He smiled, choosing to be completely oblivious to my murderous glare. Ren turned to greet Lisa, and as the two girls spoke, Blake whispered in my ear.

"Don't worry. I'm sure you still have a tiny chance to win."

He held up his fingers to demonstrate just how little he thought that was, and my jaw twitched along with my fist.

"Why are ya doing this," I asked, even though it was a stupid question.

"Because I want to win, and seeing you twisted like this is worth every second."

Giving my shoulder a clap, he turned his back on me to speak with Ren and Lisa as Ivy, and Chantry joined them.

Marching away, I wandered over to the beer pong game and tossed my money down to play the next round. Making Ren jealous was the only card I had left. Blake had charm and impeccable timing, and Nash would take what he wanted until she finally caved. Neither of those things would work for me. I wasn't like that, at least not with her.

She could be spitting mad as long as she looked at me like she had the other night. I did a quick scan of the room. Now I just needed to find someone to help me.

Chapter 29

Ren

I'd been dreading this moment but couldn't take it any longer. I had to break the seal and use the bathroom. Pushing through the crowd that had doubled in size since I first arrived, I noticed Ivy making headway with Zigzag. They were talking and laughing, so I gave them their space. Chantry had found a couple of her friends that went to this school, and she was happily chatting in the corner.

As usual, I felt like an outsider. I should be used to this feeling, it wasn't new, but I'd secretly hoped this party would be different and

I'd have a great time, feel confident to talk to new people and maybe dance or try something crazy like play a game of pool. Instead, I watched everyone around me get hammered while I stayed sober until I was no longer involved.

I kept an eye out for Blake or Myles as I moved from one open space to the next. Was it stupid of me to still be looking for Myles? Oh, it definitely was, but I still did it. I stared at a guy chugging two beers at once while making a complete mess of himself. Avoiding him as best I could, I stepped around him and ran straight into a solid chest.

"Hey, watch where you're...."

I looked up and locked eyes with Nash. My body flushed as the memory of laying over his lap skipped across my mind like it was playing fucking hopscotch. Of course, he was here. I'd hoped he wouldn't be, and when I hadn't seen him all night—even though Vicky was floating around with her group of Chaos Creators—I thought I'd lucked out.

"You were saying," Nash said, his mouth pulling up at the corner.

"I was saying watch where you're going. You almost ran me over," I said, then gasped when his arm snaked around my waist and pulled me into his body. "What the hell Nash? Have you been drinking, or are you just this stupid? I don't want anything to do with you. Why is that so difficult to understand?"

I expected the glare and the threats, but I wasn't ready for him to drop his head to the side of my neck and inhale. An uncontrollable shiver started all over my body, and my stomach flipped and twisted into knots.

"Keep telling yourself that, Princess, but we both know better. Remember, I heard your moans and felt you wiggle under my hand. If you want, I could take you to a room right now and finish what we started." His warm breath fanned my ear, and I could just make out the hint of alcohol.

"I'd rather eat chocolate-covered dog shit. Now let go of me before your girlfriend sees and thinks I have something to do with her boyfriend being a jerk who can't keep his hands to himself. She's already a pain in my ass, I don't need her having anymore reason."

He chuckled, and the deep sound vibrated against my neck. It took all the willpower I had not to rub my legs together. Nash lifted his head just enough that our eyes once more found one another, and all I could hear was the pounding of my pulse in my ears as it drowned out the thumping of the loud music.

"I told you I was going to fuck you."

"And I told you I'm not interested."

We were at a stalemate, neither of us pressing forward or yielding, and even though Nash's terrifying aura made me want to slip around him and hide, I knew I couldn't. Nash was a bully, and if he thought I was scared, it would only feed the need to keep pushing me around. I refused to give him that satisfaction.

"You'll change your mind, Princess, and when that day comes, maybe I'll be the one not interested."

Nash stepped around me, and his hand caressed my body, leaving a searing sensation. After the other day, that feeling was committed to my memory. I took a shuddering breath.

Just walk away, don't look back.

Why couldn't he leave me alone? He had a fucking girlfriend, and whether I liked her or not didn't matter. There was no way I was getting between that mess. No, scratch that. Even if they were no longer together, I wanted nothing to do with Nash. He seemed determined to try and break me just because I stood up to him, but I never would. One of us would end up killing the other.

I slipped into the bathroom and took my first deep breath since I arrived at the party. After using the toilet, I washed my hands but couldn't bring myself to head out into the group of partiers.

"What was I thinking," I said to my reflection. I sat down on the edge tub and put my head in my hands. For once, I wanted to feel normal, like a teenager that did normal teenager things, but I wasn't normal and wouldn't know the meaning of the word if it hit me in the face. I was the girl that people avoided inviting to parties or did, but only so they could make fun of me. There wasn't a cool bone in my body. I wasn't gorgeous or popular or really anything else. I was this bore, that didn't drink, smoke or do drugs. I studied hard and was in bed when I was supposed to be. I was genuinely the kid everyone else hated.

Wiping a tear from my cheek, I couldn't help wondering about what Myles said earlier. Could he be telling me the truth? Could he actually be the one person that is interested in me despite all my strangeness? It seemed far fetched.

A hard knock at the door made me jump.

"Just a second."

Standing, I glanced at myself in the mirror before opening the door and stepping out into the attack of the Chaos Creators. That could be a video game. Vicky was leaning against the wall with her girls fanned out beside her, each wearing an identical scowl.

"Wow, you look like a happy bunch."

I stepped away from them as Vicky stuck her head in the bathroom.

"Ew, were you shitting in there?" She yelled, drawing looks from all those standing around.

A couple of kids swung their phones my way as they laughed, and I could feel the heat radiating up my neck.

"No, although it is a natural bodily function. Maybe that's why you're always full of shit. You're backed up," I snarked. "Try some fiber. I've heard that helps."

Vicky's grating voice called out as I walked away.

"Oh yeah, then why do you have shit on the back of your dress. I didn't think that rag could look any worse, but you pulled it off."

Even though I knew better, I looked. As soon as I did, her horde of cackling bitches started laughing. I barely restrained myself from tackling her to the ground. I could clearly see it in my mind.

"Don't think I didn't see you with your hands all over my man. I warned you what would happen if you went anywhere near Nash."

If she saw us, she must have noticed that I stood perfectly still with my hands in fists at my side while he did the touching. She'd have to be blind not to have seen that. That she was coming after me instead of Nash showed her insecurity and said so much about their dynamic. I oddly felt sorry for her.

Vicky was snarling at me like a dog, and I sighed.

"You know I'm not the problem here, but if you need to blame me, come at me. Just make sure you're ready, Vicky. It's in my nature to be nice, but thinking that is a weakness would be a mistake."

I held her glare, then turned around, ignoring whatever she said next. It was obvious she would retaliate. The question was how and when.

The house was way over fire code by now, and people blocked the way back to my corner perch. Grumbling, I made a couple of turns and spotted Blake's back as he leaned against the wall. I walked up behind him and went to tap his shoulder but stopped and held my breath as I heard Lisa speak.

"If you like Ren, why are you flirting with Tiffany," Lisa scolded.

"Whoa! Who said anything about liking her?"

Stupidly my heart rate picked up, and my stomach tightened into a knot. My hand instinctively ran down the front of the dress he'd given me.

"Then what the hell is going on," Lisa asked, the question and I wanted to know the answer as well.

"It's a bet, that's all."

"A bet?"

"Yeah, a bet. Me, Nash, and Myles are trying to see who can fuck her before Christmas. The first one to get her into bed wins."

Pain gripped my chest, and just like that everything made sense —the sweet smiles from Myles, the muffins, the sudden interest in doing better in school. Blake offering to drive me to town and buying me this dress, and of course, Nash's over-the-top advances. I was being played, but not the way I had thought. I was nothing more than the butt of a massive joke. I should have known.

"Well, everything certainly makes sense now," I said. Blake

jumped and spun around, his eyes wide as his face drained of all color. "Don't worry. I'll find my own way home."

"Oh shit, no, Ren, I'm sorry, I...."

I held up my hand to stop Blake from speaking and suddenly wanted to rip the dress he'd given me off my body. How many people knew? Did they all have money down on how quickly the new girl would give in to the Kings? I'd almost fallen for it. I thought Myles liked me even if Blake was just flirty and Nash was an ass.

"Just leave me alone, Blake. I never asked to come here, and certainly didn't ask to be your friend or become the school joke. I don't want to hear anything else you have to say to me."

Pulling out my phone, to call an Uber, as I spun around, I pushed through the groups of drunken people and saw Myles flirting with a girl. When he spotted me, he leaned down and whispered in her ear. Her eyes glanced my way before she laughed.

The last bit of hope I held that Myles felt something for me flew out the window. It seemed like all the eyes in the room were staring at me. My adrenaline spiked, and tears stung my eyes. They'd always been laughing at me. It was my fault for hoping things would be different here. I'd let my guard down just enough and he almost had me fooled.

I slowed to say something and spotted Axel sitting on the couch. If they wanted to play this game, then so could I. Stomping over to Axel, he stared up at me with bloodshot eyes, obviously drunk.

"Whatever I did, I didn't do it," he slurred.

"Are you dating anyone?"

"Um...no. Should I..."

I didn't wait for him to finish and sat down on his lap. Wrapping my arm around his neck, I kissed him hard. He was a terrible, sloppy kisser and tasted like beer, but I didn't care. I'd learned some very important things since I arrived. One of those things was group dynamics. Axel's group and Nash's didn't like each other. No, they hated one another. Why? Who knows, and who cares. What mattered now was sending a loud and very clear message.

"What the fuck?" Myles growled from beside me.

He grabbed my arm and dragged me off Axel's lap.

"What the fuck yourself."

I jerked my arm out of his hold. The anger was spilling over the edges, but there was hurt underneath as I stared at his stupid face. He'd gotten to me, and I was angrier at myself for letting it happen. My chest ached, and even though I knew he was a jerk, the look in his eyes pulled me in. Earlier tonight, I was so sure he was telling the truth. I was so close to giving him another chance.

"Axel is bad news. Ya don't want to be around him," Myles growled, his eyes heated as he stared over me at Axel.

"Fuck you, man." Axel jumped to his feet and yanked on my arm as he pulled me to his side. I really didn't want to be near him. The kiss was to make a point, but I wasn't suddenly team Axel. "If the hot new girl wants me over you, so be it."

Myles stepped into Axel's personal space, the two of them going nose to nose.

"You touch her, and I'll destroy ya," Myles said, his voice so threatening that it made me shiver.

I saw Nash behind Myles and knew this was turning into far more than I intended when I sat down on Axel's lap. Before it could get any more out of hand, I pushed on Myles's chest and forced him to back up.

"You mean he's bad news like you, Nash, and Blake all betting who could have sex with me before Christmas?"

Myles's face turned as white as a ghost as his mouth fell open.

"Got nothing to say to that? No witty comeback about how you haven't been playing me since day one? How you made me the joke of the school?"

I didn't know when the DJ had turned off the music, but the silence of everyone watching was deafening.

"Shit...I...," he said, his voice sounding guilty as his eyes darted away from mine.

Good, he should feel guilty.

"Fuck you, Myles. I stupidly thought you might care about me." My lower lip trembled. "What did I do to make you hate me so much?" Why did people have to be so terrible? I couldn't escape them no matter how hard I tried.

"I don't hate ya," Myles said, and he sounded sad and sincere.

"You're a good actor Myles, really good, but I don't believe you." I shook my head and stepped away from him. I needed to put space between us.

I looked around the room. Vicky was smirking in the corner, and I knew by the glint in her eyes that she had known all this time.

"You can all laugh it up now. Jokes on me. Ha ha ha. The stupid new girl was fooled. Not sure who just won, but congratu-fucking-lations."

I pointed at Myles and then Blake and Nash.

"Unless it's for a project, I don't want any of you to speak to me anymore. I mean it. Stay the fuck away from me. I don't care if I ever see any of your faces again."

Pushing my way through the people blocking the door, I opened it and skidded to a stop as Sheriff Morrison stepped up onto the top step. Oh, this night just keeps getting better. I figured he was here for a noise complaint or maybe for Ivy if he found out she was here.

"Perfect. Just the person I was looking for."

"What?"

I looked at him and the deputy leaning against the cruiser with flashing lights.

"Yeah, what?" Myles said, and I glared up at him.

"I said don't talk to me."

"I wasn't talking to ya. I was talking to the Sheriff."

Myles shrugged, and if I weren't standing in front of the one person who could actually put me in jail, I would've strangled Myles.

I swore in my head.

"What would you like, Sheriff?"

He hooked his thumbs in this belt and smiled.

"I told you, you have a curfew."

"Sure, everyone does during the week, but no one does on weekends, and how did you even know I was off the property?"

He smiled, and it sent a chill down my spine.

"A Sheriff never tells their secrets, but we need to get going. Your curfew is every day of the week, your father's orders. And, this time, I'm taking you back to the academy. Let's go."

This was what I got for going to a party. Big mistake, just like everything else lately. Sometimes I couldn't help wondering if I was the mistake.

Chapter 30

Myles

I watched Sheriff Morrison walk away with Ren and had a bad feeling.

"Whoever said Sacred Heart parties were boring fucking lied. That was amazing," Axel said, and of course, the football team and all their groupies laughed.

Spinning around, I glared at the large group, who quickly fell silent. My reputation for inflicting pain wasn't limited to Wayward. My eyes landed on Blake. He stood with his arms crossed and stared down at his sneakers.

"It was you," I growled. "What the fuck did ya do?"

I knew it had been him. One look at his guilt-ridden face, and I knew. We'd been best friends for over a year now, and I'd seen that expression more than once.

Blake rubbed the back of his neck.

"It was an accident, man. I was talking to Lisa, and Ren was behind me. I—"

Not waiting for him to finish, I jumped at him and took him to the ground, my fists flying.

"Yer an asshole! Ya knew I fuckin' liked her!"

"Fuck you. It was an accident! Get off me."

Blake got a good hit in on my ribs, making me groan as we rolled around on the floor.

People scattered in all directions as we fought. My blood pounded hard, my heart harder still as the anger rode me. The hurt-filled look in her eyes as they shimmered with tears gripped my heart and squeezed it inside my chest. There was no way she was ever going to give me another chance. Her walls slammed into place right before my eyes, and it was all Blake's fault. No, it was Liam's for even suggesting the bet. Where the fuck was he, I would happily punch him in the face too.

Blake's nose was bleeding, but I didn't care and raised my fist to punch him again.

"You shouldn't have agreed to the bet if you liked her," Blake said, and my fist shook.

"Aye, yer right about that. I also shouldn't have trusted ya to be me friend."

Pushing myself up, I stomped for the door that Nash was blocking.

"Are you idiots done?"

I glared at Nash, just as angry with him and his part in all of this.

"Good, then both of you are coming with me. We need to talk," he said.

"I don't want to go anywhere with any of you, especially him."

I pointed my finger at Blake.

"Does it look like I give a fuck?"

Nash crossed his arms over his chest, and my teeth audibly ground together.

"Whatever," I said.

Liam and Theo seemed to materialize out of nowhere and walked down the steps to the crowded parking area. The way people parked, it looked like they were drunk before they arrived. Not one vehicle was lined up in an orderly fashion.

"Myles, you're upfront with me," Nash said as we walked down the road to Nash's pickup truck.

We didn't say anything else until we got inside.

"Blake ruined the bet, so we'll either need a new one or pay everyone their money back," Liam said, and I turned around to glare at him from the front seat.

"Forget the fucking bet. We have a bigger issue," Nash said. He looked at all of us like we were stupid. "Does anyone else find it strange that Ren not only has an early curfew but that Morrison knew she'd be at the party?"

"Maybe Ivy told him," Theo offered.

"Possibly, but we all know that girl avoids her father, and he didn't seem to know his daughter was hiding in the corner."

Nash started the truck and pulled onto the road, following the police car.

"Now that ya mention it, when I was out with Ren the other night, he was in the parking lot like he was waiting for us. I thought maybe he'd stopped in to get takeout, saw Ren, and decided to speak to her."

"He also pulled us over the night the four of us were in town. He ordered us back to the academy and followed, which was strange," Blake said from behind me.

"Exactly. Who the hell is this girl? I looked up her last name, and Davies is nowhere in any major families with any pull. If it weren't for the fact she was in the school, I'd say she didn't have any influential or criminal background at all."

"Then why all the extra hassle," Theo said. "And what's with the early curfew? That's very strange."

"It's almost like her father is scared she'll be seen or maybe attacked," Liam said, and we all fell silent. I really didn't like that thought process. If someone hurt her, I'd kill them with my bare hands.

"I'm not even that important," Nash finally said. "We need to get her to talk and tell us who she really is."

"I don't think she knows," I said, shrugging. "Either that or she's a damn good actress. She didn't even know that the school was for us types. She looked like she was gonna faint when I told her."

Nash tapped his fingers on the top of the steering wheel.

"Maybe we're being played, not the other way around."

"Oh, come on, ya don't really believe that?"

Nash looked over at me.

"It's a possibility. You've had your head up your ass where this chick is concerned from the moment she stepped on school property."

"Fuck ya, Nash. I'm so sick of being accused of shit lately. I might like her, but I'm not an idiot, and I know what I saw. She was shocked and terrified, and no one could pull that acting job off."

"I have to agree with Myles on this one. She doesn't strike me as the type to hold back who she is. If anything, she is too honest, over-sharing, and a whole lot innocent," Theo said, acting as the voice of reason before I punched Nash and forced him to drive off the road. Theo was always the one that analyzed people far deeper than than everyone else. Funny enough, Ren reminded me of Theo or maybe Theo reminded me of Ren. Point was, she had that same quirk to her, and I loved it. Fuck. Fucking Blake. I should've just told her about the bet, I knew shit was going to go bad.

Nash looked in his rearview mirror.

"That's what you believe?"

"Yeah, it is. I think Myles is correct, Ren doesn't know who she is, or if she does, she doesn't understand the significance."

"Hmm." Nash suddenly slammed on the brakes, all of us jerking in our seatbelts. He pointed at the small highway picnic area. "There's the cruiser," he said, cranking the steering wheel to drive into the lot. My adrenaline spiked as I stared at the dark car.

"What the hell is going on?"

I didn't wait for the truck to stop moving before jumping out. Running over to the car, I peered inside, but no one was there, and my fear made it hard to think as all the worst-case scenario's raced around my brain.

"Let go of me, you asshole!"

Ren's angry voice reached me, and I sprinted toward the sound.

"I told you we need to get a few things straight," Morrison said.

"You're hurting me."

I was going to kill him. There was a rest stop building with maps and a bathroom, and I raced around back, the guys following close behind.

"What's going on here," I asked, taking in the scene.

The deputy sat on a picnic table while the Sheriff held Ren's arm. What the hell had they been up to?

Morrison rarely looked shocked, but his eyes went wide as we ran up to Ren and came to a stop. I would've smirked at the annoyed look in Ren's eyes if she hadn't been in such a dangerous situation.

"Go home, boys. This has nothing to do with you," Morrison said as his deputy stood from the picnic table and wandered over with his hand on his gun.

Ren was still pissed off, but she also looked relieved. That was all I needed to see.

"Naw, I don't think so."

"I second that," Nash said. "You planning on shooting all of us? That may be a little hard to explain to our parents." Nash nodded toward the deputy.

"No, of course not. Nick is just protective. We weren't expecting anyone."

"I can see that. What exactly were you doing, Sheriff," Nash asked, and as much of a dick as Nash could be, I loved seeing the fear flicker in Morrison's shit-brown eyes.

"Just having a friendly conversation."

"You could have a friendly conversation in the police car. You didn't need to pull into a deserted rest stop for that. So I'll ask you again, what the fuck are you doing?"

"I need to speak to Ms. Davies...alone."

Nash stepped forward, and my muscles tensed, ready to jump in.

"Yeah, I don't fucking think so. Let go of her arm."

Ren pulled again, and this time Morrison let go, but his hand balled into a fist.

"We need to speak, Ms. Davies," Morrison said. "It's important."

"No, we really don't." She backed up until she was surrounded by the five of us. "I'd rather not speak to you ever again."

"Are you going to force me to arrest you?" Morrison glared at Ren.

"You won't be arresting anyone tonight. Run along, Sheriff, before I decide to make a few calls and see what you're really up to," Nash countered.

Morrison's face turned a violent shade of red.

"Fine, don't say I didn't try to warn you. You'll regret not listening to what I have to say," Sheriff Morrison said and stomped away, his deputy following.

Once we were certain the cops were gone, Nash turned his glare on Ren.

"Well, Princess, you going to tell us what the fuck that was all about?"

"I don't know," Ren said, her eyes still following Morrison.

"I call bullshit." Nash took a step toward Ren, and I stepped in between them.

"Let it go for tonight. We can discuss it more later," I said. Nash rolled his eyes.

"Whatever, let's go."

"I'm not going with you guys. Thanks for the assist, but I'll walk from here."

Ren marched away, and Nash shook his head, mumbling about a fucking pain in his ass. He stomped toward her and lifted a squealing Ren up and over his shoulder.

"Put me down," Ren growled and smacked Nash's ass.

"Not a chance, Princess. We didn't just save your ass from Morrison to have him pick you up again on the side of the road. You're getting in the truck, and that's final." Ren's hand smacked his ass again. "Keep that up, and I'll fuck you in the bed of my truck."

Her hand stopped mid-strike, which I was just as happy about. If anyone was fucking Snowflake, it was me. If I had to fight Nash to make that happen, I would.

"Asshole." She grumbled and crossed her arms instead.

I smirked. That was my Snowflake.

Nash was right. We needed to figure out who she was and why no one had ever heard about her or her family. It was hard to be a ghost in our world, but she seemed to be more of one than just her white hair and seductive silver eyes. She was a mystery that we needed to figure out for her sake and ours.

Chapter 31

NOVEMBER 24 – THURSDAY 2:00 PM

Ren

I ignored the millionth phone call from my father and tried once more to focus on my Spanish assignment. The same sentence ran loops in my brain. I could see the words, but nothing registered. I'd never struggled in a class before, but my mind was scattered.

Despite the brain fog, it was nice to have my room to myself with everyone away for Thanksgiving—another oddity for me. Our Thanksgiving was held in October, so when everyone ran out of class last Friday, saying see you in a week, I needed to ask why.

After the party at Sacred Heart, Vicky had been surprisingly quiet. A quiet Vicky was dangerous. I looked over my shoulder and refused to close my eyes at night more now than when I first arrived.

Ivy and Chantry swore they didn't know about the bet, but they'd also been extra quiet. A weird tension had settled between us for reasons I couldn't fathom. I believed them but felt like they were leaving something out. It could just be me. My ability to read people lately was definitely turned upside down.

No matter how many questions the guys asked, I didn't speak to them the entire ride back to the academy. I also ignored them all week despite being forced to sit beside them in class. Of course, they tried to engage me in conversation and followed me to class like my own personal stalkers, but I didn't say a word.

Myles and Blake were the worst. Blake kept apologizing and insisting that he'd been part of the bet, but he didn't mean what he said to Lisa about not being interested. I didn't get it. The game was over. Give up already. Myles had at least figured out that I didn't want to talk, but that hadn't stopped him from sitting at my table during lunch. It also didn't stop him from following me to another table when I moved until I gave up. He'd also show up at the end of class to walk with me. I was starting to wonder if they were worried about Sheriff Morrison more than they were letting on, and if so, why?

I hated secrets and I was surrounded by them.

I kinda wished I had listened to whatever Morrison wanted to say. It was driving me crazy, and I kept replaying it over and over in my mind. Morrison only told me that I needed to listen to him, I was in danger, and that my father knew best. Of course, I was in some mysterious danger my father had us wrapped up in. My mum's murder was proof of that. The conversation with Myles about the school and who attended was at the forefront of my mind. Every conversation I overheard I wondered if it was code and found myself googling everyone's last name. I was the one turning into a bloody stalker.

Who was my father, really? Just some paper pusher at a large corporation was an obvious lie.

My phone rang again, and I growled as I stared at the caller ID.

"Oh my god, take the hint."

I locked my phone, sending the call to voicemail, only to jump at the sound of someone knocking. Marching for the door, ready to give my father a piece of my mind, I whipped it open. The argument died in my throat as I stared at Dean Henry.

"Ms. Davies, you look like you wanted to say something?"

"No, sorry. I thought you were someone else."

"Your father, perhaps?"

I crossed my arms.

"Does everyone know my personal business?"

His eyebrow rose, and I wanted to cut out my tongue for snapping back at him. So far, I hadn't gotten into any trouble with the Dean, but that could change, which wasn't a path I wanted to travel down.

"If by personal business you mean the car waiting outside to pick you up, then yes."

Dean Henry folded his hands in front of him, and even though his voice was even and calm, it felt like a scolding.

"What do you mean by car?"

"Mr. Davies has been trying to reach you. A car is waiting to take you to Thanksgiving dinner. Before you stomp your feet and refuse to go, the kitchen is closed, and the staff have all gone home to spend time with their families. You will do the same. Unless, of course, you want detention and a mark on your record." My mouth fell open. "You have fifteen minutes, and make sure you dress nicely. Have a good evening Ms. Davies."

I watched Dean Henry walk down the hallway. Well, that was a grade-A bully maneuver if I'd ever seen one, and way more effective than anything Vicky or Nash had pulled so far. Closing the door, I went to my dresser and rifled through the drawers trying to find something that Dean Henry would consider nice. What did that mean? Formal, semi-formal, business casual.

I finally decided to modify the outfit I had purchased with Myles. The skirt and top were a little too sexy for Thanksgiving dinner, but it would be perfect if I wore a black knit sweater.

I dressed as fast as I could and tossed my hair up with a fancy clip before putting on some eyeliner and a pair of shoes I bought to go with the ensemble. There that was as good as it was going to get. I looked good for only fifteen minutes of prep time.

Slipping my arms into my coat, I grabbed my phone and purse and walked out the door. It was strange not to hear any noise. There was no music playing or laughter filling the air. The silence was startling now that I'd grown used to the hustle and bustle of the dorm. It made me feel safe and not so alone—a stark contrast to home, when I had only my thoughts to occupy me as Mum slept.

Pushing out the large doors into the cold November air, my eyes landed on the black car, and it finally dawned on me that I would have to face my father for the first time in weeks.

Taking a deep breath, I opened the back door and found the car empty of other passengers. Figures. He couldn't be bothered to show up himself.

"Ms. Davies," the elderly driver said as he turned around in the front seat.

I slipped into the car and closed the door, happy to be out of the bitter wind.

"Yes, I'm Ms. Davies. You can call me Ren."

"No can-do, Ms. Davies, but you can call me Styles," he said, smiling, and the corners of his eyes crinkled.

"Styles? That's an interesting name."

His warm expression was infectious, and I found myself smiling back.

"My name is Harry Styles. I'm sure you can see the resemblance. I'd hate to be mistaken for the superstar," he said, starting the car.

I laughed as I buckled.

"Yes, I can see how that would happen."

"Any particular music you'd like," Styles asked as we left the academy.

"I'm good with whatever you choose. Thanks, Styles."

He laughed again.

"Harry is fine, Ms. Davies. I'm not sure I'm cool enough to go by Styles these days."

"I think you're plenty cool."

I stared out the window at the landscape passing by. A thin layer of snow coated all the trees. It snowed in the morning only to melt by midday and then fell again at night to start all over. My view of the lake was much clearer now that the leaves were gone. I wondered if it ever froze over and what was on the other side.

"You're not like the other students I've driven around from Wayward," Harry said.

"You mean I'm not an asshole," I blurted out and Harry burst out laughing.

"Something like that. Well, settle in. We have about a half-hour drive."

Harry turned on a local station playing a pop song, and I let myself get lost in the music. I should have been figuring out what the hell to say to my father when I saw him, so I didn't punch him.

It would be nice to have one moment, one meal, that didn't end in all-out war. Was he forgiven? Not even slightly, and I had a million questions. Leading with, what the hell did he do for a crime family that could've gotten Mum killed? Was it really random? Was the robbery and murder why he rushed us out of town? Also, why did I have such a strict curfew? How did he know where I was, and why keep sending the Sheriff after me if he couldn't be trusted? I looked at my phone and narrowed my eyes. Was he tracking me?

I looked over my shoulder, out the back window and half expected to see the Sheriff's car, but no one was there.

The anger began to bubble again, but it was Thanksgiving, and if there was any day of the year to put my snark aside for a few hours, it was today. I pinched the bridge of my nose and tried to think of anything that wasn't violent. I would have a nice meal and then... shove the pumpkin pie in his face if he didn't answer my questions. That felt like a good compromise.

Then another startling thought decided to kick open the door in my mind. What the hell would I do if he was using this to introduce me to a new family? I had no proof of any other family, but it was the only thing I could think of that would keep him away from his only daughter for nearly a month without any contact. Even back home he would wander in a few nights a week to have a conversation, eat a meal and spend the night. It was never to help me with mum, but he'd still make the point to be around. Here... he'd become a ghost.

My palms began to sweat, and my knees bounced with every passing minute.

We pulled off the main highway and drove up to the large gates of what looked like a hotel. There was no way this was my new house. Was it? Leaning forward as Harry pulled up to the guard booth, I stared at the metal gates with a fancy C in the middle, and my stomach flipped as little light switches began to turn on. We were already on the move and through the closing gates with the armed guard when I decided it would be better to take my chances with the elements than eat a meal with my father's boss.

Mr. Collier, aka Count Dick, was not someone that I wanted to see on Thanksgiving. I didn't want to see him ever again, especially not on a holiday where I'm supposed to be thankful for the things I have and the people in my life. My father had been normal until he went to work for Mr. Collier. That was the start of it all going downhill.

If I ever found out that this man was the reason for what happened to my mum...I honestly didn't know what I'd do. I couldn't trust the Sheriff, but there had to be someone that would listen to me.

Harry pulled the car around the massive fountain in the center of the drive, the water had been shut off, and it looked as sad and lonely as I felt.

"Would you like me to open the door for you, Ms. Davies?"

I unclipped my seatbelt and opened the door.

"Thank you, but I'm fine. You don't happen to have an invisibility cloak or something I could borrow?"

"I think you're mistaking me for a different Harry," he said and winked, making me smile. I liked Harry.

"Do you have a card in case I ever need to call for a ride?"

"Are we discussing a situation that may require a car your father doesn't know about?" His bushy brows drew together over his eyes. I blushed. With a flick of his wrist, he produced a business card. "Only for emergencies. I can't be getting fired for no good reason."

I took the card from his hand and quickly tucked it into my coat pocket.

"Thank you, Harry."

"I'll be back later to pick you up."

"Oh?"

I'd foolishly assumed I would sleep in town at my Dad's house since I didn't have to return to school until Monday.

"Yup, I have orders to be here for midnight. Are you sure you're not from a fairytale? You won't turn into a pumpkin in my backseat, will you?"

"I don't think so, but there is always a first time."

"So no Prince Charming?"

I gave him a small smile. "No, definitely none of those in my life. Not sure they exist or if they became extinct long ago."

"They're out there, you wait and see."

I nodded, but wasn't sure I believe him. Pushing open the door I stepped out into the cold air and stared up at the gigantic house. The home was as intimidating as the man I'd met. The doors were black and gold with the same golden *C* raised in the center of the metal. When I looked from one side to the other, the home stretched on for so long that the windows looked like tiny pinpricks by the end. All the lights were on. What a waste of electricity. All this place needed was blood-red roses crawling up the walls to fit any villain in a fantasy book.

"Who the hell needs this much space?"

The front door opened as my foot landed on the top step, and I froze as I stared into Nash's cold blue eyes.

"Happy Thanksgiving, Princess. Welcome to my family home."

Chapter 32

R^{en}

"Oh, hell no."

I turned to march down the stairs, fully prepared to call Harry back. He couldn't have gotten that far.

Nash grabbed my arm before I managed to make it down one step.

"Hold up there, Princess."

If looks could kill, he would've been dead when I looked over my shoulder.

"I should've known you were Count Dick's son. This makes so much sense now."

The corner of Nash's mouth pulled up into the closest thing I'd seen for a genuine smile from him.

"Did you just call my father Count Dick?"

"What if I did?"

He let go of my arm and lifted a shoulder in a shrug.

"I like it, it's fitting, and I wish I'd thought of it."

That made me turn and look him up and down. I hated that he actually looked sexy away from school without his normal glower and threats. His eyes seemed sorta happy as he stared at me. Was he just as miserable as I was? Maybe he lashed out to cope. Nope, I wasn't going there. We had nothing in common. That was dangerous thinking. They'd made a freaking bet about who could sleep with me first. Laughter echoed outside and Nash turned to look at the door and I took the moment to let my eyes travel up and down his body, when wanted to hit myself.

I could still be the better person here.

"You look nice," I said, as he turned to face me and his eyes widened in shock like I'd told him to fuck a duck.

He wore tight black dress pants—that hugged his ass far more than dress pants should— with a black button-down shirt open at the top. A steel grey vest, black shoes, and the thick silver rings he always wore finished his look. His blue eyes seemed brighter today, and I swiftly looked away to stare out at the yard suited for a palace.

"You look beautiful, Princess," he said softly, and despite the cool air, I wanted to fan myself.

"Don't let your girlfriend hear you say that. I already get enough of her, 'Stay away from my man rants'...oh shit...Vicky. Is she here too?" My shoulders slumped.

Nash laughed this time, a rich sound that matched everything surrounding him.

"No, she's with her own family."

"Thank the sweet baby Jesus. I can only take so much of the Chaos Queen."

Nash laughed again, and I found myself smiling. I shouldn't be smiling at him. He'd been a jerk to me from the first day I arrived and then had the nerve to spank me. Can we say humiliated? My smile fell as I glared at him.

"Myles is right, you do have an adorable glare," Nash said, and I stopped glaring like I'd been caught with my hand in the cookie jar, making him chuckle. "So tell me, do you have a nickname for everyone?"

"Almost everyone."

He stepped in dangerously close and dropped his head to my ear like at the party.

"What do you call me, Princess?"

I swallowed down the sudden nervousness conjuring all sorts of images I shouldn't be having for this jerk.

"If I told you, I'd have to kill you."

Nash slowly straightened up, and even though he hadn't touched me, it felt like his hands were caressing my entire body.

"Hey man, what's takin' ya so...long? Snowflake?"

Myles stepped outside, and Nash turned so I could see him. I hadn't spoken a single word to any of them in over a week, but it looked like I would be forced to tonight.

"Ya wore the skirt," he said, and smiled. "Yer fuckin' stunning." Myles eyes locked with mine.

I quickly looked away. I couldn't let myself go there again, and the butterflies had already taken flight.

"Thanks, Myles. Is everyone here?" I asked, wanting to change the topic.

He was wearing the exact opposite of Nash with his steel grey suit and black vest. I was feeling wildly underdressed and simultaneously wearing way too many clothes. I needed to scrub how sexy they looked from my mind, but I knew that was never happening, stupid traitorous thoughts.

"Aye, we're all ere and our parents." He rolled his eyes. "Lawrence coulda left me Da an Devin at home, an I wouldna complained."

"Have you been drinking? Not that it's any of my business, but your accent is really thick tonight."

Myles blushed and stuffed his hands in his pockets.

"Bein' around that lot will make ya want ta do a lot more than drink, but aye, I should cut meself off." He continued to stare at me, and it took more willpower than it should've to ignore him. He'd lied to me, over and over again.

"Come on in. I promise a truce for tonight." Nash held up his hands.

"Fine. Deal."

I stepped past Myles, and it looked like he wanted to say something, but he looked down at the ground instead.

"I'll take your coat," Nash said as I stepped inside the house.

He took it from me like a gentleman as it slipped down my arms. He was acting way too nice, and I stared at his back, wondering what the hell he really wanted from me.

"What do you want, Nash?"

"Nothing. I told you we have a truce, remember?"

My eyes bounced around the overly lavish foyer. This place reeked of Mr. Collier. It screamed intimidating, and I'm better than you with all my money and arrogance. Every corner had something that looked more expensive than the one before.

"You ready for this?"

"I'm not sure how to answer that," I said, and he smirked.

Myles held his elbow out for me like a gentleman, and I stared at it for a long time.

"There be no ulterior motive.

I slowly slid my arm into the crook of his. He laid his other hand on mine. He was warm, and yet a shiver traveled down my back. I turned my head away from his sweet face before my resolve weakened.

Nash pushed open a tall door—that was unnecessary unless you played in the NBA. Beyond the door were two very distinct groups. It reminded me of those family dinners I'd seen on television where the parents were at one table while the kids were at another. Liam, Theo, Blake, a pretty girl around ten with fiery red hair, and a young boy of around six were at one end of the table with three empty seats. At the other end sat Count Dick at the head, and no one else I recognized other than my father.

My father was laughing at something way too loudly, and his face flushed red, clearly drunk. All the goodwill I'd gathered to play nice flew out the fancy door. My father looked my way smiling as he pushed himself up and almost knocked over his chair.

"Ren, my daughter, you look amazing." Everyone awkwardly looked in my direction as I stepped away from Myles. "I knew this was the school for you," he said, trying to walk toward me, but he had to stop and grab a chair to keep from falling over.

Tears stung my eyes as I watched him wobbling, and I refused to take one step in his direction. My family was reduced to an ill mother who was murdered and a drunk for a father. At the moment, I didn't feel like I had anything to be thankful for.

When my father was close enough, he grabbed me in a hard hug that I didn't reciprocate, but he didn't seem to notice or care.

"So stunning," he slurred. All I could smell was the expensive scotch on his breath. I recognized that odor all too well. His eyes were as red as his cheeks. "It feels like forever since I saw you."

"Well, it has been a month, but that shouldn't feel that long for you. You've certainly gone longer."

He snorted a laugh instead of recognizing what I said as an insult. I could feel everyone watching us, and I hated it.

Parents shouldn't embarrass their children like this. Why was I forced to tell him that he was cut off? It wasn't fair, but my instinct was to ask Mr. Collier not to give him any more. I'd been the ref before, ensuring my father didn't stumble into my mum's room drunk. I always got him to sleep it off in a spare room while I stupidly held out hope that the stress of my mum's illness had started him down this road. Obviously, I was wrong, or maybe the ship was so far out and lost at sea that it didn't know how to get back to shore. Either way, I couldn't be his lighthouse or anything else anymore. It was time I looked after myself first.

"Has it really been that long?"

"Yes. I haven't seen the new house yet, or did you forget that as well?"

"I sent you pictures," my father said, touching my shoulders.

I would've pushed his hands away, but I was pretty sure I was the only reason he was upright. I couldn't do that to him, even if he chose to embarrass me.

"I sent pictures...that's all you have to say? I've never seen the new house. That means I don't know where you live. I haven't been able to arrange my room. Does none of this strike you as strange?" His forehead creased as he thought way harder than he should have for the simple question. "Did mum's things arrive? Did my stuff? Do you even know? Do you even care, or are you so busy with whatever Mr. Collier has you doing that you don't have time to care anymore?" I slowly backed away from his touch, disgusted to be called his daughter. "What am I saying? You already proved you're too busy to be a father," I whispered harshly.

"Hush now, it's Thanksgiving. We can talk about that later. We're here to give thanks and eat a grand feast," he said and waved his arm like he was showing off the table and almost hit me.

"I already had my Thanksgiving when mum was alive," I said. "This is not my Thanksgiving and I have nothing to be thankful for." I kept my voice low, but could feel the guys staring. They were so still it was like they'd been turned into statues.

"Well, this year you get two," my father said happily and once more missing the point of the jab. I felt like I'd been stabbed in the stomach.

"Come, Mr. Collier has been excited to have you join us."

"I bet he is," I mumbled under my breath as my eyes flicked toward the man at the end of the table.

He watched us, continuing a conversation with another person pretending he wasn't fully invested in what was said. That man made my skin crawl. There was something evil in his eyes that I couldn't explain without sounding crazy.

"Come say hi, be polite," my father said.

I really didn't want to, but my mum had brought me up with manners, and you didn't walk into someone's house and ignore them. That was rude, and I wouldn't tarnish her memory.

Head held high, I walked down to the far end of the ridiculously large dining area, and Lawrence smiled as he stood. If he thought I was going to hug him, he had another thing coming. Instead, he held out his hand like last time. I didn't know who this man was or what crime he was involved with, but he fit the profile of every mob boss in my mind.

Reluctantly, I placed my hand in his as he lifted it to his mouth to kiss. I tugged on my hand as soon as his lips left my skin, but he held tight and turned my hand over to look at my finger.

"It healed nicely, not even a scar," Lawrence said, his voice soft, and a shiver raced down my spine.

"It was a small prick. They don't tend to leave a lasting impression."

I tugged on my hand, and this time, he let go. I knew where Nash got that look from now. It was more intimidating on his father.

A pretty brunette sitting two chairs down snickered and then covered it up by coughing. The man next to her, whom I assumed was her husband, patted her back.

My father cleared his throat when Mr. Collier continued to stare at me like we were playing a game of chicken.

"Let me introduce you to everyone." My father held out his hand to the couple closest to us. "This is Bridget and Emmet Hicks and their eldest daughter Nora." I nodded in greeting. "Beside Nora is Owen McCoy and his eldest son Devin."

Not sure why, but I instantly disliked Owen and Devin. They didn't share the same comedic energy or warmth that Myles had.

Jerk or not, he wasn't cold like these two, who reminded me of Lawrence.

"Across the table, you have Ella and Ethan O'Brien. You already know all the boys from school, but the young lady at the end is Sienna Hicks, and the youngest at the table is Filip McCoy," my father said, each person raising their hand in greeting.

"My name is Lip," Myles's little brother said, his lower lip pushed out in a pout, making me smile.

"Nice to meet all of you," I said, walking the plank back to my end of the table.

It was too quiet, and I hated the click of my shoes on the fancy floor as all the guys continued to stare at me. There was only one spot left between Nash and Myles, and they stood and pulled my chair out together. I looked from one to the other.

"Are you two okay?"

"Just trying to be gentlemanly, my father insists that we treat our guests well," Nash said, and if I hadn't been standing so close, I would've missed the subtle eye roll.

Stepping around Myles to sit, the adults began talking, and the room was once more filled with noise. They adjusted my chair, and I waited until they sat down to speak.

"I really hope the two of you don't do this all night. It'll get weird quick."

"No promises, Snowflake," Myles whispered.

Ignoring him, I smiled at the two youngest across the table.

"Hi, Sienna," I said.

"You look extremely handsome in your suit, Lip."

He lost the pout and sat a little straighter.

"I'm a ladies' man. That's what Mrs. O'Brien says." Lip hooked his thumbs into his vest.

"I can see that," I said, smiling. It was easy to tell he was related to Myles. He had a slightly darker eye color but the same smile and warmth.

"I think ya have a few more years before ya have that label," Myles said to his brother, who stuck out his tongue.

"How would you know? She never says that to you," Lip said, and Myles grumbled as he took a sip of water.

"I love your hair." Sienna's eyes were filled with excitement as she stared at me. "I'd love to dye mine. I hate these plain red curls, but my mom says I'm too young. How did you get it so white and silver? It's so cool."

I glanced at the guys, who were very quiet as they stared at me. Even Theo, who never seemed interested in anything, was staring at me with a piece of bread halfway to his mouth.

Grabbing my water, I took a mouthful of the cool icy liquid, hoping to wet my parched throat.

"Um...well. It wasn't by choice." Sienna's lips pinched together as her eyes narrowed in confusion. "It's a condition called Marie Antoinette Syndrome, an autoimmune disorder that can be triggered by extreme amounts of stress."

"What's autoilloon," Lip asked, making me smile.

How did you describe this?

Theo came to the rescue.

"You know when you cut yourself, and the cut heals?" Lip nodded. "With some autoimmune diseases, your body is too eager to fix what's wrong and ends up hurting you more," Theo explained.

"Like you attack yourself?"

"Yes, exactly like that," I said. I could still see the confusion in his young face.

"Oh," Sienna said. "How much stress?"

"Enough with the questions, Sienna," Liam said, shutting down his younger sister.

"What? I'm curious?"

Liam opened his mouth to answer, but I spoke first.

"It's fine, Liam, but thank you."

"Alright," he said.

Other than the very awkward truck ride home from the party, I'd never spoken to Liam. He seemed laid back like he didn't have a care in the world, or at least he gave that impression.

"It started after my mum got sick. It felt like it turned white overnight, but it took months. I tried to dye it back to my normal hair color for a while, but eventually, I decided that if people wanted to make fun of me, they could, and I didn't care. I am who I am."

"Did...." Sienna looked up the table at my father, and I knew what she was wondering without asking.

"My mum didn't make it," I said but left off how she passed away. This was already a sad topic without adding murder to it.

"I'm really sorry." Sienna's eyes dropped to the table, her shoulders rounding. "I can't imagine losing my mom."

"It's alright, don't feel bad asking. I love that you like my hair. Most people find it spooky."

"I don't," Myles blurted. "I think it's beautiful."

He shoved a piece of bun in his mouth like he was trying to shut himself up.

It drove me crazy that my attraction to him was still just as strong even after everything. It was annoying, and I wished there was a switch that would allow me to shut the feelings off. As our eyes met, my heart sped up, and I had to force myself to look away from his tempting amber stare.

"Everyone, may I have your attention, please." Lawrence stood at the head of the table and held up his glass of wine. "The food is about to be served, but I wanted to make a toast. At this time of year, we take account of our blessings and have more to be thankful for this year than ever. Our businesses are doing well, and we have a new family added to the fold. Welcome, Neal and Ren Davies."

That was the worst toast I'd ever heard. What happened to health, love, and being happy to share this time with those that mean the most?

I lifted my glass of water to toast, but Lawrence caught my eye and grabbed a bottle of wine off the table as he walked toward me. I didn't like the look of this. Sure enough, he leaned over me, his chest pressing into my shoulder, forcing me to move away as he grabbed the empty wine glass. He held both in front of my face as he poured.

I sucked in a surprised breath as some wine splashed out of the glass and landed on my bare leg.

"Sorry about that."

Lawrence sat the wine glass down and grabbed my napkin. Before I could react, he was wiping at the spill on my leg, his finger running along the inside of my thigh. I jerked my leg away from his touch and ended up leaning into Nash.

Myles was glaring at Lawrence, his eyes murderous as he turned the knife in his hand like he planned on using it. For just a moment, I could picture him shoving the knife in Lawrence's eye and continuing to eat as if nothing had happened.

"I can do that, thanks," I said, grabbing the napkin in his hand. There was a distinct shift in the energy around us as he glared at me and held on to the material.

I felt Nash stand up behind me.

"I'll take the wine and fill everyone else's glasses. The servers are coming in with the food."

He held out his hand, and Lawrence's lips twitched like he was holding himself back from saying something.

The dark gleam in his eyes told me I never wanted to find myself alone with him. The fact that it was Nash standing up to defend me instead of my father pissed me off. If he could sit there with all these people and let this man openly grope his daughter, he was not the father I wanted.

Lawrence's mouth slowly turned up in the fakest smile I'd ever seen. It never reached his eyes, and all I saw was a maliciousness that promised pain.

Myles held his knife so hard that his knuckles turned white as he stared at Lawrence. I caught his eye and, not even sure why, subtly shook my head no. The room felt like a helium balloon filling, just waiting for a spark to make it explode.

"Yes, of course. It is Thanksgiving, after all. Servers, you may bring in the dishes," Lawrence growled and sauntered away.

The tension balloon popped, and I sucked in a deep breath. My eyes found Myles, but he was looking up at Nash, who was still standing behind me. It was as if Myles was willing Nash to sit down with his eyes, and my respect for Nash grew a tiny bit. I thought dealing with my father was an issue, but I could honestly say that I would never want to call that man my flesh and blood. I was positive that the only thing comparable to being related to him was walking hand in hand with Satan through the bowels of hell.

If the last few minutes were any indication of what was to come, then the night would not get any better.

Chapter 33

Ren

I shook my head in total disbelief at Theo.

"Are you kidding me? This is not even a debate. A quokka is far cuter than a bilby, I don't know how you can even say that. They look like someone got drunk and mushed a rat and a rabbit together into one body."

Theo laughed.

"Fine, I'll give you that one, but nothing beats the axolotl. They always look like they're smiling and waddle when they run underwater," Theo argued.

I screwed up my face, thinking about what he said and picturing them in my head.

"Okay, they're pretty cute, but not the cutest. I'm still ahead by one point."

Theo leaned his arms on the table, his stare intense.

"Fine..." One of his eyebrows arched above his glasses. This was the first time I'd seen him with glasses on, but I had to admit they looked sexy. "The fennec fox," he said, then sat back and smiled.

My mind whirred as the image of the adorable fox popped into my head. He had a point. Their little faces and great big ears were so darn cute. And that was before they curled into a tiny ball and peeked over their bushy tails. It was one of my favorite slide show screensaver images, but I couldn't let Theo win.

"Will this never end?" Blake complained. "I think my ears are starting to bleed."

"Please...you're just jealous that you already lost and are no longer in the debates," Sienna snarked, making us laugh as Blake glared at Liam's sister.

"I can't believe this is even debatable," Nash said. "After the 'Best way to crush grapes for wine' and 'Is grave robbing actually archaeology' debate, I thought I'd seen it all."

"I'm not," Liam chimed in. "I watched Theo debate 'Why it is that deliveries on a ship are called cargo, but deliveries in a car are called a shipment,' which was then replaced by 'Why it is that a driveway is where cars are parked, but a parkway is where cars are driven,' try sitting through that insanity for two hours," Liam said, making Sienna and Lip giggle.

"It's official, you two are just fu—" Nash glanced at Lip and Sienna. "Weird," he finished before stuffing the last of his pumpkin pie into his mouth.

"I'm finding this kinda hot," Myles said from beside me, and even though I'd managed to ignore him most of the evening, I stupidly looked at him now.

He was resting his head on his hand while his elbow was on the table as he stared at me. It was totally creepy and yet completely adorable. I looked away before he could lure me in with those eyes.

"Okay, enough stalling, or I win this round," Theo said.

I tapped my chin and then smiled wide.

"House hippos."

"What?"

"That's the cutest thing. I'm so winning with that one." I sat back and mimicked his pose.

"What is a house hippo?" Theo removed his glasses and rubbed at his eyes. "I've never heard of such a thing. It has to be made up."

"It must be because you're not from Canada. We know all about them. In fact, they are very popular," I said and managed to keep a straight face.

"A house hippo," Lip asked, his eyes wide. "What is that? It sounds so cool."

Holding my hand out, I mimicked the size of the small hippos featured in commercials back home.

"They're no bigger than this," I said, my voice going low like this was a coveted secret. "But they still look like a normal hippo."

"Really?"

I nodded.

"Really, and they're super smart and will hide in cupboards and steal your food like a pesky mouse. They're very aloof, but if you can stay awake late at night and pay attention, you'll see their shadows on the wall as they sneak around."

Lip's mouth fell open as he leaned in close, and even though Sienna was trying to act uninterested, she had also gotten closer.

"Did you have one," Lip asked.

"We all have them back home. They help keep your house safe and will make a strange call that will wake you up right out of a dead sleep if someone dangerous breaks into your home," I said. Cue the aching pit in my stomach at the mention of people breaking into homes.

My father chose that moment to once more laugh way too loud

at something and grab at the table to keep from falling off his chair. The constant throbbing pain in my chest bloomed like a fresh wound all over again.

"Ren?"

At the sound of my name, my head snapped up to look at Lip.

"I'm sorry, what?"

"Can I have a house hippo?" His voice was soft, his eyes hopeful as he stared at me.

"They're hard to come by here, but I'll see what I can do."

"Yes!" He squealed, drawing the attention of the adults at the other end of the table.

Lawrence stood, and I immediately went on guard as he marched closer. My mother always told me to trust my instincts, that if I learned to listen, they would never steer me wrong, and Count Dick was setting off all the alarms. He didn't have to say a word for me to know he was up to no good.

He didn't touch me like I expected, instead laying his hand on Nash's shoulder.

"Son, can I speak to you for a moment." His voice was so low that with all the other noise in the room, I barely heard him, yet I still felt the weight of his words like concrete boots.

"Yes, of course. I'll be back," Nash said and stood, but he was easy to tell that he was tense.

Even an unobservant person could see that his shoulders were tight and his eyes were guarded, but the twitching muscle in his jaw really gave it away.

There was a knock on the table, and I saw Blake and Theo's mum, Ella, signing with her hands to her sons. I'd learned earlier that Ella was born with hearing but lost it due to a severe illness at Lip's age. What was fascinating was that every one of the guys knew how to speak to her in ASL. I loved that. Liam, Nash, and Myles didn't have to learn, but they wanted to. Nash said it was never a question of if, and now I wanted to learn too.

Myles was much slower with his movements as he joined in, and there was something endearing about his struggling to keep up.

I watched Ella and Theo and knew it was an argument by the look on their faces.

I had a feeling what it was about even though I couldn't understand what they said. I was having the same concern. Count Dick was up to no good.

"If you'll excuse me, I need to use the little girls' room," I said, but everyone seemed focused on the silent conversation.

Sneaking out into the hall, I went on the hunt. Why I was doing this, I didn't know. It wasn't like Nash had been nice to me. He'd been a jerk from the moment we met, and that was before he decided to spank me like I was some spoiled child.

Yet, my feet never hesitated as I slipped from one hallway to the next, trying to locate Nash and Lawrence. What the hell I would do when I found them was a whole other story. I didn't have a plan. I just knew I needed to find him and stop whatever Lawrence was going to do.

This place was impossibly large, and I was ready to give up and find my way back when the sound of muffled voices ahead caught my attention. Being small had one advantage, I was light on my feet. I quickly marched for the sliver of light from a cracked door, casting a shadow on the hallway floor.

"What did I tell you would happen if you ever embarrassed me in front of the rest of the families again?" Lawrence growled.

"And here I thought I was saving you from embarrassing yourself," Nash said, and I bit my lip to keep from laughing.

"This is my home, and I can do what I want inside these walls," Lawrence said. That statement was ominous, and a shiver raced down my spine as he spoke again. "You need to be punished."

"I'm shocked, especially when you were the one making a fool of yourself in front of our guest's father. I doubt Mr. Davies enjoyed you feeling his daughter up any more than Ren did, or was assaulting a minor in front of everyone what you were going for?"

"She is legal age," Lawrence said, and I covered my mouth as my food wanted to reappear.

"So that really was your plan? See if you could get the new girl to fuck the rich old man? Sounds cliché to me, even for you," Nash's tone was sarcastic as hell, like he was baiting his father. I hated that he was making me root for him. He'd been as big of a jerk to me as his father.

I didn't have to be in the room to feel the simmering hostility turn into something far deadlier.

"I thought you were learning respect, but I see now that was all an act. You will learn your place son," Lawrence growled.

Without even thinking about the consequences, I pulled out my phone and opened it to a random screen so it was glowing in my palm as I pushed open the door.

"Oh, thank god," I said.

I knew that Lawrence had been ready to hit Nash, but it didn't look like Nash was going to fight back as he stood with his hands at his sides and his head held high. Lawrence stepped back and smiled at me as Nash looked over his shoulder.

"I'm so sorry. I didn't mean to interrupt your meeting, but this house is insanely large, I mean it's beautiful, but I got myself all turned around." I held up my phone. "I was just about to call for help. How embarrassing would that be?" I smiled, even though I wanted to punch Lawrence.

"Were you trying to get back to the dining hall," Nash asked.

I pretended to be embarrassed and looked down at the ground, knowing that Lawrence would love the act. I didn't really care if he liked me, but I needed to pull off the perfect damsel.

"Actually, Nash, would you show me to the washroom first?"

Nash looked back to his father, and the man's eyes shifted from his son to me. Lawrence sighed, and I knew I'd stopped whatever was about to happen here, but for how long was hard to say.

"We always like to accommodate our guests. I'd be happy to take you," Lawrence said, smiling.

"Thanks for the kind offer," I said, my stomach churning danger-ously with the thought. "I've been trying to pin Nash down to talk to him about our upcoming biology assignment. He's been very busy, and it's due next week, so this will be the perfect time for me to get a few things straight."

Nash's eyes narrowed at me, but he didn't blow my cover or call out the blatant lie.

"Then yes, by all means, steal away. I'm thrilled that a top acad-emic mind like yourself is ensuring my son stays on the right path. I keep telling him that if he plans to take over the family business, he needs to be more dedicated to his studies."

There was no way around wondering what exactly the family business entailed. You didn't own a house like this without having a ton of money, and I wouldn't be surprised to find out that it came from the blood of others. I hadn't been able to stop thinking about my conversation with Myles. Who were these people, and how did my father become involved with them?

"I've made it my personal mission to make sure he has top grades even if it is selfishly because the project also has my name on it," I said and the earlier creepy smile Lawrence gave me returned. Goose-bumps rose on my body and I had to force myself not to rub at them.

"Yes, you've been very helpful and we wouldn't want my grades to slip now," Nash said and made a show of smiling wide as he held out his hand to lead the way, but his eyes were flat and cold as he looked at me. I swallowed hard as I realized my heart had been battering the inside of my chest. At least I could thank Mr. Chicotelli and his drama classes back home for something. Not allowing my fear to control me when the lights were brightest was a skill set all on its own. A superstar I was not, but by the look on Lawrence's face, I'd convinced him, and that was all that mattered.

Nash led me the opposite way that I'd arrived at the office, and we turned the corner at the far end of the hallway. Glancing up at him, I wanted to ask what the hell that had been about, what his father did for a living, and how he was involved, but the words wouldn't come. There was simply no good way to ask if you were the son of a mob boss and if he would kill me if I found out the truth.

Instead of slowing, my heart pounded faster as we walked along the empty, quiet halls. Looking over my shoulder, I wondered if this had been a good idea. Now that I was alone with Nash, the tension I usually felt around him was back and buzzed under my skin. A small scream ripped from my mouth as Nash snatched my arm like a snake snatching it's prey and hauled me inside an open door. I would've fallen if he didn't have such a strong hold on my arm.

The door closed, and we plunged into complete darkness. My eyes searched for him even though I knew he was right in front of me. As panic set in, I pushed at his chest and grabbed for the door blindly.

Nash grabbed my arms and spun me around as he slammed my back against the wall. One of his large hands clamped over my mouth, and I bit back the whimper of terror forming. Why had I thought Nash was any different than his father? That he needed me like I was some savior? It was stupid, and I'd put myself in the predator's clutches.

I wanted to scream hysterically and draw attention, but I knew how far away we were from everyone else. I hadn't heard a single noise the entire walk, and my legs trembled.

A light turned on, and I stared at Nash's hand as he removed it from the light switch.

"Are you going to be a good girl and not scream if I remove my hand?" I nodded as much as I could. "Good."

His hand slowly slid across my mouth, his thumb lingering on my bottom lip as his blue eyes penetrated my soul. My heart went from galloping to stopping dead. The soft light accentuated the scar that ran down his cheek and was the only imperfection in his otherwise flawlessness. I didn't know why, but I wanted to run my finger along it. I now knew without asking that it came from his father. I would've put money on it. My scars weren't on display, but they marred me just the same.

"Stop looking at me like that," Nash snarled and slammed his hand on the wall beside my head. I jumped at the loud bang.

"Like what?" I said, my voice wavering as I tried hard not to sound as terrified as I was.

"Forget it. Just tell me who the hell are you, Davies." Nash said, but I didn't know how to answer his question. He knew who I was.

"What do you want me to say? My name is Kayleigh Ren Davies. I'm seventeen and from Alberta, Canada. I don't know what else you want to know."

He shook his head. "What about your family?"

"What about them?"

Nash growled as he wrapped his hand around my throat. Pressing myself back into the wall, I hid my fear, but he didn't squeeze. His fingers were soft on my skin, and a shiver raced down my back.

"I want the truth, Princess. Who are you? What connections does your family have? What is your father holding over my father's head?"

Again I didn't know how to answer him. I was as confused about this new world I'd been dumped into as he was that I was here.

"All I know is that my father works for yours. I swear to you. I don't know what else you want me to say."

"Do I need to spank you again, Princess? As much fun as I had the first time, I'm not sure now is the best time for round two, no matter how much I'd enjoy watching this short skirt of yours riding up over your ass," he said, and his voice deepened with the suggestion. He licked his bottom lip and I didn't know you could be terrified out of your mind and still think someone was sexy, but Nash managed to make me feel exactly that.

He licked his lip, his eyes breaking the staring contest, only to look down at my chest. My fast breathing made it rise and fall faster, and his heated stare wasn't helping.

"You'll never do that to me again," I said, and I wanted to smack myself.

It was like I couldn't help pushing his buttons. Maybe I wanted to. I didn't know anymore.

"You can wipe that scowl off your face. I know you liked it, Princess."

He leaned in closer, and I looked away from him when I thought he would try to kiss me. Instead, his lips brushed my ear as he softly chuckled. I shivered.

"I heard you, remember?" He whispered low, and a spark of desire churning in my gut turned my blood into scalding lava. It was too hot, and my hands curled into fists as I forced myself not to react. "I felt you wiggle under my touch. I know you wanted me to slip my fingers inside and make you come on my lap just like that with your ass in the air. You're not such a good girl under this perfect persona, are you, Princess?"

"I don't know what you're talking about. I didn't want you to touch me."

"Keep lying to yourself, Princess, but I know better, and one day I will break your resistance. I always keep my promises, and I did promise to fuck you, didn't I?"

"We'll have to agree to disagree, because that's never happening," I said. His lips touched my ear and my knees shook.

"Liar," he whispered, he slowly pushed his body away from mine.

Disappointment washed through me, which was insane. The corner of Nash's lip pulled up like he was snarling.

"I'll ask you one last time, Princess. Who are you really?"

He released my throat, only to trace a line down my side until his hand rested on my hip. Just like the other times he'd touched me it felt like his hand was searing me through my clothing.

"I already told you."

No one had ever touched me as intimately as Nash. He acted like he had the right, and it pissed me off, but under the anger was the weight of his words. I hadn't completely hated him spanking me. Disgusted with myself, I tried to brush his hand off, but it had the opposite effect, and he tightened his hold.

"Can we go now?"

I pushed at him again, and he gripped my other hip so I was more trapped than I was a moment before.

"Keep struggling and see what happens, Princess," Nash said. His eyes grew darker and unbelievably sexy with his thick lashes. "You have an affect on me." He glanced down and even though I ordered myself not to look my eyes didn't behave. Sure enough the dress pants were tented with an obvious hard-on and I swallowed the lump in my throat. "On second thought, you should struggle, I could use the fun."

I crossed my arms over my chest.

"Whatever." Sighing, I held perfectly still. I didn't doubt him or what he threatened and I was stuck until he opened the stupid door and gave a little shrug. "I don't know what you want me to say Nash. Also, we both know that whatever was going on between you and your father was no meeting," I said, changing topics from the sexually charged one.

Nash's hands tightened a little more on my hips as his eyes searched my face like he was scanning me.

"If you think you know so much, and what you say is true, then why interfere? We're not exactly friends."

"Because I got the feeling you may need me to." His eyes narrowed into such thin slits that I couldn't see the blue. "And I don't like bullies."

My eyebrow raised as I pointedly looked at his hands digging into my hips, and to my surprise, his grip loosened.

"Look, I don't need to be anyone special to know that your father is a grade-A asshole. So be angry at me if you want, but I would've done the same for anyone else. It's a character flaw of mine," I said.

Nash let go and pushed himself away from me, but I could still feel the impression of his fingers and knew that I would for a very long time.

"That is a very dangerous character flaw, Princess. Doing shit like that will only get you killed, and I don't need you saving me. Understand?"

"A simple thank you would've sufficed," I said, tempted to smack him. My hand twitched with the thought, and I shivered, wondering what would happen if I did.

We felt like competing planets or the sun and moon trying to occupy the same space. As long as we followed our orbital track, all was fine, but the moment we were set on a collision course, bad things were bound to happen.

"I have nothing to thank you for. Thanks to you, it will only be worse when everyone is gone and no one is here to save me but me."

My arms fell to my side, my mind trying to picture what he meant.

"Just because you want to be the hero doesn't always make you the hero in the story, Princess." Our eyes remained locked as he reached out and opened the door. He stepped out into the hall and then looked at me. "Are you coming, or do you plan on wandering the halls for the rest of the night?"

Nibbling on my lip with the sudden stupid worry about what Lawrence would do to Nash later, I stepped out to join him. Nash didn't say anything else, but there was a change in him for the rest of the night. The glimpse of the decent and funny guy that lived under the asshole exterior was completely gone. With one short meeting, his father had wiped it away.

It was as if he'd shed that persona and slipped into a suit of armor, and that worried me more than anything else. Could two vastly different people live in the same skin without one being swallowed by the other? And if that happened, I had a feeling I knew which personality would prevail.

Chapter 34

DECEMBER 2 – FRIDAY 9:38 PM

N **ash**

I wiped the latest round of snowflakes off my face. It was steadily coming down, but I didn't feel the cold. Not anymore. It was hard for me to feel anything other than focused determination. The last of the other students inside the study hall wandered out, and I watched them from my hidden perch behind the bushes.

I quickly texted the guys to meet me and got a bunch of question marks back, but I knew they would come. Every stalker movie I'd ever watched came to mind as I stared through the tall window at the warm glow of the study hall that doubled as our library. I couldn't see Ren, but I knew she was in there. Her books were still strewn all over the table like she was trying to recreate a scene from Harry Potter. All she needed was a black cat to sit on the desk and a moving staircase in the background to complete the picture.

Who chose to willing study this late on a Friday night? A mocking voice in my mind asked if I was much better standing in a leafless bush while I watched Ren work. That little voice could fuck off. What I was doing had a purpose. What she was doing was just insanity. Live a little for fucksake.

She wandered out of one of the aisles, her nose dutifully buried in the book, her face intense as she read. I'd never met someone like her, and I wasn't sure I liked it. She was practically unflappable and pushed back at me as hard as I did her. The bigger issue was that I hadn't found any information that led me to believe we could bribe or intimidate her. I mean I could always threaten to kill her, but I preferred not to go that route, at least not yet.

Worse, I still hadn't found anything on her or her last name. Every search ended up at a dead end. She was a ghost, a no one, just a person that poofed out of thin air and plopped into the center of my school like magic. That screamed one thing to me—witness protection.

No matter. I would find out Ren's secret, even if it meant prying it out of her the hard way.

"Nash?" Liam was the first to arrive.

"Here."

I stepped out from behind the bush and made my way down the path to greet Liam.

"What the hell are we doing?"

"We'll wait until the others have arrived," I said, my breath rising like a steady stream of smoke. "Did you set our little moles scurrying and entice them with the cheese I promised them?"

"I'm not sure moles eat cheese, but yes," Liam said, shaking his head. "I'm hanging around Theo too fucking much."

"Stop fucking him, and that will happen pretty quickly." I shrugged.

"You wouldn't say that if you had gotten a blow job from him, the things he can do with his tongue...."

"Okay, enough. You're my bros, but I don't need to know the deets on what you do behind closed doors," I said.

"Who said the doors are closed?" Liam smiled as I stared at him.

"I have nothing to say to that. Here they come." I nodded toward the pathway from the front entrance of the dorms.

Blake and Myles wandered up, looking cold as they shivered with their hands buried inside their hoodie pockets.

"Where's Theo," Myles asked as we converged.

"He had something else to attend to tonight, but we don't need him for this." I pulled out the handful of black ski masks from inside my jacket.

"What exactly are we doing," Blake asked as I handed out the masks.

"Ren is the only one left in there, and we're going to pay her a visit," I said.

"Oh, hell no, count me out." Myles threw his mask at me, and I glared at him. "And don't be giving me yer evil eye. I just got Ren to start talking to me again."

"I'm not sure you can count, 'Leave me alone, Myles,' as speaking," Blake said, earning himself a dark glare from Myles.

I tossed the mask at him again, "I don't care if you got her to get down on all fours and bray like a donkey as you fucked her. You're doing this. It's an order."

"Are ya purposely trying to fuck up my chances with her forever," Myles asked, his hands in fists as he stepped into my personal space.

"Get out of my face Myles or are you challenging my authority as your King?"

Right on cue, the lights I'd paid to have shut off clicked, and the normally bright pathway leading from the study hall switched off. In five minutes, so would the ones inside. I stood my ground with Myles, our noses almost touching as we stared at one another.

"No good will come of doing this, Nash," he said. "She is not like us. She doesn't know shit about shit."

"I have to agree with Myles on this one. What are we hoping to accomplish by scaring the shit out of her? That is your plan, right? To scare her into talking," Liam said, pulling his mask into place.

"We need answers. You all saw my father at Thanksgiving. When have you ever known him to bring someone into the inner circle, let alone call them family and then let them act like that at his table? Ren talked back to him, and her father was loaded before the first course was served." Myles stepped back and shook his head. "Myles, I'm telling you, she knows something."

"Naw, I don't think she does. I've talked to her more than any of ya have, and there is no way she's lyin'," he argued, holding his arm out to the main building. "I've interrogated enough people to know the signs."

"She could be a really good actress or you're too busy thinking with your cock to see her for what she is." Myles glared, but I didn't give a flying monkey's uncle of a fuck. "I told you what she did in the office with my father. He was completely convinced and didn't hit me that night when he called me in later. You also can't tell me that at seventeen, she hasn't seen anything to do with the business. We all saw shit by the time we were old enough to walk. The girls are usually more protected, but they still know."

"Maybe yer Da knows, can't ya ask him? I know he's a fucking dick, but can't ya just say ya have a concern and see how he reacts?" He put his hands on his hips.

"Of course he knows, the point is he obviously doesn't plan on telling me and that means we can use whatever that knowledge is. We don't have time to argue over this. Here comes Cory and Ivan." I lowered my voice so the two guys approaching wouldn't hear me. "We need to know why my father is acting strange about her and her father. They could be used, or they could be a threat."

"And I'm tellin' ya she doesn't know anything. This is not going to get us anywhere," Myles argued quietly.

I knew Myles liked her, but I'd assumed it was an infatuation that would come and go. Now I wasn't so sure. He'd never argued over a direct order before.

"Fear has a funny way of bringing out the truth, and since I'm not about to drag her out to the cabin and put one between her eyes without a scrap of proof, we need to get it out of her somehow. You're with me, Myles, or you're out, and I mean all the way out."

"Yer a bastard Nash, a right fuckin' bastard." Myles pulled the mask on, cursing me under his breath the entire time.

"Yeah, I am, but it's also why I'm the next King. I'll do what needs to be done, no matter what."

"Here," I said, tossing Ivan and Cory masks as they stepped up to the group. "Only Ivan and Cory will speak since she doesn't know them and will recognize our voices. They've already been instructed on what to ask. You two good?"

"I'm fine," Ivan said, his eyes filled with excitement.

"I'm always down for whatever," Cory answered, pulling the mask into place.

"Good. The lights are going to shut off any second. When that happens, we run in and fan out at the front of the study area. I'll lock the door so she can't get out. Now, the lights will only be off for a minute before the backup generator turns on several emergency lights. Let's scare that info out of her. We need her to think that she either tells us or dies."

The guys looked at one another, and I could tell they were still uncertain, especially when I pulled my knife.

"I'm not going to stab her. It's only to scare her into thinking I will," I said, and they noticeably relaxed. "She may hold the key to my father's secrets and how to take the regime down. Is that not worth it?"

They reluctantly nodded, and I knew they would do it, but it burned my ass worse than poison ivy that they hesitated. Ren Davies was not coming between me and my guys. I'd make sure of that.

Stepping up to the door, I peered through the glass panel and saw Ren sitting at a table, her fingers like little worker bees on her keyboard. The old clock on the wall showed the second-hand closing in on the twelve.

I looked over my shoulder at Ivan and Cory. "Don't fucking touch her," I said. I wasn't even sure why I gave a fuck if they did, but I didn't like the idea of them pawing at her. The why didn't matter. I waited until they nodded.

I counted the seconds with the clock, and with a click and a hum, the power shutdown, and the entire building went dark. Yanking open the door, the guys tapped me as they passed to let me know they were through, and I flicked the bolt at the top of the door, which I knew she wouldn't be able to reach.

"Hello," Ren said, her voice shaking slightly. "Who's there," she asked, but none of us said anything. I trusted that the guys would be in position. "There is security all over this property," she said.

Yes, and I paid them all to stay away from this building and ignore anything happening inside, but I didn't tell her that. There was a loud whirring sound as the generators kicked in, and two lights highlighting the only two exits in the place turned on.

Ren shot to her feet as she stared at us. "Who the hell are you, and what do you want?" I didn't say anything but spun the knife in my hand. "I asked you a question," she said and once more shocked me with the ferocity in her tone. I had to give her marks for bravery.

"We have seen you around school." Ivan put on a thick Russian accent. He was one of my best moles and deeply embedded, but still just as loyal as the day I recruited him.

Ren's eyes flicked to my spinning blade. "Okay?"

"I've looked into you, Kayleigh Davies, and couldn't find anything." Ivan stepped forward and crossed his arms to show off a set of brass knuckles.

"Why is everyone so concerned with my family name," Ren asked.

"Someone else was asking about you? Who was it," Ivan asked, and I smirked under the mask.

"It doesn't matter. The point is I'm no one special. My father works for the Collier family, and that's all I know."

"I think you know more than you're saying." Ivan took another step, and Ren's body stiffened. "There is a group in this school that we don't like very much, and you could be the one to solve all our problems."

"I don't understand. I just want to do my schoolwork, get good grades and then get the hell out of this place and leave all of it behind," Ren said.

Did she not understand that when you were born or brought into a family like ours, there was no leaving unless you were in a body bag? I hated to admit that I thought Myles might be right, but we might as well continue to be sure.

"What do you think, boys? You think she knows anything?"

"I think the bitch is lying," Cory said, and Myles's hands balled into fists. I caught his eye and shook my head no, but I knew if Cory were stupid enough to grab Ren for real, he would be a dead mole.

"So do I," Ivan said, stepping closer until only the table separated them. Ivan stood a solid six-eight and played on the basketball team. Seeing him tower over Ren made her look ridiculously small. "Maybe we should have some fun with you. Maybe loosening up your legs will loosen your mouth."

Ivan was laying it on thick, but it worked. Ren's eyes went wide, and she stumbled backward, hitting her ass off the table behind her.

"I swear I don't know anything about anything. I just learned—"

"You're fucking lying," Ivan bellowed, and Ren's face drained of all color. A tiny ball of guilt formed in my stomach as I stared at her terrified face. Myles was right. If she was acting, she was damn good at it.

"Get her boys," Ivan growled. "And fuck her up good."

Ren screamed as she ran around the table and took off into the darker corners of the tall bookshelves. She sprinted for the emergency exit as expected, but I'd already handled that. The bar folded down when Ren slammed into the door but didn't budge. She bounced off like a cartoon character and landed on the floor. The stupid little thread of guilt bloomed again and tried to worm into my brain, and I had to punt it aside. I needed answers, and she had them.

The guys fanned out, and the game was on. She got to her feet and took off across the massive room toward the stairs. I was pretty sure it was Liam who jumped out of the dark and blocked her route up. Skidding to a stop, she whipped around and ran for the cover of the tall bookshelves, her white hair streaming out behind her like a beacon.

Howling like a wolf, the other guys followed my lead, each making a noise that echoed in the cavernous hall. I jogged softly to the far end of the shelves and started back while the others took different rows. Ren's scream jolted my heart, so piercing that I was torn between carnal excitement and feeling like this had gone too far.

"Get away from me," she roared. There was a crash and thudding as books landed on the floor. Bending low, I looked through an empty gap in the shelves as a blur of feet and skirt went running by while who I was pretty sure was Cory curled up in the fetal position on the floor.

Pushing away from the shelf, I ran in the same direction as Ren, impressed with her speed. She reminded me of one of those white rabbits used as bait for greyhounds. Her small body streaked out of the cover of the shelving. I chased her, watching as she looked back and tripped over a chair. She screamed as she sailed through the air and landed with a bang on one of the many tables in the center of the room.

The first time I'd been forced to chase down prey like this was shortly after my tenth birthday. My father felt it was time I learned what the grown men needed to do to hold the reins of power. I remembered that night so clearly.

They pulled a girl out of a cage. She was dressed in all white, and her blonde hair fanned out around her as she ran. I felt so empowered. My father trusted me with knowledge the others wouldn't understand this young. I was special, I was important, and she was the enemy. Then I learned that she was just some girl, a waitress at a diner who didn't have much money and was offered the chance to make enough to pay her rent in the building owned by one of the other Kings. She was no enemy, and we weren't doing anything for the greater good. It was all for sport. That was the first time I saw my father beat and rape a woman.

As Ren's pain-filled scream reached me, my body shook, but not with pleasure or a sense of power—not this time.

She rolled off the desk and kept running, despite the obvious pain as she held her arm and limped like she'd banged her shin or maybe her foot. Myles looked over at me, and even though I could only see his eyes, he was telling me to stop this shit.

I opened my mouth to call off the chase when Ren ran into one of the dark rows on the other side and began screaming hysterically.

"We're going to fucking kill you," I heard Ivan say, and in a blink, Myles was whipping past me like I was standing still. The other guys and I ran toward the screaming, stopping at the end of the row. The scene unfolding before me was something I hadn't expected, and now that it was happening, I didn't know what to do.

Ivan and Myles stood back as Ren screamed at the top of her lungs. She was clawing at the bookcase, books falling to the floor like rain, but what she was saying hurt parts of me I thought were destroyed.

"No, let her go! Don't hurt her. Let go of my mum, please, let go of her. You're killing her! Mum! Let me out of here!"

Ren slammed backward into the shelf behind her and rammed forward at the unmovable wooden tower in front of her with a loud thud. She was going to hurt herself while caught in a memory, something about her mum so traumatic she was in a full dissociative meltdown.

I only recognized it because I had a few myself until my heart hardened and my mind locked away traumas I never shared, not even with the guys. My father said I was weak, and piece by piece, I locked it away until my mind and heart were steel vaults and my fists just as hard.

"No! Stop it! You're killing her! I'll kill you! Let me out of here, and I'll kill you, you fucking assholes," she shrieked. Ren's nails scraped down the wood, leaving grooves in their wake. Her eyes were wild as she screamed and thrashed back and forth like she was trying to break out of something. Her hand clutched at her heart, and she stopped.

Ren looked right at me. Silver eyes filled with a twisted and toxic combination of fear and hate burning in their depths before rolling back in her head as she collapsed to the floor.

Myles was fast and caught her before she could hit her head. My own heart felt like it was trapped as it pounded out of control. My ears rang with the sound of her voice.

Myles gathered her into his arms and marched toward me. I knew before he reached us that he was furious, and the only thing stopping him from jumping on me was Ren in his arms.

"I told ya this was a waste of time. I told ya I didn't want ta do it. Ya forced me, and ya did this ta her. I will no do it again fir ya," he growled, his accent thick with his rage. "If dat means I'm out, den I'm out. But don't ya fuckin' dare do somethin like this ta her again, or I swear on me mother's cold dead body, I will come fir ya."

He ripped the mask off his face and slammed it into the middle of my chest, forcing me to step back. "Yer me brother and me king, but if I wanted ta be like me Da then I'd just follow me Da. Ya told me ya wanted ta do better than yer father, so be better." He looked down at Ren and then back up into my eyes, and all I saw was disgust. "Now I'm no sure who is worse."

I kept my face blank as I pulled off my mask and glanced at the other guys. Blake marched away with him, unlocking and opening the door. He slowly pulled off his mask and turned to look at me.

"I'm sorry, Nash, but I agree with Myles. Yes, we've done far worse things, but to people who were either really bad or coming after us, Ren is neither. Where do we draw the line between what we do for the betterment of The Last Rank and just being an asshole?" He shook his head. "All I learned tonight was something terrible happened to her. You may be right, she may know something that will help our cause, but if that's true, it's locked in her mind. She's not trying to hurt us and...I'm not doing anything like this to her again. I never thought I'd see the day I'd have to tell you that."

Blake marched off and pushed open the door, and I looked at Ivan, Cory, and finally, Liam.

"And what do you three think?"

"I don't know her, so it's just a job to me. She was scared, but I thought that was the point," Cory said and shrugged.

I turned to Ivan.

"What about you?"

"I think Blake is right in saying that if she knows anything, it's locked behind whatever trauma she has. Her entire personality shifted, and her eyes went blank when she ran into me. It was like a light switch. I'd look into that," Ivan said calmly. "The night wasn't a total loss."

"The two of you can go," I said, watching Cory and Ivan leave before turning to my best friend.

"And you? You've been pretty quiet."

Liam sighed and rolled out his shoulders.

"I will always follow you, and if you want my honest opinion, then I think you're right to be concerned."

"Really?"

"Yes, but for all the wrong reasons. I don't think Ren is the threat, at least not directly," Liam said, and I tapped my chin as I thought.

"You mean she's a victim like us?"

"Her father is a waste of space and doesn't strike me as a top-level leader. What I do find peculiar is your father's actions. Lawrence and Mr. Davies know something. If they know something, then the information is out there, but Ren doesn't have it. All I saw tonight was another one of us with scars lining her soul and haunting her mind." He clapped me on the shoulder. "I just hope we haven't pushed her too far to figure that out. I'm not sure I'd forgive myself for that."

Liam wandered away, and the lights flickered and came back on as the door clicked closed behind him. How did I remain who I needed to be to remove my father and rule yet not become him? It felt like I was walking around with a blade to my throat and one at my back, and no matter what I tried, I lost.

Walking over to the seat Ren had occupied, I sat down, looking at the scattered books and the backpack lying on top.

"What the fuck am I doing?" I mumbled, annoyed with myself yet still feeling like this needed to be done.

Grabbing the books and laptop, I stuffed them inside the empty bag. Opening a smaller pocket, I went to put away her snow tiger pencil case. My thumb ran over the image as I remembered the feel of her skin under my fingers at Thanksgiving.

"Fuck."

I tried to stuff the case in the pocket, but there was a book in the way. I pulled it out and realized it was the same journal I'd grabbed from her drawer. Sitting back, I flipped open the cover.

Asshole I was, but after what I had done tonight, this was the least of my crimes. If it helped me solve the puzzle...so be it.

Chapter 35

Myles

Ren twitched and mumbled, waking me from my light dozing. I'd passed out with a girl before but willingly slept with one, no—that required way more emotional involvement than I wanted to invest. But, laying here with Snowflake felt perfect. It felt like the world had stopped, and I could envision taking her to a lodge and hiding out from the world.

She mumbled again, the words inaudible, yet each small whimper ripped my heart apart a little more. Kissing the top of her head, I held her tighter.

"I've got ya, Snowflake," I whispered until she settled. "I won't let anything happen to ya ever again."

Her body suddenly jerked, and she sucked in a deep breath. I knew she'd just woken up even though I couldn't see her face. The light was on in the bathroom with the door open a crack so she could see, but I was spooning her and didn't want her to think she was in Ivan's grasp.

"Shhh, it's okay, Snowflake. I promise not to let anything hurt ya," I said, hating that I would be the one to tell her what happened and why.

I shouldn't have done it. I should've put my foot down as soon as I knew what Nash wanted to do, but he was my King, my boss, and my friend. I was raised to follow orders, not give them. Kicking all that in the face was something I'd never done before. To do so would typically mean a bullet between my eyes, but I'd never let him push me into the likes of that again where she was concerned. He wanted to torture anyone else, I didn't care, but Snowflake was a different story.

"Myles?"

Ren's voice was soft and shaking, like she was cold or maybe terrified. I really hoped it was the first.

"Yeah, it's me, love."

Sitting up, I grabbed the small blanket she had folded on the bed and felt her eyes on me as I laid it on her. She snuggled into the fuzzy material, and I'd never been jealous of a blanket before, but I was now. Laying down, I wrapped my arm around her and cuddled as close as possible.

"What's happening? Am I dreaming?"

I smiled. At least she didn't say nightmare.

"No, I'm actually here."

"And where is here? The last thing I remember was...." Ren sucked in a sharp breath and pulled on my arm like she would get up and take off.

"Please don't. Just lay with me. I swear to ya, I'm not going to do anything to hurt ya or that ya don't want."

It took a moment, but she finally relaxed into me, and I released the breath I was holding.

"Why should I trust you?"

It was a fair question and yet it hurt that she felt she needed to ask it. "I haven't done anything to warrant yer trust, not yet, but I'm hoping ya will let me start right now." When she didn't move or yell to get out, I continued. "Yer in your dorm room. I'm totally breaking the rules to be in here with ya but I wasn't leavin' ya alone," I said.

"My fingers hurt. I feel bruised."

My jaw clenched, the muscle twitching at the memory of her clawing at the bookshelf as she slammed back and forth. Burying my head in her hair, I let her sweet scent fill me as I tried to relax. I wanted to stay like this and breathe it in forever.

"What happened? I...I swear I was in the study hall, and then... there were these guys...and," her voice cracked before a muffled sob escaped her lips, and I didn't think I could hate myself any more than at that moment.

"Before I tell ya that, I need to start at the beginning. I have ta tell ya things that no one other than a few of us knows. I need to tell ya things that are dangerous and can never be repeated. I want to show you how much I trust ya, Snowflake, but are ya willing to take the risk of knowing? Or would ya like me to leave?"

Ren was quiet for a long time, and I just let her think. She'd proven she was highly intelligent, and whatever she chose, as hard as it may be, I'd respect it. It was the least I could do at this point.

"Okay, tell me, but you better make sure Vicky can't hear."

Unable to help myself, I kissed the top of her head and smiled.

"She's not here."

"Oh," she whispered.

"Don't worry, I promised I wouldn't do anything ya don't want, and I keep my promises."

Ren nodded, her body relaxing, and I molded mine to hers like she was a piece I'd been missing.

I figured I could tell her most of what had happened to get to this point without getting myself into too much shit.

"Alright, I'm not sure why because I really shouldn't, but I trust you," Ren said, and I held her tighter, unable to get close enough.

No sweeter words had ever been spoken to me.

"Aye, I've been an arse, but I wanna start over and lay all my cards on the table with ya." She nodded slowly, and if my arms weren't already a vise around her body, I would've held tighter. "As ya know, I wasn't born here. I was born in Ireland and came over almost two years ago so my father could be closer to the boss or, as we call him, the King."

"King? Why does everyone like throwing around that word so much? Are we talking like royalty?"

"Aye and no. Not by any standards that heads of countries would want to recognize."

Ren looked over her shoulder at me, and even in the dim lighting, I could see her beautiful silver eyes that reminded me of liquid metal.

"You're confusing me."

I wanted to kiss her so badly and forced myself to swallow the razor-like dryness scratching down my throat.

"We're mafia Snowflake. All of us are Irish mob and have been for generations. When Nash's great-great-grandfather was in charge, he created a smaller group of the most powerful families to act as a council. He would still be in charge, but he saw the value in having families wanting him to succeed so the entire group flourished." I wet my lips. I was in it now. No point holding back. "Skipping ahead, there have been other leaders, but Lawrence wanted the title back for his family. He clawed his way to the top, then killed his father and brother to ensure no one else in his family could fight for leadership."

"I knew he was evil," she said. "I can see it in his eyes."

"Aye, he is. Long ago, we were a secret society, a cult with blood sacrifices and ceremonies. No one even remembers, but there are old books on it. None of the other leaders took it seriously until Lawrence took over. He re-established the secret society and forced the five most powerful families to join if they wanted to continue to rule with him, my father included. He calls the group The Order of Kings." I licked my lips. "Two of the families are still in Ireland and the other three are here."

Ren looked over her shoulder at me again and slowly shifted around so she was on her back. My body roared to life, wanting to forget all of this dark bullshit that had plagued me from birth and just lose myself in her.

"So you're saying that Nash's father is the head of the Irish mafia and opened Pandora's Box?"

"Aye, exactly. He does terrible things, demands loyalty, and gets others to do terrible things that he can use as blackmail. Like running illegal businesses, guns, and drugs weren't enough. He murders, traffics women and children, and does unspeakable things to people just for amusement."

Her mouth dropped open, and she stared up at me so intensely that I was afraid to blink. My heart pounded hard as I waited for her to respond.

"And my father is part of this? He's taken up with Lawrence and doing all this terrible stuff?" Her eyes were filled with so much sadness and heartache that I would've taken it all as my own to keep that look away.

"That I don't have a definitive answer ta, but my guess would be in some capacity, yes. Only Nash is allowed at ceremonies. Ya have to be eighteen, but he's never seen your father there, so he's not one of the inner leaders and yet is treated like royalty." Her eyes widened. "Please don't be scared. I mean, ya have every right to be, but...please try not to see us differently. None of us chose to live this life, none of us chose to do terrible things in honor of loyalty to a man that is certifiable, but we do, and we are if we want to survive."

"Why hasn't someone taken him out?"

"Assassination?"

She nodded.

"It's not that easy. Even if we killed him, one of the others would step into the role, and that could get messy and start family wars."

Her eyes searched my face, and I wish I knew what she was looking for. I wish I knew what to say to make her feel safe.

"I'm not scared, even if I should be. I think I'm broken Myles. I have trouble feeling much of anything anymore."

She looked down, and I ran my thumb over her lower lip, unable to stop myself.

"Yer not broken, yer perfect," I said, and her cheeks pinked with a hint of a blush.

"I'm not sure what else to call it. I came here not knowing anything or anyone. I got to know you before you dropped this bombshell, and other than some odd quirks that now make sense, the school is like any other. The people inside these walls are no different from those back home. The thing is, Myles, I'm still trying to wrap my head around possibly seeing all of your faces on an FBI's Most Wanted list for who you are and what you do...I don't even know how to compute that."

"I know."

"Doesn't it scare you? To run drugs, collect money, and...well, you know."

"It used to, but I think somethin inside of me broke a long time ago too."

I almost jumped out of my skin as she touched my cheek. Grabbing her hand, I kissed her palm and held it so I wasn't as tempted to pull her under me and kiss her until she was gasping for air.

"So you weren't exaggerating about everyone here and their families?"

I shook my head.

"Some have parents who are crooked politicians, lawyers, judges, and even police officers."

"Like Ivy's father?"

"Aye, but the rest are all mafia and major crime families from all over the world. We are talking Irish, Russian, Italian, the Cartel, and Hell's Angels. Ya name it. This place is neutral ground. No one is allowed to start a war, attack this place, or pull strings to take over another group by using their children. The rules are very strict, but just to be safe, the guards walk the property at all times, and cameras are everywhere. The school is run by a group called the Superintendents, and they don't mess around. The name doesn't sound scary, but they are deadly and have been facelessly running this place for generations. They have wiped out whole families—that no one would dare take on—for disobeying the rules. There is some shit we can get away with, but nothing major can happen on the property, or you pay the consequences with your life."

"They sound terrifying."

Ren looked around the room like they were hiding in a corner.

"They are, and you won't see them coming. People go missing, but you always know it's the Superintendents."

"Why is it that I suddenly feel like I'm at the hotel from the movie John Wick, and this place is not as safe as it is supposed to be?"

I chuckled at that, but it wasn't far from the truth.

"Aye, a lot like that, which makes what Nash does so dangerous," I whispered, fearful to even talk about this on property.

"What does he do?"

"He created a group, his own order, called The Last Rank. It's made up of those of us who are oppressed by our families and want a way to take over or to get out."

"He's a smuggler?"

I laughed hard at that.

"No, he's more like a ringleader of unruly cats."

She smirked, and I loved how she nibbled on her lower lips as she thought.

"So, when you said you hurt people, you meant for the mafia? Like collecting payments for them, not just working for a local bookie."

"Aye, I'm afraid that my lifelong membership to the fucked up world of shadows was decided for me the day I was born. I need ya to understand that we don't get to choose this life, and to refuse is certain death. Our families don't mess around, blood or not."

She wiggled around, and at first, I thought she would get up, open the door and order me out. Instead, she rolled onto her side and looked me in the eyes. I loved that she didn't look horrified or that she was judging me. She was as rare in her heart as she was in her looks.

The desire to touch her became too much, and I ran my knuckles against the soft skin of her cheek.

"Why do you do that?"

Her voice was nothing more than a whisper.

"Do what?"

"Look at me like that? You look at me like...."

"Like yer a glittering diamond that fell from the sky into this dark school?"

Her eyebrows rose.

"I was going to say something a lot less dramatic," she said, the corner of her mouth curving up.

Fanning my fingers out, I cupped her cheek and knew I'd remember this moment for the rest of my life, even if I never got to touch her like this again.

"I stare at ya like this Snowflake because, from the first day we met, I knew there was somethin different and unique about ya. I was drawn to ya, and I've been makin' a fool of meself ever since, hoping ya would give me a chance. I want to show ya that I'm more than just what I've been labeled. My entire life I have worn one label or another, but no one knows the real me, not even the guys, at least not fully."

"You've kind of ruined the way I see you all on your own, you know?"

"Aye, I know, but I'm praying you'll find it in ya to give me a chance to make it up to ya."

She sighed, breaking eye contact, and my heart sank.

"I'll think on it. So what happened with the bet and tonight? I want to know what the hell is going on."

"The bet was just dumb. We're always bettin' on something, call it boredom or just stupidity, but we love to challenge one another, and you became that challenge." She looked down, and I tilted her head up to look at me. "I never should've agreed. No, I never should've let it happen at all, but it was second nature and...."

"I was new, and you didn't know me."

"Aye. I said yes and have regretted it ever since. I do have a reputation, I cannot deny that, but I never set out to play ya, Snowflake. I swear to ya on me ma's grave and I loved that woman with my whole heart."

My thumb ran along her lower lip, and I knew I'd beg for a kiss. I didn't care if I had to get down on my knees and cling to her leg. I wanted her so badly that I would do whatever it took to have her. I forced myself to look into her eyes to keep from grabbing her as my pulse raced through my veins and made it hard to concentrate, along with other body parts coming alive. I was suddenly thankful to be contained in my jeans.

"As for tonight...I wish I could say that I heard ya screaming and ran in chasing off the bad guys, but the truth is...I was one of the guys in a mask."

Her features darkened, her eyes narrowing into a harsh glare as she sat up, crossing her arms over her chest. I sat up but made sure that I was still touching her. I wasn't letting her go without a fight. Not again.

"Look, the thing is...I can't even begin to explain to someone that hasn't lived it just how dangerous our lives are, and some of our parents are monsters. I saw it in your eyes at Thanksgiving and you said it yerself. You see through Mr. Collier and my father to the evil that hides under the perfectly unwrinkled suit and tie."

Her body relaxed a little, her features softening.

"When I arrived, Nash and the others brought me into his group, the one working to ruin Lawrence and some of the top families, but we are taking our lives into our hands by doing this. Things will never be clean and simple with who we are, but abuse, rape, torture, and sex trafficking, all for money and pleasure, are not things we ever want to uphold. I'm not excusing Nash, he can be a dick of epic proportions, but he takes abuse every day, so hopefully, others won't have to."

Ren bit her bottom lip, and I loved how she instantly seemed concerned.

"I'm pretty sure I saw that, but Nash can also be so...volatile and unpredictable."

I shrugged.

"I'm not sure what to say other than he's a dick because he has to be, and it comes with certain emotional and mental costs."

"Okay, I can understand all that, but...I still don't understand why he feels like he needs to torment me."

"The way yer father was treated at Thanksgiving is strange for Lawrence. We would've said yer father was someone special, but we can't find anything on him or yer family. Lawrence has been almost nice. He never treats newcomers well or anyone with a modicum of respect unless it's for his own gain. I've seen him put a bullet in a man's head for far less than getting sobbingly drunk at his table."

Ren's eyes lowered, and I immediately wanted to hit myself for being so tactless. Reaching out, I gripped her hands, and her eyes slowly lifted to mine.

"And Nash thinks I know why his father is acting this way, right?"

I nodded.

"He thinks that even if you don't realize what you know, you know it, and he wanted to get it out of you. Fear is a tool, and sometimes we use it, but I'm really sorry. I didn't want to do it and told him I'd never do it again."

Ren slid off the bed, and I held onto her hand a little tighter in a panic.

"I just need to pace. I like to do it when I think."

Letting go, she crossed her arms over her chest and marched from one side of the room to the other as she tapped her chin and mumbled under her breath.

"Are ya mad at me?"

"For which part?"

My face heated up, and I rubbed the back of my neck.

"Any of it."

Ren stopped pacing and glared at me, but the look softened the longer she stared.

"Honestly, I should be livid and never trust you again. I should open the door, order you out and tell you I never want to see you again."

"Aye, ya should."

"Myles, the six of you brought on a panic attack, and I can barely remember what happened, which is terrifying because it means Nash could be right, and I'm repressing. But, I don't think him scaring the shit out of me and making me relive the worst moment of my life is helpful."

"Aye, I agree. It was a stupid long shot we never shoulda tried."

She sighed and ran her hand through her hair.

"But I'm going to make a couple of assumptions here, and tell me if I'm wrong. One, you're supposed to listen to whatever Nash tells you, and two, by the look on your face, you hate all the shit that has happened."

"Aye, and aye. All I wanted was to get yer attention. Ya make me feel so much like a pup that knows nothin'."

She cocked her head and looked at me before her mouth turned up in a small smile.

"That description suits you."

I rolled my eyes at her.

"Aye, it probably does. No need to rub it in, though."

"I think I can get away with calling you whatever I want for at least a week after what you've done."

She put her hands on her hips, challenging me, and I loved it.

"Aye, fair enough."

"Okay, then you have work to do to rebuild my trust. But I don't hate you, just what you did."

She resumed pacing, and I sat there stunned, not even sure I heard her right.

"Are ya sure?"

"Do you want me to hate you? Do you want me to grab whatever "

"Well, no...."

"Then leave it be. The fact that you told me and didn't try to lie and say that you weren't one of the guys tells me a lot. Most guys would've made themselves out to be the hero, not the villain."

I laughed as I stood and leaned against her desk.

"I might have the face of an angel, but a hero I will never be."

"So for now, let's concentrate on what my father is up to 'cause I don't understand any of this."

"Nash has a theory," I said and knew that if Nash heard me talking about this, he'd knock all the teeth out of my head, but it was worth the risk. "He thinks yer in witness protection and an important piece that could help his father in a power play move."

Ren stopped moving, her face draining of all color, and I rushed to her, convinced she would faint again.

"Are ya okay?"

I gripped her shoulders as Ren looked up at me, and I could feel the light tremble under my fingers.

"My mum was murdered."

"What? When? I thought she was ill."

She wiped at the tears sliding down her cheeks.

"Five days before I came here. She had been sick with cancer for a long time, but I genuinely thought she was on the mend. It was my birthday, and we sat in her room eating all my favorite takeout food. She'd managed to sing me happy birthday. She also gave me this." Ren dug under her shirt and held up a chain with a small pendant, a blue stone with an R. "It was around ten, my mum was resting, and I was reading when these masked men broke into our house."

"I'm so sorry."

Her shaking worsened, and her breathing was so quick that she was nearing another attack. Scooping her into my arms, I sat on the bed and held her to my chest.

"Yer okay just breathe, Snowflake, yer gonna pass out again if ya keep that up."

I took long, deep breaths, and Ren eventually relaxed.

"My mum ordered me to go into the closet and get her a gun. I didn't know we owned one, but I would do anything to protect her. But once I was in there, she hit a button, and the closet turned into a safe room I didn't know existed. I was trapped in this small prison while the men...." I held Ren tighter as a sob gripped her, and she covered her mouth. "But...what if they weren't there for her? What if they were there for me? What if I got my mum killed?"

I rocked her like a child.

"No Ren, no matter what happened, none of this is your fault." I held her until she stopped crying. "Can ya think back? Was there anything weird in your life, or did the men say anything you heard that could give us a clue?"

She shook her head.

"The only thing weird was that my father had a job at a marketing firm. He did graphic design for printing jobs. Then one day, he came home and said he'd been offered a job with Collier Inc. I didn't even know he was looking for a job. I have no idea what he does for Nash's father, but he changed after that."

I kept rocking her, never wanting to let her leave this room.

"Changed how?"

"Workaholic, and he liked to travel before, but we never went anywhere after that. He became cold and distant and barely spoke to me and my mum. It was like...like he just..." She stopped as she cried a little more. "Like he just stopped loving us. It was like one day a switch flipped, and he wasn't the dad I remembered."

"Was there anything else ya can remember?"

"When I was in the safe room, I couldn't hear anything, but I found a monitor and was watching." She stopped, and I didn't press as she cleared her throat, collecting herself. "One of the men had a tattoo on his forearm. It looked like a polar bear, maybe. I'm not sure. God, this is frustrating."

"That's okay, Snowflake. We'll figure it out."

I kissed her temple, and she leaned away from my body, her intense eyes searching for something.

"What—" I started, but she grabbed my face, and my heart leaped from my chest.

"I...umm...."

"Just do it," I whispered, unable to peel my eyes away from her lips.

Her cheeks pinked to a deep rose, and I was ready to grab her face when she touched her lips to mine. The world could've exploded, and I would've been none the wiser. How was it that one person, one moment, could feel so life-altering?

I was nothing more than a shadow floating around aimlessly in a world that never belonged to me. A puppet in a game far greater than myself for so long that I forgot I should want more. I was playing a game, and doing all the right things, holding the remote but never in control.

With just a touch, she ignited a new desire inside me. Wrapping my arms around Ren, I deepened the kiss, begging entrance to her mouth.

"Open for me, Snowflake. Open your mouth like a good girl," I whispered, nipping at her bottom lip.

Her lips trembled slightly against mine like she was nervous, but before I could ask, she opened her mouth and ran the tip of her tongue seductively along my lip. My heart stopped altogether, and I forgot to breathe as my brain zeroed in on nothing but the taste of her.

"Good girl," I said and kissed her hard.

I couldn't get enough as I drank her up and swallowed down her moans. She was making me unbelievably hard. My entire body strained, and even though I knew I shouldn't, I shifted us around and laid her down on the bed, settling myself between her thighs.

Ren kissed me as if we'd always been lovers like I'd kissed her a million times before, and she knew exactly what I wanted and liked. When her hands gripped my hair, I almost lost my senses completely and quickly broke the kiss. It was impossible not to want more when I stared into her eyes, to bury myself inside her and stay locked in here all night.

"Fuck," I growled, and—with self-control, I didn't know I had—pushed myself up and off her body.

Ren was panting hard, and the top few buttons on her blouse had popped open, giving me a delicious view of the white bra underneath. So close, so fucking close.

"What are you doing," Ren asked, sounding like I'd smacked her instead of doing the right thing.

"I can't do this."

She grabbed the top of her shirt and held it closed. Her eyes were snapping with anger that made me want to say fuck it and get back into bed despite all the reasons why that would be bad right now.

"I see," she said.

"No, no, I don't think ya do. Ya see this." I pointed to the massive bulge in my jeans. "This is not letting me think straight. I want ya so fucking bad."

Ren's eyes followed my finger. I saw her swallow, and her eyes got a little bigger, but when she bit her lip, I had to step back. I needed the space to try and think straight.

"I don't want ya to think I'm doing this for some stupid bet, and I've barely started to earn yer trust. I want to do this right for once because...fuck...because ya mean more to me than a one-night stand."

The iciness melted from her eyes.

"So what you're saying is you don't want me to strip down and get in the shower right now?"

"What?" I gasped and took another step back. "Sweet Mary and Joseph, ya can't be doin' that to me."

I glanced at the door, tempted to escape. I wanted to do right by Ren, but fuck even I had my limits.

Her laughter filled the room as she grabbed her hoodie off her desk chair and pulled it on.

"I was joking, and I love it when you're all riled up. Your accent is sexy. Is this better?"

"Aye, a little."

Ren used a hair elastic on her wrist, and with a quick twist, her hair was up in her usual messy fashion on top of her head. She still looked adorable, and it didn't help a ton to cool myself off. I would need an ice bath. Forget the cold shower.

"Turn around."

I didn't bother asking why and spun around, shutting my eyes just in case I could suddenly see backward.

"Okay, you're safe."

I opened my eyes, and she giggled at me.

"You're crazy," she said, shaking her head and smiling.

She'd swapped out her kilt for a pair of blue, fluffy pants with little snowflakes all over them. Stepping up to her, I tucked a stray piece of her hair behind her ear.

"Yer so fuckin' beautiful," I said.

Ren cleared her throat and broke our stare.

"Oh shit, my books and laptop. I left everything there. I have to go get them."

I stopped her before she could run off.

"Don't worry. It's taken care of. You'll have yer stuff back tomorrow, but it's all safe."

"You sure?" She crossed her arms.

"Aye, I'm sure." I stuffed my hands in my pockets. "Did ya want me to go now?"

Ren looked between the bed and the door so many times that she looked like she was watching a tennis match.

"I'm not sure. I want you to stay, but I'm not sure that's a good idea."

"Yer probably right." Stepping in close, she looked up at me, and for the first time, her eyes were completely unguarded. With my hands cupping her face, I dropped my lips to hers for a quick kiss. "I asked ya before, and ya said no, but I'm gonna ask again. Will ya come and watch my lacrosse practice?"

"If I do, I'm not turning into some groupie, you know."

I now had a new goal to turn her into a raving fan that would drop-kick a mascot. Okay, that was a bit extreme, but a great visual.

"It's just practice."

"Fine, I'll watch."

I gave her another kiss and stepped away, knowing I'd stand in this spot all night.

"I'll give ya the details tomorrow over breakfast. I'll meet ya here with a feast." I held up my finger before she could argue why that was not a good idea. "No arguments. I'll be here at nine."

Stopping at her bedroom door, I looked over my shoulder, and she was touching her lip where I'd just kissed her.

"I really am sorry for earlier and promise to make it up to ya. Sleep well, Snowflake, and if ya change yer mind and want company, ya know how to reach me."

"Night, Myles."

Closing the door took a shit ton of effort. I stood in the hallway, my body alive with excitement. Could I really be getting my chance? Fuck, if so, now I would be waiting for the other shoe to drop.

I glanced up at the ceiling. I had the worst luck. Fucking Murphy's Law.

"Yer a bitch, Murphy. Just sayin, it would be nice if for just this once ya weren't a cunt."

Chapter 36

Ren

The shrill sound of a whistle told me I was heading in the right direction. I hadn't been in this building yet and was astounded at its size. It was easy to get lost, and after taking a wrong turn, I stopped to memorize a map.

My phone dinged again, and I groaned. I loved Lizzy, but holy hell, when she wanted to know something, she was worse than a dog with a bone.

I pulled my phone out and looked at the twenty messages of her poking at me. Sighing, I opened the chat.

L: Hello

L: Don't you dare ignore me, woman!

L: Answer the question

L: Poke

L: Poke

L: Poke

L: Keep ignoring me, and I'll do this alllllll night long.

I believed her too. A few months before I left and everything with my mum, I saw her call the local township nonstop about unsafe conditions at the park until they had the police speak to her to get her to stop calling. It didn't work, she became more persistent, saying she knew her rights and someone was going to get hurt, and they needed to add four lights to the trail. She insisted it was the perfect spot for someone to be mugged or worse and wouldn't let up. A month later, there weren't just four but ten new lights. Activists everywhere needed her on their team.

R: I got your question, and I'm only ignoring it because I don't know what we are yet. I haven't agreed to be his girlfriend, girl, arm candy, baby mama, queen or anything you want to add to that list.

L: LOL! That's quite the list, but FINALLY, I thought my birthday would come faster than your text.

R: You're a dramatic biotch, but I LV U

L: I know. So what is the holdup? Why haven't you said yes to that gorgeous golden-eyed god?

R: Okay, Myles is never meeting you. His ego is already far too big for compliments like that.

L: LOL! Stop stalling. You can give me the deets, are you leaning towards dating him? Are you going to give him your V-card? Let's get on with the show.

R: Lizzy...stop pushing. I'm not ready to jump into a relationship with someone or have sex.

L: Yes, because you've had so many relationships, and you're seventeen. Come on, girl. I keep telling you that you won't be disappointed.

R: Stop pushing, or I'll stop answering your messages, and you can forget about me visiting for Christmas.

L: What??? Fine, I'm sorry, but gurl, let's get real. GEG is a keeper. I mean, he brought you waffles and pancakes with all the sides...need I say more?

R: What the hell is GEG?

L: Golden Eyed God, I thought that was pretty self-explanatory.

I shook my head and pictured her face all screwed up, like I was the one being insane and unreasonable.

R: He asked me to date him yesterday at breakfast, but I told him I'd give him an answer after Christmas break. That's not far away, and it gives me time to get to know him.

L: OMG...Fine, but tell me this...is he a good kisser?"

I sent a shrugging emoji and laughed as she sent me angry faces.

> R: I gotta go. I'm meeting the GEG to watch his lacrosse practice.

> L: Oh, lacrosse...I love him already.

> R: LVU

> L: Right back at you, Boo

I'd already passed the doors to the pool and another that led to a weight room, but there were also two gyms, a hockey rink, and a relaxation/rehab clinic. It was an entire complex, complete with concession stands that were open when there were games. Wayward may not have been my first choice, hell, they weren't even my last, but it was obvious they poured a vast amount of money into every aspect of the school.

Would I admit that to my father? Hell no. If he'd spoken to me, explained why we needed to come here, visited, or called me like a normal parent, I would've, but we were so past that now. He'd lied to me repeatedly, ignored my phone calls and texts, ripped me away from the only home I knew, and hid who he really was from me, which may or may not have gotten my mum killed. At the moment, I loathed even the thought of him.

The sound of thundering feet got louder, and a group of guys wearing two different colored uniforms raced by the double doors. They looked like streaks as they passed. My pulse spiked, and my stomach seemed to have perma butterflies since Friday for more than one reason. Not only was I toeing the waters with the idea of a boyfriend, which I'd never had before, but it also felt like I was standing on quicksand trying to get my bearings only to have my footing shift again.

If you were in quicksand, you shouldn't struggle because you sink faster, but I wasn't sure standing still would be effective for what I was going through.

My journal had mysteriously disappeared on top of everything else, but I knew Nash had it. My bag was left at my door for me to find Saturday, and nothing made me feel sicker than for him to read all that personal information. For anyone to see how much I'd struggled and feared, what I had wished for on my darkest day. It was all laid bare on those pages because it was my personal space, and I never intended for anyone else to see it.

Conveniently for him, I didn't have a class with Nash today, and he wasn't in any of his usual lurking spots. Okay, lurking wasn't exactly accurate, but I liked the visual.

I glanced at the glass cabinet I was walking passed and skidded to a halt as I stared at the stunning trophies, shiny as mirrors, but the team photos had me looking closer.

There was a tall trophy with a picture of Nash, Liam, Myles, Blake, and Theo posing for the camera. I'd never watched swimming, but as my eyes roamed over the picture, I could certainly see the appeal. I caught myself smiling in the glass and quickly wiped it off my face. This was ridiculous and exactly what I promised myself I wouldn't do—no gooey and squishy girly reactions.

"What are you smiling at, Princess? Do you like something you see? I can give you a up close and personal view."

My entire body jolted like I'd been electrocuted by Nash's voice next to my ear.

"Someone needs to put a fucking bell on you," I growled, my eyes flicking up to the blue ones staring back at me in the glass. Where the hell had he come from? Maybe lurking was the right word after-all. He was close enough that I could feel the heat from his body, but he didn't touch me.

"Myles told me it was you the other night," I said a sharp edge to my tone.

His eyebrow lifted, but he wasn't shocked.

"I know. He also told you who I am and what I do."

"But you don't care?"

"Not really, unless you plan on squealing like a little piglet." He casually shrugged. "If you threaten my secret, though, all I can say is Myles will cry many tears over your missing body. If he comes for me...well I'm sure you can put together the rest. Don't test me, Princess."

My breath froze in my chest, and my eyes widened as I stared into his. Was he serious, or did he want a reaction out of me? Would he really kill me and Myles if I said anything?

"Let me guess, I'm an asshole," he mocked in a higher voice that I presumed was supposed to be me but sounded more like Vicky. "I'm joking, kinda. I mean, what's the worst you could do? Run to your daddy? Oh, that's right, you two aren't speaking. Shucks, sorry, that's rough." The sarcasm was so thick it could have been cut with a knife, and the comment hurt, just like I was sure it was meant to.

"I didn't realize you got your rocks off by picking on others...like your father. I guess I was wrong." The smirk fell from his face. "Oops, was that hurtful? Oh, I'm sorry."

I glared at him, my pulse thrumming faster with each beat of my racing heart.

His chest touched my back.

"You think you're a badass, don't you, Princess?"

"I don't like being tormented for no reason, and I'd also love to have my journal back."

I watched him, feeling like a wild animal in a trap, as he pursed his lips and softly blew cool air on my neck. As hard as I tried, I couldn't stop the shiver that raced down my spine.

"Who says I have it?" He said, but the smirk in the glass told me he did.

"Do you want me to hit you," I asked, my teeth clenched as much as my stomach.

"I'd pay money to see you try, and then what you'd do when I punished you for it. I'd be far more creative this time around," Nash said, and I didn't doubt he would follow through.

I shook my head at his reflection. Continuing the argument

seemed pointless, we'd just go round and round with the same threats.

"What do you want, Nash?"

"So quick to get rid of me, but I know better. You can keep your feelings for Myles, I don't care, but I know you want to fuck me."

"Gee thanks for letting me keep my own emotions, how fucking kind of you. And, you keep dreaming. Just don't when you're with Vicky, that's disgusting." I made a gagging sound.

Nash chuckled, and I squeezed my fists tight to keep from moving away from him and the charge in the air that seemed to follow.

"I did think you might want this back."

He wrapped his arm around my body, his hand gripping my journal. This felt far more intimate than him simply handing over a book, but I was too stubborn to move away. That felt like defeat when it came to Nash

I gripped my journal, but he didn't let go. There was no way he took it and didn't read it, but if I showed that it bothered me, it would only give him another win. That was something I refused to do.

"Did you have fun reading it?"

"Meh, you put me to sleep with all your poor me, life is terrible, and art talk. I mean, really, could you get any more boring?"

"Give me my fucking journal, Nash."

I was getting pissed, and it was harder to hide.

"But you have such a nasty tongue I'm not sure if I should give it to you," he mocked, gently tugging against my hold. He was messing with me, and the temptation to punch him in his sexy face intensified.

"And here I thought you liked a nasty tongue. I mean, you are with Vicky after all," I said, my lip curling up as I glared at him.

And just like all the other times that I said her name, she appeared like magic. I really needed to start saying Jason Mamoa instead.

"What's going on here," Vicky said, her voice barely containing her rage.

If her sudden appearance bothered Nash, he didn't let it show. He also didn't move away, which felt awkward as hell.

"Just giving Ren her biology notes that she was so kind to lend me."

I rolled my eyes.

"Yes, how very kind of me. Maybe next time, ask to borrow them," I said, tugging on my journal.

This time he let go. He slowly stood straight, and I wanted to gag as he stepped up to Vicky and smiled. Keeping his eyes on mine, he kissed the top of Vicky's head. I had no idea what he was trying to accomplish, unless he wanted me to throw up.

Vicky was definitely blind because she melted on the spot like she was made of butter. It was, smack my head, worthy. An idiot could see he was putting it on and was as fake as a three-dollar bill, yet she was lapping it up.

"Hey baby, you want to go get some dinner," Nash asked, and I was seriously considering majoring in acting. Not showing any emotion was real work.

"Of course I do, and maybe we can have some dessert when we get back to my room," she giggled.

"You two love announcing your sex life. Would you like me to stream it for you again?"

Vicky turned her evil Gollum glare on me. I half expected her to hiss, 'My precious,' as she grabbed Nash's arm.

"You're just jealous, Freak."

"Of you two? Not a chance, but I'll give you a heads up that if you pull that shit again, I'll make sure the dean gets a framed copy of the two of you." I smiled, and it wasn't fake. "I'm sure you can find some dark and disturbing hole to crawl into for a few seconds."

"Keep it up, and you'll make an enemy of me, Freak," Vicky said, taking a step in my direction, but Nash grabbed her shoulder and held her back.

"Oh, you mean you've been nice so far? I couldn't tell, with your resting bitch face, my apologies."

Nash chuckled and Vicky glared up at him. "Don't worry, baby. People like Ren always get what's coming to them," he said.

He smirked at me, and I was tempted to rub my ass at the memory of him spanking me. He'd do it even if I didn't provoke him.

The door to the gym opened, the sounds of squeaking shoes and yelling getting louder and echoing along the hall.

"Hey, Snowflake, ya comin'," Myles called out, and my stomach fluttered.

I brushed by Nash, knowing that would piss him off to no end. I knew I was playing with fire, but I was enjoying it way too much.

"Let's go, baby," Nash said.

I glanced over my shoulder, feeling a tiny hint of jealousy. Oh, hell no. I whipped my head around, my lips curving up as I saw Myles in his uniform.

"Were they bugging ya," Myles asked as soon as I got to him, and my appreciation for his powers of observation increased.

"Not really. Vicky is always a pill, but Nash gave me this." I held up the journal he'd stolen. "He was very Nash about it, but nothing I couldn't handle."

"No doubt, Snowflake. Yer like a gale force wind. Come on in. I've got twenty left of practice, it's a short one today."

Even with the lacrosse mask on, I could see him smiling, and I stuffed my journal into the pocket of my hoodie to try and hide my nervousness.

He was so cheesy and...I kinda loved it.

"Ya can sit up there," he pointed to the bleachers with a few dozen people scattered around.

"McCoy, get your ass back into line," the coach yelled, and I quickly walked over to the bleachers, not wanting to be in his coach's crosshairs.

Settling myself on the top row, I tried to figure out what they were doing. Even though lacrosse was popular back home, it wasn't a sport I watched. I quickly did an internet search of lacrosse, and a list of terms, equipment, and rules popped up. I was a total geek and totally interested in Myles.

There was no denying that now, but a small voice still screamed that it was dangerous to want him, and he would do nothing but hurt me. I lacked a role model the last few years, and my trust-o-meter was way off.

"Myles is so hot. I'm dying. His ass is perfect," a girl I didn't recognize said and then giggled with the girl beside her.

A flare of jealousy pulled its head from the sand in my gut, and I glared at the back of their heads. Is this what it would be like from now on if I dated him? Would I turn into Vicky, looking over my shoulder at the next girl with doe eyes for him, wondering if she is the one I lost him to? Then I'd have to give myself a pep talk. It wasn't my fault, but really it was since I should've known and never gotten involved with him in the first place.

"I can't decide if I like him or number twenty-two better," her friend said.

I almost stood up and marched out. I was way out of my depth here. I wasn't sure what made me think I was ready for this.

The only thing that kept me from doing that was thinking about Saturday with Myles. We spent an amazing and relaxing day together, and for once, there was no anvil falling from the sky to crush our happiness. But I couldn't help that I still looked up.

I needed to get my own room. It was freeing not having to schedule a shower. Rubbing at my hair with the plain white towel that the school was obsessed with us using, I wandered out of the bathroom as a sharp knock sounded at the door.

"Hey Snowflake, it's just me."

I smiled like a hopeless romantic at the sound of his voice. Opening the door came with a series of emotions that ranged from fucking terrified to *paralyzed stupid with butterflies. In a blink, Myles cupped my face and dropped his lips to mine.*

Moaning, I opened my mouth for him, and we stood there kissing for so long that my lips were swollen and sore.

"Ya taste as sweet as ya smell. I want to lay ya out and devour ya, Snowflake, like yer a fucking buffet."

I shook my head at him. He said things no one else could get away with without looking like a creeper, but somehow it came off as adorable.

"You're crazy."

"Ya keep saying that, but as long as I'm yer kind of crazy, I don't care."

Just like that, he did it again.

"You remember to bring breakfast?" I looked at his empty hands.

He stepped back outside the door and bent down to pick up three large bags of food, and my mouth fell open.

"Was there ever really any doubt that I'd come through?"

"Myles, who are we feeding? You have enough there for an army." Following him to the table, he sat the bags down and pulled the containers out.

"Until I know what ya like, I will bring ya everything." He smiled wide, and I stared at his face trying to decide if I should accept this version of Myles that no one else seemed to see.

I grabbed his arm, and he stopped unloading the bags. He glanced at my hand and then my face. His eyes were wide and worried.

"What's wrong?"

"I need to know something, and please be honest with me."

Myles turned and rested his hands on my hips like he'd done it a thousand times.

"Anything, you name it."

I licked my lips and breathed deeply to steady my out-of-control heart.

"I need to know how many people you've done this with. I don't want to know how many girls you've eaten with or been with sexually." I looked away from his eyes. "Just that you've acted like this..." I waved my hand at the food and then at him, trying to convey what I meant. "And it didn't work out?"

"Oh, that's easy, zero."

"Zero?"

"Aye, zero. If ya want me to be honest, I couldn't give ya a number for the other even if ya asked." He let go of my hip and rubbed the back of his neck. "I've admitted that I was a player, but not now, now with ya, Snowflake."

"So you were a love em and leave em type?"

He blew out a long breath, and I liked that he was at least as uncomfortable as I felt.

"Aye, mostly parties and random hookups."

"And how many of those random one-night stands are going to mock me in the hallway or want to beat me up?"

"All of them," he said, and my mouth fell open. Myles laughed, and I crossed my arms, glaring. "I'm jokin', but yer face was precious." My expression didn't change, and he sobered. "One and only one. I decided it was best to keep stuff like that outside of my own school. Like Pam, she's from one of the other academies and we met at a party."

"Good to know." I hated the jealousy burning inside of me. "So, who was it then?"

Myles cleared his throat.

"It was Vicky's friend Raquel."

I scrunched my face up like I'd just sucked on a lemon. I wish he hadn't been quite so honest, but I guess it was better to know.

"Yeah, no worries. I make that face when she sits at the table too." I laughed at that.

"Are ya worried?"

"Technically, we're not together, so I'm not sure I have a right to be worried or pissed about anything, but it's better to know the odds before making decisions."

"Stop." Myles cupped my face again. "I'm not a calculus equation ya need to solve." He kissed my lips softly and stared into my eyes for what seemed like forever. "I want ya. I have from the first second I laid my eyes on ya, and don't be trying to figure out when I'll be leaving. That only starts us on negative energy."

. . .

T he sound of the whistle and the players giving one another high-fives yanked me out of my daydreaming. Shit, I could hardly remember what I was watching. He was number five, and I'd seen him run up and down the gym and toss a ball to other players, but that was about it. I hoped he wasn't about to quiz me.

The coach dismissed the group, and Myles peeled away. I figured he'd head to the locker room, but he ran right to the bleachers.

"Oh my god, he's coming this way," the girl a couple of rows down sounded like she was about to faint.

Myles ran up the bleachers taking them two at a time, and stopped one row down from me. He peeled off his helmet, and it was like I had stepped into a commercial as he ran his hand through his wet hair.

He was saying something, but I hadn't heard a single word as my mind played that image on a loop in my brain.

"Snowflake?"

"Hmm? Yeah?"

"Did ya hear what I asked ya?"

It felt like all eyes were on us, and it was way too warm.

"Umm, no..." Myles smiled wide, then leaned over, and I quickly moved away. "Get away. You're disgustingly sweaty."

Being on the top row had one distinct disadvantage, a wall behind me, and Myles only stopped moving when he was hovering over my lips.

"When I get ya naked, we're gonna be far sweatier."

Everyone within earshot just heard that, and embarrassment flared in my stomach, but it was quickly squashed as he nipped at my bottom lip. I gasped and opened my mouth. That was all the invitation he needed. His lips were warm against mine. I'd never dreamed that kissing someone would make me feel this fuzzy all over like a charge was under my skin, but not in a bad way.

He broke the kiss the same way it started, by nipping my bottom lip.

"I'm going to get showered and changed. Then we'll get dinner. I won't be long."

Turning, he sprinted down the stairs as fast as he came up, and I didn't take my eyes off him until he disappeared.

Only then did I realize that all eyes really were on me and even a couple of phones. I looked around, and everyone quickly turned away, pretending they weren't watching except the two girls. They looked to be in as much shock as I felt.

I'd never wanted to be the center of attention, and I definitely didn't care if I was dating the popular guy. Dating hadn't been on my radar besides Rylan, but he'd shown what an asshat he was. As the smile pulled at the corner of my mouth, it felt good not to be laughed at for a change.

Chapter 37

Nash

Mrs. Grey paused at the end of the desk, a handful of assignment results in her hand. She gave me her usual evil eye, and I gave her the same passive look I always did in return. She was a tough teacher. I'd learned that her parents were part of the Russian mafia, low-level but loyal. Unfortunately, or maybe fortunately for her, they were killed when she was in her twenties. She lost all clout and ended up teaching at her alma mater.

"She's a good influence on you, Collier, best mark you've ever had," Mrs. Grey said, placing my assignment in front of me.

"Keep up the good work, Ms. Davies. I wish I could clone you." She adjusted her glasses before walking away.

"You are quite the suck-up," Axel said mockingly, spinning around in his chair.

I got way too much amusement from Ren ignoring him, especially after that kiss at Sacred Heart. Myles wasn't the only one ready to kill Axel that night.

Axel knocked on the table, and I sat back to watch the show. One of Ren's eyebrows rose as she glared at Axel's hand.

"Is there something you'd like Axel, other than to insult me, that is?"

Ren slowly lifted her head, her eyes clearly saying fuck off. I'd seen that look a time or two myself already. The issue with staring at her or spending any time around her was that I could clearly remember every word of her journal. There was some seriously sad shit in there, and how her mother died made me more certain about my theory. Maybe she couldn't remember what happened in her family or was too young. Either way, I was more determined than ever to figure out who she really was because a Davies, she was not. Despite what I said to her, I felt... something, protective maybe, after reading it. She may not have suffered the same abuse I did, but the darkness pulled at the same corners of our heart.

"When are we going on a date," Axel asked, and my attention snapped back to the conversation.

"I already told you that we're not."

"I know private spots we can go if you want to skip to the end of the date," Axel said.

Okay, this was getting sad, even for Axel. I'd watched him try to worm his way into a date three times since the party at Sacred Heart, where she was clearly just using him to make a point. The only one who didn't seem to understand that was Axel. But I was up for watching another round of him making an idiot of himself.

"Axel, give it up. I'm never going on a date with you. It was one kiss, nothing more. Besides, you just called me a suck-up. What makes you think I'd want to date someone that insulted me?"

"Come on, that was just a joke. What do you have against me? I can be a lot of fun." He leaned on the desk, and I couldn't hold it in any longer.

"Dude, just fuck off already. She said no, she has the last however many times you asked. Take a hint," I said and sighed, bored of this conversation. The guy had no game and it seriously fucking hurt my eyes to watch this pathetic, bullshit.

"How about you mind your own fucking business," Axel growled, his chair scrapping as he stood up.

"Oh, don't give me a reason to fuck you up," I drawled, slowly pushing to my feet.

"Gentlemen, is there a problem in the back," Mrs. Grey asked.

"Axel, I'm dating Myles. So no, I'm not going out with you. Okay, there, it's out there."

"What?" Axel and I said at the same time. "Since when?"

"What does it matter? The answer is still the same. No, I won't be going on a date with you."

Ren closed her books and stuffed them in her bag. There was a strange heaviness in my stomach, and even though I didn't want her, I wasn't sure I liked the idea of her around all the time hanging off of Myles.

"Then why did you kiss me?" Axel's indignant voice rang out, drawing more curious eyes.

"Are you really that stupid man?" Crossing my arms, I glared at the blockhead. "She used you to piss off Myles, which was obviously effective." I had to give it to Ren, it was an impressive powerplay.

"Is that true? Did you use me?" Axel growled.

Ren straightened her back and tossed her backpack over her shoulder.

"What if I did Axel? You've never kissed a girl just because you wanted to get under her skirt but had no interest in her as a person? You've never said everything you think someone wants to hear to get a date, only to use them and throw them away. Never asked a girl out and then didn't show up just to make a fool out of them?"

"That's different."

"Your dick, or lack of it, doesn't give you the right to treat people like shit. As for you and me, you were drunk. I gave you one kiss, no promises, and certainly haven't led you on since. So for the last time, no. Leave me alone or I'll go to the dean."

Damn, she could give it. Axel's face went a violent shade of red. He opened his mouth to say something else stupid.

"Fuck you," Axel huffed, like he thought that was the greatest insult in the world.

Even if no one else did, I caught the shift in his eyes and tone. His muscles tightened, and his fingers twitched. I may not be sure about her becoming Myles's girl, but if she was part of my circle, she was under my protection. I didn't offer the same protection to Vicky, but that was something I didn't plan on looking at too closely.

"Do it, Axel, and you deal with me instead," I said, stepping closer to Ren.

"I'll ask again, do we have a problem, gentlemen," Mrs. Grey said from the front of the room.

"You lost. Get over it and move on." I never took my eyes off Axel as we stared at one another but called out to Mrs. Grey. "No, no problem. We're having a friendly discussion."

It was technically against the rules to fuck with the head of another family, even if he wasn't what I'd consider major league. Axel was the son of the Slovenian mafia boss. They were a smaller group, known for being dangerous, but I wouldn't just stand here and watch.

"Whatever." He rolled his eyes and turned around.

I stuffed my laptop in my bag and could feel Ren's eyes on me. The bell rang, and I grabbed Ren by the shoulder, guiding her out the back door and away from Axel.

"Why are you pushing me?"

"You don't know when to keep your mouth shut, Princess, and

one of these days, it'll get you into more trouble than you can handle."

"If you mean I stand up for myself, then yeah, I guess I do. That won't stop, no matter how many names people call me or how many times I'm threatened. It certainly won't stop even when guys in masks try to scare the shit out of me."

I smirked at her pointed dig. We drew a few looks as we walked past. Most looked worried like I was taking her out behind the school to beat her to death. On the one hand, it was good that everyone thought I could and would follow through, but it also bothered me. It meant the only thing separating me from becoming my father was desire, and I was terrified that one day I'd wake up and that last piece of me would disappear.

"When did you start dating Myles," I asked, not removing my hand as we walked.

I couldn't figure out why her dating Myles bothered me or why I felt protective now. I blamed the journal making me see her as more than another chess piece.

"Technically, we're not." She sidestepped, and I let my hand fall away from her shoulder, but I walked with her all the same. "Why do you care?"

"Myles is one of my best friends and important to many things in my life. I like to know when there are major changes. Girlfriends tend to fuck things up and make my life more difficult." I said.

She looked up at me like I'd just spewed dog shit.

"Yes, like I'm the one stalking you," she drawled, and I narrowed my eyes at her. "Not that I owe you anything, especially after what you did, but I told Myles I would give him an answer after Christmas. Axel doesn't need to know that. Happy now," she said, pushing open the front door of Morisward Hall, and we stepped outside into the harsh wind.

"Yes."

We were getting our first real snowfall this weekend, not just flurries, and I was looking forward to the blanket of white. Most couldn't handle it or just didn't like the cold and snowy months, but I loved to lay in the snow until my skin stung and then hop in my hot tub, feeling like my skin was going to melt off. It was cleansing.

Rory pushed his way out the doors of the building we were heading and walked toward me. He glanced at me but looked down at his phone as he continued his walk. As we passed, he ran his shoulder into mine, and I felt his fingers slipping into my hand, leaving a piece of paper behind.

"Hey, watch where you're walking, asshole," I yelled and stuffed the note in my pocket.

"Sorry, man," Rory called back and kept going.

"Fuck some people," I growled, making the exchange look authentic. When I told him I wanted the information fast, I hadn't meant for him to hunt me down at school, but he was effective.

"Done harassing people," Ren asked as I caught back up to her.

"He ran into me."

Ren's eyebrow arched up, and even though she didn't say anything, I felt like she was scolding me.

"Why are you following me anyway?"

"I'm not, just heading the same way, and you're the one that waited for me. Besides, I can't help that you're short with tiny strides." I smirked as she glared up at me.

I yanked open the front door to the main building.

"You going to sit with us for lunch?"

"Me, sit with you and Vicky for lunch?"

"Yeah."

She smiled wide and then laughed.

"Not even if pigs learn to fly or hell freezes over. Maybe not even during a zombie apocalypse."

"Harsh Princess, but I know you're lying. You'd happily fuck me with zombies walking around, missing body parts, and watching us through a window while wanting to rip the skin from our bones. It would be an ultimate fuck you."

Her face scrunched up like she was trying to picture that

scenario. She looked adorable, and I liked that she imagined fucking me.

"You have strange fantasies, Nash, like seriously, that's fucked up."

I had a quick comeback ready to go, but Ren's name was bellowed like a fog horn in the foyer, and all the students froze as all eyes turned in our direction. At first, I didn't know who screamed until I spotted her father leaving the secretaries office.

"Dad?" She sounded as confused as everyone looked.

He stomped toward her, his eyes wild like an animal, but she didn't budge. She walked away from me, meeting the threat of her father head-on. He looked like a man pushed to the brink sitting on the edge of insanity.

"There you are. What the hell did you do," he screamed, and Ren looked around at the growing number of people watching.

"I don't know what you're talking about."

"Don't play stupid with me." He held up a thick pile of papers that looked like a statement of some kind from where I was standing. "You fucking maxed out your credit card! And what the hell is all this stuff? There is one thousand sweaters and pairs of underwear and socks. There's enough soap, shampoo, and pillows to start your own store, and why the hell are there five hundred cases of baby formula and diapers?" With each word, his voice got a touch louder.

I was as fascinated as everyone else. Why did she need all those things? Crossing my arms, I watched the show. Each one of these interactions gave me a little more insight into Ren Davies and her family.

Ren snatched the papers from her father's hand and shook them at him.

"This is why you're here? This is what finally made you come here?"

"Two hundred-thousand dollars Ren. Of course, I'm here," he said, and she slowly shook her head.

"You want to know why?"

"Yes, I demand to know why!"

She slammed the papers against her father's chest, and he stepped back from the sudden blow.

"Fuck you! If you can't figure it out for yourself, then there is nothing left to our relationship. I'm happy Mum's dead, so she didn't have to see the waste of space you've become," Ren screamed, her face twisting with pain as her eyes filled with tears.

I knew he was going to hit her. I'd become perfectly honed in on what someone looked like before they struck. I lunged forward and grabbed Mr. Davies' arm as he raised it. My fingers dug in hard, and I knew there would be a bruise on his skin.

"Do it, and it will be the last thing you ever do." My whisper was as lethal as a gun, and I meant every word.

Mr. Davies shocked expression turned to me.

"Nash?"

I jerked him closer, and he suddenly didn't look so cocky.

"I don't care how much you suck my father's dick or what you do for him to be in his good graces." He winced as I squeezed harder. "If you lay one hand on Ren, for any reason, I will rip your arms from your screaming body and cook them over an open flame so you can smell your flesh burn. That way, you'll know what you smell like in the flames of hell before you die." I glared into his wide, terrified eyes. "Don't test me, Davies, I can make what my father does look like childs play."

Ren was the only other person close enough to hear what I said, and I could see her mouth fall open.

"Nash, I don't need you protecting me," she whispered, her lips hardly moving.

"Mr. Collier, Mr. Davies, and Ms. Davies, we will take this conversation into my office," Dean Henry said.

I wasn't sure when he came out or how much he saw. I wasn't sure I even cared. The anger was burning so hot that I could picture following through on my threat for no reason other than watching him scream.

I released Mr. Davies' arm.

"I've said all I need to say."

I marched off, pushing my way through the crowd of people to find Vicky waiting by the open cafeteria door. She was in her Queen Bee stance. Arms crossed, eyes narrowed, with a foot and a manicured nail tapping.

"Say one word to me right now, and I'll rip your fucking tongue from your head," I said as she opened her mouth.

The consuming rage was bubbling up, and I needed to calm down. I marched out the side door of the cafeteria to get some fresh air. Myles and Theo were walking up the path, talking.

"Who the fuck pissed in yer cereal," Myles asked as I stomped up to them and cut them off.

"I just had to do your job for you." I poked him in the chest. "And stop hiding shit from me," I growled, wanting a fight.

Myles looked at Theo and then back at me.

"What the fuck are ya talkin about, man?"

"Just now inside, Ren's father was going to hit her, and I was the one that stopped it. That's your job now, right? And why did I find out the two of you are, sort of together, from her and not you?"

I shoved him, and he stepped back. The confused look on his face quickly shifted to something much darker. I could always count on Myles to match my anger. I hated how he hid his inner demons so much easier than I could.

"Did ya say her father was going to hit her?"

"Yeah, and I stopped him." I pushed him again. "Then the Dean took both of them into his office."

"Stop fuckin' pushing me, man."

"Nash, this is ridiculous. We never give you a rundown of who we're sleeping with," Theo said.

"I'm not even sleeping with her, and what do you care?"

That was a question I couldn't answer.

"I'm sick of all the secrets," I said.

"Are we doin' this again?" The anger in his voice was getting more prominent. "Why is it that yer suddenly thinking I'm not trust-worthy?" I did trust him. So much that I knew I could push him, we beat the shit out of one another and have a beer later. "Are ya gettin' as paranoid as yer old man?"

I took the bait for what it was and jumped at Myles, tackling him to the cold ground. I landed a right hook at the same time he did. The packed earth was hard and hurt like a bastard as we rolled around, exchanging blows, but neither of us gave an inch.

"Should we stop them?" I heard Theo ask.

Myles caught me across the jaw with his elbow rattling the teeth in my head, but he groaned as I got a knee into his side.

"Fuck no, this is awesome," Blake answered.

"Too bad there aren't more people out here I could take bets," Liam chimed in, and the running commentary was enough to snap me out of the moment.

Now that the rage was used up, I didn't bother to land my next hit and pushed myself off Myles to flop beside him. He had a split lip and some blood trickling from his nose.

"You look like shit," I said to him.

"Ha, speak for yerself. Ya look no better," Myles said and smiled.

"Sorry, man, you know I trust you with my life, right?" I watched his face closely, and the humorous smile slowly fell.

"Honestly, sometimes I wonder." He pushed himself into a sitting position and stood, holding out his hand.

Grabbing his hand, I let him help me up but didn't let go.

"I'm sorry. I just...fuck, it's just me, and I needed this...fuck...."

We stood like that for a few seconds before he nodded.

"Here, you can tell me what it says." I pulled the paper Rory had given me from my pocket and handed it over.

Myles took the small square piece of paper and opened it. There were days that I loved who we were and what I was born into. There were some days that I wouldn't trade at all. We were at the top of the food chain, and with that came privileges others couldn't even fathom. But then there were days when I'd trade every last cent and all my power to feel real peace.

"So what does it say?"

"We have a problem to take care of," Myles said, handing the note back.

R en "I want her grounded," my father snarled.

Dean Henry raised an eyebrow at my father as if telling him to watch his tone. He squirmed in his seat, and it felt far too good that he was getting the same scrutiny I would.

"You want to ground me?" I held my arms up to show where we were standing. "I can't get any more grounded than this. You already shipped me off like I meant nothing to you and then tacked on a ridiculous curfew, making it impossible for me to do anything with any friends I meet." I crossed my arms. "What's next on your agenda to ruin my life?"

Dean Henry smacked his hand on his desk, and we both jumped. "That is quite enough from both of you."

Dean Henry casually sat down, and my conversation with Myles came to mind. Who ran this place? What ties did they have that they kept the worst of the worst in line? And how did Dean Henry not seem frazzled by what he saw?

"Now, Mr. Davies, I understand that you're upset with what your daughter has done, but there are better ways to get to the reasoning than shouting down my building and causing a scene." He tapped his fingers on his desk and it seemed loud and a lot more threatening than it should in the quiet office. "We do not tolerate such behavior. I would hate to see you banned from the property."

"I'm sorry, I...." My father ran his hand through his hair. "I've been very stressed lately."

"Oh sure, apologize to him," I said, crossing my arms. "Figures."

Dean Henry's stern expression found me, and I shifted uncomfortably in my seat.

"Ms. Davies, tell your father why you maxed out his credit card."

It was tempting not to say a word, but the longer the dean stared at me, not blinking, the more creeped out I became.

"I did it to get your attention. It was payback. You dropped me off here and never showed me our new home, didn't let me know if anything of mine or Mum's arrived safely. You sent me a few pictures and said you hoped I was having a good time. That was all before you dragged me to a Thanksgiving dinner, got drunk, and then shipped me back here rather than take me home and spend time with me."

I held my hands in front of me, hating the tears that had started to flow like someone had turned on a tap.

"Don't you get it? Mum just died, and you ripped me away from the only home I've ever known and the only people I'm close to. The one time I really needed you to be present you...." Shaking my head, I wiped away the tears. "It doesn't matter. You're happier drinking your problems away, and I don't know why I expected it to be any different with me now that mum is gone. I thought maybe you couldn't deal with her sickness, but... I'm starting to feel like there was more to you staying away, and I'm part of that reason."

"You're talking foolishness, I didn't think you wanted me around. You told me not to visit," he said, and I rolled my eyes.

"Well, I can see why Mr. Collier likes you. You're good at following orders."

I so badly wanted to ask what the fuck he did for him, but this wasn't the time. Not in front of Dean Henry when I wasn't sure what his role was besides Dean. For all I knew, he could be the head of the secret group Myles mentioned.

"See what I mean...she makes no sense," my father said. "One second she wants me around and then insults me with the next breath."

Dean Henry held up his hand and stopped any further complaints.

"Ms. Davies, what did you purchase with the money?"

"I bought necessities for those at a homeless shelter and a battered women's shelter. I didn't spend the money on myself. I bought a few items like new school shirts for me, and that was it."

"Well, I think what we have here is a standard misunderstanding and lack of good communication. Mr. Davies, did you have anything you'd like to add?"

"Only that I'll be away for Christmas on business, so you'll need to stay here. I've already called Nadia and told her you won't be visiting." My mouth fell open as he stood. I didn't think he could find new lows, and just like that, he kicked me in the teeth when I was already down. "I'll talk to you soon, Ren, and we'll discuss your punishment for what you did. I need to think on it. Have a good day Dean Henry," my father said like he was ending a business meeting.

As quick as he came, he was gone and left the office door open behind him. I stared at it before slowly turning to face Dean Henry, who was watching me closely.

"Am I in trouble?"

"No. I do not police family affairs, only what happens inside my walls. You are free to go."

I looked around as I stood, and everything suddenly felt more tangible. Reality had finally settled in. My father was worse than I thought, and I was trapped here like an animal tempted to chew off my paw to escape.

Dean Henry called out to me as I reached his office door. "Ms Davies?" I looked over my shoulder at him. "For what it's worth, I personally feel you used the money on a worthy cause, even if your actions were guided by anger. You may go," he said, his voice soft and yet still as commanding as ever.

"Thank you," I said, and slipped out the door.

Chapter 38

Ren Christmas break had officially begun, and even though I was tempted to stay in the art room after class, I was determined to visit my family over Christmas. Well, Lizzy, her mum, and my Aunt were the only family I had left as far as I was concerned.

It didn't take long before everyone knew about my father's tantrum or the fallout afterward. Myles didn't like it, but he agreed to smuggle me off the property to the airport. Vicky couldn't know anything about my plan, so I couldn't pack until now. I knew the bitch—who was swinging from my last nerve—would say some-

389

thing to the dean, or worse, hunt down my father. I wouldn't put anything past her at this point.

I shivered as I walked into the dorm, shaking off the bits of sadness that had clung to me since my conversation with my father. I was going to see my best friend. Nothing could've cheered me up more. The elevator seemed super slow as it made its ascent. The door dinged open, and there she was—I just couldn't escape without seeing Vicky.

"Well, if it isn't the queen of misfits." She tapped her chin as I stepped out. "You're just like that movie where all the misfit toys get discarded into a pile where nobody wants them." Her lips pulled down in a mocking frown. "So sad, poor little Ren here all alone."

"Aren't you forgetting something?" I said, and Vicky stupidly looked down at her suitcase and then smoothed out her expensive coat. "Your broom...how will you get home without it?" Vicky just glared at me, so I continued.

"Have fun making someone else's life miserable. I will be happily relaxing without your shrieking voice and bitch scent," I said, walking away.

"At least my family wants me. I can't say the same for you," she called after me.

I didn't bother to slow down and heard the elevator door close moments later. Normally, a comment like that would bother me, but I knew the truth. My mum had loved me with her whole heart, and even when she was at her worst, she always made Christmas special.

Whatever was going on with my father was bigger than me. He would have hit me if it hadn't been for Nash, which was so out of character. His entire personality had changed in the last five years. The more I replayed our conversations in my head, the more apparent it was that something was happening with him.

I'd spent those years being the parent and caring for my mum. I couldn't start that all over again with my father and keep my sanity. Some days it felt like I was clinging desperately to it with my fingertips, and it was still slipping.

"Hey, Ren."

I turned at Ivy's cheery voice and watched her waving as she jogged down the hall with Chantry.

"Merry Christmas, Happy Holidays, Happy Hanukkah, and any others I missed," Ivy said, gripping me in a hug. She held me so tight it felt like she would break my ribs, but her joy was infectious, and I found myself happily hugging back.

Releasing Ivy, I hugged Chantry. She'd started to warm up in the last couple of weeks, but getting more than a handful of words out of her was still my mission.

"You two look happy," I said.

"Yeah, my dad agreed to let me visit my older sister for Christmas since I haven't seen her in three years. She lives in England, and I've never been there before." The excitement was pouring off of Ivy in waves.

"I'm so happy for you. That's going to be an amazing trip. What are you doing, Chantry?"

"Going home to visit my family in Japan. My dad is here for business, so he's picking me up, and we're flying home together," she said, her voice still no more than a whisper. I hoped to hell I never had to hear her in a noisy place.

"Wow, Japan and the UK, they both sound wonderful." I smiled as they stared. "Oh, you want to know what I'm doing?" I waited until the hallway was clear to speak. "I'm flying home to visit my aunt and best friend," I said softly.

"Does your dad know?" Ivy whispered back, getting in on the conspiracy vibe.

I shook my head.

"He's not speaking to me, and he's going away for work, so...I'm doing what I want."

Life was too short, and I refused to stay locked up like a prisoner.

"You're so much braver than I am. How are you getting to the airport," Ivy asked as Myles walked through the door to the girl's wing.

He looked delicious in his jeans and hoodie with a long stylish coat open over the top. It was like he was strutting down a runway as he walked toward me, smiling. The bruise on his cheek and the cut on his lip were almost gone now. Was it terrible that I would've loved to see Nash and Myles fighting? Rolling around on the ground, muscles straining.

"I think I know now," Ivy said.

"What?" I whipped my head around to look at them as they giggled, making my sudden hot flash worse.

"Hi ya, Snowflake," Myles said, handing me a coffee.

When I took it from his hand, he wrapped his other arm around my waist and tucked me into his side. He smelled so good, and just being around him made me want to curl up in his warmth and kiss him until we passed out.

"I missed ya."

Of course, the only thing my brain came up with was to smile stupidly back and say, "Thank you for the coffee."

"Well, I think that's our cue to go. I just wanted to catch you before we left," Ivy said, and Chantry nodded.

"You two have a wonderful holiday and send pictures. I can't wait to see everything," I said as I stepped away from Myles to hug them.

It felt oddly normal when I returned to his side, and I wasn't sure what to make of these newfound feelings. I wasn't used to being touched other than the odd hug, but he always wanted to have contact with me. Even while studying, he needed to be close enough that our shoulders or legs touched, or he'd hold my hand. It was awkward at first, but now I looked forward to the little touches and stolen kisses.

The skeptical voice in the back of my mind kept telling me to be careful, but I needed to learn to take some risks to have the life I wanted. So far, Myles was proving himself trustworthy every second we were together, and I didn't hear any rumors of him hitting on anyone else. I needed to start trusting myself and people again, or I would have a sad life.

"Did you tell them where you're going," Myles asked when we were in my room.

"Yeah, was I not supposed to?"

I put my coffee down on my desk.

"Look, I'm not going to say don't tell them about yer life, but everything ya know and say can be used against ya. Words and knowledge are just as powerful as any weapon."

Myles walked us over to the table and sat down, pulling me onto his lap.

"Mmm, ya smell so sweet." He kissed the side of my neck. "One day, I wanna take ya to Ireland and show ya around. We still have my old home there."

My eyes fluttered closed as he continued his soft kisses until our lips met, and a moan escaped my lips.

"You keep doing that, and I may miss getting a flight."

"That's me plan," he teased.

Clearing my throat, I gave him a quick kiss and stood before I really did end up staying.

"Tell me what I should be worried about with Ivy and Chantry."

I wandered over to my bed and pulled the suitcase out from underneath. Light blue was definitely not the color I would have chosen. It had been used once and looked like I'd beaten it with a black baseball bat.

"For starters, Ivy's father is not a good man as ya've seen with yer own eyes. I think he plays too many sides and doesn't know who he owes more to. It would be easy for Ivy to slip up and mention where yer goin'."

He sipped his coffee while I thought about what he said.

"So they may not be a direct threat, but what they know or who may see their phones could be."

"Aye. As for Chantry...I'm not really sure. She keeps to herself. I know her family is Yakuza, but not much more than that. I keep an eye on what everyone does."

"Don't you get tired of all this? I mean, I just learned about my father's involvement, and I wish I could go back in time and forget."

I leaned against the desk, watching Myles closely. His finger softly tapped on the table, and his face was haunted.

"Aye, I do. The things I've done and will do are just part of me now. The death, blood, pain, fear of getting caught, and waring with my morals...ya either get used to it, or ya die. My father would shoot me between the eyes if he thought I wanted to run."

My mouth fell open in shock. I'd met his father, and he gave me the creeps, but shooting his son for not wanting to be in the business was next-level crazy.

"We have a saying in our group for why we do what we do. For the Deserted, For the Power, For the Blood of the Fallen. We do this for those that wanted to leave, to take control, and for those that gave their lives needlessly. Like your mother...like mine," he said, taking another sip of his coffee.

The reminder hurt, but the fact that half of what the guys did was to stop things like what happened to my mum helped on some level.

"Do you want to tell me what happened to your mum?"

"Aye, but not today. I do want to show you this." Myles dug into his pocket and pulled out a folded piece of paper.

"What's that?" I asked, as he held it out to me. He smiled, but didn't say anything further. Taking it from his hands I gave him a skeptical look before focusing on what the paper said. "Oh my god, Myles! This is fabulous," I said. Excitement bubbled in my chest and I couldn't stop smiling at his mid-term grades. He had a, B or better in all his classes.

"The Dean says I can stay on my teams, and that's because of all yer help." Myles grabbed my hand and pulled me close enough that I was standing between his legs and staring down into those amber eyes that I couldn't get enough of.

"I'm so happy for you, and you did all the hard work, not me."

"Aye, maybe, but I can tell ya that I wouldn't have put as much effort in or saw the value in doing so without ya."

Cupping his face I kissed him and for the first time since I arrived, hope bloomed in my chest.

"So Snowflake, are ya ready to give me an answer bout being my girl?"

There were so many variables and forks in the road that I just couldn't say yes as much as I was tempted to.

"When I get back from Christmas, I promise to give you an answer," I said, kissing the top of his nose and then heading back to the suitcase.

"Fine, I guess I can suffer a few more weeks."

It was unfair that someone as sexy as he was could pull off the perfect pout.

"I'm sure you'll survive."

Opening my dresser drawer, I grabbed a pair of underwear. I stared at it and held it up, pulling the material apart to show the entire crotch area cut out.

"What the hell?"

Tossing it on the dresser, I pulled out the next one, and they were the same. I threw it down and grabbed a third set, and they'd also been cut.

"Bitch," I growled.

"What's wrong?"

I spun around, fuming, and held up the black pair of lacey underwear.

"This is what's wrong," I said.

Stretching the crotch area, I showed off the hole. Myles's hand froze with his coffee halfway to his mouth as he stared wide-eyed.

"This is unbelievable. I can't believe she did this."

"I'm sorry, what's the problem," he asked, and my brows knit together.

"The entire panty area is missing."

"Yeah...again, I'm not seeing the problem. Are ya gonna wear 'em like that?"

Myles sat his coffee down as he licked his lips.

"No, of course, I'm not."

"But they're all like that?"

"Yes."

"So yer gonna to go commando?"

Grabbing my tank top from the dresser, I whipped it at his head. "Jerk."

Myles caught the material out of the air, his laugh ringing out, and as pissed off as I was, I couldn't stay angry, staring at his amused face. I ended up giggling along with him and then sighed. Vicky was creative. A total bitch move, but creative.

"Is anything else of yours cut?"

Myles stood and came over as I pulled open the rest of the drawers and did a quick inspection, but all seemed fine.

"No, just the underwear. Damn her, now I have no panties."

Myles picked up the icy blue pair I had on the dresser.

"Again, I'm not seeing the problem with this," Myles said, grinning.

I tried to snatch the underwear out of his hand, but he held them over his head.

"You're not keeping those."

"I sure am. Consider it my payment for smuggling ya out of the academy and taking ya to the airport."

He smiled, and I couldn't believe he wanted to keep a pair of my underwear like a prize. I wanted to smack him and order him to give them back. It was a pervy move, but the thought of him holding a pair of my underwear while he jerked off was next-level hot.

"Fine, but no one, and I mean no one, ever sees those. If they end up here at school in the cafeteria or on one of the teacher's desks, we will have a very serious conversation that will end with my foot up your ass."

"Yer so fucking cute."

Grabbing my chin, he dropped his lips to mine. It was more aggressive than the other kisses. He was so forceful that I stepped back, but he followed till my legs hit the bed. When his hand gripped my hair, I moaned as he pulled my head back until our kiss broke. Those amber eyes were dark like brandy and just as intoxicating. His lips hovered just over mine as the butterflies fluttered in my gut. Was this what passion felt like?

I wasn't ready for sex, but all I could picture was him peeling that coat and hoodie off so I could touch his skin.

"Ya make me wild, Snowflake."

My stomach pulled tight, and embarrassment flooded my body as he brought the blue panties to his nose but kept his eyes on me. A sound far more animal than human rumbled in his chest. I shivered and bit my lip. He broke eye contact to follow the action, and heat flooded my face.

"Wanna give me a used pair?"

My mouth dropped open with his question.

"Um, no."

"I'll steal a pair from ya one day Snowflake," he said.

I cleared my throat and forced myself not to push for more. I wanted to try things that other girls my age were already doing, what Lizzy had done, but a part of me was holding back for so many reasons.

Before I could say anything, Myles eased back and released his hold on my hair. Taking a shuddering breath, I leaned into his hand as he rubbed his thumb along my cheek. The room was so quiet that the pounding of my heart filled my ears.

"Ya better get packed before I change my mind and keep ya here."

Myles walked back to the table, but my feet were rooted to the spot, eyes glued to his back.

It was obvious now that I wouldn't be free of these feelings. An ember had become a spark, and a spark, was now a small flame, but with each passing day, that flame grew. Soon it would be out of control, and that terrified me.

Still breathing hard, I turned around and packed my bag. Luckily, Vicky hadn't bothered to touch the boy shorts I slept in sometimes. They would do until I got to Lizzy's and we could go shopping. Myles turned on some music, and I glanced over at him as he stared at his phone, tapping his foot to the song.

"I think that's it," I said, stuffing the last sweater into the top and zipping it closed.

"So you remember what I told ya about where to go," Myles asked.

He stood and walked over, taking the large suitcase from my hand.

"Yes, I need to follow the hallway that leads to Ivy's room, but at the end, I make a right and follow it to the emergency stairwell. I take it outside, and you will be waiting for me."

"Aye."

"So tell me again why I'm going that way, but you're going out the front?"

I slipped on my coat and made sure to grab my toque and gloves.

"I want them to see me leave and think I'm headin' home. If we walk out the front door together and they're watching ya as closely as I think they are, then they're gonna have Sheriff Morrison on us before we make it out the gate."

"I still don't understand what my father could've done for all of this to happen, and he won't return my texts. I hate this. I feel like I'm in an exotic cage filled with the offspring of killers."

"It's not just the parents that kill, Snowflake."

My hands stilled on the large white button on my coat. Raising my gaze to Myles, I searched his face for an answer. Was he one of those people? He didn't give anything away, but I already knew.

"Do I want to know how many names are on a missing list because of you?"

Fear should've been ravaging my body, but I still saw him the same. What that said about me was something I didn't want to study too closely.

His eyes softened.

"Any is too many, but my father doesn't see it that way. Are ya wanting an exact number?"

"No, I don't think I do. I'm not sure how I feel about you taking someone's life. You're seventeen and don't want to tell me how many people you've had to...you know. There is something messed up about that."

"This is who I must be, Snowflake. I make no apologies for what I've done and will do. I've let ya into my world and told ya more than I've ever told anyone outside the inner circle. So if ya can't handle being with me, all I ask is that ya forget what I told ya and never speak to anyone about it." He sighed and looked down. "But I hope that's not what ya decide. I really like ya, Snowflake."

"So what would happen if I didn't want to be with you and knew all this? Would Nash or someone else come for me?"

"Nash would say yes. My father would say ya should already be bleeding on the floor. I say I would rather have yer trust."

There was so much weight to his words that I felt them pressing in on my heart, making my stomach churn. My life seemed so sheltered compared to his and Nash's or really any of them. I couldn't imagine the secrets they've had to keep or the things they've seen. Hearing the rumors about those born into a life like this was one thing, but seeing it with my own eyes was entirely different.

Our worlds were so far apart, yet they'd collided, and now I wasn't sure I wanted to give that up, even knowing what I knew. I waited for the guilt of that knowledge to smack me in the face, but nothing happened.

Stepping closer, I slipped my arms around his waist inside his coat. Myles looked down into my eyes, and I felt compelled to ask a question I never thought would leave my lips.

"What would you do if someone hurt me?"

The dark gleam in his eyes made my blood quicken in my veins.

"I would knock on the Devil's door and happily accept whatever fate awaited me if it meant it was my hand that stuck the blade in the fucker's heart."

There were no words to describe what I felt as I searched his eyes. They held no humor, and when he touched his lips to mine, the desire was still there, but he didn't press further. It was more of a promise than a kiss.

"No one will ever hurt ya, and if they did, they'd have to deal with me. I will make them beg at yer feet for forgiveness, Snowflake, while I burn their world to the ground. Call me a monster if ya want, but nothing would stop me. Not even you," he whispered against my lips.

We stood motionless, our eyes locked. I broke the stillness and kissed Myles hard, hugging him tighter. At no time in my life had I felt safer. Even if it was nothing more than pretty words, they were the sweetest I'd ever heard. Cupping my cheeks, Myles kissed me back, and his tongue was relentless as he explored my mouth, stealing my moans.

"Fuck," he growled, breaking the kiss and touching his forehead to mine. "We really need to go before the last of my willpower snaps."

Nodding, I stepped back but laid my hand on his chest.

"I believe you would do that for me, and...."

Myles' finger was soft as it touched my lips and halted the rest of my sentence.

"Ya never need to thank me, and if yer gonna ask me not to, ya might as well save yer breath. Come on, let's get out of here."

"Okay."

Within seconds we were out the door and smuggling me off the property.

Chapter 39

R **en**

Making the final turn, we veered into the departure area and pulled over to park.

"Are ya sure ya don't want me to come with ya?"

I laughed at the quirky lop-sided smile plastered on Myles's face.

"Yes, I'm sure. But no worries, I'll bring you back something very Canadian, and I already promised to send pictures."

"A few sexy ones would be nice too." He winked as I glared. "I'll take that as a no."

I shook my head at him, leaning in to give him a quick peck before pushing open my door and hopping out.

Myles got out and pulled the heavy suitcase out of the back of the truck, sitting it on the ground for me. Grabbing me before I could touch my luggage, he pulled me into a hug, and every sappy movie I'd ever watched where two people said goodbye at the airport flooded my mind. How had this even happened? I'd been so determined to keep him at a distance, but somehow he picked the lock on my emotions and snuck inside.

"I'm going to miss you, and thank you for helping me."

"I'm going to miss ya too, Snowflake. Be safe," he said.

"I will."

Cars were lining up behind us, and I smiled, wanting to remember this sweet moment that was so new for me, carrying it with me on my flight. As I wheeled my bag through the glass doors, the putrid scent of too many people and jet fuel hit me making me gag.

Looking around for a company I recognized, I finally spotted one from ads in Alberta. The airport was packed with people heading somewhere for the holidays, and it was easy to tell who was escaping to an exotic destination as they stood in line with flowered shirts and flip-flops. They looked like they were going to run off the plane and straight onto the beach.

There were only a couple of people at the linkup to purchase tickets, but the line for the security area looked like a snake that went on forever. My first time flying had been on a private flight, and we drove right up to the plane. This was very different, and I felt a trickle of fear when I realized what I was doing. I hardly knew what to ask for because I'd never traveled alone, hell other than to the movies or the mall, I'd never gone anywhere alone. Nervousness took over, and even though I'd contacted Lizzy, and she was going to borrow her mum's car to pick me up, I looked over my shoulder to the drop-off area, wondering if Myles was already gone.

No, I couldn't let fear of the unknown control me. I needed to think of this as an adventure.

"Next."

I whipped around to see the woman behind the counter staring at me. She looked like she'd sucked on lemons for breakfast while she summoned me with a crooked finger. I tried to smile at her, and she glared—not a great start.

"Hi there, I...."

"Passport."

"What?"

"I need your passport." The annoyed expression that seemed permanently molded to her face never changed as she held out her hand.

"Oh, okay. One sec."

"You should have it ready next time."

"I'm sorry, this is my first time. I didn't know."

I dug around in my small backpack for my passport.

"It's on the sign."

The woman pointed to the triangle-shaped sign on the counter that said in bold red letters to have your passport ready. I swallowed hard as a bead of sweat trickled down my back. My fingers touched the rough exterior of the passport, and I pulled it out to hand over.

"Sorry."

Could I feel like any more of an idiot? Was this why people dreaded going to airports, or was this just the beginning, and it would only get worse? That was a terrifying prospect.

"Where to," she asked, her unsettling gaze focused on her computer screen.

"Alberta, Canada," I said, but she looked up at me.

"Which one? There is more than one airport in Alberta."

"Oh...um...the one that's in Calgary?"

"Are you asking me or telling me?"

I sucked in a deep breath so I didn't go postal and jump over the kiosk at the woman who was being extremely rude for no reason.

"Did I do something to you to offend you?" She opened her mouth but didn't say anything. "I just told you this is my first time flying. I'm sorry, I'm not a pro and don't know exactly what to say. If you wouldn't mind helping me out a little, it will probably make everything go smoother, and maybe I won't walk away thinking this is the worst experience of my life," I said, managing to keep calm.

I was ready for her to have a meltdown and call security. I would end up on the local news and could already see the headline: *Canadian Teen Loses It at the Local Airport on the Ticket Agent. Guess They're Not so Friendly, Eh?*

"Please, just help me. My mum passed away a couple of months ago, and this is the first time I'm going home to visit her grave and see my Aunt, my only living relative other than my father, who thinks that spending time with his only daughter is too much work over Christmas."

Tears filled my eyes as my bottom lip trembled, but I refused to let them fall.

"All I want is a flight to Calgary, and I don't care what airport. I'll figure out how to get where I'm going once I land."

"Okay," she said softly, her eyes that had been so hard and cold softened enough for me to see she still had a soul and working here hadn't sucked it all out of her body.

"Do you want a round trip?"

I nodded as her fingers traveled across the keys.

"We have a single economy seat on the 9:15 pm flight returning December 27th or a single seat in business class at 10:25 pm returning December 28th."

"The economy is perfect, thank you."

I pulled out my wallet and slid the shiny credit card from where I kept it. How did this thing and the money it represented mean so much more to my father than I did? I was his flesh and blood. At one point, he knew that and acted like that, but not anymore. The last of the father I knew was gone.

"That will be nine-hundred and sixty-two dollars," she said, and I held out the card for her to take.

She reacted like everyone else when they looked at the platinum card. Swiping it, she hit several buttons, and her eyebrows went up. I didn't like that look. She swiped it again before her eyes found mine.

"Do you have another card?"

"Why is this one not working? It should, I checked the balance this morning, and there was plenty of room."

"It has a block on it. No transactions can be approved without calling the number on file," she said, her voice sad.

She turned her screen enough to point out the box with the number. My fist tightened until my fingernails dug into my palm as I stared at my father's cellphone number. My bank account only had a few hundred dollars, as I'd never needed to worry about a bank balance. That earlier trapped feeling flooded my system like a tidal wave crashing into the shore and dragging anything in its way back out to sea. I was on the sand and should've expected the wave, but I hadn't. I never thought he'd cut me off like this.

The ticket agent laid the credit card on the counter.

"For what it's worth, I'm sorry. I lost my mom three years ago, and it still hurts."

"Thanks."

I stuffed the useless card back into my wallet and walked like a zombie past the couple standing behind me, their eyes filled with pity as they watched me.

Stepping out into the cold air, I pulled on my toque and sat on a bench. No one else was stupid enough to sit outside with the bitter wind, but I didn't care. I stared at my gloved hands in my lap, the dejection overwhelming me. I'd been so strong for so long, but I didn't want to fight for everything all the time anymore. It was tiresome. I was tired.

A droplet fell on my gloves, the glistening tear just a tiny dot, and I felt just as small and insignificant. I hated to do this, but I pulled out my phone and called Myles.

"Hey, Snowflake, did ya make it through security okay?"

The sound of his voice made mine shake.

"No, can you come back, please? I'm really sorry." I swallowed the sob.

"Stop apologizing. I'm turning around now. What happened?" I heard the truck slowing and the clicking of its turn signal before it revved as he picked up speed.

"He blocked my card," I said, wiping away the stupid tears I never wanted to shed for my father again.

"Oh shit, I'm sorry."

"Thank you, Myles."

"Do ya want me to buy ya the ticket?"

"As sweet as that is...no," I said.

"Are ya sure?"

"I'm sure. I'll see you soon."

I hung up before I lost it and started bawling like a lunatic. I hadn't realized how much I was looking forward to going home and seeing Lizzy and Aunt Nadia and visiting my mum's grave. It felt like the grieving I needed to do had been ripped away from me along with everything else. I wanted to take flowers and sit at my mum's grave while I told her everything that had happened and how much I loved and missed her.

I didn't see or hear Myles pull up, but he was suddenly kneeling in front of me, his warm hands on my frozen knees. I hadn't noticed how cold I was.

"Come on, Snowflake, let's get ya warmed up." Myles helped me to my feet, and I sucked in a deep breath of his cologne. "I already put yer bag in the truck."

Wow, I really had been out of it.

Hopping up into the truck, he closed my door, and I leaned my head against the glass. Moments later, Myles was in the cab and wheeling us away from the curb to leave the airport behind.

"I'm sorry, Snowflake," he said, reaching out to grip my hand.

"I know. I just need a day to process."

I held his hand tighter.

We pulled around to the backdoor, where I'd made my escape earlier. My father knew how to keep me where he wanted me. I had no one to visit, didn't know where our new house was, and had no money to travel. I guess it could be worse. I could have no place to go at all.

"Did you want me to come in with you," Myles asked, and I gave him a little smile.

"No, I need to be alone, and I need to call Lizzy and let her know I'm not coming. Girl talk with lots of crying, nothing you want to see," I teased, trying to make light of what had happened.

Myles gave me a lopsided smile for my effort, but his eyes still seemed worried.

"I'll be fine, I promise. I'll text you later."

I reached for the door handle, but Myles stopped me, his hand gripping mine firmly.

"Ya said that yer mum loved Christmas. Tell me what the two of ya would do."

"Oh...well...we would make fun ornaments for the tree and bake and build gingerbread houses." I giggled at the memory of the badly charred cookies that always made us laugh. "We always had a wonderful meal. Even when she got really sick and couldn't help make it or keep it down, she wouldn't take no for an answer and sat in the kitchen with me all day, walking me through how to make everything."

Myles's thumb rubbed the back of my hand, and I watched it move back and forth, the simple action so comforting as memories flooded my mind.

"The last few years, my father wasn't around for dinner. I don't know why I thought this year would be different. But Lizzy would come with her parents and little sister, and my Aunt was there too, so we still had a warm house filled with smiles."

I settled back into the seat and watched the white snowflakes fall, illuminated by the truck's headlights.

"After everyone left, we would give each other a gift, and I'd help my mum get bundled up, then we'd sit outside drinking hot cocoa with lots of marshmallows, just talking. She could hardly stand, let alone walk, but she refused to let a holiday or birthday pass without making it something to remember. She was my hero, and I miss her so much," I said, closing my eyes as the emotion poured out of me. Tears silently slid down my cheeks.

"Yer mum sounds like a beautiful soul." I nodded. "Yer like yer mum Snowflake. I see the same kind heart in you."

"You haven't seen me really mad yet. You may change your mind," I said, and Myles laughed.

"Aye, I may, but I doubt it. The goodness in ya runs deep like a river of pure white. This world is so dark, Snowflake. Please don't ever lose yer beautiful heart. It gives me hope that I'm not forever lost." Myles leaned in and kissed my forehead. "Ya better go in before the guards come over to investigate."

Myles got out and once more handed me my suitcase.

"Thank you again for...well, for everything."

"Text me," he said.

"I will," I said and walked toward the door. I punched in the code that Myles gave me, the light on the keypad turned green, and the door unlocked.

When I got up to my floor, I stared at the pink wreath I hated, and the next wave of emotion washed over me. With a burning rage born of the helplessness I felt in my soul, I ripped the wreath off the door and smashed it over my leg. It bent in half, and I pressed it together until it was a pink half-moon.

Unlocking the door, I tossed the wreath in Vicky's trash and went straight for her closet. There they were, the holy grail of Vicky's closet, her shoes. The wild rage rolled over me again as I pictured her smug face laughing as she cut my underwear apart.

Grabbing the first pair of high heels—Jimmy Choos—I screamed and strained but ripped the heels off before tossing them onto her bed. Reaching in again, the next pair to touch my fingertips were Miu Miu, and even though someone somewhere would faint to see it, I pulled the heels off them as well. I didn't stop there. Every pair I touched was ruined until I was out of breath and stumbled back to sit on my bed, completely spent in every way possible.

Vicky was going to kill me for what I did, and she probably owned the gun to do it, but I still couldn't bring myself to care. Standing, I grabbed the frame that held the picture of my mum and me before she got ill. We looked happy, and she looked healthy. Gripping it to my chest, I lay down and closed my eyes.

Tomorrow was another day and another battle, but for tonight I'd cry and grieve for who I'd been and who I needed to become to survive.

Chapter 40

Ren

I jumped when someone knocked at the door. I'd gotten used to the ultra-quiet of the dorm, no one but me and the ghosts of those who walked the halls before me.

There was a set schedule for food, but other than that and a handful of students, I didn't see a teacher or the dean. The knock came again.

"Snowflake, are ya in there," Myles called out, and a smile spread across my face.

I hadn't seen him since the airport, but we texted every day, and it was becoming routine to talk just before bed to say goodnight.

"Coming."

I opened the door and was breathless within seconds as he grabbed me and kissed me like we hadn't seen one another for months, not days. His hands were warm on my skin as he held my face. I registered the click of the door and that we were moving, but my mind was light with excitement.

"I know ya wanted yer space, but I couldn't stay away any longer. I was going crazy," Myles said as he picked me up and laid me down on the bed.

He groaned, and I pulled him down on top of me. The ball of heat in my stomach burned bright whenever he was nearby. His weight was as delicious as his lips tasted. My nails drew soft lines along his neck, and he shivered and kissed me harder. I couldn't have said how long we laid like that when he grabbed my hands and held them above my head as he buried his face into my neck. My heart thundered in my chest, the thumping so loud I would swear someone in another room could hear it.

"Fuck Snowflake, I want ya so fucking bad. I just need a second to get myself under control."

I could feel him through his jeans pressing into me, and I had to fight the temptation to play with fire and rub myself against his hard cock. My logical mind screamed that it was a bad idea while my hormones begged me to do it.

Logic won as he pushed himself up and off my body, and I shivered without the extra heat. Myles stepped back until he sat on my desk where I'd been working.

"God, I just want to stay in bed with ya all fucking day. Make ya come on my fingers and...." Heat rushed to my face and flooded my body. "Snowflake, I swear yer a drug in human form."

He was always so dramatic, but I couldn't say I didn't like it. Myles was the one person who made me feel anything other than lost. Somehow, even when he did the stupidest shit, he found ways to redeem himself and made me feel special.

I stepped between his legs and loved the look in his eyes that told me I was everything to him. He rested his hands on my hips, and I knew I was falling for him a little more each day as the voice in my head warning me to be careful got quiet.

"What happened to your eye? It looks bruised," I said, gently touching the swollen area around his eye.

"Ah, it's nothing, just a disagreement with my Da, but we got it sorted."

My face sobered, and he quickly changed the subject.

"Blake, Theo, and Liam wished ya a Merry Christmas. Apparently, they are having way too much fun scuba diving and taking a ton of pictures on Grand Turk Island. They left these for ya."

He held up three envelopes and laid them on my desk.

"Are you sure you're okay," I asked as he stared down at the gold envelope on top.

"Aye, I'm perfect."

I searched his eyes, but whatever happened with his Da, he didn't want to tell me.

"So, no Merry Christmas from Nash? I'm shocked," I said teasingly.

Myles smirked.

"He'll come around."

Reaching around him, I grabbed the card I'd finished making and held it up between two fingers.

"This is for you."

He looked genuinely shocked.

"Thanks. Do ya mind if I open it once we are outside?"

"Sure, but why are we going outside?"

I stepped back as he scooted off the desk and stood, forcing me to look up at him.

"That is a surprise, but ya need to dress for the cold. Don't be giving me that look. It's a nice surprise, I promise."

A giddy eagerness filled me as I darted away and ordered him to turn around. Laughing, he complied so I could pull on long underwear and my jeans. The key was to always layer in cold weather. Once changed, I tied on my boots while Myles held my coat in one hand and my toque and gloves in his other.

"You know you're going to ruin your bad boy rep if you keep up all this nice stuff, right?"

He held open the coat to help me into it.

"Snowflake, if ya haven't figured it out by now, I'd do anything for ya, and I don't give a flying fuck what anyone thinks. It's the bonus of being a bad boy. No one says shit to ya, even if they want to. Come on. I can't wait to show ya this."

It was as if we'd traveled back in time and were just kids as we jogged down the hall laughing. Taking the back stairs, we snuck outside. Myles held my hand as we navigated the icy patches and walked the path beside Wayside Hall.

We rounded the corner to the quad set up for students to mingle and hang out outside, and I skidded to a halt. The inground firepit area was decorated with fresh green garland and little lights on the lamp posts so they looked like candy canes. There were two lounge chairs beside the brightly burning fire. The soft sound of crackling and the scent of wood felt like home.

Myles gave my hand a gentle tug, a smile plastered on his face.

"What is all this?"

"I know ya miss yer mum and the traditions ya had, but I thought we could make some new ones while still celebrating the old."

As we got closer, I saw tall heaters lit to take the chill out of the air and a small table set with bowls of art supplies.

"I'm not very crafty, but Mrs. Frey said ya'd find all this useful to make an ornament."

My hands covered my mouth, and I lifted my eyes to Myles.

"You did all this for me?"

He smiled wide.

"Aye, and I have a couple more surprises yet. Here, sit down."

Laughing, I did as he said and sat while he grabbed a tall thermos from under the table and two mugs. He quickly poured two hot cocoas and made me laugh harder as he grabbed an unopened bag of miniature marshmallows stealing a handful to shove in his mouth before adding some to the mugs. Sitting down, he pulled a blanket out of nowhere and laid it over us.

"Myles, this is incredible. I don't even know what to say."

I was at a loss for words to describe how his doing this made me feel. Light was breaking through all the dark in my soul, and it was all because of him—someone I least expected.

"No need to say anything. I couldn't have ya alone on Christmas."

Taking a sip of the cocoa, I savored the sweet, rich, chocolatey taste. He nailed it. This was fabulous. Everything about tonight was incredible, and I rested my head on his shoulder.

"Thank you, there is nothing I can say to repay you for this moment."

Holding out my hand, I watched the snowflakes fall onto my glove while the orange flame of the fire danced in the background.

"This is priceless to me."

"Good, 'cause I have a whole meal being delivered out here in about half an hour."

Lifting my head, I glanced up at him in wonder.

"My answer is yes."

"For what?"

"That question you keep asking me, my answer is yes."

I smiled and laughed as it registered what I meant.

"You're going to be my girl?"

"Let's not use labels, but yeah, I will date you, officially."

He leaned in and kissed me.

"Best Christmas gift ever."

Epilogue

DECEMBER 25 – SUNDAY 1:02 AM

Nash

The door softly clicked as I unlocked it and peeked inside. All was dark except for the moonlight shining in the window. Closing the door behind me, I walked over to the bed and stared down at Ren's sleeping face. Her expression was relaxed, and her fair hair fanned out on the pillow. She held the comforter close to her chin like she was prepared to jerk them back if I tried to take them from her. That thought made me smirk.

It was tempting to crawl into bed with her just to see what she would do. My lip lifted with the thought of her snuggling into me, thinking I was Myles, only to wake up and realize her mistake.

Her breathing was perfectly even. The long slow breaths and moving eyes told me she was dreaming. Bending down, I inhaled the smell of her hair. Myles was right. She smelled like cherry blossoms. The sweet scent was addicting, and I fucking couldn't stand it. I didn't want to be in this room hovering over her like a stalker, but here I was.

Tracing my finger down her soft cheek, I took this quiet moment between us like a thief.

"Do you dream of me, Princess," I whispered.

She mumbled something, her brows knitting together, and I smiled. Even in her sleep, I could piss her off.

"Merry Christmas, Princess."

On my way out, I laid the card and small box on top of the pile of envelopes on her desk. I tapped the top, still unsure if this was a good idea. Looking over my shoulder, I knew I was going to leave it.

I had one more stop tonight and needed to get going before it got any later.

Leaving as silently as I arrived, I walked down the eerily quiet hall. When I got out front, I jumped into the van I'd rented for the occasion and flicked on the windshield wipers. There would be a solid foot of snow on the ground when everyone else woke up to open gifts and give each other kisses. That was not my family. It hadn't been since my mother took off.

I understood why she did, my father had always been a cunt, and that hadn't changed. What I didn't understand was why she didn't take me with her. That pissed me the fuck off. Yes, he had a long reach and a lot of money, but my mother came from a powerful family. If she really wanted me, she could've at least tried.

Glancing in the rearview mirror, I smiled at the eyes staring back at me.

"Oh good, you're awake. I have a question for you. Who would fuck you up more, me or my father?"

A muffled response came from behind the layers of silver tape I'd wrapped around his head.

"Sorry can't hear you, but the correct answer is me. You'll learn the hard way that you never should've crossed me."

Smirking, I turned on the radio and headed for the cabin.

Merry fucking Christmas to me.

I F YOU LIKED BOOK 1 BE SURE TO LOOK FOR BOOK 2 - DEFIANT KNIGHT

.

EDITOR'S NOTE

Announcement:

Myles McCoy officially belongs to me and only me, the great and wonderful, Rita Mudawar and no one else! He is mine! I licked him all over. Stampsies no Erasies! Don't make me pull out my kiddie pool and cucumber to fight a biotch. lol!

__Brooklyn Cross does not approve this message.__

THANK YOU

Thank you to all those that decided to pick up this book and read it. It is only with readers continued support that Indie Authors, such as myself, are able to keep writing which is why your reviews mean so much to us. If you enjoyed this book, please consider leaving me a review.

ABOUT THE AUTHOR

Writing is not just a passion for me. It is a lifeline to my sanity.

I have always loved writing but suffer from severe dyslexia and short-term memory retention issues. I struggled in school while I worked every night on re-training my brain.

I was frequently treated like I would never succeed, and I found myself putting my love for writing on a shelf.

Even at the age of six, I found it easier to communicate with animals than people, which was a big reason why I was drawn to dressage horseback riding. I remained focused on my passion for riding until I had to step away from the competition world for personal reasons.

Today, my desire for writing and storytelling has been rekindled. I have published multiple books and will never let anyone or anything hold me back again.
I am a proud romance author who offers my readers morally grey heroes, a ton of spice, epic journeys, and redemption stories.

-Follow Your Dreams-

Brooklyn Cross

Made in the USA
Middletown, DE
07 September 2024